I0587366

THE BATTLE FOR METAGORE

THE BATTLE FOR METAGORE

D. L. STEWART

A LANDS OF THE ABYSS NOVEL

Copyright © D. L STEWART 2019

The right of D. L STEWART to be identified as the author of this work has been asserted by them in accordance with the Copyright, Designs and Patents Act 1976.

All rights reserved. No part of this publication may be reproduced, transmitted, or stored in a retrieval system, in any form or by any means, without permission in writing from the publisher, nor be otherwise circulated in any form of binding or cover other than that in which it is published and without a similar condition being imposed on the subsequent purchaser.

All characters in this publication are fictitious and any resemblance to real people, alive or dead, is purely coincidental.

Cover and Interior Design by Eight Little Pages

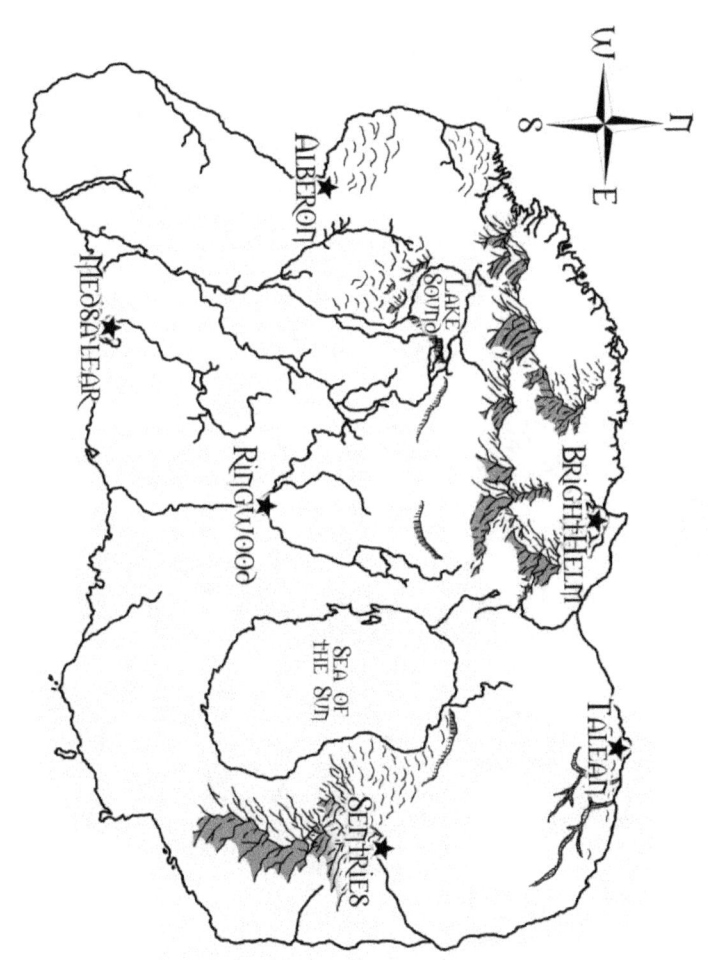

A Lord's Ceremony

It was a fine first morrow of the Batell Moon. The sweet aroma of freshly baked bread, roasted meats, and stewed vegetables lingered through the crowded courtyards and gardens within the stone walls surrounding the castle in BrightHelm. The mountains rising in the distance beyond the capital were mere silhouettes covered in an overcast sky and dampened by a fine morning mist.

Inside the white marble castle, an elderly elven lord—Lord Brighton—stood in front of a mirror, adjusting the belt buckle on his tabard. "Thou dost swear, every year thou hast to loosen this damn thing."

"You still look astounding, my love," his wife, Kalama, said and giggled as she braided strands of his hair.

Brighton turned his gaze from his waistline toward his wife, still in awe of how she could look as young as when they had first met centuries ago. Her skin was as smooth and bronze and her body as toned and firm as it had always been.

His gaze trailed back to his reflection in the mirror. He had not noticed any weight gain over the past year—then, of course, he never did. His appearance remained regal and proud, but his posture had slouched. His hair had darkened to a light gray and had grown as coarse as the beard he had neglected to keep groomed. His skin wore wrinkles where it was once tight and smooth.

Glancing at the many rings lining his fingers, he reflected on all the things he could once do with his hands. All the fighting and training he had done while he was still young and possessed a perfect body. All the structures he had worked on as a young lord to construct the city surrounding them. All the fun and crafty things he had done with his older children while they remained at home. Unfortunately, time had passed, and his hands weren't as steady as they once were.

Kalama noticed the sadness permeate Brighton's face. She tried to comfort him as she finished his hair. "We all grow old. Some merely show it more than others."

Brighton turned and looked at his wife, then tucked a feat of her dangling red curls behind her ear and smiled. "You could be philandering around these streets, making merry and chasing men far younger than thee, but thou suppose you see something in thine old self, aye?"

"I do not see an old man in front of me; I see an old heart still burning with passion for what he loves," she responded as she gave him a slight hug. "Besides, I am going to be sitting beside Duke Kaprin, who is by far one of the youngest of your dukes, and trust me, he does nothing to warm my soul."

A slight laugh slipped from Brighton's mouth. "Thou can have thy seat if thou wishes."

"It is not a matter of significance, my love. You can sit on your throne, and I on mine." She paused as she grabbed a silver and ivory circlet off the vanity. "Now, finish getting ready. Your kingdom awaits you."

Brighton took the crown and placed it upon his graying hair. Staring into the mirror once more, he spotted all the imperfections of his once-fair skin, the dark veins running through his sagging flesh, and the blacken scabs of sores on his face from being in the sun for too long. The gloomy sight did nothing but bring awareness to his struggling breaths. His eyes sat low as he continued to reminisce about the past and realized his years of being alive was soon going to come to an end. He slowly put on his pauldrons and bracers as he continued to stare at his withering reflection.

†

Outside the castle, at the front of one of the courtyards, stood a large wooden stage. Upon the platform sat seven people, ranging in size and race, along with two giant trolls—suited in dull gray armor—standing guard on either side.

Lord Brighton sat in the middle of the six others; his beloved wife and his five grand dukes accompanied him. He stood from his throne and trudged to the front-center of the stage. "Welcome to the seven hundred thirty-fifth annual New Life Festival!"

The attendants shouted with joy and aspiration.

"Thou would like to thank ye for coming out and celebrating with us. 'Tis been another blessed year for Metagore, and thou art sure we're going to see many more to come. We're going to start off this year, like many years before, with a few words from our grand dukes and their visions for the upcoming year. So, if ye would please, help thee welcome up Grand Duke Azreal."

The crowd continued to cheer and applaud as a djinn, almost three legs high and wearing a maroon pteruges, stood from his seat and maneuvered to the front of the stage. Duke Azreal hailed from the desert provinces of Talean, east of BrightHelm. His blue skin, taut against his sculpted figure, had been molded from years of training with his father's army as a child. His hair, gray as the sky above, draped over his shoulders and hung midway down his torso.

"It is a beautiful day, is it not?" Azreal asked, then paused for a moment to allow the crowd to respond.

"Duchess Anina and I have been working on a trade agreement with the Kingdom of Direfell. You all are probably wondering why. It is quite simple. Emperor Berez does not know how to rule over his land, or how to keep his people safe. He summoned for me three moons ago, asking if I would be gracious enough to help him protect his land and keep his people safe. Over the past few moons, we have been working on an agreement with him. We will send him two hundred of our best warriors. In exchange, Emperor Berez has agreed to house and feed them, free of charge. He has also offered to pay us a green chip per head that we send him."

The crowd roared in excitement.

"Thus, growing our purse and allowing us to refortify our capital cities and spend more on supplying our knights with better weapons and armor."

The audience continued to cheer. The guards patrolling the courtyards bellowed a shout of excitement.

"The deal has not transpired into motion, but within a few moons we will be sending over a shipment of warriors to help defend their land." Azreal bowed before the crowd. "Thank you all so much for your time and patience. Have a great New Life."

Azreal turned around and returned to his seat.

Lord Brighton shuffled to the front of the stage. "It is always nice to be able to help our allies from across the Abyss. Next, thou would like to introduce Grand Duke Darius."

Lord Brighton turned as Darius ambled to the front of the stage.

Duke Darius was a tall and muscular demon, three links taller than the average of his kind. Scars littered his dark, ashy skin. His eyes burned a fiery red, and his head housed two horns growing from his forehead, curving backward as a ram's, surrounded by waves of raven hair cascading past his shoulders. Upon his bare left shoulder rested his pet salamander, Meek, continuously emitting flames keeping both Darius and itself warm.

"I hope you all have had a fantastic year," he said in a deep voice. "I am the new duke of Sentries, replacing Duke Riray after his fatal loss in battle this past year. In this upcoming year, we, the Senturians, will be mining deeper into Mount Dumas's core, thus allowing us to be able to make our blades more lethal and our shields even stronger!"

Darius thanked the crowd as they cheered and returned to his seat as Lord Brighton shuffled toward the front.

"Ye all give it up for Grand Duke Darius," Brighton said as he gestured toward the large demon. "He kept his speech short, didn't he? Now, the next person to come up is Grand Duke Moll'ar. So, if ye all would, make him feel welcome here in BrightHelm."

Lord Brighton returned to his seat as Moll'ar approached the front of the stage.

Duke Moll'ar was a morling with a sculpted body. He had dark, tan skin with circles integratedly woven together and branded into his arms and chest and eyes that sparkled like emerald gems. He wore a leather outfit decorated with beads and feathers. He had long, wavy, brown hair cascading to his shoulders, accented by a headdress made of red and black feathers.

As Moll'ar approached the front of the stage, the women in the crowd grew extremely loud, taken in awe of Moll'ar's flattering looks.

"*Sré omd herizh*. Which means: 'hello and welcome' in Oacari," he stated as he smiled at the crowd, allowing them to quiet down before he continued. "This past year has been a great one for us in Alberon. The Gods of the Eight Divides have blessed us with beautiful weather and so many wonderful crops. In this new year, we are goin' to expand our farmlands into various settlements in Feather's Bow and Pixdale, thus, givin' the tribes outside of my capital more jobs and easier access to the food supply. In the year to come, we will be workin' the lands and gettin' them prepared for next year's crops, and in two years, we will have double the plantation space and double the produce!"

The crowd cheered and celebrated as Moll'ar turned and gave a slight nod toward Brighton before walking to his seat. The venerable lord stood from his throne and scuffed back to the front of the stage for the fourth time.

"Thank you, Grand Duke Moll'ar," Lord Brighton said and looked at the crowd. "Isn't that going to be great? Double the food? The look of some of ye, ye couldn't handle double the food."

Laughter flowed through the audience as Brighton

tugged on the belt wrapping around his restrained gut.

"Next, thou would like to introduce to ye, Grand Duke Kaprin from Medsa'lear."

Lord Brighton turned and motioned for Kaprin to go on up as he sauntered to his seat. As he walked, he saw Kalama glaring with annoyance as Kaprin pranced forward.

Duke Kaprin was a head taller than his lord, with webbed fingers and toes and blue scales covering his body. His eyes shone as black as night and protruded from a fish-like face, with fins on both sides and a crest adorning the center of his scalp. Being a cryter, Kaprin had both lungs and gills for breathing in and out of water.

Kaprin bowed deeply to the crowd. "Aye, thank ye for comin' out. 'Tis a beautiful day, isn't it?"

The crowd responded with cheers.

"'Tis past year hasn't been the best for Medsa'lear, but the next shall be better," he shouted as if giving a pep talk to the crowd. "We have seen evidence that the megalodons are approachin' closer to our shores. More than likely, they are lookin' for food."

The crowd gasped and grew frantic, shouting remarks of concern.

Kaprin desperately tried to get the crowd under control. "Calm down! Calm down! Aye, I beg of ye to calm yeselves! There is no need to panic! They will become motionless if they try to venture onto our lands. Now, I have assembled some of my best fishermen that I, myself, have trained. We are goin' to hunt 'em down, and we are goin' to kill 'em! We're goin' to make our oceans safer, and once we rid the megalodons from the Abyss, we shall feast upon their flesh," Kaprin shouted with his fist raised.

He returned to his seat as Brighton, once again, traipsed to the front of the stage.

Lord Brighton pointed toward the cryter. "Give Grand Duke Kaprin another round of applause."

As he had asked, the audience erupted into cheers and claps.

"Now, will ye all help me welcome forward Grand Duke Galach?"

Duke Galach was a treefolk and the tallest of the seven on stage, standing shy of three and a half legs. A thick, bark-like shell covered his body, while his seeded core pumped a dense, sap-like fluid through his veins.

Galach stood and approached the front of the stage, shook hands with Lord Brighton, then commenced his speech.

"Good morrow, dear friends. During the past year, thou has had a group of djinns and liches working on a special elixir. An elixir that can revive dead trees and make them stronger than they were before. Once we have completed the crafting of thine elixir, we shall begin testing in Black Rain Forest. If it works as we have intended, 'tis will bring all the dead, soot-covered trees back to life. They will bear leaves and fruits. They will stand tall and house some of the most durable wood in all thy land." Galach paused for a moment. "We are so close to completing thine elixir that within a few short moons, we will begin testing, and within the next few years, the trees in Black Rain Forest will be revived and stronger than any other tree in Ringwood, and within all of Metagore."

The crowd, who had been silent throughout the speech, cheered as Galach turned and headed to his seat.

Lord Brighton stood, shook the towering treefolk's branch-like hand once again, and returned to the front of the stage for the last time.

"Thou knowest ye all may not be interested in reviving dead trees, but to our treefolk community, this new elixir will change the way they live—capable of becoming stronger and living longer. Plus, the lumber from the new trees will make for great, powerful, defensive walls around our beloved cities. Doesn't the new year sound amazing?" Lord Brighton paused to let the crowd cheer for the grand dukes one last time. "Thou's not going to keep ye much longer; thou knowest most of ye are wanting to feast. So, one quick thing. We will begin blasting into some of the rock structures in MireBane this upcoming year. Graphite is abundant in MireBane's lands. We will harvest it, and we will manufacture it! So, this new year is going to be filled with glorious things for all of Metagore! Enough with all this squiddle, who's ready to feast?" Lord Brighton shouted, causing the crowd to erupt louder than they had before.

As the crowd dispersed into an adjacent courtyard and began feasting, Lord Brighton and Lady Kalama remained upon the stage, standing amongst their grand dukes.

"'Tis an honor, thy Lord, for thou to have thee; but thou cannot stay," Galach said, gracefully thanking their host. "Thou must fare-thee-well and return to thy Woodite people and carry on thy's duty as grand duke." He turned to the others that stood beside him. "Thou hopes ye have a blessed year. Thou shall see ye again next year, whither we can reunite as a kingdom once more, but for now, thou must fare-thee-well."

After saying his goodbyes, Galach maneuvered through the crowd and out of the castle's courtyards.

Brighton rested his blue-eyed gaze on the remaining four dukes. "Thou dost hope that ye can stay for the remainder of the festivities."

Darius scrunched his brow as he looked at the crowd. "I suppose I can tarry for the day, but tomorrow I must make my way back to Sentries," he grumbled, as he stroked his fingers through his beard followed by cohesive responses from the other grand dukes about their respective regions.

A smile grew on Brighton's face as he nodded, pleased they would stay a bit longer.

"If ye must, then so be it, but whilst ye are here, let's go feast 'til our hearts are content," he said with a chipper voice, tugging the strap of his belt.

Wooden tables where the congregation could enjoy their meals filled the many courtyards surrounding the castle. Hundreds more tables containing a vast variety of entrees and appetizers lined the curtain walls. Hung on the wall, high over the tables, were banners, each with an emblem representing one of the six provinces of Metagore.

Prepared meats ranged from roasted catoblepas ribs rubbed in a crust of garlic and herbs, to plates of suckling boar garnished with mint leaves. Other tables housed soups and stews or held fresh fruits and vegetables. For desserts, there were all sorts of pies and cakes, jams and jellies to go with the newly baked bread, and an assortment of wines and cheeses.

†

Azreal fixed himself a platter of honeyed coatl strips and a few pieces of freshly baked bread, then left the castle and toured the city.

Merchants and shopkeepers, who could not afford to set aside their work for the day to attend the festival, filled the streets. Even though the capital was the center of the trade markets and regulations within Metagore, most townsfolk worked in small, family-owned businesses, struggling to make enough coin to feed their loved ones.

Not far from the castle, Azreal strolled into a parlor, where the barber was shaving the beard off a troll.

"Morning, my good gentlemen," he greeted them as he set his plate of food on an empty side table.

"Morn, Duke Azreal," the barber replied as he wiped the excess cream from the troll's cheeks. "Sounds like the festival is good this year. Ya enjoyin' yer stay here?"

"Aye, I always enjoy my time at the festivals. And I do believe I saw a fire breather walking around the courtyards."

The barber chuckled. "The food is sure to stay warm then."

"You do have a valid point," the djinn replied with a laugh of his own. "Speaking of food, I have brought you both a plate."

He reached over the platter and raked the air above it. The plate of food seemed to pull apart from itself, until there were two identical saucers, each appearing to be the same in size as the original. Then once more, he raked the air above both platters, creating two more the same as the firsts.

Azreal retrieved one of the platters.

"Thank you for your services to this kingdom, though little it may seem."

"Thank ya, Duke Azreal. But why a third?"

"Take it home to your family. I am sure they would appreciate a well-cooked meal," Azreal said, smiling as he headed toward the parlor's door. "Have a wonderful New Life and a blessed new year."

Azreal left the shop and visited multiple homes and other public establishments, using his magic to multiply the food for the city's inhabitants and proclaiming everyone should be able to celebrate the holiday, including the ones who could not afford or manage the trip to the castle.

†

Inside the castle's infrastructure, Lord Brighton and the remaining three grand dukes fixed their plates and found themselves a seat amongst the crowd. Different entertainers—fire breathers, jugglers, musicians—were amongst the congregation making their rounds, interacting with the joyful citizens, keeping their spirits high as they laughed and rejoiced on such a splendid holiday.

Kaprin took a seat beside a group of elves—appearing to be housemaids from their dull, woolen garments—and enjoyed his fish stew.

"Have ya e'er encountered a megalodon y'self?" one of the elves asked Kaprin.

"Have I?" Kaprin responded, pausing for a moment, as if to remember if he had. "Have I?" Kaprin repeated, but this time with a chuckle. "Aye, let me tell ya somethin'. Durin' the last moon, me and some of my finest fishers were out sailin' off the coast of Seaford. Out of nowhere, somethin' hit our ship and caused us to spring a leak. We started to take on water rather quickly. So, I decided to turn the ship 'round, hopin' to make it back to shore before we took on too much water."

Kaprin paused as he took a bite of his stew.

By that time, everyone close enough to hear had silenced, eavesdropping on the story.

"One of my men noticed a fin circlin' 'round the ship. Eventually, the fin vanished beneath the waves. A few moments passed, thence at once, our ship took another hard hit, thence another. With each hit, our ship became more and more destroyed, takin' on an even greater amount of water." He paused again to take another bite. "We started to sink, so we all abandoned ship. After all my men had fled, I followed behind, jumpin' into the water. And that's when I saw it: the biggest sharks that anyone ever did see."

"How many were there?" one elf asked in awe.

Kaprin focused his gaze on the elf. "There were three. Three of the most terrifyin' sea creatures were out to get us. When I surfaced, I started swimmin' toward the shore. I swam faster than I have ever done before in my life." Kaprin paused for a moment and fell into a deep thought as tears glazed his black eyes. "I could hear the screams of my men, one by one, as their lives were taken by those monsters. But I just kept swimmin' toward the shore, never lookin' back." Kaprin paused once again—a tear making its way down his scaly skin—and scanned the audience he had accumulated. "Once I reached land, I turned, and I saw it: an enormous fin sticking out of the water. The megalodon had came almost all the way to the shore with me, but it retreated, not wantin' to go farther."

"Astonishing. I bet that must have been terrifying," a

djinn mentioned, who had been sitting behind Kaprin and listening to his story.

"Aye, 'twas terrifyin', but more so, 'twas heartbreakin'. I lost five great men that day to those beasts," Kaprin added, being sure to look at everybody in the eyes. "That's why this year I am goin' back out there with more men. 'Tis go 'round we will be prepared, and we will capture the megalodons infesting our waters."

†

Across the courtyard, as Kaprin continued telling his fictitious stories, Moll'ar feasted upon a slab of catoblepas ribs. From the way he scarfed it down, it would appear to be his first meal in a long time … or the last.

Darius sat beside him.

"Slow down," Darius said, then chuckled. "There's no need to eat so fast; there'll be plenty for another round."

Moll'ar set down the ribs for a moment—still chewing on a large piece of meat—and looked at Darius.

"Back home I just get to enjoy the fruits of my own labor. Do not get me wrong, I am blessed with our crops, but I try to enjoy every opportunity I get to eat a well-cooked slab of meat from time to time," Moll'ar responded as the raw juices from the meat progressed down his chin.

A troll sitting across the table from Darius and Moll'ar spoke with a raspy voice. "Duke Darius, why dost ya travel here with a pet?"

Darius quickly swallowed his mead.

"Most are unaware, but demons are cold blooded. Thus, is why we live in warm climate regions. Meek helps keep my body warm when I'm in colder climates, such as here in BrightHelm."

"If ya would wear a shirt, ya would be warmer," the troll replied and laughed.

Darius took a bite from his duba ribs, then scoffed at the troll.

"I don't wear shirts. They restrict my movements in combat."

"Men like us do not fight in combat," Moll'ar responded before patting his mouth dry with a handkerchief. "That is why we have armies."

"If war is brought onto my land, you can hold my words as true; I will be out in the field with my knights, with a blade in my hand."

"Aye, same as if a war crosses into Alberon; I will pick up my shaft and fight. But there has not been a war in Alberon in almost seventeen hundred years, since the War of Snakes to be exact."

"Unfortunately for Sentries," Darius grumbled, "it's only been a hundred and eighty years since my father last brought foreign armies onto our lands to fight their wars."

†

In an adjacent courtyard, Brighton and Kalama sat at a table with their ten viscounts and a few wealthy elves from the city.

"'Tis been a grand ol' day thus far. The festival is magnificent, my Lord," one of the viscounts said.

"Thank you, but if it were not for the great people of Metagore, 'tis festival would never take place," Brighton said humbly.

The viscount gave a slight nodding toast. "If it weren't for your great leadership, my Lord, Metagore would still be a land filled with bickering and wars."

"Thank you for your gratitude. 'Tis much appreciated."

Brighton took a sip of his wine, then a bite from a slab of an achlis tenderloin. After a few bites of his steak, he began to cough. At first, it was a slight, dry cough but soon developed more viciously.

"Are you all right, my love?" Kalama asked as she stood from her chair.

Having turned slightly paler than usual, Brighton gained control his cough.

"Thou art fine, my dear. Just got a little choked up, that's all."

Kalama took her seat but cautiously kept her gaze on her beloved as he continued eating.

"How is little Aden doing these days, my Lady?" Mela, a young, rounded, elven lady asked.

Mela didn't hold any titles to her name and plenty were more well off financially than her, but her grandfather was the eldest and the head of the viscounts, and that was enough to land her a seat at the Lord's table.

"He is doing just lovely," Kalama replied, glancing around, trying to find her youngest son, but to no avail. "Him and Eira are running about these courtyards somewhere, probably with their brothers and sisters."

"That's good to hear. Did they all make it home for the festival?"

"Yes, they did," Kalama responded as a smile grew on her bronze face.

Most of her children were grown and with families of their own—too busy to travel home more than once or twice a year. Kalama knew they would be leaving after the festival concluded in two days, but she enjoyed their presence while they were home, even if they wanted to see old friends more than their own mother; she couldn't blame them, for she might as well have done the same.

A slight tremble swept over Brighton's body.

"'Tis grew cold quite rapidly, wouldn't you say?"

Kalama and the viscounts looked at each other with confused and concerned stares.

"My Lord," one of them began, "are ya sure ye'r doing fine? Yer pash is starting to redden."

"Thou art fine, thou assures you," Brighton responded as he wiped a few beads of sweat that had accumulated from his ribbed brow before beginning another coughing fit. He grabbed his wine and took a large gulp, then stood from his seat and turned his attention to the crowd. "Thank ye for coming out and enjoying this fine morrow with us, but thou dost believe thou's going to retire thyself to thy's solar." Brighton paused to cough once more into his hand. "Enjoy the remainder of the festivities. Ye may carry on as ye were."

"My love, are you sure you will be fine?" Kalama asked as she stood from her seat.

"Thou art fine, my darling. The changing of the air is drying out my throat, that's all," he reassured her as he began to walk toward the doors of their castle.

As he trudged, he glanced at his hands, where the bloody mucus dripped from his fingertips.

Darker Days

Three days had passed, and the grand dukes had left for their respective regions. Unfortunately, Lord Brighton had not ventured from his chamber during that time. He spent the majority of his days in the garderobe, spewing every grub he had tried to intake. The rest of his time was spent lying in bed, being too weak to traverse the castle.

Kalama sat beside her husband, brushing his forehead and cheeks with a damp cloth while he lay asleep. At the foot of the bed sat a young boy twirling his red hair around a finger as he studied his father's sicken state.

Kalama gazed at Brighton's closed eyes. Warmth filled her body as she remembered the day they had met, of how he had protected her and helped with their escape from the Penéné prison. His passion had sparked the desire within herself to leave her home in Fintan and move to Rigdale. Their burning love and his comforting embrace had been enough to make the chill of the night bearable.

Their relationship had grown as a fanning flame, dancing and swaying as they twirled in the castle gardens for the first time as man and wife. Their desire to be with each other had burned bright and jumped with life as they formed a family of their own, with eleven children.

As Kalama continued to softly pat her husband's face with the cloth, desolation crept over her. Her husband's pale complexion had lost its color. His visible blue veins appeared like frozen spider-webs under ashy skin. The tips of her hair burned with embers as she realized her beloved would not always be with her. His time would come to an end, and she would have to go on with her life, living in the debris left behind from their fondest memories, but with the absence of his warm touch.

Knock, knock

Kalama turned as she extinguished the small flames in her hair. A young, pudgy, elven lady slowly opened the door.

"Mela, enter."

"Morning, my Lady," Mela greeted her as she entered the room, carrying a covered platter. "I have brought our lord his morning meal for when he awakes."

"I am sure it is a lovely meal, but you did not have to bring it. I am sure one of the servants could have brought it. After all, that is what they are for."

Mela set the platter on a bedside table. "I am aware, my Lady. But this way, I feel as if I'm helping our lord return to good health."

Kalama forced a smile and nodded. "I will tell him it was you who brought it." She turned her stare toward Brighton's resting body. "But it may be of no use." Kalama slowly closed her eyes, then reopened them as a tear creeped out. "His breaths have become slower, and I fear for the worst."

"My Lady," Mela said, gently grasping one of Kalama's hands, "don't speak of such ill fortune. Our lord will be in good health soon."

"I hope you are right, but I foresee darker days on the horizon."

†

In the absence of their lord, the city of BrightHelm grew weary. Rumors of someone poisoning their noble lord spread rampantly through the capital and the vast majority of the kingdom. Mass fear of their lord dying soon sparked chaos to rampage through the streets.

The Duchess of BrightHelm denounced accepting the crown if matters worsen, leaving the viscounts—in the hopes to try and ease the fear of the townsfolk—to schedule a meeting amongst themselves.

In the throne room of BrightHelm's Kingdom Hall, the ten viscounts and viscountesses convened around the outside of a large, horseshoe-shaped stone table. The viscounts were in charge of enforcing the laws set in place by their lord and distributing punishment when such laws were violated. The viscounts were all elves—seeing as how BrightHelm recognized elves as being the superior beings of intellect and decision making—and most hailed from wealthy families who had paid their way onto the council. Others followed in their parents' footsteps, taking their seat once they had passed away.

The head of the council, an older elf named Efar, led the meeting. He was the eldest, with his wrinkly skin and his balding head of short white hair, and he had sat on the council for over seven hundred years.

Efar stood from his seat and stooped over the table, unable to hold himself upright in his old age, and addressed the council. "We hast all heard of the agauw news of our majestic lord being venenated," he said in a soft, haunting tone. "Wherefore is the reason we are gathered here on 'tis morrow. In the melpomenish scenario of our lord's departure, we shall need to appoint a new lord. Thou propose to each our own, who art willing to take upon the duties of lord, present unto thee a statement. Then anon we shall cast silent ballots, which to each our own shall cast for who we believe to be the next lord, but thou cannot vote for thouself. 'Tis there anyone that revokes the process?"

The nine other viscounts agreed upon the process.

"Thou shall start, then we shall make our way 'round the table to thy left. Thou believes thyself shall be the new lord, if fate may bend its wishes, because thou art a man of dignity and perfection. Thou hast served on the council for centuries, helping the denizens of Metagore reap what they hast sowed, 'tis which are peace and fulfillment of thine duties and obligations for thy kingdom. May it happen, whilst thou art lord, no more children shall pingle or be forced to kiss the jack's foot when thoust dines. Elect thou, and ye shall be blessed. Gramercy, and may the Eight bless ye."

Efar sat down in his chair and turned to his left, where a young elven lady named Xoe stood.

"I pass on the opportunity presented before me, for I do not wish to have this kind of responsibility laid upon me," she stated before sitting down, and the next stood.

Senson, Xoe's twin brother, rose from his chair. He brushed his brown hair from his face as his vibrant blue eyes looked at the others and a broad smile stretched across his face.

"I agree with Efar; our children need to be fed. Better yet, our children need better education, like what I had when I studied at the institution in Whitefall. Education shouldn't be just for the endowed but for everyone who lives in this beautiful kingdom." Over the course of his speech, Senson's voice grew stern. "Plus, even more so than our children, our knights need to be better taken care of. They risk their lives fighting so that we may stay safe, and when they return home, they have to scamper around, pillaging to find a job so they can live out of the cold and support their families. We should praise them like gods, not like worthless pawns! If I'm elected as the next lord, I will provide our knights with a greater purse, and for the ones wounded in battle and can't work, the crown will fill their purse even greater for their courage and honor. Thank you."

Senson took his seat as Ramous—one of the wisest elves in the kingdom and one of the prestigious scientists in all of Metagore—stood and propped himself up on the table.

"I was listening to Duke Kaprin at the festival—the feather-headed bedswerver that he is—state he had evidence that megalodons are moving closer to our shores." He paused for a moment as he ran his hand over the top of his thin gray hair. "This is a real threat, and in my studies, megalodons aren't the worst of what's out there. Some creatures could swallow a megalodon whole. What's worse? These monsters are moving closer to our shores and are going to cause enormous problems if we don't do anything to stop them. It will prevent fishers from going out to sea. If other lands hear of the matter, they could cut off their supply from us, which would affect everyone in Metagore, not just Medsa'lear. If you all crown me as lord, I will devise a plan to put blockades in our water to keep them from getting to our lands. Even if I am not elected, these creatures are going to become a major issue, and we need to take action soon. Thank you for your time, and please vote with a wise mind," he concluded as he sat.

Next was Coi, the shortest and the second oldest member of the council. She looked at each of the other viscounts.

"All that hast been proclaimed are all things that any of us can accomplish if we art elected. Ye should cast a vote in my name, because I believe I care more for this land and its inhabitants than any of ye. We need a person who loves Metagore and wants the best for it. I am not stating ye do not relish 'tis beautiful kingdom of ours. What I am saying is I care for it more than any of ye could e'er imagine, and I dost think I would be a better ruler than any of ye. Gramercy," Coi concluded as she bowed slightly, then sat as she brushed her long raven hair out of her face.

Barinthus, a slender, dark elf with black hair and yellow eyes, was the next viscount to stand and give a speech.

"We have incredible military units all over Metagore, but we're not using them. We send them to other kingdoms to help protect their lands, but they're not guards for other lords to use. They are knights—our knights! Why aren't we using them as such?" Barinthus shouted as he slammed his fist on the table. "If you elect me, I will use them as such. Eventually, our population will outgrow our lands, and our resources with be dwindled to nothing. We will need our military to advance into other kingdoms—ones we are foolishly protecting—and take them from their incompetent leaders. Our primary focus should be on our land and on our people." He paused before concluding. "Thank you all."

Cornelius, who was the youngest and looked upon as a child, stood and nervously presented his proposal.

"Greetings. I agree, yet disagree, with Barinthus. I accept the fact they are our knights and we need to focus on protecting ourselves before we try helping other nations. Wherefore, I disagree regarding using them to force control over another land for our own benefit. We have plenty of unused lands we can utilize, and it will be millennia before we will need more land. We can worry about expanding when that time comes. If I am elected, I will build our defenses and put our military to good use—defending our kingdom, not foreign lands." Cornelius took his seat, relieved he was done with his speech, then quickly stood. "Thank you," he rattled off, then sat once more.

Kaafel was a former warrior of the Alberian army, with scars wrapped around his wrists—same as all Alberian warriors—and was the next to give his speech.

"I've trekked four of the regions of this kingdom, and the wildlife I've encountered in my journeys were far worse than any military I've clashed against. If I am sworn in as the new lord, I will be sure the wildlife threat is taken into consideration. We will be able to safely travel our lands without the fear of being attacked by a chimera or a nundu. Elect me, and let's take back our kingdom! Thank you."

Kaafel sat as Thoaral rose from his seat. Thoaral, just

as Xoe, wished not to be nominated.

Edorin, the last of the viscounts, poised his old, obese body and began his speech, slumped over the table.

"Why do we, as a kingdom, have six militaries? If you all elect me, I shall construct a single base for a centralized military. With a unified military, our knights will be exposed to the same resources and the same training. Thus, it will provide us with a stronger military. So, elect me, and let us make our kingdom stronger than e'er before. Gramercy."

Edorin rested his corpulent body into his seat.

Efar stood back up. "The next room holds a podium with sheets of parchment, along with a quill and ink. In the same order, one by one, we shall goest and cast our ballot. Remember, ya may not vote for thyself."

The eldest viscount left the room and casted his vote. The remainder of the council followed suit, each returning to their seat at the table after their cast had been made.

A New Seed

The ten viscounts sat around the table in the throne room, each having cast their ballot for the new lord. In front of Efar rested a small wooden box. He lifted the lid and removed the rolls of parchment.

"In thy hands, thou holds the fate of Metagore."

The old elf placed the votes onto the table, unrolling them one at a time.

"One vote, Cornelius. One vote, Barinthus. One vote, Senson. Two votes, Senson. Three votes, Senson. Two votes, Cornelius. Three votes, Cornelius. Two votes, Barinthus. Four votes, Cornelius. One vote, Kaafel. Five votes, Cornelius."

Efar, disappointed that he had not received a single vote, forced a smile.

"Congratulations. With half of the votes, Cornelius, ya shall bear the crown if fate falls unto yer shoulders."

Cornelius raised his young, rounded head from the table toward Efar, numbness spread through his body. With his skin turning paler than usual, he stood from his seat.

"Thank you all for believing in me." He paused, his stomach tightening as the news settled in. "It is a great honor. I hope to be able to lead this kingdom as well as Lord Brighton has done before me. Again, thank you."

Cornelius reseated himself. His body trembled in anxiety as he wiped the sweat from his palms onto his maroon viscount robe. The voices of the others drifted away as thoughts raced through his mind, and his vision narrowed onto the table before him.

As Efar and the others discussed the terms of Cornelius's coronation—if the worst were to come upon their lord—their young duchess with short chestnut hair and green eyes rushed into the room.

"Lord Brighton has left us in his sleep!" Duchess Zorie's panting voice sputtered.

The council gasped in sorrow.

Efar stood from his seat and shambled toward Zorie. Grabbing her smooth hand, he stated in a soft voice, "Duchess, we pay our deepest condolences to ya and thy Lady Kalama."

"Thank you, Efar. Have you all decided who will be appointed as the next lord?" she questioned as she glanced around the throne room.

"Aye, we hath reconciled on a new lord."

Cornelius stood, still wiping his nervous hands on his robe. "I am, my Duchess. I did not expect to take over so soon, but I am ready to take up the reins of this kingdom."

"Congratulations, Lord Cornelius," she spoke, dismay still filling her words. "I will start preparing for your coronation, and I shall send for the grand dukes at once."

†

A full moon had passed, and once again, guests from all across Metagore filled BrightHelm's castle courtyards, this time to honor the crowning of their new lord. In the front of the central courtyard sat a wooden stage—the same platform from the New Life Festival four weeks prior. Upon the stage stood an archbishop wearing a black hooded robe, with a table to his right. Beside the stage stood a group of elves with an assortment of instruments: drums, flutes, and small horns.

The elven band played a soft melody as the nine viscounts entered the courtyard and continued onto the stage. Each viscount was appointed a ceremonial item to carry: a bowl of chrism and a sponge, a collection of flowers and herbs from the six different regions, a chalice of dragons' blood, and a silver and ivory circlet crown. As they reached the stage, one by one, they set their item upon the table beside the archbishop.

With the viscounts leaving the stage and taking their seats next to the three grand dukes who were able to make it in time, the band changed their tune to a more regal tone with an upbeat tempo. From the back of the courtyard, Cornelius entered wearing a large navy cape with golden, floral print-lined edges supported by golden tassels tied together around his neck. Under the cloak, he wore black slacks and boots. He took his time passing the visitors, to wave and greet them and occasionally hugging and kissing some of the guests on the hand. Once he had reached the stage, the band silenced.

Cornelius knelt in front of the archbishop as the priest stepped forward and removed the cloak from the young elf, leaving his back bare.

The gaze of the archbishop's skeletal face scanned the massive crowd gathered to witness the ceremony. "Thou art here to unveil unto ye, Lord Cornelius, thy newly appointed lord."

He motioned with his bony hand as Cornelius rose to his feet, still facing the archbishop.

"Sire," the archbishop began, "art thou willing to take the oath?"

"I am willing," Cornelius responded with power in his voice.

The archbishop's yellow eyes stared at Cornelius. "Will thou solemnly promise and swear to govern the inhabitants of all of Metagore according to the respective laws and customs of Alberon, BrightHelm, Medsa'lear, Ringwood, Sentries, and Talean?"

"I solemnly promise to do so," Cornelius answered.

"Will ya, with all of thy power, cause law and justice to be executed in all of thy judgments?"

"I will."

The archbishop turned to the table and grabbed the sponge and soaked it in the bowl of chrism.

"Let thy head and heart be anointed," he said as he patted the sponge on Cornelius's forehead, then rubbed it on his chest.

Cornelius smiled as the scented oils trailed down his body.

"Cleanse thy mind and soul, and lead with pure intentions."

After cleansing Cornelius, the archbishop grabbed the flowers and herbs and placed them on the stage floor in a row, grouped by the region they were from.

"Thou cannot rule over land thou has not trekked over. By traversing these weeds, thou art traversing over all of Metagore."

Starting with the ones brought from Alberon and ending with the ones from Sentries, Cornelius walked across the limbs, being sure he stepped on each individual weed. The twigs and stems crunched under the weight of his boots, the leaves laying submissive before their new lord.

Once he finished, the archbishop waved his left hand over the weeds, igniting them into a blazing fire.

"As these grasses burn, may thy passion for ruling over thy kingdom burn."

After finishing the statement, the archbishop waved

his hand over the weeds once more, causing the fire to dwindle and cease to exist.

The priest grabbed the chalice of dragons' blood and handed it to Cornelius. "The drinking of the chalice will empower ya with the strength of the mighty dragons."

Cornelius looked at the sloshing crimson fluid in the goblet. His face scrunched with the thought of partaking in the haram act of drinking one's blood, formal setting or not. He raised the chalice and pressed it against his lips. With a quick gulp, he swallowed every drop of blood. Puckering from the horrid taste, he handed the chalice to the archbishop, who placed it on the table.

"May thou rule with the strength and power, as the mighty dragons rule over the mountains." The archbishop then picked up the circlet as Cornelius knelt before him. "The crown of thy lord, we pass from one to the other. We place it upon thy head, to guide thy kingdom to a glorified state of peace."

After the crown had been secured upon Cornelius's golden hair, he rose to his feet while the archbishop tied the cape around his neck once more.

The crowd cheered loudly as the archbishop began to speak. "We crown thee with a crown of glory and righteousness. May ya obtain a kingdom of high strength. Go forth beyond the clouds and rule thy kingdom with philotimy."

The elven band played a lively melody as Cornelius turned and faced the crowd, catching a glimpse of the former queen in the front row, distinctly still mourning the death of her husband. Cornelius walked off the stage and toward Kalama.

"My Lady," Cornelius greeted as he approached her and her youngest children. "My condolences for your loss. Lord Brighton was an honorable man, and he will truly be missed by the masses. I could never replace what Lord Brighton was, but I will do my best to continue to lead this kingdom to better things. And I hope I'm not stepping over any boundaries, but if you wished to remain in the castle, you may. I will have the maids fix up a different chamber for myself."

Kalama glanced at the young lord as she held her youngest son and daughter close to her with her arms draped over their shoulders. She stared at the young ruler with a furrowed brow. Thoughts of Brighton's murderer still being loose and she could possibly be next, haunted her mind. Now, on top of that worry, the kingdom she had grown to love was left in the hands of a child.

"My Lady?" Cornelius agged on. "If you wish to stay elsewhere, you may."

Kalama slowly closed her eyes. "I think I will stay elsewhere. I need to be around my family right now." Kalama glanced around the courtyard as she stared at the place she had made her home for centuries. "Not all this. I am sure Noelle will take in her mother."

"As you wish, my Lady," Cornelius concluded, then trudged through the crowd, stopping to greet the guests as he exited the courtyard.

DEVIATING THE COURSE

Ten days after his coronation, Lord Cornelius gathered his grand dukes and the remaining councilmen in the throne room. They sat around the large horseshoe-shaped table with Cornelius sitting on his throne in the center of the group. The new lord eyed the fourteen in accompany, his stomach tightening with nerves. Clearing his throat, Cornelius stood from his throne.

"Duke Kaprin, Duke Galach, I am glad you were able to make it to the meeting. You both were missed at the coronation."

"We would like to hath been there, thy Lord," Galach apologized. "But trekking through those forests is a rigorous and slow task."

"Well, you are here now, and that's all that truly matters." Cornelius paused, pursing his lips, then continued. "To start, I would like to thank the viscounts for voting me to be your new lord. I would like to ask who voted for me, and why?"

Tapping his face with his webbed fingers in a fidgeting manner, Kaprin restated his lord's question. "Aye, why *him*?"

Ramous raised his hand as he sat slumped in his seat. "I voted for you, my Lord, because I think we should protect our lands from the creatures in the depths of the Abyss, to the armies across it."

"Thou casted a ballot for ya," Efar spoke in a soft voice after clearing his throat. "Ye'r youthful and outwitted, and thou believes the decisions ya make—with some guidance from thy council—shall be for the greater good of thy kingdom."

Coi raised her thin, wrinkled arm. "I could not vote for thyself, thus I cast a ballot in yer name, my Lord."

"I too voted for you, my Lord," Senson stated. "I just think our warriors will be in safe hands with you as lord."

Lastly, Xoe raised her hand. "I also voted for you, Lord Cornelius. I voted because you are younger than any of us. You have a different outlook on situations. You haven't been a viscount for long, so you are not strongly influenced by the old ways of doing things."

Cornelius nodded slightly, still nervous with the thought of being lord. "Regardless of the reason, I would like to say: thank you."

Azreal, sitting through the statements with a concerned look, spoke up. "I object to this outcome."

Everyone in the room, shocked by the outburst, turned their attention toward the mighty djinn.

"Who was even up for a vote?"

With a slight tremble in his voice, Cornelius replied, "All of the councilmen."

"Just you ten?" Moll'ar questioned as he leaned forward onto the table, his green eyes piercing through his dangling, long hair. "Who voted? I know I never cast a ballot."

"Again," Cornelius responded, becoming more anxious with the friction building in the room, "just the council."

Growing anger emitted from the grand dukes' faces.

"Why didn't we have a say in the matter?" Kaprin hissed angrily. "We are the grand dukes! 'Tis should have been an issue which we cast a ballot, not all of ye!"

Efar stood and shouted back at the cryter across the table from him. "'Tis the way we hath always elected a lord!"

"What 'bout the duchess?" Kaprin retorted. "Is she not entitled to the crown?"

"She did not want the responsibility of bearing the crown," Cornelius interjected into the discussion.

"But why were our names not mentioned for a cast?" Darius shouted as he joined the debate. "We five have ruled over land! We have commanded armies and have made trades with other kingdoms! What has the council done?"

Efar's face became ruddy with anger. "Only an elf can hold the position of lord and bear the crown!"

Darius's brow furrowed as his anger raged. "Why? Why does it have to be a pathetic afterling—a fucking *huma*—instead of a powerful demon?"

Efar, defending himself, continued. "We elves are not *pathetic*, nor are we afterlings! 'Tis hast always been an elf from the council to proceed the lord, and thus the way it shall remain."

"Lord Brighton was the only lord that Metagore had known," Azreal pointed out. "This kingdom should not be governed the same as Rigdale was before it. We are supposed to be a united kingdom, not lessers to the Sword and Crown. My father did not stand for it, and neither will I."

"Yer father was a dangerous man," Efar hissed. "Thou doesn't know why our late lord let him remain as the head of Talean for so many centuries."

"My father was a great ruler, way before Lord Brighton was ever born."

"Yer judgment is clouded by yer relations," Efar shouted. "Duke Valek raised up two rebellions during our lord's reign."

"There is no evidence he started any rebellion," Azreal rebutted, defending his father. "We were at war with Penora, and our men fought just as the other armies had done."

Efar's sagging brow sat low over his eyes. "How many of yer Golden Men died in those wars?"

Coi stood from her seat. "'Tis kingdom will be

governed the same way as it hast always been, 'til the high lord wishes it to be changed."

Darius slammed his giant fist on the table, causing a crack to spread across the stone tabletop and fear to grow upon the viscounts' faces. "I pledge we change that rule! I pledge that we, the grand dukes, have a place on the ballot and that we have a chance to cast a vote ourselves!"

Kaprin leaned over the table and glanced at the giant demon. "Aye, I second that."

"Enow!" Cornelius shouted, getting everybody to quit their arguing. "Now that Lord Brighton has passed, I am the new lord. End of discussion!" Cornelius glanced around the table, sweat building upon his forehead and hands, growing fragile from the uncertainty of how the group would react.

Thoaral glared at the grand dukes. "Lord Brighton was venenated, and we needed to elect a new lord quickly. So, we carried on with our duty and crowned Cornelius as our new lord."

"Aye," Efar added, "Lord Brighton was venenated, and now that Cornelius is lord, we can begin our search for the culprit and sentence him to retribution."

"Have you not started questionin' suspects yet?" Moll'ar raised his voice, his tan face turning red in anger. "Lord Brighton was poisoned six weeks ago! What have you been doin'?"

"We were busy preparing the coronation—" Efar started to answer.

"That's bullshit!" Darius responded in fury as he

stood and slammed his fist onto the table once more, causing it to frush from his strength, and a large piece of stone crumbled from underneath his hand. "Your first order should have been to find out who poisoned our lord, not sit around a table with your thumbs up your arses!"

"We couldn't go on without a lord," Edorin stated in a loud voice as he, too, stood.

"We could've stepped in 'til the matter was settled," Kaprin rebutted. "'Tis is why we are here."

"We can't go back and change what has been done. Let's move on from—" Cornelius interjected, trying to take charge of the room once more, but their escalating debate diminished his attempt.

"No!" Darius persistently shouted. "This is bullshit! I demand a revote!"

The room erupted in a clash of voices, all fifteen of them stating their opinions—so much so, it was impossible to decipher what any were saying.

"Enow!" Efar shouted as his haunting voice echoed through the room. "What has—"

"I think you poisoned our lord," Azreal cut him off.

Efar stood flabbergasted. "'Tis is obscured."

"Is it now?" Azreal asked. "You are the head of the council. What you say goes, amongst them."

Distrusting, Efar's deep-set eyes narrowed. "What motive dost thou have to venenate Lord Brighton?"

"Now, that is the question, is it not? Why would you poison the most honorable man in all of Metagore?" Azreal questioned as the gaze from his white eyes met

Efar's.

"Thou did no such thing!"

"Enow!" Cornelius shouted once more, but by then too much turmoil had filled the room, rendering him powerless of regaining any control.

"Nay!" Kaprin blurted. "'Tis a reason why he hasn't started the investigation. Think 'bout it. He murdered our beloved lord so he could take the crown. He thought that since he was the eldest, he would be a sure win in the ballots."

"'Tis a falsehood," Efar said, trying to defend himself as he eyed at the other viscounts.

Barinthus looked at the others. "That actually makes sense. Did he not seem as if he was trying to rush the ballot casting? And didn't it seem like he was dragging out the coronation?"

"Aye," Kaafel replied. "I think you are right."

"We will look into every possibility in time," Cornelius managed to rejoin the conversation, "but today I would like to discuss my vision for the future."

Darius quietly stood, pushed in his chair, and approached the room's only exit.

"Duke Darius, where are you going? We have matters to discuss," Cornelius questioned the massive demon.

"You said you wanted to discuss your vision for the future," Darius responded to the youthful lord and shook his head. "I don't think I should be present then."

"Don't be ridiculous. You are one of my grand

dukes, so of course you should be here," Cornelius replied. "Now, will you take a seat please?"

"No!" Darius shouted; his head extended outward from the base of his shoulders, striking fear into the young lord and his council. "I will not follow under your rule. I did not vote for you, and I don't think any of you should have the right of passage to the crown. So, as of this moment, I am removing myself and Sentries from being under your rule."

"If ya deviate from Lord Cornelius's rule, prepare yerself for severe consequences," Efar threatened.

Darius glared intensely at the aged elf as Moll'ar stood.

"Alberon, as well, leaves from under your rule. Nothin' held against you, my Lord, but I wish to not be involved in this quarrellin' dispute."

Efar's pale face grew rosy as he became more furious than ever. "Ye all cannot survive away from the established nature of the MCA."

Darius, still snarling at the room as he stood by the exit, pointed his finger at Efar. "That is where you are wrong! You all cannot survive without *us*."

Azreal, enjoying the divide in the room, spoke. "I agree with Darius. Without us, BrightHelm is nothing—*Metagore* is nothing." He paused, contemplating what he was to say and studying the expression upon Darius's face, trying to conclude what the outcome of this meeting would be. "Until something is done about the murder of Lord Brighton and a revote for the new lord is cast, Talean will no longer be under BrightHelm's control."

"Is this how you all feel?" Cornelius asked, feeling overwhelmed and devastated by the hate he was receiving from his grand dukes.

"Aye," Kaprin replied. "I believe any of us would make a better lord than ya. 'Tis to my point, Medsa'lear shall be its own kingdom as well."

Cornelius hung his head in humiliation. The turn of events his meeting had taken saddened him. He glanced upward at the towering treefolk on the far end of the table. "Duke Galach, what say you?"

Galach rose from his chair, his head nearly reaching the ceiling of the throne room. "Thou art loyal to the ways of the land. Thou shall remain by yer side, thy Lord."

Cornelius grinned in appreciation that one of his grand dukes remained on his side. "Thank you, Galach." He looked at the other four grand dukes, then continued. "If you all are going to stand against me, then be prepared to fight."

"You dare threaten the Senturian army?" Darius shouted at the young elf. "You will be sending your knights into a slaughterhouse if you wish to hold a blade against us."

Cornelius—for the first time, seeming to fit into his role as lord and less of a shy child—narrowed his eyes onto the hard face of Darius. "There has been unity amongst the regions for centuries, and there will be unity amongst them again, even if I have to claim it myself."

Moll'ar joined the conversation once more. "Without food bein' brought to you from Alberon, your armies will wither to bones."

"Aye," Kaprin chimed in. "Without us, BrightHelm is nothin'. We will team up, us four against you two, and we shall prevail."

Darius's beady red eyes fixed themselves upon Kaprin's scaly figure. "Who's teaming up?" he asked sharply. "Sentries stands alone! We will overthrow the Sword and Crown, and if anybody gets in our way, we will annihilate them as well."

The grand dukes and the council of viscounts all erupted into another huge argument.

After a few minutes of hectic chaos, Cornelius silenced the room. "Enow! If it is a war you all want, then a war you all shall receive." The young lord paused as he studied the grand dukes' expressions. "You all have six weeks to return home and build up your armies. For after the last setting of the Crahesh moon, the Helanian army will start their advancement into your lands and bring peace back to this kingdom."

"Aye, 'til the end of the next moon as ya bid," Kaprin responded as he stood and gave a graceful bow.

"But my lord—" Efar exclaimed, but Cornelius raised a hand to silence him.

"You are all dismissed," Cornelius announced as he lowered his head in disappointment.

The grand dukes and the councilmen shuffled from the room as Cornelius motioned for Efar to remain at the table.

Glancing at the elderly elf, Cornelius spoke softly. "I did not think my first ruling would be that of war amongst the regions. What have I gotten myself into? What if I can't be the lord that Metagore needs?"

"Ya shall be a great lord," Efar stated as he patted Cornelius on the back, trying to reassure the younghede. "Thou art confident that ya shall prevail, and ya shall once again bring peace to thy kingdom."

"I hope you are right," Cornelius said in a broken voice. He paused, soaking in the situation, then continued. "Schedule a city announcement for dawn break."

RUMORS OF WAR

As dawn broke the next morning and the mountain peaks glistened peacefully in the rising sun, the denizens of BrightHelm were anything but calm. Townsfolk from the city, as well as traveling villagers from outside the city walls, frantically tried to find any truth to the unsubstantiated rumors of war following the lord's meeting with the grand dukes. The upcoming late-notice emergency meeting scheduled to take place at any moment did nothing to alleviate their fears. Speculations and blob-tales were well underway on whether Cornelius would be a good ruler or not, and some families in the city had begun making long-term plans on what they would do if—and when—war did fall upon them.

If one were to listen to the right gossipmonger, they would hear of how mercenaries and dreshdis, and even the ellestrians of old myths, were on their way to sell their services for the upcoming battles and how Cornelius had plans to denounce the crown himself during the meeting, though many would say otherwise.

As everyone gathered in the streets in front of the kingdom hall—tension and anticipation building—the doors on the second-floor balcony opened. Out stepped a giant troll suited in metal armor stamped with the insignia of BrightHelm—three crossed swords pointing downward and a crown resting under the center blade. Following behind the troll was Duchess Zorie dressed in a formal, white laced gown with floral, golden trim.

Zorie stepped up to the balcony railing. "Our lord wishes to address all Helanians," she stated as Cornelius joined her out on the balcony.

Cornelius placed his hand on the small of her back. "Thank you, Duchess."

The young lord then placed both hands on the railing in front of him. Scanning the aroused audience, the terror and anger in their eyes struck a nerve in his throbbing chest. He patiently gathered his thoughts, mentally preparing to speak. Beads of sweat formed on his smooth brow as his legs grew weaker.

After a brief moment of analyzing the crowd, Cornelius spoke. "Good morrow!"

The squiddle and spreading of rumors amongst the townsfolk halted.

"Investigations are underway for the murderer of the late Lord Brighton. The culprit will be found, and they will be persecuted. In other matters, I am sure you all have heard there has been a divide amongst the regions."

He paused to take in a deep breath as the crowded street in front of him grew loud with anger—near-instant pandemonium.

Shrieks and shouts arose from the crowd, and hostile muttering sprung from the revelation of the fear on everyone's mind. The masses seemed to become one entity as they threw accusations toward their new lord.

"Enow!" Cornelius shouted. "There is no need to fear for your safety; BrightHelm is a fortress. So, as long as you all remain inside these city walls, there will be no harm brought to you or your belongings." He regarded the emotion of the crowd as they continued to echo threats and hurled trash and pebbles toward him. "For the nearby villages in Nuwulf and of the such, we will be opening shelters for the residents who don't feel safe out from the city. I can assure you all this situation won't last long and that Metagore will return to its peaceful state soon."

As he concluded, a small stone struck his pale cheek directly below his right eye. Cornelius flinched, tucking his head under his arm as his guard swiftly forced him and his duchess inside the building while the young lord wiped the small stream of blood from the fresh cut.

They hustled downstairs and into the throne room, where sat the nine members of his council, his marquess, and Lady Kalama.

"My Lord," Efar gasped in shock when he saw the red smear of blood on the elf's cheek. "Who durst strike thy holiness?"

"It was just a frightened citizen. Not a big concern," Cornelius responded as he dismissed the accusation.

"If it continues, my Lord," Barinthus chimed in, "you cannot keep being kind and forgiving to these people."

"I do not feel threatened by a few restless souls. I do not condemn them for their actions. I might've done the same if it were I who stood in that crowd."

In a loud, firm tone, Barinthus tried to persuade the young lord to see the matter as he did. "But, my Lord, there are more villagers than guards. If you are too gentle, they will see it as a weakness and will try to overthrow the crown. Look at your grand dukes; they sensed the weakness, so they preyed upon it like a strix when it smells blood."

"There will be no more speak of the matter," Cornelius ordered, silencing Barinthus. The gaze from his gleamy blue eyes glanced at the still-mourning widow. He couldn't begin to fathom the heartache she had been coping with the past few weeks. He looked back at the viscounts. "We need to find out who is responsible for the murder of the late Lord Brighton. If any of you gain knowledge, please present it to me so appropriate actions can be taken."

"My Lord," Ramous spoke up, "I have some information you may find intriguing."

Kalama, who had been sitting motionless and staring at the floor between her feet, glanced up with curiosity lingering in her ruby eyes.

"I was doing some investigating of my own, and I came across not one, but two Lord Chalices," Ramous stated as he pulled two goblets out of a small burlap sack.

Kalama's glare narrowed onto the two cups as she rose from her seat and circled the large table, not taking her eyes from the objects. Once she had reached the chalices, she picked them both up and analyzed their every detail.

"There is only one Lord's Chalice," she said with a seemingly disillusioned look on her face. "Have I been mistaken all these years?"

"No, my Lady," Ramous responded. "There is only one; the other is a fake."

Barinthus snatched one of the chalices from Kalama's grip and inspected it. "How can you be certain?"

"Yes," Kalama concurred, "how can you tell which is real and which is the fake? They look identical."

"They are identical, except for one minor detail," Ramous responded as he took the chalice from Barinthus. "You see the rings on the inside of the chalice?" He paused to point out the faint circles to everyone. "These are called flutings, or ridges. They form on both the inside and outside of horns as they grow. With this one, the ridges are just rings, meaning the horn expanded from the tip as it grew." Ramous set down the chalice and retrieved the other from Kalama. "This one, on the other hand, its ridges are a constant spiral."

"So, what are you saying?" Cornelius asked with his vision glued on the two chalices, studying their every curve.

"The horns used to craft the chalices came from different types of animals," Ramous answered. "The Lord's Chalice is made from a bicorn's horn to purify any liquid that gets poured into it. That way, my Lord, you don't risk the chance of being poisoned when drinking from it." Ramous shook the chalice in his hand. "This chalice, by the way the ridges are spiraled, looks like it may have come from a chimera."

Kalama's hair began to smoke as her anger grew. "So, someone switched the chalices and poisoned my beloved Brighton?"

"That is what it would seem, my Lady," Ramous responded, dreading the chance of a raging fire to combust from Kalama's anger.

"Who was in charge of setting the tables at the feast?" Cornelius asked.

"I do not know," Kalama stated, her body growing tense, trying to control her emotions. "But it would have been one of the castle maids, probably one who works in the kitchen."

Cornelius nodded slightly, then looked at his council. "Go and find out who set the tables so that we can continue on with our investigation. You are dismissed."

Kalama and the council all rose from their seats around the large table and exited the room.

Cornelius, still seated beside his duchess and marquess, watched as the others left. Feeling nervous, he stood from his throne and paced around the room.

"How's your military?" he asked his marquess, Tylon, who was slouched in his wooden seat.

Tylon was over twice his lord's age but acted not of honor or nobility, but as a careless, arrogant child. Strands of gray peppered his black-as-coal nott-headed hair, and his dark-red eyes blended with his ash-gray skin. Upon himself, he wore a thin layer of chainmail, covered by a tunic with small, metal scales, resembling those of the mighty dragons.

Tylon spoke with subtlety as he looked upon his tensed lord. "We have an active military, my Lord. We will prevail against the other armies with ease; that I am assured. Beyond the clouds, we shine."

"Aye, that's what I wanted to hear," Cornelius responded as a small smile managed to surface onto his white face. He continued to pace around the room for a bit longer. "You two are dismissed." He waved off his duchess and marquess as he turned to his guard, who had been standing by the door. "Ser Trolgar, I need you to escort me to the temple."

"Ya carriage 'tis not here, m'Lord. 'Tis at the castle," his guard replied.

"Then we shall walk."

"As ya bid, m'Lord."

The giant troll escorted Cornelius through the city

streets where a massive crowd of townsfolk was still gathered. The majority of the people yelled vulgar insults toward their new lord, while the remainder were in a state of panic and asked a large variety of questions concerning their safety.

Cornelius followed close behind his guard, hoping to avoid any more objects that might get thrown his way. He was worried how the crowd would react to the news and feared the threats to come, but he believed Trolgar would keep him safe. Just looking at the troll's dark face and getting caught in his yellow beady stare would steer anyone from causing mayhem.

After they had arrived at the temple, Cornelius turned to his guard. "Stay posted by the door, and don't let anyone enter. I will return shortly."

He left his protector's side and entered the temple.

The temple was a large, circular building with eight, elegant, stone pillars circumventing the inside walls. Located in the middle of the room was a pedestal holding a large bowl of chrism. A chiseled design adorned each of the pillars, each representing one of the Gods of the Eight Divides the inhabitants of Metagore prayed to: Afria, Artus, Iden, Libras, Nya, Taac, Trillis, and Zallah.

Cornelius shuffled toward the center of the temple and splashed his face with the chrism. He then approached one of the pillars and knelt before it. The stone shaft featured a chiseled outline of an elf with a sun cresting around its head to represent Afria, the Goddess of Peace.

He began to weep as he prayed. "Afria, I kneel before you, holy and clean, so that I may ask a favor of you." The young lord, broken in voice, wiped the pouring tears from his blue eyes. "I have done nothing wrong, but the safety of this kingdom is at stake. I bid you, please bring back peace to this great land. Bring us back to the time when we could roam this land worry free. Bring us back to the time when we stood strong as one. Aye, most of all, bring us back to the time when we were united with love." Cornelius sniffled as he continued to wipe the tears from his cheeks. "If I must hand over the crown and step down from the throne, I will."

As he prayed, a cold breeze rubbed against his pale face, followed by a daunting, feminine voice. "You will find your peace rather soon, young one."

Cornelius jolted his head around, but the temple was empty. He glanced up at the pillar as he gave a slight smile, believing he had heard the goddess's voice.

"If I must, for the land to be unified once more, then I shall. I am willing to do whatever it takes to bring back peace to this once great land. I just bid that you lead me with your helping hand. To the Eight, I bid unto thee."

Cornelius rose to his feet, left the temple, and had Trolgar escort him to his castle.

THE YEOMAN

By the sixteenth day of being the Lord of BrightHelm, Cornelius had begun regretting taking the seat of the throne. Maybe he should've relinquished the opportunity and waited until he was much older and more experienced with giving orders. Or perhaps, he should've withdrew when his grand dukes caused an uproar and let one of the more qualified leaders rule the land, but if he had, then everyone would have seen him as weak, and his actions would have disgraced the other viscounts.

After eating his morning meal, Cornelius traipsed to the throne room and met with his council, but at no surprise, no one had any leads on who the culprit could have been. The most prominent lead they had was the possibility of it being one of the housemaids—one of the many people Cornelius interacted with on a daily basis.

One of the individuals who had access to every room in his castle was most likely the cold-hearted, ruthless being who poisoned Lord Brighton.

†

Later that afternoon, after a disappointing meeting with the viscounts, Cornelius sat in his cabinet writing on some parchment; his untouched lunch sat beside him, growing cold. The thought that someone who had access to his food could possibly be the killer made his stomach churn. He had checked and double checked his cup. He knew there wasn't any possible way there could be any poison in it; however, as of the moment, he had no means of making sure the food couldn't be tampered with.

As Cornelius decided to go to the kitchen to personally fix himself some lunch, someone knocked upon his door.

"May I enter, my Lord?" Ramous politely asked as the door opened.

"Aye. Come have a seat." Cornelius tidied his desk, setting all the parchment into one stack and placing his plate of food on the other edge of the table. "You bring good news, I hope."

Ramous pulled out a chair across the desk from his

young lord. "I do. But I'm not confident that it will amount to anything in the grand scheme of things."

"Alright. Well, out with it. What news do you bring?"

"I am still uncertain of who was in charge of the setting of the tables, or even who switched the chalices. But I do know that just a fake grail doesn't poison someone; it's what's in it."

"So, are you saying you know who poured the drinks?" Cornelius asked, the gaze from his crystal-blue eyes piercing through his golden bangs.

"It was your yeoman, Daeavar, my Lord," Ramous responded.

Cornelius gave a quick, subconscious glance at his chalice, then shunned it away and swallowed nervously. "I trust you've put him into custody?"

"Not yet, my Lord," Ramous cautiously replied. "We felt it would be best if you knew who poured the drink first and to see what actions you wished to take upon him."

Cornelius's eyes widened in fear. "Guards!"

His cabinet door opened as two massive, heavily armored trolls entered.

"One of you go to the buttery and bring Daeavar to me. The other, go prepare one of the keeps in the dungeons for him."

"Aye, m'Lord," the larger troll acknowledged. "We shall go at once."

Once the guards had left the room, Cornelius sent Ramous to muster the other viscounts and have them meet him in the throne room in an hour's time.

Before Ramous could exit the cabinet, Cornelius stopped him. "The next time you have accurate suspicions of a murder suspect at hand, do not wait for my agreement before taking them into custody."

"Sorry, my Lord. It won't happen again," Ramous responded before exiting the room.

Cornelius stood from his desk and paced around his cabinet, deep in thought on what course of action to take next. He knew he would have to begin the process of some form of trial, but the idea of potentially having to sentence someone to death—no matter the reason—two weeks into his lordship, put him on edge. He wondered how his subjects would perceive him, be it cruel or weak, and questioned what position he had put himself into, agreeing to take the late Lord Brighton's place.

During his pacing, Cornelius continued to glance at his untouched meal, worried he'd be at risk if he ate. He heard a knock on the door as he reseated himself, signaling the return of his guards and Cornelius's first prisoner to the room.

"Enter," Cornelius said as he tried to retain his composure.

"We bring ya Daeavar, just like ya hath commanded, m'Lord," the smaller troll said as the two guards shoved a shackled elf-like being into the room.

They pushed him with so much force, it caused him to collapse onto the floor in front of Cornelius's desk.

"M'Lord," Daeavar stated with a tremble in his

voice. Still on his hands and knees, he looked up at Cornelius as his raggedly brown hair fell to the sides of his face. "What hath thou done to deserve this treatment?"

Cornelius scowled at his yeoman. "You are being held accountable for the late Lord Brighton's death."

"But thou would ne'r—"

"You will stand in front of the council later today."

"M'Lord, thou promises to ya, thou hath done nothin' to be at fault for Lord Brighton's death. He was a dear friend o' thine."

"The council will determine your fate." Cornelius looked at the guards. "That is all. Escort him to the throne room, where he will await his trial."

The two trolls hoisted Daeavar from the floor and escorted him from Cornelius's cabinet.

†

An hour later, Daeavar stood in the center of the large, horseshoe-shaped table in the center of the throne room. Shackles bound his wrists and ankles, chained to a metal band wrapped around his waist. Two giant trolls stood slightly behind him. They were different from the ones before, but they were as intimidating as the first.

Around the table sat Lord Cornelius, Duchess Zorie, and the ten viscounts, including the newest viscountess who had replaced Cornelius: Mela.

"Welcome," Efar stated. "Do ya knowest why thou

hath been brought hither?"

"Somethin' to do with Lord Brighton's death, thou dost believe," Daeavar responded in a brittle voice.

"Aye," the duchess replied. "You are being held accused of poisoning our beloved lord, and for his death. How do you plead?"

"Thou … Thou didn't do it. Thou assures you, thou speaks the truth."

"So, you didn't taint Lord Brighton's wine or meal?" Cornelius asked.

"Nay." Daeavar paused. "Thou art tellin' ye, thou hast nothin' to do with his death."

Senson spoke up. "Did you ever feel rejoiced that he was poisoned?"

"Nay, not at all."

"You work in the castle's buttery, correct?" Edorin asked.

"Aye."

"How long have you worked in the buttery?"

"Just o'er forty years."

"And how close were you to Lord Brighton and his family?"

"We were really close. He always invited thee to family feasts and treated thee well, better than his other servants."

Edorin's face grew peculiar. "I believe you are married, correct? What does your wife do?"

"Aye, she's a backstress."

"What role did she play in your plan?"

"Ya leave her out o' this. She hath done nothin'

against her lord," Daeavar snarled, angered Edorin would even consider his wife having something to do with Brighton's murder.

"Do you think one of the other housemaids would have poisoned Lord Brighton?" Mela, the newly appointed viscountess, asked.

"Nay. We are like a family. Thou doesn't think any o' 'em would hath done anythin' to harm Lord Brighton."

"But you just stated that he treated you better than the other maids," Xoe stated. "Do you not believe *that* would give one reasons to seek retribution?"

"Nay, ne'r. Aye, he treated thee better, but that's not to say that he treated e'rone else badly. He treated us all like family. He spent countless o' time with each o' us, gainin' knowledge o' us personally. Brighton 'twas a great Lord. Thou can't reconcile why anyone would want to kill him. But to proclaim that one o' his servants hath done such a thing, 'tis just preposterous."

"Calm yerself, Daeavar," Coi said. "Did ya set the tables at the New Life Festival?"

"Nay, I did not."

"Do you know who did?" Thoaral added.

"Nay. Thou was inside pourin' drinks. So, thou knowest not who all was outside preparin' for the feasts."

"Did you pour Lord Brighton's drink?" Kaafel asked.

"Nay."

"Nay? If you poured drinks all day, then how can you be sure you did not pour that particular drink?"

Kaafel responded.

"Thou was in the buttery, pourin' drinks; 'tis m'job. The Lord's drinks are o' a different cellar, and thou was too busy that morn to hurry back and forth between the two."

"So, who was in charge of the Lord's wine cellar?" Kaafel continued to question.

"That knowledge wasn't given to thee. Another housemaid maybe, or possibly a townsfolk that volunteered to help."

"You might have let a commoner handle our Lord's drink?"

"Thou didn't assign 'em work. Thou done what was asked of thee—m'job. For all thou knows, ya could've poured the drink and poisoned him yerself."

"I did no such thing!" Kaafel shouted in anger.

"'Tis all the same to ya, thou art innocent as well, but here thou stands bein' accused o' it."

"If you didn't poison Lord Brighton," Ramous began, "did you switch the chalices for someone else to have the opportunity to murder him?"

Daeavar's face twisted in confusion. "The chalices were switched? That knowledge hast ne'r been given to thee."

"You handle the chalices, correct?" Ramous asked.

"Nay. Thou only pours the drinks that are brought to thee, but thou manages not the glasses at any other point."

"Do you know who handles the dishes?"

"Nay."

"Where would one find any form of poison?" Barinthus asked, trying another approach of the interrogation. "Or do you supposedly not know that either?"

"Ya can find some at a local drug cart," Daeavar responded bitterly.

"What carriage sells poisonous drugs?"

"The cart by the west gate hast some potent drugs, that thou guesses could become deadly."

"Is that where you got the poison at?"

"What? Nay! Thou hast told ya, thou didn't do it!"

"Then how would you know such a fact, that the cart by the west gate, in particular, sells deadly drugs?"

"Any drug can be harmful," Daeavar said as he grew petulant. "But thou dost buy remedies from there, for personal use o' course."

"What kind of personal use?" Barinthus questioned, hoping Daeavar would break from the pressure. "Poisoning Lord Brighton?"

"Nay!" Daeavar shouted. "Thou takes 'em for heart problems."

Lord Cornelius rose from the table. "That will be enough questioning. We will all discuss a verdict, then your sentence will be agreed upon."

Cornelius, along with his duchess and viscounts, left the room to review the situation in private, while Daeavar remained standing in front of the two trolls, in the center of the table.

Thirty minutes later, the council returned to the room and took their seats, while Cornelius remained standing.

"We could not come to agreeance on if you were guilty or innocent, so we have reached the conclusion that the gods shall decide your fate."

"What dost that mean?" Daeavar asked in a trembling voice.

"If you are guilty, your sentence will be death. But if you are innocent, you will be a free man to go back to work in the buttery for all of your days."

"What dost that hath to do with the gods deciding m'fate?"

"You will be thrown into the Pit," Cornelius stated as Daeavar's face turned to terror. "If you survive the hour, you will be free, but if the gods find you guilty, then your sentence will be the death that you will succumb to."

"What shall be m'opponent?" Daeavar asked in a tremulous voice.

"A manticore," Zorie softly spoke.

Daeavar collapsed to the ground. His body became numb, fearing and knowing there was no way he could survive against a manticore for five minutes, let alone for an hour.

"May the favor of the gods be on you," Cornelius concluded, as he motioned for the guards to take Daeavar away.

FEEDING LIBRAS

It had been eleven days since the grand dukes met with their newly crowned lord and his viscounts, since Darius decided to rebel against Lord Cornelius's authority and bring upon the first civil war amongst the land in centuries, and since Darius had crowned himself as the Lord of Sentries. The morrow came, and he arrived at the Northern Brim dividing Sentries and Talean. Upon reaching the wall, a young succubus rode up beside him on a nightmare.

Her name was Ky, the Duchess of Sentries. Her green eyes were vibrant, and the sun had glazed her hazelnut skin. Her hair, black as night, lay straight to her shoulders, with golden beads adorning the tips. Her back housed a pair of wings with feathers matching that of her hair. She wore a tight black-and-blue dress, open in the front, exposing her sculpted abdomen, but modest enough to cover her rounded breasts. Her boots complemented the dress. Golden armlets and earrings helped accent her dark complexion.

"What are you doing all the way out here?" Darius asked as she approached him.

"I am just seeing you a safe return to the kingdom, my Lord," she said, her voice soft and heavenly.

"Aye, I am safe." Darius stared into her seductive, green eyes. "So, tell me, Ky, why are you *really* out here? You would find me just as safe at the manor."

"Yes, I could've," she responded, her face shadowing with concern. "Is it true that we are at war?"

"It is true, but how did you hear word so soon?" Darius questioned her.

"We received a letter from Azreal a few nights ago, asking for peace between our lands."

"Who knows of the letter?"

"Marquess Lucius is the one who retrieved the scroll, but besides him, just you and I."

"Once you have arrived home, summon Lucius to join you in my cabinet. I will accompany the two of you after I return in a few days, but first I am going to survey the Brim to see how it is holding up," Darius said as he looked at the massive wall of metal stretching from the Sea of the Sun to the Abyss Ocean.

"Will do, my Lord," Ky said, then rode off.

Darius sat outside the wall, watching his duchess disappear through the rough terrain of Thieves' Hill, before turning his steed around and entering the structure.

†

A week later, Darius sat at a table in the hall of his estate, writing a letter, when Ky entered accompanied by an elder demon, Lucius.

Lucius was much shorter than his lord. His horns were small spikes, no longer than his thumbs. He was clothed with chainmail on his left side and leather straps on the right. He wore thick, leathery pants and boots. His skin was dark as ash, and his eyes burned a fiery red.

"You summoned thee, my Lord?" Lucius asked as he pulled out a chair for Ky, then seated himself.

"Aye," Darius responded, then continued with a snarled voice. "I heard you retrieved a letter from Azreal."

"Aye, my Lord." Lucius removed a rolled-up sheet of parchment and handed it to his lord.

Lord Darius,

The Kingdom of Talean wishes not to be at war with the Senturians, but rather at war with the Helanians. If you accept this letter as a treaty for peace with us, the Taleanics, we will gladly provide you with all you could ever ask for, to further aid in your attempts to take down Lord Cornelius and overthrow the Crown and Sword. Once we are successful in our conquest, we will step aside and bow to you as our gracious and almighty lord.

   - Lord Azreal and Duchess Anina

Darius crumpled the parchment and tossed it on the table before grabbing the letter he had written. He rolled it up and handed it to Ky. "Send this to Azreal as my response."

"Right away, my Lord." Ky took the letter and stuck it in her dress, then stood and left the manor.

Darius stood and scuffed to a giant map of the six kingdoms hanging on one of the walls in the hall. The tapestry was torn in spots with loose strands of fabric dangling from the rest of the map. The ink had faded, but the colors of each region were still noticeable enough to stand out from the tan background.

"I want you to form two calvaries." Darius pointed toward the bottom of the map, at the land connecting Sentries to Ringwood. "I want one army to travel into Ringwood, then up to BrightHelm."

"You want them to go through Black Rain Forest?" Lucius questioned.

"Aye."

"It would be quicker to go north around the sea. Going south would be nearly forty leagues farther. That's another two days ride, when they could have already taken Ringwood."

"Aye, I am aware. But I want them to go south, in case one of the other kingdoms surpasses the Southern Brim. We will have a higher rate of confronting them out in the field, instead of waiting until they are at the walls of our city."

Lucius nodded, understanding Darius's tactic.

"Now, the other, I want to head to the Kingdom of Talean." Darius moved his massive finger from the south of the map toward the north, just above Sentries. "Once they've reached Talean, I want them to obtain every bit of resources they can commandeer, drain them dry. Once they have supplied themselves with what they need, I want them to travel west to BrightHelm, where we can then flank Cornelius and his *puny* army. Once we have taken the throne from that huma child, the six kingdoms will be mine." Darius paused and stared at the map, then turned to his marquess. "Go summon all the citizens who are without family to the throne room."

"For a tribute, my Lord?" Lucius asked sternly through a smile creeping onto his face.

"Aye, it's been ages since one was needed, but in these trying times, we do not need to anger the gods."

"Aye, I will go right away, my Lord."

†

Later that day, as the sky darkened and night began to spread over the heavens, Darius, Ky, and Lucius sat upon their seats in the throne room, awaiting to meet the potential sacrifices. Before the tributes were allowed entry, forty of Darius's best knights entered the large hall first and lined the walls. Following the armored knights, eighty-three potential sacrifices entered, along with another forty knights.

Different emotions filled the citizens. The offering repulsed a few of them, thinking they shouldn't be offered to the gods just because they were without relatives. The majority were frightened for their lives—one was so nervous, he fainted upon entering the room. A few tried to resist entering, hoping to escape their possible fate of being chosen, but the knights wrestled them to the ground and forced them to comply, as the others had done.

"Welcome," Darius greeted them as he stood. "War is amongst us. And for us to have the gods' mercy, we must offer up a tribute." Darius raised his jubbe of mead. "This is why you all are here; because none of you have a family that will be burdened by your death." Darius took a swig. "One of you will have the honor to be a hero for your kingdom. So, if any of you is willing to volunteer, please speak now." He paused, awaiting a response. "If no one volunteers, we will randomly select one of you. No one?"

"I will be the tribute," a raucous voice from the back of the crowd said.

"Who said that?" Darius asked as he looked around, trying to find the disembodied soul.

"I did," a venerable minotaur knight said as he raised his hand.

"Ser Parellus?" Darius couldn't comprehend what his eyes and ears were telling him. "But you were not selected to be a tribute. You are a knight, a protector of this realm. Besides, you have a son who is alive and well."

"I understand, m'Lord," Parellus responded. "But I am reachin' the age where I must soon lay down my blade. So, why should I live while any of these youngins be sacrificed? I signed up to be a knight willin' to give m'life for this realm. What's a bet'r honor than doin' just that, givin' m'life for the glory of the gods? So, if you will have me, m'Lord, I will take on that responsibility."

Darius nodded. "If you wish to be the tribute, then the tribute you shall be."

The rest of Darius's knights ushered everyone out of the manor. The group, along with some citizens who had not been invited into the estate previously, followed Darius and his knights up Mount Dumas's narrow, rocky ledge.

†

After a couple of hours of walking, Darius and the crowd reached the break of the volcano's crater, where it met the rivers of lava flowing through the Keep of Ashes and into the Sea of the Sun.

"We have arrived," Darius announced as he faced the audience. "Come forth knights, with the ritual items."

Three knights, dressed in black suits of armor, stepped forward and stood beside their lord. One carried a chalice filled with mead, the second held a bowl of chrism, and the last had a bundle of anthurium leaves he had picked on their way up the volcano.

"Bring the tribute forward," Darius commanded.

Two more knights stepped forward, escorting Parellus. Instead of delivering him to Darius, they brought him to two large stone pillars with a chain hanging from each. They first removed Parellus's black armor, leaving him stripped bare before the crowd. They latched his hands in each of the pillars' chains so he would be facing the crowd, then placed his feet in a clamp attached to the ground between the two posts.

Darius turned to the fiery, lava-filled crater and lifted his hands in a worshiping manner. "Libras! Nya! Taac! ... Libras! Nya! Taac! ... Libras! Nya! Taac!" he chanted. "Libras, we know you are within us, and we acknowledge the blessings of strength you bring us. All hail Libras!"

"All hail Libras!" the crowd reiterated.

Darius turned and took the chalice of mead. He then turned to face the crater and lifted the goblet. "Libras, share in the drinking of this great mead! Give us guidance in this war, and share your strength to all those who have assembled here on this night. Take this mead from man, as we have taken it from the land."

Darius turned and raised the chalice for Parellus to consume its liquids.

"Stop! Stop!" a young voice shrilled.

Darius turned and gasped in shock as a young minotaur weaved through the large audience.

"Why have you interrupted us?" Darius asked,

enraged.

"Don't go through with it. Lord Cornelius wouldn't approve of the sacrifice."

"Lord Cornelius? He is no longer your lord, I am!" Darius bellowed, infuriated someone would mention Cornelius's name.

"Artekus, 'tis all right. I wished this upon m'self," Parellus said as he forced a smile, trying to calm his son.

"I won't let you go through with this," his son said as he ran to his father and tried to pull open the shackles.

"Knights, apprehend him immediately!" Darius roared.

As he had ordered, two of his knights ran up and retained Artekus as he screamed and flailed.

Darius unsheathed a sword draped around his waist. It was one of six swords Lord Ozir had forged centuries ago when the six kingdoms of Metagore had united. The sword had an ebony hilt with two embedded diamonds and an obsidian-tipped blade that was five links long.

Darius approached Parellus's back. While holding the sword in both hands—one on the hilt and the other on the blade to make his cuts precise—Darius carved a symbol into the back of Parellus. The symbol was an upside-down triangle with a line jutting from each side and a circle cut into the center.

"Strength, powerful and strong. The weak fall, on his back they rest," Darius proclaimed as he engraved the image into the minotaur's back.

Once completing the design, Artekus slipped free

from the knights who had been trying to retain him. He lunged forward and grabbed Darius's arm to try and pull him from his father. Darius's strength was too much for the boy, as he whipped the boy around him, causing him to fall to the ground. As soon as the child hit the ground, he jumped up and lunged at the demon once more. This time, however, instead of grabbing Darius's arm, he found himself struck by the mighty sword.

As Darius pulled the blade from the boy's abdomen, the knights picked his gasping body off the ground.

"Leave him be," Darius commanded as he approached Parellus again. "I'm sorry you had to witness that, but your boy brought it upon himself."

Parellus was in tears. Though he had been weeping due to the agonizing pain he was enduring, something sounded different in his cries. They were cries of mourning.

Darius proceeded the ritual by cutting another symbol, but this one on the front of Parellus's torso. The symbol appeared as an X, with a diamond for the bottom half.

As before, as he engraved the image into Parellus's chest and abdomen, Darius chanted. "War, the sting of a dragon's fang. Blood and sweat tastes the blade."

Once he finished engraving, Darius approached one of his knights and grabbed the anthurium leaves, then stepped up to the one with the bowl and soaked the petals in the chrism. Once the leaves were thoroughly soaked, Darius returned to Parellus, whose body hung lifelessly due to the loss of blood and the searing pain.

Darius proceeded to rub the chrism-soaked leaves across the wounds of Parellus.

"Cleanse thy blood, for only thy purest is best for the gods."

Once he had finished, two knights unlatched the chains supporting Parellus and carried him to the edge of the crater and sat him down as Darius lifted the boy and chained his helpless body to the pillars.

"Please take this additional sacrifice, as we ask for forgiveness on his behalf."

Darius stabbed the boy in the heart and twisted the blade until he could see the life leave the young minotaur's body.

Darius slowly removed the blade, wiped the blood onto the legging of his pants, and returned it to its sheath. He approached the edge of the crater, beside Parellus and his knights.

"From the gods to the land, we eat. From us, on the land, to the gods we feed," Darius proclaimed while raising his hands once more. "The gift of life, for the blood on a knife. Come forth ol' great one, come forth in acceptance. Hail to the beast, hail to the Gods of the Eight Divides. Libras emerge from your slumber. Emerge as we fall!"

Darius and the crowd knelt, waiting for Libras's acceptance of the tributes.

Nothing happened.

Darius grew tense and angered that Libras had denied the offering due to the interference. Darius clenched his fist and pounded the molten ground.

"Libras!" he yelled, enraged, demanding the god to take the sacrifices.

A strong gust of wind blustered from the cave on the other side of the volcano's crater as a sonorous rumble emerged from its depths. Thick smoke built up as if the volcano was preparing to erupt.

It was hard to decipher anything through the burning smoke billowing into their faces, but they could see two massive, crimson red eyes staring at them from across the mouth of Mount Dumas. His appearance was so sudden and his exit so swift, the spectators could hardly tell what had happened at first. Upon mighty wings, with a wingspan of over three rods, the dragon took flight from the volcano, smoke following in his wake.

He was silent as the night, until, with a tremendous roar, he circled and dove for the sacrifice, grabbing Artekus and tearing him from the chains binding him to the pillars, causing them to crumble from his mighty force. They watched as Libras flew higher and higher into the sky, his maroon scales seemingly black as he vanished into the night. They heard another roar and caught a glimpse of the young minotaur's body plummeting to the land. The body fell onto one of the knights with so much force, it killed the knight in the process, splattering those nearby with their blood. Libras swooped and snatched Parellus from the ground. The gusts from his wings pushed everyone onto their backs. A couple of unfortunate civilians were too close to the edge and found themselves tumbling down the steep ledges of Mount Dumas.

As fast as he had appeared, Libras—their God of War and Strength—vanished back into his abode in the mountain. There heard a deep rumble from the depths of Dumas, along with screams from Parellus before the dragon's sharp fangs silenced him.

Darius stood and faced the crowd. "Libras has granted our request! Tonight we feast, for tomorrow we will prepare for war!"

The crowd cheered with rejoice as they followed Darius and his knights to the manor where they would enjoy a generous banquet in his hall.

Sibling Rivalry

Eleven days after returning to his manor in Talean, Azreal prepared for his meeting with Berez, the Emperor of Direfell. He sat at the table in the great hall, beside him sat a lamia, Anina, who was his half-sister and who he had named his duchess. Pale-green scales covered her lanky body, topped with long auburn hair. At their feet were two large canines known as droyaids, covered in thick plated hide, laying guard to their masters.

On the table in front of Azreal sat large mounds of coins—silver and gold pieces—along with some blood pennies. His large fingers pushed around the piles on the golden tabletop as he occasionally glanced at his spindly sister.

He grasped a stack of blood pennies and jingled them about. "Do you know how Talean became the richest city in Metagore? Probably even in all the Abyss?"

Anina's yellow snake eyes trailed over her brother's figure and spoke with insolent toward him. "We stole from other realms to fill our purse."

Azreal's white eyes looked fiercely at her. "No. We negotiated with the realms, and the ones that stood against us, we forced ourselves upon them."

Anina crossed her arms and looked away, disgusted with her brother's rulings and tactics. "'Tis all the same. Our armies rampaged and pillaged their lands, raped their women, and killed their ungrown."

"The realms needed to be put in check," he snarled. "Now they come to us for support, offering chips and pennies."

"And you will thus turn around and give it to stronger domains as payment for an attack on the weaker, so they will send us more chips and pennies," Anina hissed, as they had never seen eye to eye on the matters of the kingdom.

"It is called supply and demand," he barked, then calmed himself before continuing. "After all, that is how you run a business."

The two grew quiet, ignoring the other as they waited for their guest to arrive. The concept weighed heavily on Anina's mind to expose Azreal for his mendacious actions, but along with the idea, she worried what would happen to her if she laid bare his double-dealing ways. He would have her killed if he even knew of her thoughts; others had died for less.

They didn't have to wait long before someone finally knocked on the door.

"M'Lord, Emperor Berez has arrived," a guard said as he entered the hall.

"Send him in," Azreal responded.

"As ya bid, m'Lord."

The guard left the room, then reentered a moment later with a hobgoblin dressed in red and gold garments.

"Emperor Berez, take a seat," Azreal stated as he motioned for him to sit.

"Gramercy."

Berez pulled out a chair across the table from the djinn and his duchess.

"So, hath ya came to an agreeance with the terms of our treaty?" Berez asked, smiling, confident that Azreal was a man of his word, and he would help defend his people.

"I have not," Azreal said as he surveyed the many coins setting upon the table before him.

Berez was shocked—so much so, he swore under his breath. In his attempt to try to be polite, he responded, "'Tis there somethin' grea'r that ya wish to obtain, Grand Duke Azreal?"

"No. The situation here has changed. War has been raised amongst the provinces, and I will not have the men to spare. I will need all my knights here to defend our cities." Azreal noticed the disbelief in Berez's eyes. After all that time, they were mere signatures away from getting the nod, but matters had changed.

Berez glanced at Anina, who had been sitting with her head tilted, staring at the table, then back toward Azreal.

"I'm sorry for yer misfortune," he said dolefully, still hoping there was a chance for future discussions. "Perchance after the war is o'er, we can renegotiate sanctions."

"If all goes as planned, we should still be with firm numbers after the war. For now, I am sorry if we have wasted your time, Emperor, but after the war, we can meet up once more and renegotiate our terms."

The guard from before entered the great hall. "M'Lord, ya have received a letter from the Senturian, Lord Darius."

Azreal looked at Berez. "You may be dismissed." He then waved for the guard to bring him the letter.

"'Tis it good news, brother?" Anina asked as the guard escorted Berez from the hall.

"No, I am afraid not."

Azreal crumpled up the letter and tossed it on the table, then grabbed a blank sheet of parchment and proceeded to write another letter. After a few moments, Azreal finished the letter, rolled it up, and sealed it.

"Guard!"

The guard outside the hall's door responded as he entered the room. "Aye, m'Lord?"

"Go fetch me Rri. She is in my chamber."

"Right away, m'Lord."

"She may be hungry, so be cautious."

"Will do, m'Lord."

The guard left the room and scurried to Azreal's bedchamber.

Azreal sat with the new letter rolled up in his hand, in deep thought as he stared at it. He had hoped someone would want his aid in the war. He had preferred to obtain Darius's help, for he was formerly a skilled knight in both the Taleanic and Senturian armies and had a vast knowledge of what it was like in the face of battle. Unfortunately, the demon lord had denied him his request.

"Go retrieve me a small carrot and a slab of meat from the larder," Azreal commanded Anina.

"As you bid."

Anina slithered from her chair and toward the kitchen.

Upon Anina's absence, Azreal grabbed another sheet of parchment and wrote once more. This time when he had finished, he waved his hand over it to cast a spell, making the ink only visible to one other person. He smuggled the letter in his vest as his duchess returned with the two pieces of food.

"Here you go."

Anina handed Azreal the carrot and an uncooked tenderloin.

Azreal took a bite of the carrot as he tossed the meat under the table for his droyaids to devour.

At that time, the guard returned with a beautiful red-feathered strix with a long, shiny, golden beak splattered with a little bit of blood. As it perched itself on the guard's right arm, all four of its black talons dug deep into his leather glove.

Upon entering the room and seeing Azreal, the owl-like bird flew from the guard toward its master and landed on Azreal's shoulder.

"I hope Rri was not a bother for you," Azreal told the guard, as he scratched the strix's neck.

"Not at all, m'Lord," the guard replied as he wiped a few drops of blood from his face.

"Good. You are dismissed."

The guard returned to his post outside the hall's main entrance.

Azreal gave the first letter to his bird to clutch tightly in her front talons. He then waved the rest of the carrot in front of Rri's bulging yellow eyes for a brief second, then fed it to her. After finishing the carrot, the strix flew out an open window in the hall's roof.

"How does she know where to go?" Anina asked curiously as she watched the strix fly away.

"I have trained her in a way, depending on what I feed her, where she will know where to go. So far, I have her taught to go to the five capitals: a carrot for Alberon, apple for Ringwood, rice stalk for Medsa'lear, fish for BrightHelm, and a tomato for Sentries."

As Azreal continued to converse with his sister, the door opened once more as his marquess entered the room. Marquess Solaris was a djinn who had a lavender complexion, a long black mohawk and goatee, and an earring hanging from his left ear.

"Ahh, Marquess Solaris," Azreal exclaimed. "I was

about to summon for you."

"Is it true?" Solaris asked as he greeted him with a slight bow. "I have heard word of war amongst the lands. Tell me it is not true."

Azreal lowered his head in disappointment. "I am afraid it is true." Azreal peeked over his shoulder at Anina. "Will you leave us in private?"

"Am I not allowed to hear of these matters?" Anina asked as her face turned sour.

"No. Our discussions are not permitted for your consumption."

"But I am your duchess."

"Leave us!"

Anina shifted her distrusting eyes between Azreal and Solaris, then left the room, her serpentine body trailing behind her.

After Anina had departed from the room, Azreal continued. "Prepare our knights for an incoming attack. Fortify our walls, and do not let any army enter the city." Azreal reached into his vest and removed the hexed letter. "Take this letter, and when the time comes, follow its commands exactly."

"I will follow it strictly as it is written," Solaris affirmed as he took the parchment and stuck it in the pouch hung around his waist.

"I suspected that you would," Azreal responded as he smirked.

Man Versus Beast

In the chilled, frosted keeps of Cornelius's castle sat Daeavar, the former yeoman, forced to reside on the cold concrete floor with nothing to sleep on and not permitted a single bit of food to eat aside from stale bread and putrid water to drink. Daeavar was miserable and weak. All he could do was to ponder over the situation that had gotten him thrown into the cell.

For the past fifteen days, Daeavar had no contact with anyone except the guards. The armored trolls had no care in the world for the prisoners under their watch. They showed no sympathy for neither their isolation, nor lack of sleeping materials nor the courtesy of a simple bucket for the prisoners to relieve themselves.

The keeps were beyond chilling—enchanted by the

djinns who had helped design them—making the prisoners believe they were enduring the effects of a blizzard, causing frost to form on their bodies. Each keep had the capability of inducing the inhabitants to feel as if they had been imprisoned for years, forcing their bodies to undergo the symptoms of being in such a climate. They grew stiff and sick, and their limbs pained from frostbite. Thus, most of the prisoners never survived in the keeps for longer than a moon.

Fearing his punishment for a crime he pleaded innocent and being left without any belief or hope, Daeavar prayed to Nya, their Goddess of Life and Death, for a quick end to his undeserved suffering.

As he prayed for his life to be taken before he could suffer anymore, Daeavar heard footsteps approaching. With his head down, he could tell it was a female approaching by the sound of her traveling lightly.

Daeavar knew the steps taken into the keeps. He dreaded to face the one woman people were slow to anger. He glanced at the approaching feet. He could feel the stiffness in his neck muscles as he quivered and shook. His eyes caught a glimpse of burning embers falling onto the ground outside of his cell. His gaze traveled up a thick fur coat snug around a feminine body. He locked his sight onto the blazing ruby eyes glaring at him.

Kalama stood still before the door. Her breaths came with force as her nostrils flared, and her bronze skin glistened in the light of the flames dancing amongst her curls. Lady Kalama, who was loved as much as her late husband and her beauty never faltering, looked deadly and dangerous.

Daeavar's face was wary as he stared at her for what seemed to be an eternity in his faltered mind, but it didn't take her long to find the words through her rising anger.

"How dare you?" she shouted, her voice reverberating through the keeps.

"I—" Daeavar began but more shouts from the enraged widow drowned out his words.

"How dare you take him away from me! How dare you kill my only love! My *life*! My *fire*!" Kalama hissed and screamed, tears steaming off her bronze face. "He was the only one who understood me!" Kalama paused to reflect upon the life they had spent together. She closed her flooded eyes as she began once more, this time her voice brittle. "He took me in and made me his love forever."

Daeavar struggled to his feet and ambled to the metal bars, cringing in pain. "Thou art innocent."

He tried to defend himself but was cut off once again as Kalama's eyes shot open.

"Then you took my children's father. You took my beloved husband. My beloved Brighton! You took him away from me! You will be damned forever! Your soul will be plagued by Dézhira for all eternity!" Kalama screamed as her outstretched arm passed through the barred door. Fire engulfed her as she tried to grasp the prisoner.

Daeavar edged away in fear as her nails scraped

against one of his arms. His eyes flickered in disbelief. The soreness he had previously felt fled his mind, replaced by the dread of his once queen. He had never experienced Kalama's anger. He had always steered away from her when she looked as if she was going to explode, but he had heard rumors of how she could burn down a kingdom.

"What do you have to say for yourself, you *abomination*?" she snapped.

Daeavar, terrified of the woman he had grown to know so well over the years, slowly inched his way into one of the far corners of his cell, his face frozen in fear. He slumped onto the ground, his face brooding as Kalama scowled at him.

After a few moments of no reply, Kalama grabbed one of the door's iron bars. Steam rose from under her palm as the bar melted. She released her grip on the cell with no intention of going in after Daeavar but to solely strike fear in him, leaving him knowing she could seek revenge if she wished. She stood still—the true epitome of a fiery rage—glowering at the former yeoman.

"I thought higher of you," she said, her voice thick with emotion. "But for you to commit such a horrid crime, to my Brighton of all people, I guess my judgment failed me."

She lowered her head and traipsed away from the cell.

As she left the keeps, one of the guards who had been overseeing Daeavar unlocked the cell's door.

"'Tis time to go," the guard said as he approached

Daeavar and placed him in shackles.

As Daeavar trudged along, mostly pushed and shoved by the guard, he was in a state of shock, only able to feel his limbs burn. His frozen and frostbitten skin had begun thawing expeditiously. His strength wavered, causing the weight of the chains to force him to trek slowly, thus, the guard shoved harder. The rough ground under his bare feet felt as if he were walking on broken glass.

After leaving the keeps, the guard crammed Daeavar into a restricted caged wagon drawn by a dralion and was taken to the Pit, where he would meet his fate.

†

Cornelius sat in his cabinet a few floors above the icy keeps of his castle. Across from his desk sat Marquess Tylon.

"The kingdom is growing violent outside of these walls." Cornelius's voice sounded modulated and strong. "We need to establish order in the streets."

"So, what actions do you purpose we take?" Tylon responded, slouching in his chair.

"Send some of your knights to patrol the streets." Cornelius turned and glanced out the window. "Send orders for six guards to accompany me at all times, starting at sun break tomorrow."

Tylon leaned forward in his seat, supporting his elbows on his knees. "You wish to have six guards at your side?"

"Aye," Cornelius acknowledged as he turned toward Tylon. "I feel my safety is threatened when I walk the streets with just one escort."

"You don't feel safe in the streets?" Tylon questioned. "What about feeling safe from the dangers that lie beyond this kingdom's walls? What about the war that the grand dukes have brought upon us."

"They are no longer grand dukes." Cornelius's voice grew strident.

"Maybe not," Tylon responded. "But you haven't issued any battle plans. For pity's sake, you haven't given any command to defend our walls. How do you expect us to survive, if you don't try to protect us?"

Cornelius's face grew despondent as his stare narrowed. It was becoming harder for him to see as tears formed in his eyes. After a brief moment, he raised his head and peered toward the side of the room, trying not to make eye contact with Tylon.

"I …" Cornelius's voice strangled. "… I knew in the back of my mind I needed to do something. I knew war was amongst us, and I knew I needed to give the orders to line the walls with archers and to have you get your armies prepared." Cornelius paused to sniffle, then continued. "I had hoped it would have all blown over. That *maybe* they were just upset for the moment and when they returned to their manors, they would have forgotten about the war. I had …" Cornelius looked down for a moment, then back at Tylon. "I had hoped that I wasn't as big of a mistake as what everyone else thought. I wanted to be lord so I could help people, so I could do something that would make a difference, and this war isn't the difference I had in mind."

"I seriously doubt they've forgotten the war," Tylon said softly.

"I know. I've just been under so much stress."

"If you want people to respect you as their lord and feel safe in your own kingdom, then take charge. Even I am aware of that."

"Aye. Go and prepare the walls for defense and ready up your knights. If they wish to come here and attack us, I want us to be ready. But in the case that the thought of war had been smothered out, I do not crave to rekindle the flame."

Cornelius sat at his desk for a brief moment, glaring at Tylon who slouched in the chair.

"Well?" he asked raucously. "What are you waiting for? You wanted me to give the command, now here I am, and there you remain slouched."

Tylon released a slight chuckle. "Aye, I've already got the walls lined with archers. Plus, I have sent scouts to patrol outside our walls, keeping an eye out for any incoming attacks."

Cornelius gave a slight smile. A sigh of relief escaped him as the weight of appending doom seemed to have been lifted off of his shoulders. Then with a small chuckle himself, he continued. "This is why you still remain as my marquess. I'm glad I can count on you."

As they continued to speak, a knock came from the door as Duchess Zorie entered.

"It's time to go to Galdwulf, my Lord," she said as she gave a courteous bow to Cornelius.

"Aye, most certainly." Cornelius turned toward Tylon. "Will you excuse me? I have other matters to attend to."

Cornelius stood from his desk and departed with Zorie. Outside sat a white and black carriage, suited for the lord and his duchess—a BrightHelm banner hung on both sides. In front of the wagon sat two guards, who were holding the reins attached to two large felines—dralions.

After Cornelius and Zorie had entered the carriage and began their journey to Galdwulf, Zorie looked at Cornelius's moist face. No tears were visible, but his tense posture and the fixed gaze upon his faint face were very evident.

"Are you nervous, my Lord?" Zorie's softly spoken voice pierced through her lord's trance.

"Me, nervous? Why would I be nervous?" Cornelius responded with a chuckle, trying to not look discouraged. "I have no reason to be nervous. After all, I'm not the one sentenced to the Pit."

"No, you are not, my Lord," Zorie responded as she placed her hands on her lap and straightened her posture.

An hour's ride into Galdwulf, near the base of Mount

Eryn, rested a massive stone structure unlike any other—the Pit. With an iron-caged dome towering thirty legs over the ground it covered and wooden pews stretching as high as one could see, placed outside of the dome's structure to house the audience in attendance, the Pit was the place all battle-to-the-death fights were held. Some of the clashes were for entertainment, merely a sport for bragging rights, while others as the one being held on that day, were for punishment and judgment.

The incoming crowd started to flood the seats, filling them to capacity. Even with being shoulder to shoulder with the next, each citizen was filled with cheer. They were not bothered by the usual outcome of the brutal fights, they were merely excited for the free entertainment. It had been a while since the last gladiatorial duel. Many of the audience members didn't care if Daeavar was innocent or guilty, they were there to enjoy the sight of bloodshed.

As the crowd finished filing in, Lord Cornelius and Duchess Zorie, accompanied by the two guards, sauntered to their seats under a canopy designated for them, placed in the center.

"Welcome," Cornelius addressed the crowd, scanning the gathered audience. "Today we have come to witness the gods' judgment of the accused, who is being condemned for the late Lord Brighton's death. He has yet to confess. So, may thy gods' judgment be merciful and just. Now without further ado, enjoy the show."

The crowd erupted in a roar as Cornelius took his seat and motioned to a guard standing above a large iron gate connecting the arena to Daeavar's holding cell. The guard raised the gate as the prisoner was shoved out of the cell by another. Daeavar staggered as he was forced into the arena but managed to maintain his balance. He glanced at his wrists and rotated them for a brief moment, glad one of his captors had removed his shackles.

Across the arena, Daeavar could see two yellow eyes, surrounded by a thick coat of brown fur, staring at him through the iron bars. The beast growled and hissed as it rammed the gate—two long, sharp horns becoming visible to all who were watching.

Daeavar knew his death was imminent, and in some ways, he was glad the torture he was enduring would soon be relinquished. Nonetheless, his heart ached as it pounded against his ribs, and his limbs trembled from weakness.

As he stood in front of his gate, a low rumble came, and the ground vibrated as the guard lowered the iron gate. Still in much pain from being in the keeps, he could feel his body becoming numb. With his legs fatigued, he took a seat, wishing the guards would release the creature so his torture would end soon.

As he sat waiting, he saw a djinn lighting the beacon placed above the manticore's cell. A residue covered the torch that would burn out after an hour. He knew his time had come.

He continued to sit and observe the crowd. The

innocent townsfolk who would, in an hour's time, go on with their day-to-day tasks. His family and friends that he should be seated next to, watching another, innocent perhaps, man die for the crimes he didn't commit.

He distinguished Lady Kalama in the stands. Her eleven children's hair burned with anger and sorrow over the death of their father. Daeavar detoured his eyes, unable to look upon her as she glared at the one she believed killed her husband.

As his gaze continued to shift about the audience, a rumble came from across the arena as the other gate rose from the icy ground. His attention was drawn to the large feline as he awaited its release.

No matter how much affliction engulfed him, Daeavar decided the only way he could prove his innocence to the crowd was to face the beast and survive. He stood and hunched over. His body began to bulge and morph, forming into a bluish-gray wolf known as a raiju—an elemental creature capable of generating lightning from quick movements.

Daeavar paced from side-to-side, as sparks began to accumulate from his shoulders grinding against the side of his body.

The time had arrived, and the gate stood open. Emerging from the darkness of the cell, stepped out a bulky creature bearing two scorpion tails, bull-like horns, and wings of a dragon.

At first, the manticore just prowled around the arena, stalking Daeavar, who was doing the same, both creatures assessing the other.

After a few trips around on the ground, the manticore pounced toward Daeavar, who darted away in a bolt of lightning. The creature looked around, unsure of what had happened, smelling the faint scent of the ozone where Daeavar once stood.

The beast turned and spotted Daeavar on the opposite side of the Pit. It slowly prowled toward Daeavar, pinning him up against the wall. He pounced once more, but again Daeavar vanished in a flash.

Growing irritated, the creature growled. It approached Daeavar a third time. However, when he pounced, it swung its tails to the side.

Daeavar managed to escape being pounced on, but as he fled, one of the large tails struck him. Daeavar impacted the ground as he slid across it. He rose to his feet, limping in pain, the numbness still had not left him. He was uncertain how long he could keep running away.

Once more the beast pounced, this time landing on Daeavar. Its razor-sharp claws dug into Daeavar's blue hide. Gouges ripped into his side as blood soaked his fur. Daeavar knew death would soon consume him. As soon as he had accepted defeat, the beast withdrew his claws and walked away, only leaving minor scratches and matted red fur.

As the manticore circled the arena, Daeavar staggered along the wall, his sight narrowed and muzzle snarled as he tried to assess the reason of why the beast didn't kill him.

As time passed, the beast continued to pounce onto

Daeavar, swatting and ripping tufts of fur from him, just to release him shortly afterward. Daeavar began to think he might make it out alive—broken and gouged, but alive.

As the two circled around the arena—snow falling from the turquoise sky—Daeavar glanced at the torch. The flame had dwindled down, significantly smaller than it once was. He knew the hour had to be drawing near.

The ground rumbled as a loud echoing roar shuttered from above the Pit. Everyone glanced toward the tip of Mount Eryn as a figure flew overhead, but with the falling snow, it was hard to decipher what it was.

Daeavar, standing in awe, unconsciously morphed into his elven form. His mind filled with thoughts. Was this a sign from the gods? Were they actually going to allow him his life and freedom?

He glanced at the torch once more and gazed in amazement at the residue embers burning from the wick. He stood smiling as hope filled his mangled and bruised body. Against all the odds, he had managed to survive the hour. A feat he knew should not have been accomplished.

Joy and relief filled his body but quickly fled as a sharp pain pierced his chest. Daeavar collapsed to the ground, grabbing at his torso, gasping for air. The realization of why he had been taking medications so often entered his mind, along with the thought of Cornelius refusing him to take them while he was in the keeps.

As Daeavar lay on the ground, the beast grew tired of playing with its food and pounced onto him one last time. Daeavar managed to muster enough air to expel one final booming scream.

The beast stabbed his body with one of its tails and bit into his head and shoulders, ripping them from the rest of his shredded body.

The crowd drew still for a brief and silent moment before echoes of cheers bellowed through the structure.

Cornelius rose from his seat. "The gods have decided. We have found—"

The enraged chants from the crowd cut him off.

"The Lord's blood! The Lord's blood!"

Cornelius's guards snatched him and Zorie by the arms and rushed them toward their carriage, weapons at the ready in case the hostile crowd decided to attack.

ΠΟΤ ΑΤ WAR – DIΠ HEE'DOLU

It had been a full moon since Moll'ar and the other grand dukes had met with their newly elected lord. Upon returning to Alberon, Moll'ar continued his days as he had always done—waking up early every morning to help the farmers with their crops. He would run from settlement to settlement in his animal form to gather a list of needed supplies; then later in the week, he would return to each colony with their orders. His marquess never understood why he would do such chores, on top of his duties as grand duke, but he had always felt that helping the tribes in Alberon grounded him in a way, reminding him where he could have been if not for his status as grand duke.

While Moll'ar steered a wagon pulled by a couple of

heardbeasts delivering some manure, a satyr descended beside him on a pegasus.

Duke Pol stood slightly shorter than Moll'ar, though his chest and arms were larger and bulkier. His physical appearance led many to believe he was a dominant fighter, but he despised any avoidable conflict. Dark brown fur covered him from the waist down, the color matching his tanned skin. His scalp was bare, except for the two spiraling and protruding horns. A brown goatee lined his elongated muzzle, and hooves appointed the ends of his legs.

"*Duke Pol, what brings you out here?*" Moll'ar asked, speaking in Oacari—the native tongue of Alberon—as he stopped the wagon.

"*We received a letter from Grand Duke Azreal of Talean,*" the satyr responded. Leaning in close to Moll'ar, he whispered, "*There is mention of war amongst the people of Metagore. Why have you not brought this to my attention yet?*"

Moll'ar spoke from the corner of his mouth, trying to keep the nearby tribe members from overhearing. "*Alberon is not involved in the war.*"

Another pegasus flew in, this one carrying Marquess Terus—a stout minotaur wearing nothing but a thin loincloth and the scars upon his arms. He stood a head taller than his lord, and his skin was much darker. His hooves were freshly polished and shone brightly in the sun.

"*There is a war, and you failed to notify me about it?*" the minotaur uttered in an irate voice; his loud statement caused the tribe members nearby to start an uproar and begin panicking.

"*We are not at war!*" Moll'ar shouted, trying to be heard over the clamor of his people. He looked at Duke Pol. "*Return with Terus back to the manor. Once I finish my work here, I will meet with you both, and I will read the letter then. But until my return, there will be no further speak of war.*"

Terus scowled and muttered expletives under his breath before glancing at the satyr beside him.

Pol looked up at the incensed minotaur, then headed toward his mount. He ran his hand across his scalp, rubbing it nervously. As the two of them departed on their pegasi heading back toward the city, Moll'ar tried to comfort the restless tribe, telling them that Alberon was not at war with anyone and that there was nothing to fear. After getting everyone to settle down, Moll'ar made his way to a settlement in Feather's Bow and delivered the manure.

†

A few hours passed, and Moll'ar arrived at his manor. It stood three levels high, making it possible to see over the neighboring homes and shops from Moll'ar's study and tall enough to be able to see the manor from a distance. The foundation and walls were made of light-brown clay, and a lavish garden and fruit trees for the tribe members to eat from surrounded the structure.

Upon entering the hall, he saw both Pol and Terus sitting at the table, enjoying cold beverages.

"*Let me see that letter,*" Moll'ar stated as he pulled out a seat at the table and sat down.

Pol handed him the rolled-up sheet of parchment, stamped with the Taleanic seal.

Moll'ar skimmed it, then laid the letter on the table. "*Write back sayin' we are in agreeance with his wishes.*"

"*I thought you said we were not going to war?*" Pol questioned.

"*We are not partakin' in the war,*" Moll'ar stated. "*We have all the food and plenty of resources of our own, so we do not need to go to war with any of the other kingdoms. But if Azreal wants to make an alliance sayin' that he will not go to war with us and will help protect us if we so need it, then it would be foolish to not accept the pledge.*"

"*You trust Azreal and his Golden Men?*" Terus barked, his large black eyes locked onto Moll'ar's face. "*You have heard of the rumors said about his father. What makes you believe Azreal will transpire to be different? Food is scarce to them, and the only resource they have is a large purse.*" Terus's nose flared from his anger. "*He will use us for our resources! We should not accept his proposal.*"

"*I have sat with Duke Azreal; what is spoken about his father are just rumors.*" Moll'ar stared back into the minotaur's giant eyes. "*I do not want to go to war with any of the realms. Talean is not a threat to us, nor are they a threat to the others. If they want to have peace between our lands, then peace we shall have.*"

"*Let us look at the big picture,*" Terus proclaimed, grabbing the letter from the table and shaking it in the air. "*If you accept Azreal's pledge, then we will have a mark on our heads, as well as his. The other dukes want to control all of*

Metagore, and if they can bring the two of you down at once, they will have control over half of the land—"

"But we are not going to war," Moll'ar cut him off.

"You might not want to go to war," Terus roared as he stood from his seat and leaned over the table, "but it is not up to you if the other regions want to declare war on us! Aye, you are correct, the Taleanics are not a threat to us—they are almost five hundred leagues away. But when you pair us with them, we are a threat to the other realms! Besides, do you think Duke Darius cares who is in the war or not? No! He will overthrow whoever he wants, just because he can." Terus straighten his posture. "You should get us prepared for war because there is no stopping it from coming."

"I do not want to put our land in danger."

"Danger? You will be putting us all at risk if you agree to Azreal's plea and not be prepared for the other regions to attack us."

Confliction was clear to read on Moll'ar's face as he glanced at his duke. "Pol, what is your take on the matter?"

"I do not want us to be at war," Pol answered with apprehension, "but I will have to agree with Terus. If we do not join the war, I am fearful that it will only hurt us."

Moll'ar nodded. "Alright. Terus, gather our tribes' best warriors and prepare them to take BrightHelm."

"BrightHelm?" Pol asked bewildered.

"If we are going to be at war over the land of Metagore, we might as well cut the head off as quickly as possible," Moll'ar responded. "We hold the East and the West; now we just need to take the middle. So, go and rest, for tomorrow will sweep in as you sleep."

"*Until the sun sets in the East, we will defend and serve the West,*" Terus spoke, a smile of confidence brightening his face.

Oη Laηδ aηδ Sɛa

Two weeks after returning from BrightHelm, Kaprin, excited and eager for the war, had traversed to Seaford's dock early that morning, accompanied by his marquess, Lucan, who led their kelpies by the reins.

Lucan's race was apparent by his lack of complexion and his gaunt, skeletal figure. Though he had worked with and served under Kaprin for over a decade, he still had some of his flesh and blood attributes, as opposed to some of the older liches in the land. The marquess never delved too deeply into his magical traits; however, he still bore the mark of his people. He was covered with sores and blood blisters, as his skin was slowly decaying and becoming weaker from his magic use, and his organs and muscles had begun to fail, his body relying more and more on his magical output to survive. He had vivid yellow eyes, slit like a nundu's, which stood out drastically compared to his bone-white skin.

Persea walked toward them—a young dryad around the same age as Kaprin. Flowers bloomed from her short chestnut hair. Her eyes were as green as the vines that wrapped her thin olive skin. Her hips swayed from side to side as she approached, knowing she had the figure and the looks to appeal to anyone who glanced her way.

Kaprin wrapped his arm around Persea's waist and pulled her close, grasping her rear in his webbed hand. "Do ya have my ship repaired?"

Persea, feeling uncomfortable by his hand placement, twisted her hip free from his grasp. "You hit that coral reef pretty hard, but I managed to fix it."

"Aye, good," Kaprin said elated. "I need ya to ready-up my entire fleet of ships for war. Reinforce the rake and the mass, and add cannons whilst ye'r at it as well. Can ya do that for me?"

Her brows furrowed. "The *entire* fleet? Is it not enough for you alone to die by the waves, but you wish to sink our entire arsenal of ships in the process?"

Kaprin chuckled. "What's our rallyin' cry?"

Persea rolled her eyes as a sigh escaped her mouth. "We stand solid on land and sea."

"Aye, we stand solid," Kaprin repeated as he stomped on the dock's wooden planks, "on both land *and* sea."

"You stand as solid as a drunkard in a tavern placed

beside a vineyard," Persea chortled and teased. "But for your request, I can ready them all for you. Just give me a couple of moons, and they shall be ready to sail the Abyss."

"I'll be back to check on 'em later then," Kaprin affirmed, and leaned in just for Persea to deny him a kiss. He shrugged off her rejection as he glanced at Lucan. "Ya heard the shrub, they're not done yet. Now, onward to the city!"

Lucan scowled at his lord, unpleased by the way he disregarded others. Knowing how Kaprin had obtained the title of Grand Duke—being a descendant of a long line of Blue Fangs, dating all the way back to the original Blue Fang Officer, Lord Grakhaa—left his stomach in knots. Kaprin had no right to rule, but the Blue Fangs had corrupted the Learish government for thousands of years, commissioning who they wanted to rule, or at least who they wanted to take the blame for their actions.

Kaprin and his marquess mounted their squamous kelpies and galloped toward Medsa'lear. Their equine's hooves sunk slightly into the soggy ground; each print filled with water. The surrounding trees seemed to glisten from a recent downpour as the morning fog dispersed. The sounds of bugs and other wildlife engulfed the region as they traipsed through the swamplands.

"How many men are we sending to sea?" Lucan questioned in his raspy voice.

"I will have to analyze our numbers, but I figure half,

if I had to give an amount."

Lucan gasped, taken back by the high number. "Half? That'd be easily forty-five thousand men. We'd need a hundred ships to pack them in, and that would still be a tight squeeze."

"And yer point?" Kaprin shrugged off the statement, not worried by the numbers or the cramped storage his warriors would have to endure.

"Unless you have forgotten, we only have twenty caravels afloat."

"Then I will commission for more to be bartered."

"Where are you going to find that many ships on such short notice?"

Kaprin's face scrunched in thought. "The Valkards have more ships than they do men. I'm sure I can persuade their queen to spare a few."

"A few, maybe. But eighty?"

"Lucan. Lucan. Lucan," he said, chuckling. "Do ya not have faith in my negotiatin' skills?"

The lich's eyes narrowed as he cocked his head, uncertain if he should answer.

"I will get us a hundred ships before the dawn o' the war."

"My apologies, my Lord."

"Don't fret. I've got 'tis under wraps. Yer main concern should be if our men are ready for the war."

"They are most certainly prepared, my Lord."

"Aye, good." Kaprin stared at the path before them, a smile growing on his face. "I've been thinkin', and I believe we shall lure any incomin' attacks toward

Dravendale."

Lucan's thin brow ripped with concern. "But the hydra rests in Dravendale during this season."

"I know o' 'tis. 'Tis why we lure our enemies there, so the hydra can do our bidding, and if they so happen to kill the beast, then 'tis a win-win for us."

"But our men will be at even greater odds of being endangered."

"Aye, but they are warriors, 'tis their duty. But ehh, I suppose we can set a trap for the beast, then bait our enemies toward it."

Lucan looked quietly at his lord as they rode toward their capital. The spontaneous and irrational thinking of his lord never ceased to irritate him.

†

After Kaprin and Lucan arrived at the large wooden manor, three Learish warriors greeted them in the hall—a short, buff troll with a tall mohawk and a scar over an empty eye socket; a tall, slender ogre; and a cryter with brass-plated armor.

Kaprin gave an overly dramatic bow to meet their acquaintances. "Welcome, I'm glad ye'r all here." Kaprin, followed by Lucan, approached the table and sat across from the three warriors. "We have some matters to discuss, but first, where's Duchess Alor?" He scanned the room. "Alor!" he shouted. "Alor, come down here please."

A few moments passed, then a nude female, covered in scales dissolving into flesh, sashayed down the staircase. She was wrapped in a thin towel, while drying her hair in another.

"Yes, my Lord?" she asked in a singsong voice as water dripped down her perfectly curved body.

"Are ya busy?"

"I was only bathing."

"Come. Join us and be briefed on matters of this realm."

Slightly appalled by his lord's remark, Lucan blurted out, "She is unpleasant, my Lord."

Kaprin pursed his bottom lip, wishing his duchess would remain as she was. "Fine. If she must, then goest and clothe yerself."

"I shall return, my Lord." Alor returned upstairs, then a few moments later re-entered the hall, fully clothed.

"As ye'r all aware," Kaprin addressed the warriors, "we are goin' to war. Marquess Lucan and I have discussed some battle plans, startin' with what to do 'bout defense."

"We plan on letting the wildlife do our defending," Lucan chimed in. "Mostly, the hydra. But the hydra will be migrating soon toward Shylock, putting villages there in jeopardy of being attacked by the hydra and by enemy forces." Lucan paused, then continued in a louder voice. "We need to keep it in Dravendale. We need to trap it there, and we need to bait our enemies toward it."

"If any of ya have an idea on how we can trap the hydra and bait the enemy, we are open to ideas."

"War goin' to affect hydra's migration?" Ser Nerek, the ogre, questioned.

"What do you mean?" Alor asked.

"It moves to places seekin' food?"

"Aye," Kaprin answered. "Are ya suggestin' that we should provide food for the beast?"

"It will be too late," Alor stated. "Even if the hydra hasn't migrated yet, it wouldn't recognize the new food as being there. Its sense of smell isn't that great, and it would assume the food is in the next region. Since, to it, the area in which it is in is completely empty of food to prey upon."

"How does it know where to go then?" Ser Sillius, the cryter warrior, questioned.

"It sees heat," Alor responded. "Every living creature puts off heat, and it can sense it. The foul creature follows the strongest source of heat, which if we provide it food, the only heat would be the ones from who's delivering the food."

"What if we made fires that were contained? Then the heat from the flames would be much greater than our own," Sillius continued. "Wouldn't that be a way to trick the hydra?"

"Yes," Alor responded. "That should work. But our warriors would be endangered until the fires were lit."

"But most of our men are cryters, like our lord and Ser Sillius here; they don't emit much heat," Lucan informed his duchess.

"You are right," Alor stated as she nodded, assessing the information. "I think this plan might work. What say you, my Lord?"

"I think we are goin' to Dravendale," he responded with a smirk on his fish-like face.

"What 'bout offense?" Nerek asked.

"Ya will goest toward Ringwood and lure the Woodites to the hydra," Kaprin instructed. "And if the Alberians decide to cross the river, then the same will be done to 'em."

"What o' BrightHelm and others? Hydra can do not all our biddins."

Kaprin smirked. "I am well aware, but Lord Cornelius won't wage war on us."

"How do you know of such things?" Ser Kealin, the single-eyed troll, questioned.

"The Blue Fangs have embedded themselves beyond the clouds, most into seats of power. As for the eastern lands, they have waged war amongst themselves since the great flood. They have no time to quarrel with us."

"Ringwood and Alberon are only realms we war with?" Nerek asked.

"By no means, 'tis that true. We will attack Sentries and Talean; not by land, but by sea." Kaprin laughed. "Even I know there's no way we can get through the Brim. We'll take our entire fleet and bombard Lord Darius and his land-savvy knights, then we shall sail on toward Talean."

"We shall stand solid on land and sea," Kealin spoke

in his raspy voice.

"Aye. Yer lord knows what he's doin'."

The Moat – Wa'Lirrak

Four days after he had convinced his lord to join the war, Marquess Terus regarded the one hundred seventy thousand warriors training under his command. The majority of the fighters were morlings and minotaurs, all suited in leather and pelts of fur as they sparred with other warriors, practicing their hand-to-hand combat.

As midday approached, Terus decided to visit Lord Moll'ar's tan brick chateau manor to brief him on the state of his warriors and how his people were rallied and ready to fight for their lord. They were all proficient with long-range weapons—bows, small hatchets, and spears—as well as agile enough to deliver hard blows with the blunt ends of their maces, clubs, and halberds with dexterity.

As Terus ventured to the manor, he noticed Duke Pol exiting from the main hall, treating his hands with gauze and bandages as he walked.

"What happened to your hands?" Terus asked in a husky voice as he approached the satyr.

"Just a few blisters," Pol responded. *"I am not used to all the physical labor."*

"What? Are you laboring out in the fields with our lord?"

"No," Pol responded as he inspected his hands. *"I was out past the wall with our lord, helping him dig a moat around the city."*

"A moat, aye? A moat would help with the city's defenses. Is our lord still out there?"

"It was Lord Moll'ar's idea. And yes, he was when I left him," Pol stated as he glanced toward the capital. *"I am going back out there if you wish to follow."*

†

Outside the city, two thousand Alberians had volunteered to help their lord dig the moat. Catoblepones and herdbeast were harnessed to plows and used to break the ground, making for an easier labor for the volunteers. Though the tribe members had all willingly provided their services, Moll'ar had pronounced to pay each of them a sun coin—roughly a peasant's pay for the course of two moons. The weather-beaten denizens of Alberon put in their day's work, removing the earth from around their settlement's tall, wooden walls. They were all pleased with the generosity of their lord's pay, but most had wished to help with the trench even before hearing of the compensation. They wanted to try and protect their cruck houses that were held together with mud, straw, and manure.

On the southwest edge of the wall, against the Abyss Ocean and bordering the City of Alberon and the region of Pixdale, Moll'ar graffed the earth with his spade. Sweat drenched his long hair, plastering it to his scalp. The sun glistened off his leathery, dirt covered skin.

Moll'ar paused digging as he glanced at a young boy, approximately six years of age. The child had curly black hair highlighted with red streaks. His eyes were as green as the fields around them.

A smile grew upon Moll'ar's face as he leaned against his spade. "*How are you doin', Onnan?*"

"*I am doing just fine, Pappi,*" the young morling responded.

Onnan stabbed his spade into the dirt and jumped on it as hard as he could, trying to drive it deeper into the earth.

Moll'ar continued to smile at his son, proud of his hard work and dedication.

"*If you get too warm, go cool off in the Abyss,*" he said as he continued to watch Onnan jump onto his spade.

"*Okay,*" Onnan grumbled as he tried to pry the dirt from the ground. "*But I am fine, really.*"

Moll'ar had started to dig once more when Terus and

Pol approached their shirtless lord; the raised scars on his chest and arms accented against his ruddy skin.

"*Do you like it?*" Moll'ar asked as they approached.

"*Most certainly, my Lord,*" Terus answered as his heavy-lidded eyes glanced at the large trench. "*A moat will help out our defenses stupendously.*"

Moll'ar smiled. "*I thought it would. What I plan to do is make it fifty strides wide and fifty legs deep and have it stretch all the way around the settlement, makin' Alberon into its own island.*"

"*What about the gates?*"

"*I have a group of trolls in Redthorn willin' to build new gates. They will be reinforced with iron, and they will lower as a bridge.*"

Onnan, patting the dirt from his pants, approached his father. "*Pappi, I am hungry.*"

"*Go on home and get you something to eat,*" Moll'ar responded as he rubbed his hand through Onnan's curly hair. "*Tell your mother I will be out late tonight.*"

"*Okay,*" the boy rejoiced as he ran off.

Moll'ar turned to Terus and Pol and continued discussing the moat and the warriors Terus had been training.

†

Later that night, after most had fallen asleep, Moll'ar and his wife, Laurelin, lay awake in bed covered by a large blanket made of baku fur.

"*How is the moat coming along, Husband?*" Laurelin asked

as she cuddled up to Moll'ar, her head resting on his toned chest.

Moll'ar lightly rubbed his wife's back. *"It is comin' along just fine, but I do hope we can get it finished in time."*

"I am sure it will get completed early enough." Laurelin paused and traced her fingers along the creases of Moll'ar's abdomen. *"'Tis all Onnan has talked about today—how excited he is to help you and the serfs dig the moat. 'Tis a good bonding time for the two o' you."*

Moll'ar's gaze shifted from the overhead rafters to the black and red hair on the back of his wife's head. *"Yes, it is. And when he gets older, he can help with the farming as well."*

Laurelin tilted her head; her face was as wide as it was long, with cheekbones that rose to her eye sockets and offset by her broad shoulders. She stared into her husband's soft, green eyes. *"Do you think the moat will help keep Alberon safe?"*

"It will help our defenses," Moll'ar said and smiled. *"But we still have to have a strong military to keep us safe."*

"I saw Marquess Terus training our warriors yesterday. He is doing an excellent job with them."

"He is," Moll'ar agreed, then paused to gather his words. *"But I am the lord, and if the battle happens to come here—when it comes here—I will lead the fight."*

"But 'tis not your job," his wife said as the gaze from her hazel eyes met his.

"But it is my job to lead and protect, and I will fight to do just that."

She lay her head on his chest and gave him a slight

squeeze. *"I just do not want to lose you."*

The two of them lay in bed quietly for a few moments, but loud bursts of cries coming from a few rooms away broke the silence. Moll'ar slid from underneath Laurelin and stood.

"Where are you going?" Laurelin questioned.

"I am goin' to go check in on Athana," he responded as he exited their chamber.

As Moll'ar walked down the corridor, Athana's cries quieted, and silence once again filled the manor. He approached his infant daughter's bedroom door and reached for the handle. He paused, listening to a slight repetitive creaking sound coming from the other side of the door. Moll'ar grasped the handle and entered the room.

Inside, beside Athana's wooden crib, was a rocking chair. A young elven lady, tall and slim but more well-endowed than most females her age, sat in the chair. Cradled in her arms was the brown-haired infant, Athana, who was latched onto one of the wet nurse's teats.

Moll'ar approached her crib and leaned against it. He gazed profoundly at his child, smiling as the sight brought warmth to his soul.

Once Athana finished eating, the elven lady gently lifted the baby to her shoulder and patted her back, relieving gas from the nightly meal. She cleaned the young morling of the white bile, which came out with a burp, and turned to hand her to her lord.

Moll'ar cradled his daughter in his solid arms, then

paced around the room, rocking her gently until she fell asleep. The smile on his face never wavered as he eased her into her crib and caressed her soft cheek. He leaned forward and kissed her brow.

"I love and praise you, little one. And one day, all of Alberon will too," he whispered. Then the morling lord straightened up and looked at his daughter's wet nurse. *"Thank you for helpin' to care for her, Macci. Laurelin and I can never repay you enough for bein' here for Athana and Onnan after we found out she could not produce enough to feed them."*

"There is no thanks needed, my Lord. I would never let a child go without food if I could help it."

Macci curtsied and left the room, quietly closing the door behind her.

Vina, Oh How Thou Hast Missed Thee

After returning to Ringwood the previous week, Galach found himself wandering through the forests of Krywood, north of his capital. He had grown stressed with cluttered thoughts of war and his decision to stay loyal to the crown.

Throughout the years of being a grand duke, Galach had always seemed to walk the same path whenever he needed time alone. It was a peaceful and relaxing saunter. The route was one he had known since he was a twig of a being. Dens of wolves and dubas lay close to the trail. Galach heard knickers of unicorns and bicorns close by amongst the sounds of bugs and birds chirping.

The large treefolk felt the cooling shifts in the air as it whistled through the trees. The omniscient sounds of the swaying branches and the rustling of leaves sent shivers down Galach's wooden spine and left a sense of foresight lingering in his mind of the violent change soon to come.

He gazed upon the woods, sheer terror filling his soul. He did not witness the red and brown leaves falling to the ground, but instead, he saw the future dismay of his kingdom—the deaths of his men and raging flames brought upon his home by rabid savages. Though all of the dark thoughts clouded his mind, the aroma of the fresh morning dew wouldn't allow his mind to wander too long.

As he strolled, a decimated house built high in the trees grew closer. The building was constructed of long timbers stacked on top of each other, stretching from one tree to another. Vines of ivy draped from the spiraling staircase that led up to what remained of the cabin.

A proud willow tree protruded from one side through a crevice in the wall. Its roots had penetrated the soil floor and encircled one of the trees supporting the home's structure. Its crooked trunk weaved around the branches of the other trees as it extend outward.

Approaching the house, Galach's amble slowed, and he could barely lift his feet from the ground as he passed over. His long face ribbed as he wept, gazing upon the tree as he climbed the stairs. He entered the house and meandered toward the willow and knelt beside it, then sat on the dirt floor.

Memories fluttered through his mind. That house.

That tree. The past replayed itself. The screams and chaos. The guilt Galach felt for being absent on what would become the darkest day of his life.

"Vina," Galach stammered through his sobbing cries. "Vina, oh how thou hast missed thee."

He placed his elongated hand upon the willow's trunk, rubbed his fingers over its soft bark, and continued to weep. "One morn, thy love, we shall be joined once more."

Pausing, Galach leaned his back against the tree. He watched the thin leaves sway in the breeze as the comfort of the tree embraced him. His head lay back, resting in one of the knots in the bark. Images of his younger years flashed through his mind as he closed his wooden eye. A smile graced his coarse face as pleasant memories caused the nectar in his veins to warm his soul. Remembrances of when he would hike through the forests, exploring new depths of the region, and of when he would watch the many species of wildlife graze and take care of their young. The warmth he had felt when he had been loved by his family, and from the love of his life, Vina, crept upon him but soon faded.

With his eyes still clenched, Galach spoke to the tree again. "We're almost done with the elixir—*yer* elixir. Thou prays to the gods 'tis will help protect our lands and trees." Sap poured from his eyes. "Ya life's dream is becoming a reality. Thou just hopes thy people—*our* people—will be able to use it."

A long pause of silence filled the air.

"There's been a war brought upon our lands. Not of

foreign realms, but of thy own. Lord Brighton has passed, and the other grand dukes want to take thy crown upon thou own heads, but not thee. Power can make one do strange things, and thou wishes to hold no part in those matters. Though thou fears for thy people's safety, for thou hath not enow men to hold off the other realms. Thou believes Lord Cornelius will lead us on the right path, even if some of thy people fall in the process."

Galach opened his eyes—sap still oozing down the bark of his face—and stared past the drooping leaves, thinking of the possible destruction of his homeland.

While he was lost in thought, the sound of footsteps crunching the dead grass reacquainted him with his surroundings. Galach glanced through the opening the tree had created and gazed upon an aged female, who donned branches growing from her head, scurrying down the trail.

Galach rose to his trunk-like feet. "Until later," he whispered to the tree before exiting the old house and navigating down the winding stairs.

The elderly lady was a dryad. She had long gray hair, green eyes, and gray bark-like patches spread across her pear-shaped body, along with vines wrapped around her arms and legs. She stood hunched, straining to support the weight of her sagging breasts.

"Duchess Celsa, what brings ya to Krywood?" Galach asked as he approached the dryad.

"Duke Galach," his duchess greeted. "Darsin is awaiting you at the manor. He brings you news of the elixir."

Galach tried to rid his face of the sorrow as he forced a smile. "How long hast thou been at wait? Thou's been away all morn."

"Not long. I just left him and came straight here. Perhaps thirty minutes, if even that."

"Ahh. How did ya knowest where thou was?"

Celsa's wrinkled face grew somber. "Whenever you leave the city, you always come here."

Galach turned to the willow tree growing from the decrepit house. "Huh, thou supposes thou does."

"We must not keep Darsin waiting. I have a shrub close by to quicken our travels. It's just past the hill."

†

After returning to his large cabin-like manor, Galach and Celsa met in the hall with Darsin—a djinn much shorter than most but still stood five links taller than his duchess.

"Duke Galach, as I had told Duchess Celsa earlier, I believe we have completed the Vila Elixir," the green djinn reported. "We have tested it on some dead grass and small trees on the outskirts of Black Rain Forest. As of four days ago, I have seen buddings upon the trees. Even now in the heart of winter, the elixir is sprouting life."

A smile grew across Galach's wooden face. "'Tis it able to resurrect treefolk who hath gone from 'tis life?"

"In theory, yes," Darsin stated, then paused, biting his lips in thought. "But then again, we have not tested it on any of the treefolk community. We may have to develop the elixir a little further before it can work in that way, seeing as how a treefolk's infrastructure is more complex than what a tree's would be."

Galach nodded. "Can ya show thee where it hast been tested?"

Darsin smiled. "Of course. Duchess, do you have a tree near the sea and Black Rain Forest?"

"I do. It's on the banks of the sea, a half a league away from the edge of Black Rain. Come, I will take you there."

✝

Black Rain Forest had once been a wondrous sight to behold. Its name came from all the rich, violet blossoms that grew upon the sprawling empress and smoke trees. But since—over five millennia ago—the entire two-million gradients of land became a deserted wasteland, plagued with rotted trees coated in soot and ash, falling victim to the great flood.

Approaching the edge of the region, Galach saw small iris buds amongst the gray bark of trees barely standing waist high. The ground around the trees was dark and hard as a rock, but small blades of grass had poked through the rough terrain.

Galach knelt and ran his large hands across the grass.

His eyes swelled with joy as the blades brushed against his fingers.

"By thy gods, the elixir works," he stated in awe as he surveyed the patch of green surrounded by the dead, cold-struck ground.

Darsin grasped his hands together behind his back. "So far, the results are what we were hoping for, but we have not tested its ability to revive larger plants or its effectiveness on the soot-covered trees closer to the Brim."

Galach stood and turned to Darsin. "How long 'til ya knowest?"

"Perhaps in a few short moons, but that is, of course, if everything goes smoothly."

STARGAZER

After the tribute to Libras and a lavish banquet, Lord Darius spent the next three and a half weeks preparing his armies for the inevitable war.

On the night before the war, he stood by the window in his chamber, staring at the final sliver of the Crahesh Moon. The burly demon remained in the same spot for hours, mentally preparing himself. He knew his men could conquer BrightHelm and massacre any army that tried to get in their way, but he still felt unsettled by the situation. Maybe it was the fear of being successful in obtaining the throne for himself, and then he too might meet the same fate Lord Brighton had met before him. Or it could have been unsettled nerves, for it will be his first battle where he would not be on the battlefield.

The feeling of being useless lingered in his mind—having to rely on others to do what he demanded to be done.

As the night progressed, Darius continued to stand in the darkness of his room, the only light coming from the low flames emanating from Meek as it slept in the far corner of his chamber.

While he stared at the starry sky, a knock came rapped upon his door. Darius glanced from the window and noticed a beam of light creeping around the door as it slowly opened.

"What are you doing up?" Darius asked as Ky entered the room, the lamp in her hands illuminating her flesh.

"I could ask you the same question, my Lord, but for me, my stomach has been unsettled as of late," she responded as she set the lamp on his bedside table.

Darius chuckled under his breath. "You know I don't sleep much."

"You need your rest though. For tomorrow will be here soon, and with it a new moon—a new war," Ky replied and sighed as she sashayed to her lord, her head aligned with his chest.

"I know," Darius muttered, looking out the window.

"Why don't you tell me what's on your mind," Ky said softly as she held her tightened stomach.

Darius glanced at her staring at him with her pear-colored eyes. "What if when this is all said and done, the denizens of the six kingdoms refuse my leadership? What if nothing I do will get them to follow under my reign?"

"Like what's happening to Cornelius?" Ky inquired, knowing the answer but wanting to hear it from Darius's mouth.

"Aye. What if no matter how much power I have or my strength in numbers, they still refuse to follow under me? We'll be right where we are now, fighting a never-ending war."

Ky took hold of Darius's callused hand as she rested her head against his side; one of her wings stretched outward, enveloping his robust body.

"You will gain their trust. Besides, you have the favor of the gods."

"Aye." Darius paused, lifting his free hand and pointing out the window. "Do you see that bright star right there?"

Ky raised her head from his side and glanced at the sky. "Aye."

"That little star—the one to the left of it—that's my star."

Ky gazed at Darius's red eyes with a perplexed look. "How does one obtain a star?"

Darius curled the corner of his mouth upward. "When I was younger, my mother would tell me that star was my star. She would tell me if I wanted to grow up and become somebody—if I wanted to make a difference in the land—I would have to start out small, just like that star. I would have to work to become what I wanted, and one day I would become as big as the other stars."

"I bet you miss her, don't you?" Ky quietly responded.

Darius's face grew somber as his heart stood still, and for a moment, he only felt numbness. His hands turned to fists, squeezing them so hard Ky had to snatch her hand from his. The sense of pain and brokenness, however, seemed to flee his mind as swiftly as it had come.

"I will never forgive him for what he has done," Darius stated in a tight voice. "The cruelty. The shame and embarrassment he brought onto my family." Darius paused, taking deep breaths to ease his mind. "One day he will pay for what he has done. I hope he suffers as much as I have over the years."

"I'm sure he is suffering plenty."

Ky rested her head against his body once more, taking hold of his hand and slowly rubbing the back of it.

"His suffering has only begun," Darius snarled.

They both stared out the window at the speckled sky.

"Do you see that big star right beside mine?"

Ky amused him by answering. "Aye, I do, my Lord."

"All of my life I have been focused on being that little star because I had the potential of becoming something great. But now, I look at that big star like I used to look at my mother. She was always there beside me when I needed her; she never left my side." Darius paused. "At night I stare up at the stars, and I can't help but think that Iden has her up there smiling down on me."

Ky gave him a slight squeeze with her wing. "She would be proud of you. But it's getting late, and you need to get your rest."

Darius glanced at her with a curled mouth. "Maybe you're right. Would you mind staying? You know, to help keep my mind at ease?"

"Most certainly," Ky agreed as she turned and pranced to Darius's massive bed.

Darius approached the lamp Ky had brought into his chamber, smothered the flame, and joined her, wrapping his arm around her slender body and pulling her next to him with thoughts still flooding his mind with concerns of what the future might hold.

Sightseeing – Ekeem Latem

The morrow of the Vloth Moon and the dawn of the new war had finally arrived. Outside the wooden walls of his capital, Marquess Terus stood in front of nearly one hundred and seventy thousand Alberians from the many different tribes of the land.

The warriors were dressed in thick hide and animal pelts, adorned with beads and trinkets from their family and loved ones, while the higher ranked officials—the chieftains—wore thin metal breastplates over their suits. Sashed around their hips and shoulders were their hand-made weapons and bows. Different pigments of mud and clay were smeared across their faces, distinguishing one tribe from another—warpaint covered some entirely, while others only bared streaks across their eyes.

Terus stood firm before the warriors. *"We did not wish war on this land, but a war it wages. We must defend our fields and our villages so that the tribes of Alberon may live on in peace."* The burly minotaur raised a fist, clutching a horn tight in his grasp. *"Today you all will set forth toward BrightHelm and take the throne for Lord Moll'ar! Until the sun sets in the East, we will defend and serve the West!"*

Terus lowered his fist and blew into the horn, signaling the start of their advancement. Many warriors darted into the plains of Willowgate, stampeding through the settlements and chanting in their native tongue.

Many villagers stood outside their thatched huts and crucked houses, admiring the warriors as they marched down their paths; some offered the warriors prepared foods and gathered berries as a way to show gratitude.

The group took in the beauty of the grassy fields blowing in the wind and the rolling hills and valleys that comprised the majority of Alberon. They admired the abundant population of wildlife that surrounded them when they were away from the settlements. Their eyes beheld herds of achli and herdbeasts grazing on wheat. Overhead, coatl and perytons glided through the clear sky. Around them, the noises of nature played its beautiful melody. The nickering of unicorns and pegasi, the grunts of the catoblepone, and a slight undercurrent of growls from the lion and nundu populations in the distance filled their ears.

As they continued their first day's march, a young

girl, appearing to be in her first decade of womanhood, walked beside her commanding officer.

"*I am going to miss home while we are gone,*" she mentioned as she glanced at her chieftain's skeletal form—her dark green eyes lost behind her raven hair as the wind blew it across her bronze face.

Ixin—the lich put in charge of one of the groups—scanned the fields as his thinning, braided strands of coarse hair blew across his painted forehead. His catlike eyes sunk deep into his skull, hiding amongst crescent scars that adorned his leathery face.

"*Aye, 'tis a beaut. Now, let us keep it that way.*"

"*Aye,*" the girl responded as she fiddled with a dagger that slouched around her waist. "*I am Tera, by the way. I was told you were my chieftain.*"

Ixin peered toward the girl who was a third of his age. Her face was streaked with blue paint—two lines crossed over her eyes, with another stretched from between her brows to her chin.

"*Ya from Willowgate?*" Ixin inquired, followed by a nod from Tera. His gaze veered from the sapphire pigments smeared across her face toward the path in front of him. "*Wisdom, huh? Do ya see yerself educated in the art of battle? Or do ya think yerself as wise because ya are an elf?*"

"*I am no elf, but a morling actually, as I predict many of the other warriors are as well.*" Tera's posture straightened as she puffed out her flat chest. "*And I chose blue to represent confidence. For I know, I can hold my own in battle.*"

Ixin's left brow raised. "*Aye? Do ya not feel inferior to the other warriors? Many of 'em have been branded five or six times.*"

"Just because I am a female, it does not signify that I am weaker. No, I have never taken part in the Walk of Roses, nor have I been branded by battle, yet. But just like all of you men, I too am fighting for my missus back home."

"Maybe ya should have stayed with her," Ixin scoffed. *"War is no walk amongst roses, nor a place for a woman's wife."*

"I do believe after this journey, you will hold a higher standard of me."

"I hope that holds to be true. I would hate to have to burn yer body hundreds of leagues from home, then tell yer ol' missus that ya were indeed inferior."

"And I hope I do not have to do the same for you," Tera responded as she chuckled. *"Enough about me; what about you?"*

Ixin pursed his thin lips. *"What do ya wish to know?"*

"Your paint, it is black, symbolizing victory and that you have proven yourself in battle."

"Aye. Do ya not believe I am a notarized combatant?" he heckled. *"I was elected chieftain aft' all."*

"Aye, I know." Her words faded as she stared at the scarred ridges on the lich's face. *"But the brands on your face …"* She grew hesitant to finish her prying observation. *"They are for treachery."*

Ixin's face grew long and his voice somber. *"Aye, but that 'twas a long time ago, centuries before ya were even born."*

"What happened? I mean, apparently you have made amends."

"Aye, but that is a story for another day."

138

Small ripples traveled through the murky swamplands of Medsa'lear. The soldiers heard mouswahs and kelpies splashing in the many rivers and ponds. All that was peaceful and calm would soon be disturbed as the balance of nature was inevitably going to take a turn for the worse.

As the morning sun illuminated the thin fog, Learish soldiers marched and slithered toward the barracks where they would receive their orders. Forty-seven thousand soldiers rallied together, awaiting their commands from Marquess Lucan. The white-skinned lich was mounted on his kelpie, beside him sat fifteen large barrels of various oils.

Once all the soldiers were accounted for, Lucan spoke. "*Today* is the day that we fight! *Today* is the day that we succeed! *Today* is the day that we rule! For we are the wealth of our lands and the fruits of our labor! We stand solid on land and sea, and no one will bring us down!"

The soldiers cheered and yelled, raising their weapons and shields and bashing them together.

Lucan scanned the energetic crowd that stood before him, suited in leather and chainmail. He looked for a select few who he had thought would be good choices to help set up the bait for the hydra. He analyzed his warriors thoroughly, being precise with his selection, looking for strong, quick soldiers who didn't produce much heat—cryters, liches, and treefolk mostly. After carefully weighing his options, Lucan chose thirty men for the quest toward Dravendale. Calling them by name, one by one, the selected few separated themselves from the rest of the crowd.

Lucan fixed his gaze upon the selected. "You all are the chosen ones. Your quest will be a vital part of our survival. I am entrusting you with this great deal of responsibility because I believe you all have what it will take to succeed in the quest. Ser Sillius has been briefed and will be in charge, and he shall lead you to the desired spot for the trap." Lucan glanced over the rest of his warriors. "The remainder of you will advance toward Shylock, then to the City of Ringwood. Your primary objective is to lure the Woodite army toward the northern tip of Dravendale." Lucan pointed out the tall, slender ogre who had met him in Kaprin's manor. "Ser Nerek has been briefed on the course of action, and he will be in charge of your escapade."

Once Lucan finished addressing the crowd, Nerek led the Learish army toward the forests of Ringwood while the thirty chosen men lifted the oil barrels—two soldiers per barrel—and carried them through the gates of Medsa'lear toward Dravendale.

Through the Ashes

As the sun rose above the ocean and shined onto the treacherous wastelands of Sentries, Lucius was at the barracks of a bailey half a league outside the walls of the capital, talking to his knights.

"The gods have graced us with their favor," Lucius told his men as their squires laced the knights' boots, breastplates, and other body armor, as well as saddling their steeds. "Now we must go and take Metagore as our own!"

The Senturian knights erupted in a roar of cheers and stomps. Their battle cries echoed through the dark, stoned ground of the bailey.

"Though it will be a week or two before you are consumed by the bloodlust of battle, you will encounter dangerous wildlife throughout your journeys, so be on your guard at all times. You are only as good as you are alert. So, go out, stay focused, hold nothing back, and dominate everything that gets in your way!"

As the knights finished suiting in their armor, they, as well as their squires, mounted onto their nightmares. They were split into two groups—one headed toward the deserts of Talean, while the other toward the barren forests leading toward Ringwood.

†

Later that morning, Darius and Ky traveled from the manor toward the city's wall where they were met by Lucius and a few knights, who had stayed behind to protect the city.

"My Lord," Lucius greeted the giant demon as he stood at attention.

"Have you sent out the knights?" Darius asked as he looked up at the archers posted on the battlement, then back down at the few knights standing behind Lucius.

"Aye," the elder demon responded. "Ninety thousand men are heading toward the Kingdom of Ringwood, and another ninety thousand are moving toward the City of Talean. Just like you had asked, my Lord."

"How many knights remain?"

"We have just over seven thousand men patrolling each of the Brims, as well as four thousand posted in the baileys and battlements surrounding the city."

"Four thousand?" Darius shouted in disbelief. "Four thousand men can barely protect the city's walls. How can they be expected to protect out past them?"

"That is all that remains, my Lord," Lucius confirmed, trying to tread lightly with his words so he wouldn't anger Darius. "May I suggest that we increase our numbers with new recruits?"

Darius's brow furrowed as he shook his head, disbelieving he had fewer numbers than what he had thought to have had. "What happened to the other forty-five thousand we had when we last fought Penora?"

"They have all grown old and laid down their swords."

"All of them?" Ky asked as she looked at Lucius's dark face—her eyes narrow and concerned.

Lucius turned his attention to Ky. "The ones that didn't succumb to their wounds and illnesses from their time across the Abyss."

Darius looked at his duchess. "Ky, go gather as many citizens you can that are of age for battle and take them to the barracks."

"Right away," she said, then walked away.

Darius's gaze trailed down the street, staring at her backside as she left.

Darius turned to Lucius. "I want you to get them ready for battle. The ones that make for good archers, post them up on the battlement and out in the baileys. Send the rest out onto the battlefield where needed."

"Aye, my Lord."

Darius and Lucius continued talking—Darius wanting to make sure he had plenty of men to protect his city from any incoming attacks, as well as enough to siege other kingdoms. He didn't want to take any chances of losing the war. The gods had granted them their favor, but deep down inside, he still felt a little weary about his chances.

$$\dagger$$

As time drew on, Darius and Lucius mounted their steeds and returned to the city. As they rode down the stone road, a loud, deafening roar came from the volcano resting behind the city. Their gaze jolted to the top of Mount Dumas.

On top of the volcano, resting straight above Darius's manor, sat the majestic dragon, Libras. His fiery-red eyes scanned the city, looking from side to side as if he was searching for a particular person. From his snout came puffs of smoke. His crimson scales glistened in the sunlight. He raised his head and roared once more as a giant fireball exited his mouth and traveled through the sky. Lowering his head to glance at the city, he crept down the mountainside, only to stop halfway and then fly off.

The gusts of wind from his wings were so powerful, it knocked down a lot of the townsfolk, blew over street carts, and stirred up so much dirt and dust, the city was engulfed in a black fog for several minutes.

"What is he doing leaving his cave?" Lucius questioned in a concerned voice as he covered his eyes with his arm to block the dust. "He never leaves during the winter moons."

"The gods play by their own rules," Darius responded. "I'm sure everything will be fine. After all, we are in their favor. But I need to hurry back to the manor and check on the dungeons. Make sure you get those men trained and sent out as soon as possible."

"See it as done, my Lord."

†

Meanwhile, Dagrus—a demon with dark, matted black skin and blood-red eyes—led the group of Senturian knights through the region of Parele toward the deserts of Talean.

Dagrus had cut off his horns when he first enlisted as a knight, over a decade ago. He told everyone it would make his head lighter and would help him scurry faster. He wore black metal armor sketched with etchings of steel. His left pauldron extended past his neck, giving that side of his collar some protection. He carried a double voulge—a polearm weapon with a curved blade protruding from the tips on each end. It was meant to be used in a hacking motion; thus, each blade was sharp and curved on one side and held serrated teeth on the other.

As the days passed, the knights entered into the sand-covered valley the Senturians had confiscated from Talean in the Battle of the Burning Lands, known as the Realm of Graves.

Ribbons from the tombstones danced in the whistling wind, twirling and spinning over the graves. A few testudines—turtle-like creatures with jeweled shells, used for currency—scuffled across the ground. The smell of the rotting corpses buried just below the surface lingered through the air. Many of the men had to cover their snouts, but for others, the stench was too much, causing them to vomit on occasion.

✝

Passing over the hills at the base of the volcano—a region known as Thieves Hill—a young elf named Galzar led the other group of Senturian knights.

Galzar had joined the Senturian army a few moons prior, after his father had passed away, and he knew his mother could use the coin he would earn from serving his lord. He had long brown hair and a pair of vibrant blue eyes. His armor was made of leather, with the scaly hide from a droyaid used as a breastplate. Draped around his neck and shoulder was a longbow. He wasn't the best archer, but over the course of the last four moons, his aim had sharpened.

Galzar and his men traveled fast through Thieves Hill, hoping to avoid the packs of wild foo dogs that lurked somewhere in the region.

While they passed through, the men stopped for a brief moment to witness Libras fly across the sky. The warriors were amazed, and rumors spread quickly of why Libras had left his cave during the winter season. The most shared and well-liked reasoning was that he was going to go burn down the other kingdoms, giving them an easy victory. Others believed he may be going to Mount Eryn to mate with Tiamus, the only other dragon.

After Libras had left their line of sight, the knights continued on their journey.

$$\dagger$$

Three days later, Galzar and his knights entered the humid region known as the Keep of Ashes. No plant life grew anywhere in the area due to the humidity of the constant flow of magma within the region's rivers that emptied into the Sea of the Sun.

As the men journeyed through the land, the horses' hooves dug into the soggy ground. Areas of flames emitted from between the cracks of the igneous rocks. The men lollygagged through the region, even though it was the most humid area in Sentries, just so they could soak in the sights. There wasn't much to admire about the province itself—mostly black ashy ground with small patches of embers and flames—but the wildlife was something most had never seen. Packs of ardens tigers and wolves roamed the region, keeping to themselves unless provoked, and near the rivers of magma, salamanders infested the ground.

A Sovereign God

The afternoon of the fifth day of the war, Darius sat in his hall, dining on a tender steak and drinking some mead. Across the table sat his lovely duchess, Ky, sipping on some mead of her own.

"How are you feeling today?" Ky asked as she took a sip from her jubbe.

Darius sighed. "Worried over the war."

"Worried? But we have a mighty army and the gods' favor."

"The gods won't just hand over the six kingdoms to us," her lord stated as he took the final bite of his steak, then pushed the plate aside. "There's no certainty that we will prevail. We will have to fight for it. Then there's no guarantee that the other regions won't rebel against us."

"You worry too much," Ky said seductively as she stood and walked around the table. "You need to relax and clear your mind. I've seen our knights train, and they are the best."

"I suppose," Darius said softly, then sneered. "We need to strike fear into our enemies."

Ky straddled her legs over the arms of Darius's chair, sitting on his lap and staring into his scarlet eyes. "And how do you plan on doing that?"

Darius squirmed in his seat, trying to straighten his posture. "We need stronger and deadlier weapons that will cause more bloodshed and destruction faster."

Ky leaned in close, tucked Darius's hair behind his ear, and whispered as she grabbed his groin. "How about you show me your strong weapon?" Darius flashed a smile as he grabbed her thighs and stood from his chair. Ky kissed and nibbled his neck and ears as he undressed her with one hand while the other supported her weight on his hips as he carried her to his chamber.

†

A few hours later, Darius and Ky stared over the dark city from Darius's balcony.

"Your mother would be proud of your success," Ky said as she leaned against him.

"She'd really be proud after I take the six kingdoms," Darius responded with doubt in his voice.

"Why aren't you confident of that?"

Darius looked at Ky, then toward the darken scrow. "She never liked violence. She always said there were other ways to solve problems."

"At times, my Lord, you have to resort to violence," Ky reassured him.

"Aye, that's what I always told her. If there is to be peace, there must first be war." Darius glanced down at Ky. "And one day I won't have to be so ruthless—everyone will be too terrified to mess with Sentries. Even the gods will fear my wrath."

Ky quickly pushed herself from Darius's large body and stood in shock. "My Lord, that is blasphemous. One cannot be greater than the gods."

His face furrowed as rage built in his eyes. "Greater? No. But *feared*, most certainly."

In disbelief, Ky continued to look at her lord in slight fear of how power hungry he had become lately.

"One day, I will become a sovereign god, and everyone will worship at my feet. And you will be at my right hand, and everyone will bow to you and praise your name."

"One does not just become a god," Ky said as her green eyes shifted amongst Darius's body. "That's not how it works."

"Then *how?*" Darius's voice echoed through the dense air. "How does one become a god? Does one have to kill a god to become a god? Do they?"

Ky's head slowly lowered. "I don't know."

Darius's face went from anger to sorrow as he

grabbed Ky's fragile body and pulled her in close. "I'm sorry, Ky. I've just been stressed as of late. Do you forgive me?"

"I forgive you."

Darius peered over his kingdom as Ky rested her head against his side. "I will find out how to become a god, and I will make you my goddess."

Ky looked at her lord and attempted to smile. "I guess being a goddess wouldn't be too bad."

"No, it wouldn't." Darius lovingly squeezed her, then kissed her on the top of her head. "We will rule over the lands of the Abyss, as we have this kingdom, but for now, our focus is on taking the throne as ours."

"Aye," Ky stated. "Let's rest our concerns on the war at hand first."

"Aye," Darius said slowly as he surveyed the stone-fortress city, then quickly glanced into his chamber. "Well, I need to go do my rounds and check on the dungeons—make sure none of the afterlings have decided to die and fill the keeps with their god-awful stench."

Ky tried to chuckle. "Well, you haven't been down there to dretch them with your presence yet, my Lord. So, they should all still be doing as fine as prisoners could."

DÉJÀ VU

The sun rose over the Summerland deserts' sandhills. The Senturian knights and squires awoke from their night's rest, preparing for another long, hot day's journey.

From his slumber, Dagrus's fiery-red eyes shot open as he quickly sat up from his worn-out mat. His heart pounded fiercely as sweat trickled down his face. Trying to catch his breath, he noticed his fellow knights were well awake and packing their gear.

Dagrus frantically glanced around, trying to find his squire. His eyes focused on a small demon.

"Tyldoran, ye'r okay," he said in a sigh of relief.

"Aye," Tyldoran, hesitant by the statement, replied. "I'm fine, Ser. 'Tis ya okay?"

Dagrus scanned the legions of knights. "Aye. 'Twas a bad dream, I suppose."

Having calmed his nerves, Dagrus rose from his mat and joined some of the others, who had been munching on their rations of bread and dried fruit.

"How much longer 'til we reach Talean?" one of them asked.

Dagrus glanced over the rolling hills of sand. "If we stay moving, we should be there before the week is out."

The knights conversed while their young squires and bannermen finished packing the bed dressings and cookware and secured their mounts.

Once everything had been packed, the group mounted their horses and galloped through the brisk, morning desert.

†

After a few hours of wandering through the never-ending valley of sand, the knights noticed a long figure laying in the sand in the distance. It stretched over the rolling dunes of scorching grains, slithering like a snake to its prey.

As they approached the creature, they realized it was a long, benevolent, python-like creature known as an imugi—a proto-dragon waiting for one of the two dragons to pass so the eldest imugi could become a fully-fledged dragon itself. Usually, the sightings of such rare creatures were said to bring good luck, but the imugi seemed as if it had been struck with an illness. It lay partially submerged in the sand, as if it had fallen from the sky instead of just resting upon it. Its pain and weakness were reflected in its large turquoise eyes. Its scales lacked luster and had turned from its natural emerald color to an ashy gray.

"Another sign from thy gods," Dagrus announced as he pointed toward the sickened imugi. "Good fortune has fallen upon us, men."

The knights and squires cheered.

"Ser O'Bryon, will ya do us the honor of slayin' the creature and purifyin' its flesh so we may eat from it?"

O'Bryon—a djinn of brawns and yellow skin—rode to the imugi. He dismounted his steed and approached the massive creature. The djinn drew his long sword and lifted it over the imugi's neck. He took a deep breath, then swung the sword downward with such noble strength that his blade sliced completely through the imugi's thick scales and bones, severing its head from its elongated body.

"Be thy gods that guide us. Be thy gods that watch over us. Be no shame fall upon us," O'Bryon recited as he sheathed his sword, then placed both hands upon the scales of the carcass.

The imugi's scales glowed brightly from an internal light as green fumes rose from them. After a brief moment, the light faded, and the fumes vanished.

O'Bryon turned to Dagrus and the rest of the men.

"The flesh is cleansed of illness. We may now eat

from it safely."

The squires and bannermen worked together on preparing the imugi. A few scaled the creature, while others retrieved firewood from their travel bags. Within moments, the animal had been sliced into portions, and slabs of meat were roasting over open fires.

Once the food had been prepared, Dagrus fixed himself a plate and joined a group of knights eating by their mares. A few of them discussed strategies for when they reach the City of Talean, while others palavered about their families back home in Sentries.

"What a stroke o' luck we've had," one of the knights stated as he ate.

Lost in thought, Dagrus stared into the distance, studying something he could vaguely see—caught between being mesmerized and worried. He saw a handful of small silhouettes dancing in the sun's rays.

"Havin' the gods' favor and findin' an imugi," the knight continued. "Don't ya think, Ser Dagrus?"

Dagrus glanced at his fellow knight. "Aye." His voice trailed off as he stared into the distance once more. "Do ya see that?"

The knight turned and gazed over the sand mounds, trying to decipher what Dagrus was so focused on.

"What 'tis it?"

"I don't know," Dagrus replied as he took a couple of steps forward. "Tyldoran!"

"Ya summoned me, Ser?" his squire asked as he approached.

"Fetch me my lookin' glass."

Tyldoran sprinted down the line of nightmares and pilfered through one of the bags. He retrieved a long bronze spyglass from one of the pockets.

"Here ya go, Ser," Tyldoran said as he approached Dagrus with the object.

Dagrus turned to grab the spyglass from Tyldoran but only a couple of knights stood nearby.

"I feel sorrowed for my wife," one of the demons stated. "She is stuck at home with our son while he's startin' to cut horns."

Dagrus looked disoriented at the knight. He scanned the area to find Tyldoran amongst a large group of squires, poking the firewood, trying to keep the flames burning. Dagrus returned his gaze to the silhouette in the distance; this time they were more prominent than before.

"What a stroke o' luck we've had," another knight added. "Havin' the gods' favor and findin' an imugi. Don't ya think, Ser Dagrus?"

Dagrus glanced at him with an uneasy feeling settling in his stomach. "Aye." Dagrus paused as he looked into the distance again. "Do ya see that?"

The knight glanced at the distant images. He squinted, focusing on what he could barely see. "Are those foo dogs?"

"I believe so," Dagrus replied. "Tyldoran!"

"Ya summoned me, Ser?"

"Fetch me my lookin' glass."

"Right away, Ser." Tyldoran responded as he ran down the line of horses.

Dagrus turned to eyeball the silhouettes but instead saw O'Bryon decapitating the imugi. Beads of sweat gathered on Dagrus's brows as his heart pounded against his ribs, trying to escape his chest. The world spun chaotically around him; sounds all blurred together—the day's events molded into one cacophony of noise. He glanced nearby—his comrades preparing the massive beast for harvesting—looking for Tyldoran for a reason he could not comprehend.

O'Bryon approached Dagrus, who still stood dazed.

"Are ya all right, Dagrus?"

"Just feelin' a little odd," Dagrus responded as he took a few deep breaths. "Everything just seems vaguely familiar, like I've dreamt o' this day."

"Dreamt o' this day? Ha. The sun is gettin' to ya. Go fix yerself a plate. Maybe eatin' some grub will get ya to feelin' better."

"Aye, maybe ye'r right."

Dagrus fixed himself a plate, then walked by the horses to a group of knights already eating their meals.

"Are ya all right?" one of the knights asked.

"Aye, I'll be fine." Dagrus took a bite of his meat, then tried to change the subject. "So, how's yer family? Ye've got a little one now, don't ya?"

"Aye," the knight replied with joy, then chuckled. "But I feel sorrowed for my wife. She is stuck at home with our son, while he's startin' to cut horns. He hath been so fussy here of late. I can't wait 'til they've cut through."

Dagrus glanced around and saw Tyldoran poking the

fire. As he turned toward the knights, he saw a pack of eight large canine-like creatures creeping to their campsite.

"What a stroke o' luck—" another knight began to speak, but panicked shouts interrupted him.

Dagrus sprinted toward his squire. "Tyldoran, grab my weapon!"

The ninety thousand knights and squires turned to see what had brought about the commotion. After spotting the foo dogs, they all scurried, panicking. The squires fetched weapons for their knights while the knights re-suited into the armor they had removed for their meal.

One unlucky knight who had been struggling to tie his bracer into place on his right forearm screamed in pain as one of the beasts clamped onto his leg as he tried kicking it away. His bones crunching and the sheer shock of his limb being mauled from his body caused him to almost lose consciousness.

The foo dog placed its paws on the knight's chest, toppling him to the ground as it ripped and pulled on his crushed limb. A wet, ripping sound flooded his ears—mingled with the clanking sound of armor hitting armor—as the mangled leg detached itself at the knee. He gurgled in pain as the pressure from the creature pushing down on his chest ruptured his lungs, forcing blood to spew from his mouth, leaving him to drown as he tried to gasp for air.

A few other beasts nipped at the nightmares, stirring them up, causing some of the horses to pull their stakes from the ground and gallop into the desert trying to escape the dangerous animals, but a couple canines followed the herd, nipping at their heels.

At the campsite, the remaining foo dogs had killed several knights and squires, and with their horses gone, most of the knights near the attack were defenseless.

Dagrus was trying to save a knight from being eaten alive from a serpent—a cerastes—that had been hiding underneath the sand. As he swung at the snake's head, he noticed, across the campsite, two foo dogs were playing tug-of-war with Tyldoran, who had been lost to the bite of death.

"Tyldoran!" he shouted as he leaped over the dead serpent and tried to save his squire, knowing he was too late.

As he approached the animals, they tore his squire's body in two; his entrails poured onto the ground like chowder. Dagrus, filled with anger and sorrow, lunged at one of the beasts, slashing at it with his voulge, but before he could do anything else, the other pounced on him, knocking him to the ground. The animal nipped at his face as Dagrus tried to control its drooling muzzle away with his weapon stretched across its throat.

As the canine growled and barked, its claws pierced the openings of Dagrus's armor and flesh. Dagrus grew weak as the canine's sharp teeth drew closer and closer. Drool and slobber infused with Tyldoran's blood dripped into his eyes, making it harder for him to focus on keeping the beast from killing him.

"Die, ya bastard!" O'Bryon shouted as he swung his

sword down on the canine's neck.

Dagrus yelped as he frantically sat up. His heart pounded rapidly in his chest. Trying to catch his breath, he surveyed the legions of men packing their gear and readying their horses.

Dagrus glanced around and saw his squire placing bags onto his nightmare.

"Tyldoran, ye'r okay," he said in relief as his gaze made contact with his squire's.

"Aye, I'm fine, Ser," Tyldoran replied. "'Tis ya okay?"

"Aye," Dagrus answered. "'Twas a bad dream, I suppose."

FAMILY TIME – YAKEZH VIÐKA

"*Higher, Pappi! Higher!*" Onnan shouted as his father tossed him into the air.

The young boy's giggles brought squeals of joy from his baby sister, Athana.

The sun peeked through a sky full of wooly clouds, warming the air and making for the perfect day to play outside. Moll'ar's beautiful wife, Laurelin, asked him to take a break and spend time with his family, for the seasons were changing and the weather would soon grow cold. Moll'ar had agreed and asked for his duke to take care of any business that might crop up while he spent some personal time with his family.

They had prepared a small picnic in the garden of their manor. Athana, still trying to figure out how to crawl, rolled back and forth beside her mother on the soft grass, searching for the perfect position to watch her father and brother play.

"*You want to take a ride around the manor, Onnan?*" Moll'ar asked chipperly, staring into his son's green eyes.

"*Yeah,*" the little boy answered and grinned, showing the gap where he had lost his first tooth.

"*Are you sure?*"

"*Pappi!*"

"*Alright then, get ready and hold on tight.*"

Moll'ar sat down his son, then got onto all fours as he morphed into his canine form. The change was quick and painless, aside from the discomfort from his smooth skin rapidly growing so much fur. He had learned from a young age to not scratch his skin as the hair grew due to the unpleasant side effect of his animal form not growing the pelt properly and it causing chafing and irritation while in his elven form. He also learned that if he didn't want to fall on his face during the change, it was best to get closer to the ground.

His snout lengthened, and his teeth elongated; the transformation produced additional teeth and sharpened the existing ones. His ears shifted toward the top of his head and drooped downward, while his spine curved and sprouted a tail. His hands and feet cracked, and his arms and legs popped as the bones shifted and changed to accommodate his animal form.

Unlike most male foo dogs, Moll'ar was closer to nine links tall instead of the average height of just over seven links. His mane, along with the tuft of hair at the end of his tail and the longer fur around his legs, were dark brown, similar to his elven hair, while the rest of his fur was a lighter tint, as if the sun had partially bleached it.

Onnan grabbed a handful of his father's mane and climbed onto his back, then grasped a tuft of fur in each hand.

Moll'ar sprinted off while his son released squealing giggles from his small body.

After circumnavigating the estate's courtyards, Onnan climbed down from his father's back, and Moll'ar became elven once more.

"*Pappi,*" Onnan said, "*when can I change like you and Momma?*"

"*Well, Onnan, it takes a lot of patience and practice to get your animal form down. And even then, you have to be skilled enough to control your animal spirit, because he will try to be in control once you transform.*"

"*Can you show me? Please?*" he begged, then pouted, causing a chuckle from his mother, who had been watching them play.

"*Husband, how about you show him? You know he will eventually try to change on his own if you do not,*" she said as she picked up Athana, who was trying to reach for a small purple and red hydran beetle she had found.

"*Do you really want to learn?*" Moll'ar asked his son. "*It may be hard at first, you know.*"

"*Yes! I really, really want to try it!*"

"*Okay. There are a few things you need to know and*

understand first."

"*Well? What are they?*" Onnan replied, growing impatient with excitement.

"*The first thing, when you are one with your animal spirit, you will change back into your elven form automatically if you fall unconscious.*" Moll'ar paused, making sure his son was paying attention. "*Secondly, and most importantly, do not stay in your animal form for extended periods of time. Since you will be new to the experience and the strain of morphing, it would be best if you only transformed for a moment, just so your body can get used to the changes. Then later, slowly work your way to stayin' changed for long periods of time.*"

Onnan, with a huge grin on his small face, responded, "*I can handle it, Pappi. I am a big boy, remember?*"

Moll'ar chuckled. "*I do not think you are aware of the effects yet, Onnan. Staying in your animal form for too long could cause you to forget what you truly are—a morling—and it could cause you to be stuck in your animal form forever.*"

"*Okay, Pappi, I understand. I can stay an animal for a short period of time. Got it.*"

Moll'ar spoke in a firmer tone as he explained the transformation process. "*To train ourselves to become one with our animal spirit, we have to first understand what allows us to morph from our elven body and become one with our animal spirit.*"

"*And what is that?*" Onnan asked eagerly.

"*When Nya formed us, she made a space of inclusion in our genetics. With that inclusion, there is a massive number of possibilities that could stretch across our inner stitchings.*"

"*Yeah, yeah, yeah. What does this have to do with me*

transforming?" Onnan asked, growing impatient.

"*I am gettin' to that, Onnan. Those inclusions form a second set of inner stitchings—that of the animal spirit we are given—but these stitchings are not as active or as prominent as the first.*"

"*Okay. And?*"

"*We have to be aware of these stitching of genetics, and we have to let them take over our mind and body.*"

"*How do we do that, Pappi?*"

"*We have to have a clear mind, and the energy of our animal spirit will then envelope us. With our slates blank, all forms of manifestations, skills, and abilities can start to show through.*"

"*Pappi …*" Onnan dragged out as he waved his arms back and forth, growing bored of the conversation. "*When can I morph?*"

Moll'ar grinned slightly, noticing his son growing antsy. "*Close your eyes and clear your mind.*"

Onnan did as his father said as a smile grew across his face.

"*Search your soul for your animal spirit and become one with it. Allow it to take control of your body.*"

Onnan continued to grin. His body grew tense with excitement. After a few moments of what he determined was him searching his soul, Onnan peeked open one of his eyes. His ecstatic expression soon fled from his face.

"*I do not have an animal spirit,*" he retorted and pouted.

"*You do,*" Moll'ar replied, comforting his son as he rubbed Onnan's back. "*You just have to practice.*"

"*I know. I just want to know if I am going to be a foo dog like you or a duba like Momma.*"

166

"You will find out soon enough. Now, what do you say about us goin' and gettin' a bite to eat?" Moll'ar asked as they walked toward Laurelin, who still held Athana.

†

After nine days, the one hundred and seventy thousand Alberian warriors had marched out of the plains and into the mountains of BrightHelm. They trekked up the rocky cliffs, where powdery snow had accumulated. The wind chilled their bodies as it brushed against them. Their breaths, growing heavy after their long march, produced steam as it exited their mouths. Little rodents scampered across the snow from underneath the bushes. The peppermint aroma lingered in the air from the few cedar and pine trees lining the base of the mountains.

As night had approached, the tribe set up camp near the shores of Lake Sound. The ground was hard and unbearable to sleep on, but the warriors knew they had to sleep somewhere. Small waves crashed into the banks and ice patches shifted across the water as a morgawr dove under the water in the distance and a mortessi returned to the water for the night. Sounds of rocs squawking in the trees and of dire wolves howling in the distance rung through the mountains.

In the horizon and up Mount Hon, the warriors saw burning embers from a passing phoenix in the dark of the evening. After a few moments, the chirping of new life traveled down the side of the mountain.

As the last of the men fell asleep, they heard an increase of unicorns whickering and hooves from a large herd of kirin stampeding close to the campsite, as well as boars scuffling past the napping warriors.

Early Morning Sun

"'Tis there anything I can do for ya, m'Lord?" an elven lady dressed in thin garments draped over her shoulders and wrapped loosely around her waist asked.

Azreal, laying in a hammock outside his manor, just smiled while two attractive lamiae fanned him. Another thin and exposed female fed him small fruits. The pastel-purple djinn slowly and seductively placed the berries into Azreal's mouth, her eyes glittering with seductive lust.

"Yes. You can come and rub my neck and shoulders with oils," Azreal responded as he sat up on his hammock, and the elf walked around and began to massage him.

"Ya are so strong, m'Lord," the elf softly whispered

into Azreal's ear as she rubbed her hands down his chest and around his waist.

Bang, bang, bang

"What was that?" Azreal asked, the noise startling him.

"What was what, m'Lord?" the feminine djinn questioned while still trying to seduce Azreal as she fed him.

Bang, bang, BANG!

The noise grew louder but still seemed to be distorted and distant.

Azreal scanned the courtyards around him, but his eyes failed him as his vision faded.

BANG! BANG! BANG!

"Azreal!" a faint voice shouted.

Azreal stood from his hammock and frantically surveyed the garden.

"Azreal!" the voice shouted again, this time clearer and recognizable.

Azreal stumbled ineptly, as his sight was nearly gone; all he saw was darkness with a few flashes of light. He ran around, bumping into the skimpy servants who had been worshiping his body, knocking over one and tripping himself in the process. Azreal rolled over on the ground, his body aching from the impact. Still in a slight daze, his vision returned, and the sounds became clear.

BANG! BANG! BANG!

"Azreal, open the door! This is urgent," the voice shouted.

Azreal looked up from the floor and saw a glow from around his chamber door. "I am coming," he mumbled as he struggled to his feet and stumbled across the room. "What is the matter?"

"I know it's early, brother," Anina responded as the door opened, "but there are foreign knights riding toward the city."

The statement jolted Azreal's mind into full consciousness. "Has Solaris been notified?"

"Aye. He's the one that informed me."

"Alright, let us go to the rampart," Azreal responded, still trying to wake himself up.

He grabbed his robe and followed Anina out of his manor and toward the city wall.

†

As they approached the wall, Solaris—dressed in golden armor accented with shards of cobalt crystals, and adorned with a metallic blue cape—awaited their arrival by an outpost station.

"What are we up against?" Azreal asked as he approached his marquess.

"About fifteen to twenty legions of Senturians on horseback," Solaris responded. "I have Ser Jatus outside our walls, readying our infantry for battle."

"Twenty legions?" Azreal asked in shock. "They have greater numbers than that." He stood with a distrustful look on his face. Then a switch flipped in his mind, and his eyes widened. "Do you have my letter on you?"

"I do, my Lord."

"Now is a good time to look it over." Azreal glanced at Anina. "I am going back to the manor. I have some urgent matters that need my attention. Come and notify me of any changes to our status."

Azreal walked off as Solaris retrieved the letter from his pouch.

His white eyes skimmed the message, and his face stayed expressionless. Anina, curious as to the contents of the letter, slithered behind Solaris and gazed over his shoulder at the parchment. It was blank. Why would her brother want Solaris to look at a blank piece of paper?

Solaris finished looking at the letter, rolled it up, and stuck it into his pouch once more.

"You will want to go back to the manor where it is safe," Solaris said to his duchess. "I will inform Lord Azreal of any changes to our status."

With a concerned expression plastered upon her face, Anina did just as Solaris said without question.

†

As the morning sun crested over Qupar's dried canyons, the sky turned blood red. In the distance from the Kingdom of Talean, Dagrus and the Senturian army sat upon their steeds.

Staring at the city walls, Dagrus turned to his

knights. "Are ya ready, men?"

The Senturian knights cried out, raising their weapons.

Dagrus and his steed turned back toward the walls of Talean.

"Charge!" he commanded as he dropped his torch and pointed his weapon toward the city.

The knights, along with their squires, galloped on their horses through the chilled morning air. Dust stirred up as the hooves dug into the clay. The rising sun radiated an aura glow onto their backs; to the Taleanics, the knights appeared to be riding from out of the sun's core.

As they approached the city's wall, archers placed upon the battlement released their drawn arrows. The arrows—many enchanted with spells of fire or poison—plummeted down, striking into the few exposed openings on the first handful of now fallen Senturian knights.

A hundred thousand Taleanic Golden Men, with their swords and maces and other polearm weapons drawn, lined the bottom of the wall, awaiting the order from Ser Jatus.

"Charge!" Jatus, the Taleanic minotaur knight, shouted as the enemy grew closer.

The two armies collided with a crash. The sounds of metal clashing with metal, the shifting of armor, and the tearing of flesh rung through the air, drowning out the screams of fallen soldiers and their steeds.

As the battle raged on, the well-trained Senturians

were easily capable of fighting the larger group of Taleanics, even with the numbers stacked against them. After several long moments of blades parrying blades and thick metal plates absorbing most of the would-be deadly blows, the Senturian knights weakened. As they grew tired, they made mistakes. They moved slower and became less focus on their opponent's movements, swinging their blades aimlessly. As they became sloppy, their death total rose.

The Taleanics, both on the ground and upon the battlement, picked off the Senturians one by one until just under a couple thousand of them remained.

Lost in the bloodlust of battle, Dagrus didn't notice the shrinkage of his army; his only concern was landing his next blow. During his assault, an arrow impaled him, knitting his chaperon and neck together, but he stayed persistent with his attacks. His shield absorbed many fatal blows, leaving his body fatigued from the vibration of the impacts.

As he pressed onward, another metal bolt pierced his skin, this time penetrating through a slit in his visor and embedding itself into the upper portion of his nasal cavity. His face throbbed in pain, and his eyes puddled with moisture, but his swings never faltered, receiving and delivering many blows to the enemy.

As he slashed through the abdomen of two Golden Men, a faint shout shattered his focus. Dagrus looked toward his left. His young squire, just five hundred strides away, was on his knees arched over as he tried to pull an arrow from his fragile ribs.

"Tyldoran!" he shouted as he sprinted toward the pale-skinned demon.

O'Bryon, who had a few battle wounds of his own, cantered his nightmare beside Dagrus. "Ser Dagrus, we must retreat if we wish to live to fight another day."

"Ya goest, I'm not leavin' Tyldoran behind," Dagrus responded as he kicked up the sand behind him.

†

On the battlement, Solaris, realizing the Senturian retreat, shouted, "Quickly now! Strike them while they flee! Leave no man standing, and let no man escape!" Looking at his men, he continued, "Let loose every last bolt you have, and make them land true, men!"

†

As Dagrus approached Tyldoran, a sharp and agonizing pain pierced his foot and leg as an arrow tore his achilles. He stumbled, and his hands and face soon crashed into the dry clay. The ground thrust the bolt wedged into his visor deeper into his skull, inflicting an even distribution of pain from head to foot. Lifting his torso from the ground, he looked at Tyldoran as another arrow impaled his squire. With guilt in his heart, Dagrus watched Tyldoran topple over, with a bolt protruding from the front of his skull.

Dagrus lay silently, his jaw clenched to suppressed his grief. O'Bryon rode up to him once more, shouting and waving for him to retreat, but Dagrus remained motionless. The bloodstained djinn quickly dismounted his nightmare and picked Dagrus from the ground and saddled the demon alongside him.

As they rode off, Dagrus looked around in a daze. His plan of attack had failed his men; even worse, he had failed his lord, and he had failed the gods. He saw the rest of his knights, just a mere thousand men, fleeing as well, hoping to retreat before they met the same fate as their fallen comrades.

Hidden Agenda – Troins Kashreane'dal

"Do you think we are safe now?" Anina asked as she brushed her auburn hair from her face. "'Tis been ten days since the Senturian attack."

Azreal, walking down the street beside her, fought with the wind and secured his coarse, long gray hair in a bun. He glanced around them, noticing his citizens continuing with their daily lives; a few young djinns ran past them, laughing as they chased after their pet droyaid, its opalescent scales glinting in the sun.

"They will return," he answered. "We injured their numbers, but they cut our men down by half, and they will send reinforcements; that, I can assure you. We must remain alert and stay prepared."

As they traversed the kingdom streets, a young

messenger boy ran to his lord and duchess.

"M'Lord, ya hath received a letter marked with the Alberian seal," the young demon stated as he presented a scroll.

Azreal grabbed the letter. "Run back to the manor and carry on with your chores."

The young demon obeyed his lord and scampered to the manor.

Azreal unrolled the letter and read it to himself.

"What does it say?" Anina questioned as she tried to catch a glimpse of it with her yellow eyes.

Azreal rolled up the letter. "It is of no concern to you."

"Brother," Anina said in a hiss, "as your duchess, it has a great deal of concern to me. Why do you always try and keep these things hidden from my knowledge?"

"You are more intent in making peace than handling matters of conflict and war," Azreal retorted as her green scaly body stood firm and tall, her eyes glinting with annoyance.

"I may not like the idea of innocent blood being shed just so the arrogant bastards who sit upon thrones can say they are better than everyone else; for that, I do not apologize. I am nothing like you or father," Anina firmly stated. "But I still need to be aware of the affairs of this kingdom. It is my duty, and I demand to be in the know about these things."

"If you think you must know," Azreal snarled as he unrolled the piece of parchment, "the letter states:

Lord Azreal.

We have made it around Lake Sound and anticipate reaching BrightHelm within the next moon. We will set camp outside their walls and await your reinforcements to help us siege the kingdom.

Ixin, Chieftain of Alberon."

"*Thank you,*" Anina overemphasized as they began to walk once more. "Even if it's something that you feel I would dislike or disapprove of, I still believe, as your duchess, you should keep me informed of the comings and goings of this kingdom. Otherwise, brother, why have me as your duchess? After all, I have served by your side since you took on the oath of grand duke four years ago this moon. And it 'twas you who picked me over everyone else in Talean."

Azreal glared diminishingly at his duchess and dismissed the question, waiting a moment in silence before speaking. "I must return to the manor. Go fetch six legions of Golden Men and have them suited and waiting for me at the western gate."

"As you bid," Anina agreed, still feeling uneasy with her brother.

†

After returning to his manor, Azreal sat in his cabinet, writing a response to Ixin's letter. As he wrote, the afternoon sunlight shined through the three, large,

179

stained-glass windows—illuminating the room in a bright array of colors. Each window depicted various creatures native to Talean, with the central one holding a collage for each of the gods' seals. Azreal had never been fond of the cathedral-like feel the center window gave his cabinet, but he did not wish to anger the populace by desecrating the work of art.

In one corner of the room sat a wooden bird stand, a leg in height. Perched on top of the stand was Azreal's pet strix, Rri, along with a small, foreign roc. Rri's red feathers fluffed up and stood still as her golden eyes stared at the unwanted bird perched beside her. She remained motionless until someone knocked on to the door, and her head swiveled to see Solaris enter the room.

"My Lord," the djinn greeted Azreal. "I heard you were gathering knights to travel with you to BrightHelm."

Azreal glanced up from his writing. "Yes. Duchess Anina is getting them ready as we speak."

"What business do you have in the mountains?" Solaris asked as he approached Rri and began to scratch her neck, causing her feathers to smooth out. "We are at war with the Helanians, and Lord Moll'ar has already sent an army to raid their kingdom." Solaris paused and walked toward the desk. "We have no business traveling into Galdwulf, less alone all the way to the city beyond the clouds."

Azreal finished writing his letter and made a couple of smooching sounds. The young roc's wings spread outward as it took flight, just to land on Azreal's desk. Azreal handed the letter to the black-feathered creature—rolling his eyes toward Rri when she released a low squawk of anger—before the roc flew out the cracked window, carrying the letter in its talons.

"The Alberian chieftain informed me that they are well on their way to BrightHelm and will be awaiting our assistance," Azreal stated as he looked at his marquess. "I just wrote back, saying that we are sending them reinforcements and for them to commence with their attack on the kingdom when they are ready."

"But, my Lord, why are you leading them?" Solaris asked, concerned of the well-being of his lord. "If somebody must go, why not I?"

"I have some issues that I need to personally attend to." Azreal paused, drifting away in thought. After a brief moment, he continued, "Just promise me that you will follow my orders."

"I promise, my Lord."

"And the letter?"

"The letter too, my Lord."

"Good. I fear Anina is getting suspicious with us." Azreal stood from his desk and crossed the room to a small chest sitting next to the bird stand. He glanced at the window that sat above the chest, the seal of Afria seeming to glow brighter than the others at his thoughts. "She keeps trying to butt into the kingdom's affairs."

"Well, she is your duchess."

Azreal turned toward Solaris with a stern glare in his

white eyes. "So, she is."

Solaris looked upon his lord with worry. "I think she is far better at being Duchess than I would be as Duke."

"She does not know how to negotiate," Azreal exclaimed as he turned back to the chest and squatted down, expelling the ominous feeling the window gave him from his mind. He lifted the top of the chest and stared inside. "She would be taken advantage of if she ever became queen over Talean." He reached into the chest and removed an item wrapped in a leather blanket. "I cannot allow her to be my successor."

"I do not want to overstep my bounds," Solaris began cautiously, "but why did you pick her to be your duchess then?"

Azreal stood and stared at the window once more, remaining silent.

Solaris, trying to come to terms with what was being asked of him, broke the silence. "But *death*? Do you believe that she actually deserves death, my Lord? There is no imminent threat to your life. Does she really have to die so soon?"

"My days are numbered, and I know it." Azreal turned toward Solaris, his brow furrowed. "Now, do as I have commanded. There will be no further discussion of the matter."

Solaris hung his head, worried he had angered his lord. "As you wish."

Azreal closed the chest's lid. "I must go now." He extended his arm for Rri to climb up on it. "I will keep in contact."

He left the room as Rri perched herself on top of her master's shoulder.

After Azreal had left his cabinet, Solaris approached a bookshelf behind the desk. He skimmed through the many books until he came across one that piqued his interest. He removed the book from the shelf and placed it on the desk. He walked to the small chest and retrieved a bag from inside. He returned to the desk and poured out the many colored chips and coins that were inside the bag.

As he shifted through the jewels, counting them as he did so, Duchess Anina slithered into the room.

"Can I help you, Marquess?"

"Duchess," he greeted as he swept the chips back into the bag. "I think I have gotten everything that I need."

"What are you doing in here?" she questioned, looking from him to the bag in his hands.

Solaris grabbed the book from the desk and raised the bag of gems. "I was just talking to Lord Azreal. He wants me to go purchase more weapons and armor for our Golden Men in the chance the Senturians return."

"And the book?"

"Our lord said I could borrow it. Said it was a good read," Solaris answered as he hastily exited the room.

Anina looked out a window—through the crystal diamonds and opals on the testudine's shell placed at the bottom of it—and watched as Solaris left the manor's courtyards. She stood for several minutes, gazing upon the purple djinn as he headed southwest out of the city, an uneasy feeling settling upon her.

As the day grew on, Solaris ventured through the rough terrain of Qupar, the wind howling as it blew dust and dirt against his pastel body. A stride in front of his face, he conjured a barrier to protect his vision while he braved the gusts of wind, but his body was still left open to the numbing feeling of the harsh air; it would've drained too much energy to conjure a full-body shield against such powerful wind.

After two hours of walking through the harsh heat, Solaris discovered a cathedral that once stood tall and proud amongst the barren land but now toppled in ruins far from any village or establishment.

Four great sanctuaries had been placed in the region of Qupar surrounding the City of Talean, three leagues from the city's walls. The other three still stood in all their glory, but the one before him had fallen due to one of the great fights between Libras and the second dragon of the lands. Throughout the years, teams had been dispatched to restore the cathedral but had failed to return, and eventually, people stopped volunteering to go, for fear of what had prevented the previous teams from returning.

The entrance stood at the base of the cathedral, seeming unphased by the attacks upon the structure.

Solaris neared the entryway; the ruins blocked the

wind, allowing him to drop the barrier in front of his face. The doors, lined with verdigris metal, held unusual markings. Dried blood and sand covered their original teal coloring.

As he approached, the large double doors opened on their own, the ground shaking in the process, as if some unknown force knew he was coming. The tired djinn passed through the open doors into a dark room lined with lanterns and torches and filled with massive statues stretching from ground to ceiling; the room still stood untouched by the dragons.

The heavy doors closed behind him with a shuddering clash of noise, shaking the grounds as the djinn jumped nervously, glancing back at the doors. With the doors closed, the room's atmosphere seemed to intensify, and a faint smell of rot and decay permeated the area. Solaris took a deep breath through his mouth and examined the dimly lit statues.

The first idol he came upon was a tall skeleton with long hair and a pair of fleshless wings. It had been sculpted from an opal-colored marble stone.

He whispered to the goddess depicted before him, "Nya, please make your sting painless as you separate her soul from her body. To the Eight, I pray unto you."

He looked upon a second statue—a tall, slender, mushroom-shaped being with long arms and a headdress making up the cap of the mushroom. Trillis's statue had been constructed from the strongest wood known to man—Durbur wood, imported all the way from the Kingdom of Direfell. The wood was hard to come by and could not be cultivated anywhere else.

The djinn strolled his fingers across the statue's rough bark as he looked at the next; however, it had been knocked onto the ground. The diamond-and-citrine crystal statue lay in pieces on the temple's floor. The transparent, feminine figure's torso was headless and missing an arm, while the legs had been severed just above the knees. The orange halo that had once encircled her shoulders and head now rested as a pile of rubble scattered about the floor.

Solaris grew weary and felt a coldness consume his body. He wondered who—or what—would have destroyed a statue of the gods. The djinn surveyed the other statues, each of them constructed of different metals and gemstones—the best materials Talean could come by to honor the gods and goddesses they represented. None of the other idols seemed to be damaged in any way.

The room's light was dim enough to emanate a feeling of desolation but not enough to chase away the shadows nor hide the gouges and bloodstains on the wall.

Solaris shuddered as his gaze fell upon piles of bones near the stained walls. He glanced away, this time noticing several pairs of red eyes staring at him from behind the statues.

Pale figures slowly emerged from the shadows. The cathedral's inhabitants were poised and hunchbacked; some still chewed the pieces of meat they grasped in their claws. Soon the entire room seemed to be filled with the ashy-skinned creatures. They stared peculiarly at Solaris, with blood and gore dripping from their mouths; their fangs and claws so sharp, they could easily cut through the bones of their prey.

Upon seeing the monstrous beings, Solaris stood frozen in fear and questioned himself about why he had made the journey. He knew his lord didn't want to risk leaving Anina in charge of the kingdom, but surely there was another way they could've gone about it.

As he remained frozen, staring into the creatures' eyes, a cold breeze passed through his body. After a quick shiver ran down his spine, the sudden appearance of a closely hovering lavender-colored wisp startled him.

The feminine figure, consisting of purple smoke and gas, spoke to Solaris in an unfamiliar tongue—Gortese. *"Glo last sno'on'siy aglo orlo iy?"*

Solaris snapped from his frozen stare and flipped through the pages of the book he had taken. After finding and translating the words to mean '*You have come to speak with me?*', he responded in rough translations, *"Iy kesse—"* ('*Are you—*')

"Afria?" the wisp finished Solaris's question as she circled him. *"Yes. That is one of the many names that has been given to me by you mortals; Goddess of Peace is another."*

"Yes, I have come to speak with you, Your Holiness," Solaris responded, reading the words from the pages. He glanced at the floating torso of Afria, then toward the broken statue before looking back at the goddess.

The wisp scoffed at his shifty eyes, for she knew

what he was thinking. She spoke in a quick, agitated voice, not waiting for him to translate her words. "*I hate the way you all always depict me. You insult me by building monuments in my name without knowing what or who I am.*" Afria drifted to the toppled statue. "*I looked like a mere mortal with—What was that? A large ring around my head? Do you see a golden ring anywhere? Or appendages hanging below my torso?*" The wisp floated toward the center of the room once more. "*And now you come, not knowing who I am or who it is that you are looking for.*"

Solaris stood mesmerized by the thought of being in the presence of a goddess. The words all blended together and faded to the back of his mind as he studied her presence.

"*You did not even bother learning my tongue before coming to seek my advice. How disrespectful can you mortals be?*" Afria spoke once more, angered as she stared at Solaris's nervous posture. "*So … go on then.*"

Solaris snapped himself from his trance and flipped through the pages of the book, translating the last few words he had paid attention to.

"*I was wondering, what might be the cost to inquire the assistance from one of your dreshdis?*"

He glanced up at the wisp, waiting for a response.

"*How much is a life worth to you?*"

The djinn flipped through the pages once more. After piecing together what had been asked, he set the book on the floor and opened the bag of gems.

"*I do not want rubies nor gold,*" the wisp told him as he offered a handful of chips.

After realizing Afria wasn't going to take the coins, Solaris poured them into the bag and grabbed the book. *"What do you wish for then?"*

"For the life of Duchess Anina?" Afria began as Solaris's face grew pale with surprise. *"Four amber stones, one rose quartz, and a red diamond, all freshly harvested. And I want you to bring me the whole shell, not the chips that you mortals use."*

"How did you know who I wanted to be killed? I never—"

"I know all things that go on within the realms," she interrupted, then paused to laugh. *"You all proclaim me to be a goddess after all."* Afria circled Solaris once more, studying his posture and the beads of sweat accumulating on his skin. *"I also know that this will add three more deaths onto Talean's curse."*

"What curse?"

"I believe you mortals call it the Curse of a Hundred Rulers. Surely, you have heard of it."

"That is just a myth they started after Duke Valek's disappearance."

Afria smirked. *"So, then it is."*

Solaris's stomach grew tight and twisted in knots.

"I ... I do not know if I can go through with this," Solaris stammered.

"You are a marquess—a noble defender of the realm. You have to do nothing more than what it is that you wish to do."

Solaris lowered the book, not bothering to translate his words. "I am sorry that I have wasted your time, Your Holiness."

"Zheogla'adu dokt'iness resh gliy, yoidod iy sidths," Afria responded, then vanished into the air.

189

Solaris flipped through the book once more, trying to interpret her final words: '*Unlike you mortals, my time is never wasted.*'

The Climb – Wa'Molloc

The sun's arrays crested the peak of Mount Boden. The cold winds from the lake greeted the Alberian warriors early in the morning. Whereas they fell asleep to the beautiful sounds of the wildlife the night before, only the eerie silence and whistling winds welcomed in the new day.

On the twenty-seventh day, after eating their morning meal, the warriors prepared themselves for another hike.

One Alberian stepped away from the camp to relieve himself before starting his day's march. The chill in the air was so intense, the warrior felt a significant difference between it and the warmth from his liquids and enjoyed the small amount of steam radiating from its contact with the snow as it melted. He glanced around as he relieved himself, and his gaze fell upon a massive amount of tracks embedded into the white fluff. Each print was the size of the average elven head. In instantaneous fear, the warrior finished his business and hurried back to the others, searching for Ixin.

"Chief! There are tracks of dire wolves a few strides away from camp, hundreds of 'em at that," the warrior informed the lich. *"They look fresh. They must have passed by as we slept."*

Ixin, growing unsettled by the fact that they were so close to suffering a bloody death, glanced around to see if he could notice any significant change in the number of his men.

"Al'ight, we need to hurry and get movin'," Ixin shouted. *"Gather up yer belongin's. Ye can eat on the way."*

His people did as ordered, and all headed out, making sure they didn't travel the path of the wolves.

†

As the day carried on, the Alberians followed Ixin around Lake Sound and into the region of Whitefall—a valley resting between Mount Harod and Mount Celeren.

As they hiked the edge of the valley, Tera and Ixin talked casually amongst themselves.

Ixin's gaze veered up at the trees and saw the ruby feathers of a solitary strix among the white, snow-covered branches, staring down at him with its

192

golden eyes.

Tera glanced at the bird. "*Ya know strixes are a sign of bad luck.*"

"*That is just superstition. Why would we fly a strix on our banner if 'tis bad luck?*"

"*To ward off intruders.*"

"*Do you have no knowledge of our banner and the history it shares with our great land?*"

Tera grew confused. "*'Tis known as the Banner of the Strix, and 'twas adopted after the War of Snakes to ward off the Learish.*"

"*Ahh, but by both accounts, ya are wrong. Though we did begin flying it after the war, 'tis properly named the Banner of Addazul.*"

"*Who is Addazul?*"

Ixin's rigid face grew perplexed. "*Do ya knowest not of yer heritage or land? Addazul was a strix as large as a roc. An old god that watched over the life of our land—that 'tis 'til the Learish first crossed the Diamond and slaughtered him. Aft' the war, we flew a new banner to honor our slain god, and built the statue at the end of the Diamond River. Ya have taken part in the Cleansing, have ya not?*"

Tera remained silent, embarrassed that she knew little of her culture and shook her head.

"*Ya have ne'r wrote a scroll—a prayer—to drift to Addazul?*"

"*No. Before today, I had never heard the name Addazul.*"

"*What settlement in Willowgate are ya from?*"

"*Northwind. It is on the banks of the Riversong Stream.*"

"*Ahh, a northerner. That would explain it,*" Ixin said and

chuckled. *"Ya might as well be from BrightHelm, bein' that close to the clouds."*

As the days progressed, they trekked farther through the mountains. Their travels seemed both hurried by their unease from the distant howls in the air and slowed by the increase in the falling snow and the chilling winds. In between the eerie cries from dire wolves and the screams of the wind, they heard faint chirps from various avians populating Whitefall.

Some of the warriors startled in fear and increased their pace when a long, loud howl pierced the air.

"'Tis close!" Ixin shouted as he pulled out his hatchets. *"Keep alert!"*

A few warriors took Ixin's lead and grabbed at their clubs and bows, expecting an ambush at any moment, but after some time had passed, they relaxed, hearing the howl from a much farther distance.

"I am gettin' a bad feelin', Chief," one of the warriors said as he glanced at the barren trees and saw more strixes perched upon the snowy branches.

The warriors became warier than before. Strixes always follow death, feasting on the blood left behind on corpses. Seeing so many strixes nearby and no dead carcasses led many of the men to believe they were a bad omen.

As the day continued, the strixes became more

numerous; where there was only one or two at the start, there were now fifteen to twenty of the silent, blood-feasting birds at a time. Coupled with the howls they heard from both near and afar, the sight of the living death omens above them caused even Ixin to become anxious to end their travels.

"Our day's journey will end soon," Ixin informed his warriors, then pointed to a nearby ridge. *"There should be a landin' on top of that cliff."*

"Ya expect us to climb that?" Tera asked as she surveyed the ridge.

The graphite wall, covered in a layer of ice, had a few roots protruding from the trees that sat upon the top.

"Aye," Ixin responded. *"'Tis that gonna be a problem?"*

"I do not fare well with heights."

"Once ya reach the top, ya will be on solid ground." Ixin faced the rest of the warriors. *"Leave yer bags on the ground. Once ye reach the top, I will toss yer belongin's up before I come on my way."*

Ixin approached the rock wall, outstretched both arms, and tilted his hands so his palms faced the cliff. Flames swirled from his hands. The warmth felt nice to his thin, chilled body. The flames impacted onto the frozen wall, melting the thick layer of ice into a puddle of steaming water.

Once a clear path appeared all the way to the top of the ridge, Ixin lowered his arms, and the flames dispersed.

Ixin turned toward the warriors. *"Who is goin' first?"*

The Alberians, in groups of two and three, scaled the

cliff, grabbing ahold of extrusions in the mountain and using others as footholds. The stone was scalding and left blisters and cuts on many of the warriors' hands.

As the Alberians climbed the cliff, Ixin noticed Tera remaining at the bottom as the others passed her by.

"*'Tis ya stayin' down here?*" Ixin questioned. "*I can send a scroll to yer missus and let her know that ya were incapable of makin' the journey with the men. That is, if ya would like?*"

Tera shook her head as her body trembled and her breathing quickened.

"*'Tis not that high, is it? Only about seven legs,*" she told him, trying to convince herself she could make the climb.

Tera grabbed two pieces of field dressing from a pouch and wrapped her hands before climbing the wall. As she grabbed ahold of the extruding structures, the heat of the rocks still burned through the wrappings, causing sweat to accumulate on her palms. She took her time, carefully placing her hands and feet as she went.

Once Tera had reached the top, Ixin hurled up all of their gear, lifting the bags with his magic, then followed suit as he joined the warriors.

Tera sat on a rock, unwrapping her hands as Ixin approached her. "*Could ya not have lifted us up the cliff? It would have saved us the blisters.*"

Ixin sat beside her as he too attended to his blistered hands. "*Nay. Magic does not work on the livin'. 'Tis would have been convenient though.*"

Following a precarious climb the day prior, the warriors awoke from slumber and readied for the new day. They were still left weary as they saw more than thirty strixes peppering tree branches nearby. Their travels up the cliff face hopefully left the howls, and thus the dire wolves, behind them. But as they packed their gear, a hiss with the undercurrent of a bleating growl filled the air.

The hiss seemed to circle the air around the Alberians. Near instantaneously, all the yellow-eyed carrion birds took flight when the noise flowed through the air, a few red feathers being all they left behind. The ground seemed to rumble as the strange hiss grew louder and the unusual growl behind it became even more menacing.

One warrior shouted as the others looked his way. They found themselves peering into three pairs of eyes glowing through the whiteness of the trees.

The creature stepped into the opening, and the Alberians were in awe of the gigantic beast. The savage monster bore two heads upon its shoulders: one feline and the other of a ram. Its tail was long and scaly, with a serpentine head at the tip.

Tera stared into the chimera's eyes. Her pulse beat so hard she could feel it in her brow. All the sounds around her seemed to fade; only the sound of her own breaths remained. She stood frozen in fear, yet her body was anything but still. Her arms and legs trembled as they grew numb. After being frozen in fear for what seemed to be an eternity, she glanced at the other warriors, who were in just as much shock as her.

Ixin, in the center of the crowd, pointed his axes at the beast.

As Tera made eye contact with him, her sense of hearing returned and could hear him shouting.

"Kill that damn thing!"

Tera and the other Alberians drew their weapons and swung at the chimera with their blades. The large beast scurried to the side as a few of the swords slashed through the air, barely missing its body.

The chimera's ears pinned back as it snarled at the warriors and launched forward, breathing out a large plume of flames at the Alberians. The embers set fire to many of the warriors' pelts and leather clothes, causing them to die in a blazing fire.

The remaining Alberians circled the foul creature and swung at it from every direction. The large beast swatted its paws, gashing open some of the men, and continued to spout balls of fire. The warriors overtook the creature in a haste as their blades and clubs sliced its hide and crushed its bones.

"'Tis almost dead!" Ixin shouted. *"One last blow should finish her off!"*

As Ixin proclaimed their victory, Tera sprung forward and jabbed her dagger through the chimera's bottom jaw of the feline head as it swiped its paw toward her.

As the beast winced in pain, a minotaur warrior swung his battle-ax, impaling it into the side of the chimera's ram-like head. The creature collapsed onto the blood-soaked, snowy ground. It tried to raise itself back up, but the minotaur delivered another fatal blow, causing the beast to take its final breath.

Tera sat on a large stone and inventoried the other warriors. Thirty-five warriors had met their death fighting the creature, while another fifty were left severely wounded from the fight. She watched some of the Alberians pile their deceased comrades into a pile, while others patched up the wounded.

"When do we get branded?" Tera asked as Ixin stitched together her hip with a thin piece of thread-like cloth.

"Ya will be branded aft' ya have fought in battle; that is, if ya survive."

Tera gritted her teeth. *"A few scratches but I do believe I survived just fine."*

"'Tis 'twas no battle, and ya would be ridiculed for havin' thought that for the rest of yer life," Ixin said as he glanced at the other warriors.

"How was this not a battle? There was bloodshed, and we lost some of our warriors in the fight."

"We have nearly thirty legions of warriors fightin' against one lone chimera. Those odds are far from bein' worthy of a battle. It had no armor nor weapon to defend itself, nor did it have the brains to flee when it 'twas greatly outmatched."

"'Tis that what happened to you?" Tera asked, looking at Ixin's tense, swiveled face.

"Aye," he answered as he recollected the memory. *"I 'twas a little younger than ya. My brother and I were helpin' with some of the warriors out in the fields around the capital when a herd*

of catoblepones spooked and stampeded past us. The warriors were trampled, but my brother and I dodged the herd, and we managed to bring one of 'em down. Aft' our victory, we thought we would celebrate to honor the fallen warriors by brandin' ourselves. The Chieftain of Alberon received word of our brands and held us for mockin' and falsifyin' a sacred ritual, thus we were forced to wear these brands," Ixin finished as he pointed at his face.

"All of that because of a misunderstanding?"

"Aye. They allowed me to become a warrior because I had ne'r actually committed a crime against the capital. But my brother, on the other hand, the ridicules we received dug deep, and he ended up takin' his life a few moons aft' the incident."

"I am sorry to hear that."

"'Tis okay. Just do not go and get yer pretty face branded for nothin'."

A DEBT OWED – ALO'AƆU ΠEOSt'iƆ

Inside her manor, Anina lay coiled inside a canopy rock bed in her chamber. She held a book written in a foreign tongue, as she prided herself on educating herself on the history of the many different lands across the Abyss. She loved learning of the distant lands and planned to one day visit them all. She hoped her future travels would better prepare herself for the day when she would rule Talean after Azreal was no longer lord.

Anina was turning to a new page and reaching for a glass of red wine with her tail when a loud commotion erupted outside the manor, causing her to jump and knock over her chalice.

Her and her brother's droyaids that were guarding the estate barked and growled and then whimpered in fear. She heard the sound of townsfolk running down the streets in a panic, hurrying to get inside their homes and shops, over the baying of the droyaids. But as soon as the commotion had started, silence blanketed the air, and she only heard the gradual breeze drifting through the window.

Curious to the source of the sudden noise, Anina slithered from her bed and toward her open window. Her vibrant yellow eyes peered into the manor's desolate grounds. To her immense surprise, she saw nothing out of the ordinary on the streets or near the buildings.

Squeak

Tracking the faint sound, Anina's serpentine head jolted around, and her heart beat rapidly upon seeing the once-closed door to her room, now open. Her tongue flicked, trying to taste any new scents in the air, but she picked up nothing; everything smelled as it should. She cautiously slithered across her chamber, tasting the air and trying to feel the vibration of any sounds through the floor. Upon reaching the door, Anina looked into the corridor, neither seeing nor smelling anyone or anything out of the usual. She sighed to slow her heart rate, relieved to find nothing, and chuckled at herself for being alarmed. She reached to close the door, which a breeze from her open window must have swung open, only to freeze in fear.

From behind, she heard an unusual panting sound carrying a faint hissing undertone. She clenched her jaws and turned, her scales tightening around her body as she faced a pale, emaciated figure with dark red eyes. Upon seeing the dreshdi inside her room, her eyes widened in shock and fear; it stood two heads shorter than her and seemed to pull the shadows in the room toward it.

The former lich stood there, watching her. The magic used to keep its body alive, after the lich's death, never fully healed the massive gash stretching from its shoulder to its hip. As the savage shadow walker inhaled, the wound widened, though nothing came from it. The dreshdi hissed at her—a garbled sound from its mouth—as it cocked its deformed head. Its long, black forked tongue flicked past its jagged fangs, and its clawed hands clenched and unclenched as it stared at her.

Anina, frozen in a state of immense fear, could barely make a sound. Her hand raised to her chest, unknowingly grabbing where her erratically beating heart lay under her rib cage as she struggled to gather the courage to speak. Her breathing had increased, and the tip of her tail rapidly tapped the floor.

"How did you get in here?" she managed to stutter out.

The dreshdi's mouth opened—its fangs growing as the mouth widened—as it gave a deep, rumbling growl. Its brow sat low on its forehead, and its nose scrunched up as it hunkered low to the ground and sprung at the terrified duchess.

As it collided with Anina's terror-struck body, its claws ripped under her scales, and its jaws met with her shoulder, forcing a gut-wrenching and agonized scream from her mouth.

†

Down the passageway in Azreal's cabinet, Solaris sat behind the desk, flipping through a couple opened books and flicking his fingers at a random object resting on the desk. He was startled as a loud, feminine scream echoed through the manor's corridors. He leaped from the chair, knocking a few books and objects to the ground in his haste, and rushed down the passageway toward the duchess's chamber.

As he neared her room, he slowed down, his skin paling from the sounds from within. Her screams had diminished but were replaced with a sound similar to what the droyaids made when they had caught an animal. Noises of crunching and chewing, as well as what sounded like water dripping from the top of a roof after a good rain, came from the open doorway. An unexplained fear gripped the purple djinn as the sounds became clearer the closer he got to the door.

He turned into her room and stopped, fear gripping his chest as he gasped in shock and disgust. On the floor of her room, surrounded by a puddle of her own blood and pieces of flesh and scales, lay the former duchess. Chunks of meat had been bitten from the side of her neck, gouges of flesh ripped from her arms, revealing the bones, and slashes, as well as holes, had been dug into her torso. The dreshdi's long claws held down her face, prying into her eyes as it lowered its mouth to her chest and ate from what remained of her rib cage.

"Get away from her!" Solaris exclaimed as he rushed into the room.

The dreshdi's gaze shot toward the marquess. Blood dripped from its maw while it still held part of Anina's flesh in its jowls. Its eyes narrowed in anger as it growled at the djinn. Ripping its hand from Anina's face and splattering Solaris with her blood, the dreshdi scurried into the shadows and vanished.

Solaris stood stiff, his heart beating rapidly for what felt like hours to his petrified mind. He nervously waited for the reappearance of the dreshdi.

Solaris's gaze darted back and forth, looking at every shadow in the room, then falling upon his duchess's corpse. He noted the scratches on the floor where Anina's body lay, and her fingertips bloodied and mangled as if she had dug into the floor to try to escape the attack. The sight of her death was far more gruesome than any he had seen in battle, or perhaps it just appeared that way because he had actually known her and was the cause of her death.

The sound of frightened shrieks and screams outside the open window startled Solaris from his subconscious stare. His white eyes widened in fear as he sprinted to the window. He gasped upon spotting the pale and bloodied figure rushing from the shadows from a store below. He watched as it bounced from shadow to shadow, hissing at the townsfolk, leaving a trail of dust behind it.

After the dreshdi had disappeared from view, Solaris pulled himself from the window to look upon Anina's mutilated corpse. He shuffled toward her and dropped to his knees, guilt flooding through him as he shook from suppressed tears. With an unsteady hand, he reached out to lift her head off the ground. Her bloodied face looked unrecognizable from the holes and gashes left by the foul creature. Solaris tried to wipe the red wine pouring from her openings. He held her against his chest, wishing he could have saved her from the tragic outcome that had taken place.

"I am so sorry this happened to you," he mumbled in his sobs.

He became lightheaded at the sight of her death and lay her body back in the crimson puddle before removing his gaze from her. He looked to where the dreshdi had disappeared in the room. Anger coursed through him as he shouted in rage and rose his hand, unleashing a bolt of lightning at the shadow. With his magic, he grabbed objects around Anina's room, throwing them at the shadow, but his rage halted as a voice spoke to him.

"Kista zho'siy trase'adu iy din chidns dokt larr stis niddal iy."

Solaris spun and saw the lavender form of Afria hovering in the doorway.

"How could you do this to her? She did not deserve this!"

"Das glasa'kah?"

"I never gave you my approval," Solaris yelled at the wisp as he ran toward her and swung his fist. To no surprise, Solaris wasn't shocked when his hand passed through the smoky figure.

Afria turned toward him and spoke once more. *"Steagla'stel'diy dreal dekt'ler iy nes orlo seorlo ness ridd."*

"What?" Solaris barked. "I have read up on you. You know I do not speak Gortese, so why do you not just speak Megorie like everybody else on this forsaken land?"

Afria snickered. "The Alberians' native tongue is Oacari."

"Who gives a shit about them? The fact is that you can speak and understand Megorie, so quit speaking to me in the language of the gods."

"The language of the gods?" Afria questioned as she moved around the room. "Is that what you petty mortals think Gortese is? It is the language of the dead, not the *gods.*"

"But you are Afria, the Goddess of Peace."

"Goddess?" Her soft, chiming voice grew to a hiss. "You mindless beings think you have to give a label to everything—including the presence of something that you cannot explain, nor wrap your tiny minds around."

"But you are Afria, are you not?" Solaris asked as he analyzed the wisp's form.

"That I am, to you. To others, I go by many names."

"Then how can the Goddess of Peace take someone's life in such a cruel way."

"I am going to stop you right there," Afria said as

anger grew on her smoky face.

Her eyes narrowed and stared at the djinn as he opened his mouth to speak but no words came. A slight pressure built around Solaris's throat as he tried again to force words from his mouth; however, fear built inside him as he realized he could produce no sound. Solaris's eyes bounced around—unable to focus on one thing for any amount of time—as his heart pounded inside his numbed body.

Afria's haunting expression gleamed at the djinn's nervous state and spoke with insolence. "*You*, Marquess Solaris of the Kingdom of Talean, came to me acquiring help from my creatures of the night. *You*, Solaris, wanted Duchess Anina dead, for the simple fact that you wanted to feel as if you served your lord justly. *You*, you petty and disgraceful being, labeled me as a goddess, but here you are questioning my motives when you are as manipulating as I. I have been anointed the title Goddess of Peace by all of you serfs and laborers; that title I did not give to myself. So, you would be wise to watch your tongue around me, Solaris of Talean."

The djinn gasped—able to make a sound once more—as he ran his fingers across his irritated throat.

Afria glided to Anina's corpse. "So, now you ask me, how can I be the Goddess of Peace with an army of mercenaries? One man's peace is another man's destruction. Which side are you on?"

Solaris stepped forward. "I still never gave you the order—"

Afria's power silenced him as she reapplied pressure

on his throat.

"At least I waited to take her life on you mortals' holiday of Masida. The one day of the year that you are released from your oaths and aren't bound to live by your laws, all because it's the last night of winter. I released her from her duties to this realm and freed her from being bound a slave to the rulings of you and your wretched lord." Afria paused as she stared intently into Solaris's white eyes. "You have two moons to bring me my pay."

Once again, the djinn felt the pressure leave his throat.

"What kind of dark power is this?" he questioned as he rubbed his throat.

"Dark power? No. I am a goddess after all, am I not? I have the right to break your mortal laws of magic, and I am able to use it on what I please."

Solaris stood frozen in fear of the power the gods contained, still feeling uneasy with the scene before him and the irritating pressure once on his throat.

"*Neyadod no'a,*" Afria said, then vanished into a puff of smoke.

War Machines

As noon approached on Sentries, Darius and Ky were leaving a workshop on the eastern outskirts of the city. They had gone there to give the workers some blueprints for siege weapons Darius wanted made.

"Do you think they can build such great weapons?" Ky asked as they traversed the kingdom streets.

Darius glanced at his duchess. "They can build whatever I ask of them, no matter how large or small the weapon."

"But that's a lot for them to build," Ky said wearily. "It would take them many moons to finish such a project."

Darius snarled at the thought of it taking such a long time to complete his vision. "They will have to work harder and longer to finish promptly."

"But my Lord," Ky continued, doubting Darius's management skills, "I'm not sure that they will be able to build such larger-than-life weapons."

"If they can't build them, no one else in the land could build them neither. When we arrive back at the manor, remind me to send a letter to Queen Aerea."

"The Ajirian queen? What matters do you wish to write to her about?"

"Aye, I want to inquire from her some resources that will aid in the execution of our new weapons."

Darius and Ky continued to talk as they traveled across the capital on foot. After some time walking, they arrived at an entrance to a mine shaft attached to the southern wall of the city, west of Darius's manor. They entered the shaft, leading them toward the iron veins. As they navigated the tunnel, they heard the faint sound of metal clashing together, along with the bubbling sound of boiling magma, from deep within the mine. The orange neon lights bounced off the shaft's dark, rough walls.

Darius and Ky reached the forge of the iron vein with large beads of sweat streaming down their bodies. They were met by a large, pale-skinned cyclops, who was covered in dust and dirt—his body black from the filth of the mine.

"To what dost thou owe the honor o' yer visit, m'Lord?" the foreman of the veins asked.

"I need you to craft me some new weapons," Darius stated as he handed the cyclops two large pieces of rolled-up parchment.

The foreman skimmed the blueprints. His eye widened as he gazed upon the proposed weapons. "M'Lord, these are massive. They will need a high abundance o' iron, and the bank dost not hath enow chips to cover the expenses."

Darius nodded knowingly. "Once we take the Kingdom of Talean, our purse will be overflowing with bellies and chips and blood pennies. Plus, I am willing to double you and your men's pay for this order."

"These will be too heavy; no man could carry such an object."

Darius smirked. "Don't worry about that. Just worry about crafting those items, and I'll take care of the transportation and the use of them."

"Thou will get started on 'em right away, m'Lord."

BATTLE AT THE WALL

The ninety-two thousand Learish soldiers awoke from their slumber as the shifting patterns of light peeked through the bare branches of the forest. The brisk, foggy morning had arrived in Krywood, and the smell of wet grass and animal droppings filled the air.

"'Ight, men," Nerek began in a dark, raspy voice as he placed his helm onto his deformed skull. "'Tis day we come blade to blade with Woodites. We will suffer, but victory will be great!" He wiped away some mucus that had ran from his nose and onto his lips, then picked up his large iron mace. "Know our role ... We lure them to Dravendale, where they will take their last breaths. We stand solid on land and sea!" the ogre said, quoting the Learish motto as he raised his mace into the air.

"Duke Galach! Duke Galach!"

The shouts came from outside of the large wooden manor, along with the sound of dead grass crunching under heavy feet.

An old dryad rushed into the great hall of Galach's manor, panting profoundly. As she passed through the room, not bothering to slow down, she asked one of the housemaids, who was cleaning around the fireplace, "'Is Duke Galach here?"

"He was away in his chamber earlier, m'Duchess, breaking his fast," the maid responded as Celsa exited the hall.

A few moments later, Celsa swung open the large door to Galach's bedchamber. She scanned the room, realizing it was vacant, then ran through the manor once more. As she approached the end of one of the corridors, she heard voices chattering behind a closed door.

She slung open the door, having no time to waste to bother knocking. "Duke Galach!"

"Duchess Celsa, how might thou be o' help to ya?" the towering treefolk asked in shock of seeing his duchess panting and sweating—well aware of the urgency in her voice.

"Duke Galach, Marquess Krinn; pardon the

interruption, but I have just witnessed Learish footmen out past the city walls," the dryad stated as she tried to catch her breath.

Galach's wooden eye sockets widened as his brows furrowed. "Marquess, go gather yer men and defend our walls. See if ya can bend a knee to the Learish for our safety; if not, then goest and do what ya can to protect the kingdoms."

An elf with a head full of dark red curls stood from the table he had previously sat at and left the room.

Galach sighed. "Thou fretted 'tis morrow would cometh. Go to the stockade, and lock yerself in there. Ya shall be safe 'til thou comes down for ya."

"Right away," Celsa responded as she left Galach's cabinet and obeyed his command.

✝

Mani, a morling who had been placed in charge of the Woodite footmen, gathered his arrows from a storage cabinet under the rampart.

Mani always knew he had wanted to join the Woodite army ever since he could change into his animal spirit. He was aware the military could use his claws as well as his sword and joined the ranks as soon as he came of age. Mani always envisioned himself as a master swordsman, ranking up to the skill of his kingdom's marquess. Upon training, however, he found his skill with a bow was untested to none, and he stood out from his fellow recruits.

Mani served with his fellow archers for fifteen years; his prowess with his handmade recurve bow was legendary in Ringwood. As well as his ability to wield a bow, Mani also spent his years as a soldier, training his animal spirit to be in top shape. He was nowhere near as stealthy as he could be wielding a bow as a beast, but the years of practice had made his transformation time quick enough to surprise any enemy in a fight.

Mani approached the footmen he had been assigned and shook his dirty, blond hair out of his brown eyes. "Al'ight, men! We've got to defend the city. Grab yer weapons, and don't let any Learish pass through these gates!"

A group of fifty thousand Woodite footmen lined the outside of the western wall, forming in five rows. The first row knelt on one knee and covered themselves with their shields. The second readied their bows and rested the arrows into small notches on top of the shields in front of them. The remainder stood behind and offset the second, drawing their swords and daggers, readying to charge at the approaching army.

†

In the distance, Nerek and the Learish army marched through the dense forest toward the Woodites. They heard chants and yells coming from the grungy warriors.

Marquess Krinn stood on the battlement, holding a white banner high in the air. "We wish to not fight. Please spare our kingdom, and there will be no bloodshed."

Nerek's large yellow eyes looked up at the small elf on top of the wall. "Both armies are dressed and readied for battle. No need to play victim!"

"Duke Galach wishes to not fight today, nor ever. Let's just put our blades down and go on 'bout our lives."

Nerek's upper lip curled to one side. "Aye, ya don't have to fight."

The ogre raised his mace into the air, then gave the order to charge at the Woodites.

As the Learish stormed the wall, waving their weapons, the Woodites drew their arrows, awaiting the call. Their hearts pounded, and sweat beads formed upon their foreheads; in the midst of their fear, they stayed still and poised, awaiting the order to fire.

As the Learish army drew near, all but a thousand stopped charging.

"What are they doin'?" Mani whispered as he noticed the enemy's abrupt stoppage.

Before Mani could comprehend what was happening, from behind him, he heard Marquess Krinn shout, "Loose!"

The archers on top of the battlement, as well as the ones lining the wall on the ground, simultaneously released their arrows at the Learish invasion—both the lonely few charging them and the remainder in the treeline. The thousand Learish lowered their heads behind their wooden shields still charging the group of Woodites, a few falling to the arrows. They were only thirty strides away and quickly approaching as another swarm of arrows whistled through the air. Most of the bolts met their mark against the Learish in the treeline, causing some to fall in pain and others to tumble and never to rise again, while some arrows pierced the ground and tree trunks.

The Woodites lining the wall rose to their feet and drew their swords. The first row of soldiers broke formation and charged the Learish. They struck down the surviving Learish out in the open from the onslaught of arrows, then continued past them to the remaining warriors waiting behind the cover of trees.

The Learish engaged with the Woodites, swinging their blades and maces. Coming in contact with mostly thin plates of armor and shields, some made their way into the flesh of the enemy.

After swinging his mace and breaking a leg of a satyr, Nerek shouted to his men, "Retreat, now!"

The Learish army fled into the woods as the Woodites followed close behind.

Mani, examining the situation, yelled at his fellow comrades, "Whoa, whoa! Hold up! Come back!"

Most of the soldiers heard his orders, but a few did not as they continued to chase after the retreating Learish.

"Do we not go in aft' them?" a Woodite soldier asked.

"Nay. They are up to somethin', I just know it."

"What are ya doing?" Krinn shouted at Mani. "Go! Hunt 'em down and kill 'em!"

Mani turned and looked at Krinn. "Something doesn't feel right, Ser!"

"Ye'r not in charge, now go!"

Mani turned toward the treeline, gave a loud battle cry, and took off running; the other soldiers on the ground followed behind him. As they rushed into the forest, Nerek and his army charged the Woodites.

Nerek swung his mace around, breaking legs, crushing ribs, and smashing skulls of the enemy. He blitzed through the crowd of warriors without an enemy blade touching him.

Once he reached the wall, he holstered his mace in its sling and held his shield above him with one hand and climbed the ladder toward the battlement. Arrows bombarded his shield—some ricocheted off, chipping the edges of the shield, while others punctured the wood. One bolt pierced through as it hit Nerek's shield dead center and impaled his wrist. Nerek grunted from the pain but continued to climb.

Once reaching the top of the wall, Nerek attempted to plow through the archers. He immediately drew his mace and swung. The first couple of archers he swung at ducked and whirled their daggers at him. Nerek hopped backward, trying to avoid their sharp blades; then he ran up to one and kicked the archer over the edge of the parapet. He turned and smashed his shield into another, causing the enemy to stagger and fall off the other side. One Woodite lunged forward with his sword, but Nerek parried it with his mace, then kicked the Woodite in the groin, causing him to tumble over. Nerek raised his weapon and hammered it onto his head, causing brain matter and skull fragments to spray the ground around them.

The next closest Woodite was ten strides away, he stood there quivering in fear, knowing he was going to be next.

As Nerek approached him, the archer drew an arrow and released it, but Nerek's shield absorbed the blow. Nerek swiftly swept his mace along the ground, tripping the elven archer. Nerek stepped over the fallen warrior, and with all of his strength, he stomped in his face.

Another archer ran toward Nerek, tackling him to the ground, causing him to drop his mace. The archer unsheathed his dagger and tried to stab the giant in the chest, but Nerek grabbed the archer's wrists and flung him off his body. He scampered on top of the archer and pounded his shield into the elf's throat, tearing the flesh and causing the archer to spit up blood.

Nerek glanced up to notice a soldier charging at him with a small dagger. He pulled an arrow from his shield and jabbed it into the approaching soldier's eye, but not before the dagger had impaled his lungs. Nerek dropped to a knee, covering the wound with his hand.

"Well, well, what do we have here?" Krinn said and smirked as he walked toward Nerek. "It looks like yer time hath finally came."

Nerek lifted his head, wincing in pain, and made eye

contact with Krinn as he approached, drawing his sword.

"We might be a peaceful kingdom, but we stand our ground," Krinn continued. "We will fight for Lord Cornelius, and he will win this war."

Nerek stood, gritting his distorted teeth as he rose. Once he had both of his feet under him, he unstrapped his shield and tossed it down.

"What?" Krinn scoffed. "Do ya think ya can still fight?"

Nerek roared as he charged Krinn, who was in total amazement that Nerek could even move. He wrapped his large ogre arms around the thin elf and tackled him off the side of the battlement. The two bodies plummeted toward the earth, twisting and turning as they fell. Then, with a loud thump, the bodies slammed into the ground. Every bone in both of the warriors' bodies shattered and left them lying there as the life abandoned their inert bodies.

✝

Outside the wall, the battle still raged between the two armies. The fallen bodies were strolled all across the ground. Some were eviscerated, treading on their own entrails, while others struggled to stand, having their arms severed from their bodies. The fallen bodies groaned as they rolled about in the blood of others. Severed limbs and decapitated heads littered the blood-soaked weeds.

Mani soon realized what had happened to Marquess Krinn; hate and anger boiled within him. He turned and threw his bow to the ground and charged a nearby Learish. As he approached, he leaped into the air; his face and body bulged as he morphed into a ferocious duba.

His canine form was powerfully built, with high front shoulders that accented a sloped back. His snout was short and squared out, though his fangs were as long as his dirty, blond pelt.

By the time he had finished changing, he had already landed; Mani shook his body, getting the fur out of his eyes and released an ear-splitting growl, shaking the ground with his battle cry. He set his sights on an enemy soldier and lunged for him, knocking into him with a snarl. The soldier fell and grunted, and before he realized what had happened, Mani tore into his neck, ripping out the warrior's throat.

Mani continued to rush and tackle other Learish warriors, biting and throwing them to the ground, leaving behind a trail of blood and gore as he tore through their ranks. His pelt was stained with the blood of his enemies and matted with the mud formed from the saturated ground they stood on. After taking down one soldier, Mani scanned the area around him as he bellowed another rage-filled cry, the lifeforce from the soldier spewing from his mouth.

After killing close to a hundred Learish soldiers himself, Mani met his match as he pounced onto one of the treefolk warriors. As Mani landed on top of him, the Learish rolled over onto Mani and grabbed his body with long branch-like hands and trapped him against the ground as his fingers took root into the soil. Mani clawed at the dirt, trying to dig his way out of his grasp but to no prevail. The more he dug, the tighter the Learish's clinch became.

A Learish troll, taking advantage of Mani's exhaustion from constant struggling, approached him, carrying a battle-ax. Before Mani spotted him, the troll sliced his ax into the back of his neck, severing his head from his body.

The Learish continued to slaughter through the rest of the Woodite soldiers, stabbing and slicing them one by one, until they had all fallen. Once no Woodites remained, the Learish army rampaged through the streets of Ringwood. They looted from the vendors and overturned their carts and attacked and killed citizens who hadn't run inside yet. They struck fear into everyone's soul.

They advanced to Duke Galach's manor. They stormed the doors to the great hall, and splitting into groups, they marched down the many corridors of his mazelike manor.

One group found themselves at the end of a corridor, with a slightly opened wooden door. They approached and saw, through the crack of the door, a large treefolk sitting behind a desk. The soldiers barged into the room as a giant bird flew out a window with a scroll attached to its foot.

Galach looked up as they entered his cabinet.

"Thou's time hath came, thou supposes," he stated as he raised his crystal glass full of an amber-colored liquid in a toasting gesture.

"Ya hath made this too easy for us," a Learish said as he approached the desk.

"The seasons change, the tides come and they go, but we remain. One house. One family," Galach responded. His face scrunched as he looked at his glass. "Ya may hath broken my ranks, but ya shall not win this war. Ye art cowards and weak for attacking a surrendered city."

"Just how weak are we? 'Cause to me, ye'r the weak one. Ya will never live to witness the end of this war," another Learish said as he drew his sword.

Galach, growing annoyed with the Learish's presence, tensed up, causing his glass to shatter and the liquid inside to drip from his fist. He flipped his desk at the warriors, but they were a lot younger and quicker. They avoided the tossed desk and leaped over it. Before Galach could react, they had him pinned into a corner as two Learish swung their battle-axes. Their blades impaled into the bark on the treefolk's thick neck. Galach's lifeless treelike corpse fell forward onto the floor. The third Learish jabbed his sword into the back of Galach's head to be sure of his death.

The Last Seed

As the morning sun peeked through the branches, Galzar and his knights ventured through the southeastern portion of Ringwood. As they trotted on their mares, they saw herds of bicorns and unicorns traveling close by.

A large unicorn stallion approached one cautious knight to greet his nightmare, both equines communicating with each other. The men were wary of the nearby herds, staring at the unicorns' horns and the male bicorns.

"'Tis amazing how near they will come to us," Galzar's squire, Mivros, whispered to him, tensing slightly when a few unicorns nickered, one stallion pawing at the ground.

"These creatures have been secluded from contact with people. They don't realize how dangerous we can be," Galzar responded as a unicorn foal cantered to them to take in their scent as they passed through.

As the men continued through the forest, a large flock of startled birds flew from a nearby tree, squawking. Galzar turned his head toward the fleeing rocs and raked his gaze over their surroundings, curious as to what had disrupted the great raptors. Near the trunk of the tree the rocs had recently vacated, two large glowing red eyes stared down the warriors.

The large, serpentine body—roughly fifteen strides in length—hovered above the ground, using its long-feathered wings. Its quilled body ranged in colors from blues and greens to reds and yellows. The coatl screeched at the knights as it harnessed flames in its mouth. But the flames and shriek dissipated as it turned away and weaved around the trees, going farther into the woods.

As the coatl's tail vanished, a loud clash echoed through the region. The sound was deafening as a jolt of lightning darted along the ground behind the trees. Soon after the first thunderous sound, another booming noise came from the same area. Just as the first, another bolt of lightning danced across the grass. The second bolt, however, stopped in-between two trees.

Galzar and his men stared at the lightning as it stopped, and a long, thin wolf appeared where the streak of light had ended. The gray and white raiju glanced at the group of soldiers for a brief moment, then darted away in another flash of electricity.

Galzar turned and glanced at his men. "There are many strange things in these woods that we know nothin' about, so stay alert and keep movin'."

†

After another two weeks of journeying through Ringwood, the Senturian army arrived at the capital. The large wooden fence surrounding the city was vacant and bare, absent of any sign of life. The knights slowly approached the wall, expecting an ambush from the Woodites but were only met by a chilling breeze. The men cautiously entered through the city's gate. They wandered through the deserted streets, only to see a few of the townsfolk hiding in their homes, peeking through the windows in fear.

"Where is e'ryone?" Mivros asked.

"I don't know. It appears they abandoned the city," Galzar responded as he glanced at the imp.

"They could hath set toward another kingdom in search of a fight," Caski responded.

"You would think they would hath left some behind for defense," Galzar stated, feeling unease with the situation.

The knights and squires unmounted their steeds, leading them by the reins. The group of ninety thousand continued to slowly progress deeper into the city. No Woodite forces were anywhere to be seen, only the shooken residents who dwelled within the city walls.

As they traversed the city's dirt roads, the knights heard the whispered murmurings of the frightened citizens. The knights would pass each dwelling, and the whispers would silence, only to return after the Senturians had passed. Galzar looked around and noticed pale and ashen faces peeking through the windows and around door frames.

The Senturians continued their march until they heard faint sounds of voices coming from a few blocks away. The squires stopped and stayed with the nightmares, while the knights drew their swords and axes.

Galzar led his men around an undetermined shop. As they approached the edge of the building, Galzar motioned for the knights to halt. He crept closer toward the side of the wooden complex and peeked around to find the source of the voices. Standing down the street were twenty Learish warriors. Galzar leaned back behind cover, glanced at his men, and pointed to the bow held in his hand.

A group of Senturian archers crept to where Galzar stood, each grabbing an arrow from their quivers, then readied their bow. Galzar glanced back at the Learish. He motioned for his archers to pie-slice the corner of the building.

The archers prowled around the large shop. With their hands shaking in anticipation, they spotted the Learish down the street with their backs turned. Galzar peered at the archers and gave them the go-ahead signal to fire. Each archer pulled their bow taught, then released the arrows soaring through the brisk air and into the skulls of the Learish.

The twenty bodies plummeted forward as their weapons and shields fell from their grasps.

Galzar turned to his men. "It appears that the Learish hath came and conquered this city." His gleaming stare scanned the Senturians standing in the deserted street. "So, it appears that we need to take it away from them."

Galzar divided his warriors into four groups, each designated to a different direction. "Once you hath searched your portion of the city, we will rendezvous at Galach's manor. Any questions?"

The knights and their respective squires shouted in agreeance, then turned and marched in different directions.

Galzar led a group down the many dirt roads toward the western edge of the city. As the group approached the city's wooden wall, they spotted a garrison of Learish soldiers posted on the battlement.

"Up there," Galzar shouted as he grabbed his bow.

His men charged the wall with their weapons drawn. Arrows rained upon them as they raised their shields and lowered their heads. More Learish warriors came through the large gate opening in the wall. In total, just under two hundred Learish were pitted against Galzar and his portion of the Senturians.

Some Senturians climbed the ladders to the

battlement. A few arrows pierced the small opening between some of the knights' helmets and their back plates, impaling the lower portion of their neck, causing their dead bodies to fall helplessly to the hard ground.

The two armies engaged in close combat, both on the ground and upon the battlement. Metal and wood clashed, ricocheting off another. The many round and oblong shields absorbed the majority of the blows. The cries from the armies filled the air with hostile and terrifying sounds.

The battle carried outside the city wall and into the treeline. A group of warriors from both regions fought, studying and predicting the other's moves. They were so caught up in the moment, the sounds coming from within the forest seemed to be unheard. They maintained dodging and parrying incoming attacks.

The noise grew louder. Hooves stampeding through the winter forest, the crunching leaves, the scraping of antlers against bark all seemed to be dismissed by the warriors, not wanting to take their eyes off their opponent.

The moment came, but it was too late for the two groups of soldiers. A large herd of cervuses charged from the trees, trampling many warriors to their death. The large stag-like creatures easily knocked the men off their feet. The raging beasts' antlers impaled some Learish warriors, having just thick leather of protection.

Inside the city walls, the Senturians finished dispatching the few remaining Learish. Their swords and flails ripped the skin and scales from their enemies.

Their clubs and warhammers pulverized and shattered the Learish's fragile bones.

Galzar surveyed the dead carcasses and his remaining men, noticing fifty deaths amongst his knights. "We hath cleared them out. Time to head back to the manor."

The knights and their squires ventured into the city's center, where they discovered a wooden mansion built from large round logs.

Before entering the building, Galzar turned to his knights. "I want you all to split up and search the manor's many floors. Me and Ser Caski will lead a group to the dungeons."

†

The group of men stormed the hall of Galach's manor, each group headed down a different corridor. One of the groups navigated upstairs and found themselves heading toward Galach's old cabinet. They crept closer to the room as voices echoed out. As the door drew near, the sound of a sharp object impacting wood startled the group. The men shook off the sudden adrenaline rush, then burst into the room, swinging open the door so hard, part of it chipped as it collided into the bookshelf resting behind it.

Inside the cabinet stood three Learish commanding officers—a djinn and two cryters. On the desk sat a map of Metagore with a knife stabbed into the center of

Sentries. On the ground behind the desk rested a few small wood chips and shavings, along with a large stain.

As the Senturians incautiously bombarded the room, the Learish were caught off guard. The knights' swiftness proved too much for the unexpecting Learish commanders. Before the three warriors could turn around and draw their weapons, the Senturians knocked them down with swords stuck into their torsos.

Duchess Celsa sat in a corner of a cell. For the past two days, she had stowed herself away, trying to devise an escape plan without the Learish soldiers noticing her. She knew if she reached one of her trees, she could maneuver the forests and hide safely; but how could she exit her prison unseen?

At least two soldiers were always posted, standing guard outside her door. When they decided to share their scraps with her, the food was just thrown between the cracks of the door and walls. Her only hope of escaping was a rescue attempt. Unfortunately, she had overheard the Learish discuss Galach's death, and after two days, there had been no sign of any Woodites trying to free her. All Celsa could do was wait and die, then bear a new seed for a new beginning.

From down the stockade passageway came footsteps. The two guards didn't take notice, thinking it was just another Learish wandering around the grounds. They were too busy insulting Celsa and the other captives to notice the Senturian knights rushing up behind them.

Galzar wrapped his arm around one of the Learish's throat and stabbed him with a small dagger, Caski followed suit with the other.

Some of the inmates cheered, excited to watch the action. Others gasped and shrieked in fear of being next.

From hearing the commotion, two more Learish warriors rushed into the stockade from the stairs on the near end of the passage. As they entered Galzar's sight, he simultaneously released two arrows. Each arrow ignited in mid-flight and pierced both the Learish's skulls. Their large bodies fell to the dirt floor with a loud thud.

Caski turned and faced Celsa's cell. He opened the door and chuckled. "'Tis a shame that the Duchess of Ringwood is held captive in her own dungeon."

Celsa stared blankly at the Senturian knights and their squires approaching from where they had taken cover.

Caski's catlike eyes glowed a bright red. "Metagore will bow before Lord Darius."

"Lord Darius is a monster!" Celsa retorted in a loud, broken voice.

Caski released a purposeful laugh. "Ha! Don't ya know?" He paused as he stared into her eyes, as if he was trying to read her mind. "We're *all* monsters."

Celsa sat there, anger growing on her face.

"We are all monsters!" Caski shouted once more, this time standing with his arms spread out to his side.

"Leave her be," Galzar said as he patted Caski's shoulder. "We need to go meet up with the others."

Caski turned to follow Galzar, but before he took a step, he pointed a hand toward Celsa and released a large sphere of fire.

Celsa lifted her arms, trying to cover her face, but the fireball disintegrated her into ashes.

Caski scoffed at the sight of just small embers burning where Celsa once sat. "Pathetic."

THE BAIT

Kaprin and Alor sat in the hall of their manor, eating their dinner.

"Ya know, Alor, the last time I had seen the hydra, I sliced off three of its heads," Kaprin bragged, recalling one of his many accomplishments he tried to get people to believe.

"That's a mighty big feat," Alor replied, amusing Kaprin. "Did you have anyone with you, my Lord?"

"'Twas just me out there in the swamps of Vaseere. Just me and that hideous beast. Ya should have seen it. Its nasty lookin' face, covered in moss and weeds. It 'twas huntin' me down, and I knew it. But I had no weapon, so I just continued to wade through the water, prayin' it would leave me be."

"But it didn't. Did it, my Lord?"

"Of course not. It saw me as a trophy it could show off to all the other inferior wanderers who might be passin' by."

Alor, with a slightly indecisive look on her face—though she knew Kaprin was making the story up—asked, "If you didn't have any weapons, then what did you use to slice off its head?"

"*Three* heads," Kaprin corrected her. "And I 'twas gettin' to that. So, there I was, face to face with the beast. He tried to bite me with one of his heads, but I 'twas too fast for him. I dove under the water and swam away. I thought I had escaped, but when I surfaced, he was right there. I thought that I 'twas surely goin' to be a goner. But I grabbed hold of his neck and climbed my way up. After I had reached the head, I leaped onto a tree branch, and that's when I saw it." Kaprin paused as his mind drifted, as if he was actually looking at an object. "The gods had blessed me with a long sword. The blade was so sharp, ya could cut down a giant—no, a dragon—no, wait, a *mountain*."

"A mountain?" Alor asked as she gave a small chuckle.

"Aye, a mountain, I tell ya. I stood in that tree, and as I stood there, that beast tried to strike me, but I swung that sword, and just like that, his head fell right off. Then the bastard tried again, and yet again, he lost another head. And once more he tried to get me, and again he failed."

As Kaprin finished his story, Marquess Lucan

entered the hall.

"My Lord," the lich greeted as he approached the table. "We have not received word back from Ser Sillius or the others on the hydra situation. We should've heard something by now."

"Then goest and check on them yerself," Kaprin responded. "We cannot waste time. We need the hydra to be contained."

"Right away, my Lord."

†

Traversing the muddy swamps of Dravendale, Sillius and the thirty Learish warriors saw signs of the hydra's presence throughout the region; bones littered the ground, while the grungy waters were red from the blood. Dravendale was a large area and it boasted a vast population of wildlife, but now the whispers of trickling water were the only sound greeting the warriors. Any surviving animals fell silent, fearing the slightest sound could be its last.

The Learish spent much of the journey trying to avoid the chilling waters, occasionally wading across streams where the great beast had destroyed the bridges. The soldiers weren't only terrified of the hydra lurking around the region unseen but also the possibility of some bunyips swimming in the water; though the chances of some still being alive in the area was slim to none.

Sillius ordered the group to stop. They had arrived at a clearing in Dravendale, near the northern edge around the Bonefalls. The thirty men set down the barrels of oil, placing them in a large circle, three strides from the next. One lich walked around, igniting the barrels one by one.

Leaves and branches on nearby shrubs rustled in the still air. The thirty men watched as five large serpentine heads arose from underneath the water of a nearby pond. The beast terrified the group as they stood frozen for a brief moment, taken in awe. Water trickled down its muddy scales. One head still chewed on one of the few aquatic animals left in the region while another hovered just above the water, staring at the men with its scarred face and one lone bright-yellow eye.

The beauty of such a large, yet lethal creature mesmerized the men. Its five heads moved steadily—a few snapped at one another. The men couldn't move, couldn't think, couldn't breathe. All the while, the beast's nine golden eyes seemed to pierce their souls.

The silent stare down felt like an eternity, though it only took a moment before the thirty warriors jolted into action. Many of them drew their daggers, machetes, hatchets, and little pickaxes, while the rest were undoubtedly unprepared to come face to face with the massive beast.

The beast lunged forward, stepping onto a couple of the warriors. Its heads weaved around trees, spitting its toxic venom and snapping at nearby soldiers. One head snatched a lich by the legs, crushing his bones, while the lich pulsed flames into the hydra's mouth.

The beast released him as the flames seared its scaly face, but as the lich's helpless body fell toward the ground, his head ricocheted off a large branch so hard, it detached from his mangled body.

The warriors tried to unite against a single head, hoping that would increase their chances of taking down the beast. Two lamiae sought to constrict around one of the heads, gagging it as it flailed around. They kept their bodies locked tight as they attempted to hack it off with little hatchets.

The beast managed to slam its neck into a tree, smashing the lamiae's bodies.

The remaining liches used their powers to hurl the flaming barrels at the hydra. Most barrels shattered into its faces, imploding wooden stakes everywhere; some impaled nearby soldiers, while others lodged in-between the beast's scales. The burning oils seared parts of the hydra's hide and drenched some of the troops in an agonizing fiery liquid that dissolved their skin.

The beast, after getting hit by numerous barrels, slung its half-severed head at one of the liches, knocking him off his feet and into the freezing water. The lich bound to his feet, only to be eaten alive by another head.

The one-eyed head of the massive creature found Sillius stabbing at one of its hind legs. It roared and struck at him, but Sillius managed to scurry out of the way. The hydra—missing Sillius—bit into a tree, causing it to topple over, pinning a treefolk under the water and drowning him.

The head struck at Sillius once more; again, he escaped its deadly bite—then another—but Sillius jolted away from its massive jowls for a third time, then jumped onto the beast's neck and thrust his dagger into its lone eye. The head flung around as Sillius jumped off. He grabbed a sword resting on the ground, below the blood-stained waters. The head swung downward, spitting its venom in a blind rage, giving Sillius the perfect opportunity to slice it off.

The monstrous creature bellowed a cry of agony as the head splashed into the water. Blood squirted out, covering Sillius and some of his men—one paused to wipe the blood from his eyes, only to see a serpent tail flung at him, smashing his bones as they made contact.

By that point, Sillius was left with three other warriors. Two men had just finished decapitating the second head of the hydra, while the other attacked a leg. The beast toppled from having both of its legs on one side injured. As it fell, it caught two men and squashed them beneath its large body.

Sillius looked at his only remaining warrior with terror in his large black eyes, knowing they were not going to survive this situation.

Having taken his mind off the hydra for just a moment was all it took for one of the large scaly heads to snatch him by the waist. Sillius struggled to get free as he stabbed the beast in the eyes and nose. He felt the beast's teeth sinking deeper into his scaly skin.

Numbness flowed through his body as he became too weak to continue to stab.

As he took his last few struggling breaths, he watched his last soldier get thrown through the trees, his body splattering against a tree trunk.

THE LONELY TRAIL – WA'BÉ∂OSKI MOU

Spring had arrived, though not much had changed in the mountains aside from the top layer of snow and ice beginning to melt. It had been twelve days since the Alberians had slain the chimera. A few of the wounded had succumbed to infections from their injuries, while others had died from malnutrition. Ixin did what he could to keep the spirits of his warriors high, though their travels were long and accompanied by distant howls.

As the sun rose over the rough terrain of BrightHelm, the Alberians were already well on their way, nearing their destination.

"'Tis quiet this morning," Tera stated as they ventured over the slushed grounds.

"*Too quiet if ya ask me,*" Ixin responded. "*Keep yer eyes open. We do not know what could be lurkin' around.*"

"*I heard o' a dragon that slumbers in these mountains.*"

Ixin chuckled. "*Libras wakes in Mount Dumas of Sentries, not in these white mountains.*"

"*Nay, there is another,*" a different Alberian spoke up. "*But she sleeps in Mount Eryn, on the other side o' the city beyond the clouds.*"

The group jerked in startlement as the screeching of strixes and the loud cries of flying thunderbirds drew their attention skyward. They circled in the air five hundred strides in front of them, as if they spotted food or a dead carcass.

The hundred and sixty-eight thousand warriors from the many tribes of Alberon marched through the region of Nuwulf, curious and cautious as to what lay ahead of them. As they traversed the melting snow, paw prints accumulated in the slush. Scattered amongst the large wolf prints were tracks of hooves as large as those of the dire wolves, accented by sprinklings of blood.

"*I wish I could have seen whatever equestrian left these marks,*" Tera said, examining the large hoof markings as they passed by. "*It would have been nice to get some fresh meat for our travels. 'Tis been o'er six weeks since I have eaten a decent meal.*"

Above the warriors, the birds continued to circle the wooly sky as the splatters of blood grew and bones began to litter the ground. Most of the bones had been picked clean of any flesh, while others still held encircling strands of muscle. As the group continued onward, the bones turned to limbs, and limbs to bodies—a horrifying and disgusting mess of mangled animals soaked in their own blood with their entrails unraveling across the cold ground. The sight struck fear into the group as the stench of the rotting meat turned their stomachs.

"*What could have done this?*" Tera asked under her breath as she scanned the shredded carcasses.

Amongst the trail, dead boars and feline-like creatures were torn to shreds. Farther down, a mangled birdlike elk lay on the ground. The equine lifted its head and whimpered in pain, its numerous gashes and chewed flesh still trickling with blood.

Ixin pointed at the injured animal. "*There is a peryton up ahead,*" he informed his people as he quickened his stride through the graveyard of gore and bones.

"*'Tis there anything we can do to help it?*" Tera asked as she followed behind her chieftain.

Ixin knelt beside the pained creature, gently running his fingers across the top of its head. "*Nay, I am afraid not. His time is comin' to an end.*"

"*Should we go on and put it out o' its misery?*" another warrior questioned as he approached the two. "*We could always start a fire and eat from its meat aft'wards.*"

Ixin stood and stared into the peryton's large black eyes. "*It would be best. Its meat hast done spoiled. 'Tis be best if we leave it for the scavengers.*"

"*What about a sacrifice?*" Tera asked. "*'Tis the Day of Oblation.*"

"*Ahh, so ya northerners do know o' our customs,*" Ixin said as he glanced her way. He turned his gaze toward the strixes hovering above them, then back to the wounded creature. *"But a spoiled offerin' is not worthy for the gods. Perhaps the gods will understand and still bless us with plentiful crops for the year."*

Ixin knelt to the ground and retrieved a small hunting knife from his boot. *"'Tis will all be o'er soon,"* he whispered to the dying creature as he pushed the blade into the center of the peryton's neck, and it gave its final shuddering breath.

As he removed the blade, the sound of howling welcomed the group.

"Dire wolves," Tera shouted. *"They must be close!"*

"Watch yer back," Ixin commanded as he stood.

After giving the command, the lich stopped as he motioned for everyone else to do the same. A few strides in front of them, the leaves and branches of a shrub ruffled. Ixin retrieved one of his small hatchets and slowly approached the bush. He took a deep breath and slowly released it as he stepped forward. As he reached the snow-covered shrub; the leaves stood still. Ixin paused, trying to convince himself that it was just the chilling winds. He poked the blade of his ax into the bush. As he moved around a few branches, a small hare jumped out and ran between his legs, fleeing into the mountains.

"What the ..." Ixin exclaimed, his breathing increasing to a pant.

Tera laughed as she slapped Ixin on the shoulder. *"It 'twas just a jackal."*

"*Jackalope or not, those howls were o' dire wolves,*" Ixin responded.

Tera's gaze drifted to a small, reflective item laying in the snow a few strides away. She trod lightly to the item, bent over, and retrieved it, learning that it was a looking glass. She examined the object, then noticed a trail of fresh footprints leading from their current position. She peered through the scope, following the trail circumventing the slopes of the mountainside, leading straight toward the city beyond the clouds—BrightHelm.

"*What do ya see?*" Ixin asked as he stared into the distance.

Tera lowered the looking glass and kicked at the loose snow around one of the prints. "*BrightHelm. 'Tis a league or two away. These tracks lead back to the capital.*"

"*Let me take a gander,*" Ixin commanded as he retrieved the object from Tera. He looked through the scope just to witness the gate at the wall being closed. "*They were spyin' on us,*" he snarled as his brow furrowed. "*They will be prepared. We hast to hath the element o' surprise.*"

"*How do we do that?*"

"*We must await word of the Taleanic reinforcements,*" Ixin grunted as his gaze wandered over the mountains.

Limited Time

As morning broke, a knocking on Cornelius's chamber door startled him awake. He sat in his bed and scanned the room. Inside his bedroom stood four giant trolls suited in silver armor, with the insignia of BrightHelm stamped into the left breastplate. Relieved his guards were still in attendance, he motioned for one to open his window's curtains. The light of the new day shined through the blankets of gray skies.

More knocks demanded Cornelius's attention. "Will you please get that?" he asked one of the trolls as he rubbed his forehead, trying to sooth the oncoming migraine.

The door opened. Standing in the corridor, blocked by two more trolls, was a young cyclops.

"She may enter," Cornelius commanded his guards as he rose from bed.

"Gramercy, m'Lord," the cyclops responded as she entered. "I 'twas at the strix post checking the mail, and ya have received a scroll from Grand Duke Galach o' Ringwood."

She removed a small sheet of rolled parchment from her handbag and gave it to Cornelius.

Cornelius took the parchment and unrolled it as the cyclops left the room.

Lord Cornelius,

The Learish are invading Ringwood. Thou prays to Afria that they will respect thy surrender and leave thy homes in peace. But if thou dost not, thy's armies are prepared to do what they can to hold them off, but thou fears that thine own death is imminent. A hundred apologies, my Lord. Thou did what thou could. May the grace of the Gods of the Eight Divides be upon ya. And may ya be able to restore peace to this once beautiful land of ours.

Thy's final farewell, G.D. Galach

"My one ally in this wretched battle may already be lost," Cornelius mumbled as desolation and despair washed over him. He tossed the letter into the fresh flames of the small hearth in his chamber. He glanced at his guards and quietly commanded, "Would one of you summon Marquess Tylon to my cabinet after he has broken his fast? And have the serving maid bring mine up there as well?"

"Aye, m'Lord," a guard answered, stepping out to follow his new orders.

Cornelius, followed by his five remaining guards, headed for his cabinet. His thoughts weighed heavy over the loss of his only sure hope of reinforcements, should he be attacked. His morning meal and a fresh fire greeted him as he entered his cabinet, though his appetite had long left him. He knew anything he ate would not sit well in his stomach and likely cause him to become sick.

The weary lord reached for a piece of parchment to send correspondence to Galach, in the hopes his ally wasn't lost.

Grand Duke Galach,

It is my hope that this letter finds you and your forces in good health, though I fear for the worst. If my and your own fears are proven to be for naught, and the Learish respects your surrender, I grant you and your people permission to make way to my kingdom for sanctuary, in the likely event of a second invasion. I had hopes this war would not happen, but the word that your forces and lands were attacked dashed all hope. May the Gods of the Eight Divides watch over you and your people in the event that all was not lost, as you hopefully make your way to sanctuary soon. Please have someone bear a Woodite flag as you approach the walls of BrightHelm. Send correspondence back soon, as I will need to ready up room for your numbers immediately.

Lord Cornelius

Cornelius looked at his guards and requested one of them to send the scroll to Galach as he readied himself for his meeting with Tylon.

Moments later, a knock came upon the door, and one of the guards inside opened it.

"M'Lord, Marquess Tylon hath arrived."

"Send him in, Zulkas," Cornelius said as he looked up from his desk.

"You summoned me, my Lord?" Tylon questioned as he stood in front of Cornelius.

"Aye, I did. Go ahead and take a seat; we have much to discuss and a limited time to do so." Waiting for Tylon to sit, Cornelius shuffled some parchment around his desk and continued. "I fear we've lost Ringwood. I received word from Galach this morning, stating the Learish had invaded. He feared that his people would not be able to hold them off. I sent word back to him in hopes that his fears were all but accurate and granted him and the Woodites permission to make their way here for sanctuary."

Cornelius sat back in his chair and composed himself as a man of confidence. "I am putting the kingdom on lockdown. No one is to enter our walls unless they bear our or the Woodite's flag. I will need you to ready your men for the possible increase in forces and to ready them for an imminent attack. This war will not go away on its own, as I had naive hopes it would."

"My Lord, I know it is not my place to question your decisions, but where will you hold all the Woodites?

How will we be able to hold them all? Most dryads, and especially sirens and lamiae, can't survive the harsh colds for long. You will have many of them perish from the cold and the dryads waking back up by their trees before the week is out."

"I am aware of that, Tylon, but I cannot sit back and let what is likely our only ally in this war succumb to a death by sword without doing something. It will give them a small glimmer of hope knowing they will have some form of sanctuary should they survive the attack. I'm positive they will prepare themselves for surviving in the harsh climates, and I am not inviting them to stay here just to put them on the streets. I will do my best to give them as much comfort as my power will allow me to, and I will make sure their more delicate numbers are well taken care of."

"And feeding them all, my Lord? I mean, it is a charitable act on your behalf, but I fear their numbers will force many of our own people from their homes and leave them hungry. We are not receiving crops and quarters of meat like we were before the war; we've been cut off from all imports."

"It is not your job to worry about that, Tylon," Cornelius snapped, weary from the conversation, his nerves frayed from being on edge after receiving word from Galach. "I will handle any problems that may arise from their arrival. I would not be a good lord if I leave my people to die. I have to do something." He looked at his desk, trying to hide the despair on his face. His resolve crumbled under him, with the added worry of what he could do if Ringwood survived the attack and sought refuge in BrightHelm.

"My Lord, I do not mean to add even more stress to your already stressful duties," Tylon began, his eyes softening at the sight of his near broken leader. "But you have advisors and a council for a reason, and other people here in the castle who can help you with your duties." He leaned forward, trying to glance at Cornelius's hung head. "I am aware you don't want to leave the Woodites to their death, but we cannot possibly hold all of them—not reasonably nor safely for everyone involved."

"I will give up room in my castle if I must, but I will not leave them to die if I can help them."

Tylon sighed. "Aye, my Lord. I will go and ready our men in the event that the Woodites do survive, and I will prepare our armies for an incoming attack. Will that be all, my Lord?"

"You may leave now. Alert me when you have finished preparing everyone."

"I will, my Lord," Tylon responded as he stood.

Cornelius didn't raise his head as Tylon left. His mind, far away, as he wondered yet again what he would do and what would be sure to happen as time went on.

Walking across the stone battlement, Tylon informed the archers on the southern wall of the situation. "The

Kingdom of Ringwood has fallen under attack. Our lord is offering them sanctuary within our walls. It is our duty to provide them with whatever they need to feel comfortable." Tylon paused as he glanced down the line of archers. "But more importantly, this confirms the accusations of war amongst the regions. I urge all of you to hoard arrows. The kingdom is on lockdown; nobody is to leave. If you see anybody, and I mean anybody, beyond these walls and they're not carrying our banner or the insignia of Ringwood, shoot them down. Do I make myself clear?"

"Ser, yes ser," the archers shouted in unison.

Tylon walked west down the wall and made the same speech once more to a new crowd of archers. He continued to tour the kingdom until he reached the northeastern wall, looking over a small portion of Galdwulf and the Abyss Ocean.

As he informed the archers of their new orders, a loud screech interrupted him, echoing off the mountain ridges. A second cry followed, resounding through the kingdom; it seemed to shake the walls they stood upon. From above, a massive, opaline figure plummeted through the gray clouds. Its pale, aqua-tinted wings wrapped around the serpent-like body attached to them. The equally massive form of Libras dove after the beast. Libras shrieked a battle cry at the tumbling dragon—too gargantuan to be a wyvern but shaped just the same.

"Archers, to your posts!" Tylon shouted. "Ready yourselves! Those scales can't be penetrated by any arrow, so aim for their eyes or the membrane of their wings."

The archers around him shouted confirmations as they readied their bows. Some watched in horror, stricken by fear at the sight of the godly creatures rapidly falling toward the ground.

The white dragon, falling too fast to open its wings for flight, tried to turn its body to lessen the fall, all the while attempting to fight off Libras's attacks with its spiked tail and clawed feet. It gave off a loud snarl as it collided with one of the mountain ridges. The impact slowed its fall just enough for it to burst open its wings. The white dragon flew from its landing crevice as Libras continued his descent toward her. He shot a fiery blast at the back of the pale creature, but in retaliation, the other dragon's tail hit him, losing a couple scales as the spikes scraped across his hide.

The dragons fought, snapping and snarling at each other. They flew from one ridge to another, slowly getting closer to the wall around BrightHelm. Libras discharged bursts of fiery-red flames; the other bellowed out blue plumes of burning ice. It all seemed to happen in slow motion, though the attack only took a short amount of time. The white wyvern-like dragon darted backward, hovering above the kingdom's wall, shrieking in anger at Libras, who followed. Libras crashed into the pale beast and brought it down upon the wall.

Archers were thrown to their deaths as their footing was taken from underneath them. The clash caused the stones to crack and crumble, and the area of the wall collapsed under the many tons of weight on top of it. The impalement of the two beasts and the loud rumble of the wall's destruction drowned out the shrieks of any nearby townsfolk and the archers fleeing the area. Both dragons continued to shriek and roar as their battle continued.

As soon as they could stand on the ground, the slender, pale dragon snapped at Libras's head and swung its tail at him, causing Libras to lunge backward, giving it enough time to escape westward over the kingdom. Libras gave an enraged bellow at the fleeing figure and took off after it.

As they disappeared into the sky, many shocked archers and civilians and a destroyed wall remained.

†

Outside of the southern wall of the kingdom, around the border of Nuwulf, bodiless footprints appeared, as if by themselves, heading toward the city's wall. On occasion, flashes of leather and fur became visible, and through the thick snow, a hazy outline of a slender body ran through the region. When the slopes became a sudden drop or too steep for the running figure to conquer, grunts echoed across the landscape as large indentations of the body falling into the snow appeared.

As the footprints and skid marks approached the kingdom gates, the camouflaged illusion projected by the furred cloak fell away, revealing a hooded figure with leather boots, donning the insignia of BrightHelm upon his arm. Marquess Tylon had ordered all the scouts to wear them after the war had been announced following Cornelius's coronation, to better recognize them in the event of an attack.

"Open thy gate!" the scout shouted as he drew closer to the wall. He stumbled a few times, but never fell in his rush to the kingdom, trying to avoid roots and rocks hidden under the slushed snow. "Open thy gate!"

He flailed his arms in the air as he produced strobes of light from his palms, hoping to catch the attention of one of the archers upon the battlement.

Just as he had commanded, a knight posted at the wall opened the large metal doors separating the kingdom from the mountains that lay outside. The scout sprinted through the partially opened doors and continued toward Cornelius's castle, occasionally looking away from the street in front of him and up at the two massive beasts flying over the city.

Once the scout entered the castle, he ran up the stairs and down a corridor. As he raced through the dim passageways, he glanced quickly into the rooms as he passed by. He navigated to Cornelius's cabinet, where two guards kept watch at the door. The scout flashed his armband toward the guards, and they stepped aside as they opened the door. Inside the cabinet, he found his lord sitting at his desk with an opened book in front of him and large trolls standing in each of the room's four corners.

Cornelius glanced from his reading as the snow-covered figured rushed into the room. The scout lowered his hood, revealing his dark-purple hair and teal face.

"Anson," Cornelius greeted the djinn as he closed the large book. "What news do you bring?"

"Alberians—" Anson mumbled, pausing to catch his breath. "They are in Nuwulf, heading this way, my Lord."

Cornelius's heart grew still as he stared in disbelief. He leaned forward, propping himself up on his desk with his numb arms. He felt his stomach churn and a cold breeze caress his pale skin.

"My Lord?" Anson broke the silence, still panting from his run.

Cornelius looked at his scout, his face frozen with a grim and shuddering stare of horror. "You may go now," he stated in a broken voice.

"As you wish, my Lord," Anson nodded in agreeance and left the room.

Cornelius looked at the book's leather cover in front of him. He didn't care much to focus on the book itself, just in the general direction of it as his mind drifted away. He struggled to focus on one train of thought as his mind kept shifting from one subject to another.

Though he had received the letter from Galach of the attacks, the idea of war still hadn't fully settled in yet. Until now. With the news of Alberian forces just outside the city's wall, the idea sat heavily on Cornelius. It was actually happening. He saw no way out of the situation. The enemy was knocking on his gates, and all he could do was wait for the casualties to start accumulating.

As Cornelius sat, frozen in fear, Duchess Zorie entered his cabinet. "My Lord, we have a problem."

Cornelius raised his head, sweat beading on his forehead and nose. His eyes were glossed over from the tears. "I know," he managed to voice. "There's been a problem since I was crowned lord."

"You are not the problem, my Lord," Zorie responded with a furrowed brow. "Even if it was true, we have a much greater problem."

"I know. The Learish army has probably wiped out Ringwood, and the tribes from Alberon are charging toward us, looking for my head." Cornelius grew disgruntled with his words. "Dammit! This place is falling to ruins, and there's nothing I can do to stop it!"

"It is, in more ways than you know."

Cornelius's face grew weary. "What do I not know?"

"Part of the eastern wall has collapsed—"

"What?" he uttered in surprise. "How does a wall, a chain length in height, just collapse?"

"Libras and Tiamus, my Lord. They were fighting and crashed into the wall. A stretch of fifty strides crumbled from their attacks, and some shops and homes in close proximity to the wall were destroyed as well." Zorie paused to give Cornelius a chance to respond, but he remained frozen. "Surely, you had to have heard them. They flew right over the kingdom, screaming at each other."

Cornelius's eyes widened and his lips parted. "Are there any casualties?"

"Yes; but the numbers, I'm unsure of."

Cornelius leaned back in his chair, completely struck by the magnitude of all the news he had received within the day's time.

Bon Voyage

Deep in the heart of Medsa'lear, Alor stretched out in a large, wooden tub in her chamber. Dim candlelight shimmered off her cerulean and emerald scales and glistened across the steaming water. Her long brown hair radiated around her submerged head as it floated along the water's surface.

She lay there, enjoying the peace and serenity of the quiet manor while her lord was at the docks. Her flattened, gill-like nose allowed her to breathe underwater.

As she bathed in the tub, a powerful commotion from outside her chamber startled her. Alor emerged from the warm liquid and darted her gaze toward the door.

"My Lord, your appearance startled me," she said in quick, deep breaths as Kaprin entered.

He chuckled as he flashed her a giant smile. "Aye, I do have that effect on women, don't I?"

She smirked back. "Don't flatter yourself. I was in fear of my life." Alor chuckled. "And after seeing that it was you, I had every right to be."

Kaprin strutted past the tub and sat on a slender bed wrapped in a cherry-oak frame. "Enough with the flirtations. I will be roundin' up Lucan and 'bout forty thousand men later tonight. Aft'wards, we'll be settin' sail for Sentries."

"This late? Dusk has settled upon our land. Why not wait until dawn? It'd be much easier to sail if you could see where it is that you are sailing."

"Aye, maybe," Kaprin responded as a smirk crossed his face. "But the sooner we set sail, the sooner Lord Darius will meet his death."

"If you wish. But I would advise you to rethink your strategy."

"I've made up my mind, Alor. There's no changin' it now."

"There never is," she muttered as Kaprin stood from the bed and sauntered toward the door.

"Oh …" Kaprin paused as he reached the door and turned. "I almost forgot. While I'm gone, ya will be in charge of the kingdom."

"Of course, my Lord." Alor giggled as she lay across the edge of the tub. "I am your duchess, after all."

"Aye, and I do trust Medsa'lear will be in good hands

in my time of absence."

"Of course," she responded, tucking a loose curl behind her ear.

"Then it is, my Lady," the joyful cryter acknowledged with a grin as he curtsied and left his duchess's chamber.

Alor, still laughing from the amusement of her lord, motioned to a treefolk, who had been standing by the door, to come and let her out of the tub. Her guard did as commanded; he lifted her siren body from the water and placed her on the bed. Alor grabbed the towel draped across the edge and began to dry off. As she sat there, her fishlike tail separated into legs, and her scales smoothed out into skin.

After drying off, Alor wrapped her hair in the towel, stood from the bed, and sashayed to her boudoir to freshen up. She applied a few pastes and powders to her face to enhance her beauty. Only a few sirens used elven beauty makeup, since contact with water washed it off too quickly and tended to make it a waste of time. Alor, however, rather enjoyed the relaxing qualities it brought her as she applied them.

Once she finished applying her makeup, Alor unwrapped her lush, brown hair and proceeded to comb it with a carved piece of coral from a reef near Findail. She began putting her hair in a bun when Marquess Lucan entered after a few quick knocks on her chamber door.

Alor glanced over her shoulder at the lich, with her eyebrows raised and a grin on her face. "Well, at least you knocked this time."

Lucan's pale face turned to a faint red as his catlike eyes widened upon seeing her lack of dress. "I'm sorry, my Duchess." Lucan paused as he turned his head and blocked his eyes with one of his bony hands. "I was just comin' by to discuss what you wanted to be done with the remainin' warriors. I didn't realize you were indecent, as I had heard our lord was in here not too long ago."

"It's of no problem, Lucan. You know as well as I how Kaprin is. Now, you said you wanted to talk about the remaining warriors?"

"Aye, I know our lord wants to take forty thousand with us to Sentries, but that will still leave five thousand here at home. I was just wondering what commands I should give them before my departure. But I can tell this isn't the best of time to talk strategy. I will come back at a—"

"Lucan, it's okay. There is no need to hide your eyes or be embarrassed. After all, this is one's true body; the one the gods created. And the gods don't create things to be shunned, only things to be worshiped."

Lucan lowered his hand and glanced at Alor, who had stood from her chair and faced him. "I just thought you might find it inappropriate, my Duchess."

Alor chuckled. "Inappropriate? After being around Kaprin, everything is appropriate."

Lucan nodded slightly. "Anyways, may I ask you what command you would like for me to give our warriors?"

"For now, just tell them to hold our walls. If anything changes, I will give them their orders myself."

As Alor finished, Kaprin made his second unexpected entrance.

"Gentlemen!" he exclaimed with outstretched arms as he entered the chamber. Then, with a wide smirk, accompanied by a slight bow, he continued. "And my Lady! Fear not, for yer beloved lord has returned!" He stood and pranced toward Alor's boudoir.

"I thought you were leaving for the docks," she said as he stepped beside her.

"I will be shortly, but I had somethin' to take care of first," Kaprin responded.

Alor's brow furrowed. "Like what?"

Kaprin squinted his black eyes and tilted his head from side to side. "Oh, ya know, just somethin' that involved me doin' thin's— I, uh— I went and diddled the backstress. I mean, my death worm needed to go huntin' for some cherries before I left, and her garden is well taken care of. But anyways—" Kaprin paused as his gaze found its way toward Alor's bare chest. He quickly acquainted his right hand to the bottom of one of her breasts with a smack.

"My Lord!" Alor exclaimed as she covered her bosoms with her arms.

Kaprin grinned at his duchess. "I like the way they jiggle."

Lucan stood there stunned at his lord's action. "One of these days, my Lord, a lady may take a swing at you."

Kaprin glanced at his marquess. "Good. I like 'em

feisty." He glanced to Alor and raised his brow as he grinned, then turned back toward Lucan. "Anyways, we must go now. We can't leave Persea waiting."

The two men began to exit the room, but not before Alor reached forward and slapped one of Kaprin's butt cheeks. Kaprin stopped immediately and turned toward his duchess. He tilted his head back slightly and purred, then finished with biting playfully at the air toward Alor as she giggled.

Alor turned toward the guard as the two men exited her chamber—Kaprin marching with a high-step, always seeking attention no matter where he was at. "How that man ever became lord over anything, is beyond me."

The nude siren returned to her boudoir and opened up her wardrobe. She shifted through the many outfits, then grabbed one. She pulled the dress over her shoulders and looked at her reflection in the mirror. Alor admired the way her slender body looked in the skin-tight, brown-and-blue-laced dress, along with the way her eyeliner and bronze eyeshadow made her eyes pop.

While still admiring herself, she heard another knock on her chamber door. Alor turned to witness her guard opening the door to reveal a cryter standing on the other side. The cryter looked to have a squid-like face, with the tentacles flowing down his back like hair.

As he entered the room, he asked, "M'Lady, is Lord Kaprin 'round?"

"Our lord just left for the docks, but perhaps I could

be of some assistance."

"Aye, m'Lady. I'm Ser Sergius. I was deployed toward the Kingdom o' Ringwood. I hast came to bring news o' our victory. We hath taken the city. Now, what is the next action ya would like for us to take?"

"Did Lord Kaprin nor Marquess Lucan give you further assignment after taking Ringwood?" Alor asked as she gave him a perplexed look.

"No, m'Lady. Only to take the Woodites to the hydra, but they would not follow. So, we captured the city instead."

"What's the status of Duke Galach?"

"We slew him, m'Lady." The cryter paused, waiting for Alor to respond, but she stood motionless while analyzing the situation in her mind. "So, what do ya command us to do next?"

"Continue east toward Sentries, then north toward Talean, then back west toward BrightHelm. Once you have taken those regions, send word back. We will decide then if we wish to take Alberon or not."

"But m'Lady, I hath faith in our army, but I don't think we can breach the Brim of Sentries. Plus, even if we managed our way through, many o' our warriors won't be able to survive long in those extreme temperatures."

"I am aware of our soldiers' and of the Senturians' strength. But I believe most of the kingdoms are going straight for BrightHelm. So, their numbers at the Brim should be sparse. Our lord has also just taken forty thousand of our warriors to Sentries on ships. He will have already docked and taken the kingdom once you and your men arrive. Rest and refuel there, then make your way north."

"I understand, m'Lady."

Sergius turned and left Alor's chamber.

"Sergius!" Alor shouted before he had gone too far.

The cryter reentered her chamber. "Aye, m'Lady?"

"Have the warriors who can't survive the temperatures of Sentries and Talean stay in Ringwood, and hold it against any attackers."

"As ya bid, m'Lady."

Sergius once again left, this time not being stopped.

†

Kaprin and Lucan rode to the docks in Seaford, the same dryad from before met with them.

"Good evening, my Lord," she greeted them.

"Good evenin', Persea," Kaprin responded as he dismounted his kelpie. He scanned the dryad's figure. "Yer fern is lookin' a little dry. Maybe I could water it for ya sometime."

"My apologies, my Lord," Persea responded softly. "But your spigot could not get these swamps wet."

Lucan's eyes widened as he forced himself to contain his laughter.

"I have your ships ready, and your men are all boarded and ready to go." Persea pointed toward the docks, where twenty ships awaited their captains. "And my Lord," she continued with a smile, "I do hope you have a better score with the sea than you do with the women."

Kaprin glanced at the ships, then back at Persea. "Ha! Well, we both know this captain goes down, just like his ship." Kaprin winked at the dryad. "So, my offer still stands whenever I return."

"You are a sunken ship," Persea scoffed. "I must go turn in soon. I pray for the gods to watch over your men while you are out at sea."

"Thanks for all yer hard work." Kaprin hugged Persea and kissed her on the forehead, then began to walk down the docks.

"I thought you were going to ask the Valkards if they'd loan us some of their ships," Lucan mentioned as he followed his lord.

"Aye, I did, but they ne'r responded. But don't fret; yer amazin' lord has obtained us a hundred ships, " Kaprin stated as he pointed farther down the coast. "A hundred and seventy, to be exact."

Lucan's gaze shifted toward a fleet of gawlers—logs carved to a point at both ends, with a dug-out center and adorned with rows of seats and a mast in the center that held a square sail. Fifty warriors holding oars filled each of the vessels.

"You can't possibly expect them to sail all the way to Sentries in those. They will be so stiff and sore. Can they even stand to stretch their legs?"

"Perhaps not, and I wouldn't advise them to try. They may end up tippin' the boat if they did."

Lucan's brow furrowed. "You can't be serious."

"I said I would get us the ships," Kaprin began as he placed his hand on Lucan's shoulder, "but I ne'r promised they would be the best. Besides, what do you expect? We are in the midst of war; no one wants to help a warrin' nation."

Lucan scowled at his lord, knowing no one wanted to help him because of who he was, not because of the war.

Lucan's eyes shifted toward Kaprin. "Which ship will we be taking? Surely not one of the gawlers."

Kaprin laughed. "Nay, o' course not. I'll be takin' The Sunete. I want ya to bring up the rear in The Mibia."

Lucan turned toward a large ship and approached the plank to board it, while Kaprin strolled down the dock a bit farther before boarding another.

"Ser Tiberus, ready the ship and set sail toward Parele of Sentries," Kaprin commanded as he approached the ship's helm.

"Right away, m'Lord," a blue djinn responded, then barked orders to the deckhands.

The crew rushed around the ship, executing the orders. The boat rocked softly from the small waves, as a few of the warriors released the breast lines from the cleats. Once the crew had freed the ship from the dock, some of the other deckhands lowered the sails, allowing a small draft of wind to catch the fabric, and the ship departed. The other ships followed behind The Sunete as it left port and ventured into the Abyss.

Kaprin strutted across the deck and entered his cabin. Standing inside were two cryter warriors, who were admiring a falchion sword with an ebony hilt and two onyx stones embedded into it, resting in a glass display case.

"Is this yer sword, m'Lord?" one of the warriors asked as he glanced at Kaprin.

Kaprin approached the case. "O' course that's my sword."

"Where did ya get it?" the other cryter asked.

A slight chuckle escaped Kaprin's mouth. "Ya are not goin' to believe it, but I found it."

"Found it? Where?"

"Last spring, me and some o' my finest fishermen were out in this very boat. While we were fishin', somethin' hit our ship, almost tippin' it. Quickly aft' the impact, one o' my men ran up to the deck sayin' that we had sprung a leak in the hull. I decided to turn the ship 'round and tried to make it back to shore before any o' my men could get injured."

While Kaprin told his story, he also acted it out—moving around his hands, running in place, even jumping and staggering to emphasize the collisions to the ship.

"As I sailed toward Seaford, I saw some large megalodons in the water 'round the ship. They just circled 'round us for a period of time, but then they collided with the ship again. Each impact caused more destruction to the hull and keel. After a few hits, I realized there was no way we were goin' to make it back;

our ship was sinkin' too fast. So, we all abandoned ship; my men fled first, then I followed shortly behind 'em."

Kaprin paused to take notice of the look in the cryters' eyes, of them wanting to hear more.

"When I dove into the water, I saw five of the most terrifyin' sea creatures comin' aft' us. I started swimmin' as fast as I could, hopin' to be able to escape from those monsters. As I swam, the only thin' I heard was the screams o' my men bein' picked off by those beasts. I swam as fast as I could, but as I neared the shore, I felt the water's current fightin' against me. The waves in the water toppled over me, and I was pushed under. I glanced behind me as I was bein' spun 'round, and all I saw was a large open mouth with at least fifteen rows of the sharpest teeth I had ever seen. I was in deep fear and tried to escape from bein' mutilated by the megalodon's razor sharp teeth."

Kaprin grew still as he lowered his head.

"Before I knew it, I was bein' sucked into the megalodon's mouth and swallowed whole. Luckily, I managed to not come in contact with its teeth, but I was now trapped inside its body. I knew I wouldn't be able to survive too long inside its stomach once the acid started to pour in. As I floated 'round inside the beast, I noticed somethin' shiny layin' at the bottom of its stomach. I made my way toward the object and saw this sword. Now, I had heard stories o' this sword, 'bout how it could cut mountains with ease. So, I grasped its hilt and stabbed the side of the sea monster's gut. The creature flinched in pain as the tip of the blade pierced through its thick hide. I kept stabbin' and slicin' until I had made a big enough gap in its side for me to escape. As I pulled myself out o' its bowels, I saw the creature floatin' lifelessly in the water."

"Wait, I thought this used to be Grand Duke Kip's sword," one of the warriors interjected.

"It 'twas," Kaprin responded. "He had dropped it into the sea many years ago. Which is why I was so shocked in findin' it myself."

Writing in Blood

Following the siege of Ringwood, the Senturians spent the next nine days raiding the city, searching for any available supplies left behind from the fleeing civilians. Food was a top priority; however, some men searched for valuables to sell, books to keep for themselves, and trinkets to gift to loved ones.

As the sun rose on the forty-eighth day of the war, casting a rainbow of colors off the dew gathered upon the plants of the forest, a knight shook awake his young imp.

"Mivros, time to get up. We hath much to do and not enough time to do it," he heard his knight say through his drowsiness.

Mivros had been a squire to Ser Galzar for the past

five moons and hoped this excursion would see him becoming a true knight upon his return to Sentries.

Mivros stood from his cot—only reaching Galzar's chest. "What would ya want me to do, Ser?" he asked as his yellow eyes squinted to avoid the sunlight streaming through a nearby window.

"Patrol the courtyards. Survey for anythin' unusual that might be of some help or importance to us." Galzar paused, grinning down upon his squire. "Take somethin' for yerself, ya hath earned it."

Mivros snatched up a cloth sack, with false hopes of filling it with valuables. He tossed the bag's strap over his shoulder; it rested on top of what was once a shirt but was now a dirty, tattered mess of fibers and fabric, only barely able to hang onto his body. Holes and tears littered the garment, leaving much of him exposed to the elements. Over his shirt, he wore a grimy, old vest, flimsy and threadbare, but it helped him stay protected, even if only a little.

Mivros exited the manor. As he stepped outside, he glanced at one of the manor's seven tall wooden towers piercing through the treetops. His gaze followed along the small rope bridges that connected the tower to the manor's center building. Mivros circumnavigated the building's oddly shaped exterior, his eyes surveying the numerous small windows spread across the walls.

As he traversed the many courtyards—peaking around bushes and circling trees—he came upon the kingdom's strix post. All the carrying birds had abandoned their hut when the Learish invaded eleven days prior. As Mivros looked at the post, he noticed one lone strix perched in its nook, gripping tight a letter. Engraved below the hole where the strix sat was the word *Rigdale*. Mivros knew the letter came from Lord Cornelius and was probably of great importance to its recipient.

Mivros sprinted toward the structure, leaping into the air as he approached, hoping to grab hold of the letter, but his attempt failed. He tried jumping a few more times, hoping he would ascend higher than the last. After a few failed jumps, Mivros glanced around him, spotting a cargo wagon holding manure. He grabbed the arm of the cart and pulled it to the post, where the strix just gleamed upon him with curiosity. He placed the wagon directly underneath the red bird and climbed the mound of raw waste. The imp ascended just high enough to snatch the front legs of the owl-like creature.

He pulled the bird toward his body as he tried to free the letter from its grip. The strix's long beak hammered into Mivros's shoulder, pecking bits of skin as its hind legs scratched and clawed his arms. After a few moments of wrestling with the creature, Mivros retrieved the letter and shoved the bird into a small cage that sat at the base of the strix post. Carrying the torn letter in one hand and the birdcage in the other, Mivros returned to the manor and into the hall where everyone had gathered.

"Ser Galzar," the imp shouted as he weaved his small body through the crowd. "Ser Galzar! I have a letter from Lord Cornelius!"

Galzar's gaze found his squire heading toward him. "Why is Cornelius sendin' ya letters?"

"He-He's not, Ser. I found it at the strix post."

With a chuckle and a toast of his tea, Galzar responded, "I'm just pullin' yer horns, boy. Let me see that letter."

Galzar retrieved the scroll from his squire and read it, chuckling. Once he finished reading, he pulled the imp closer and rubbed the parchment over his fresh wounds, smearing blood over the dried ink. "Go and send it back to BrightHelm," he commanded as he handed the letter to his squire.

As the imp left with the scroll and the strix, Galzar stood and climbed onto the table where he had been sitting.

The room silenced as everyone turned to look at the elven knight.

"Raid the pantry and larder! For tonight, we ride toward BrightHelm! It will be a long, cold journey, so fatten up and clothe yeself with warmth!" Galzar climbed down from the table and turned to another knight. "Caski, go fetch me a quill and parchment."

"Right away."

A few moments later, Caski returned with the requested supplies and handed them to his commander.

Lord Darius,

We hath taken Ringwood from the Learish and Woodites, with only a few casualties suffered. We will start our advancement toward BrightHelm later in the day. I will send updated analysis once we hath taken BrightHelm.

Ser Galzar

Once he had finished writing the letter, he turned to Mivros, who had returned from outside. "Go fetch a roc, then send this to our lord."

He relinquished the letter to his squire and watched as the imp exited the hall.

†

Later that evening, Galzar gathered his men in the lobby of Galach's manor. "I hope ye ate yer fill," he addressed his knights. "It's going to be a long journey and an even colder ride. So, take advantage of yer mare's mane, and keep yer flames close. Be thy gods that guide us. Be thy gods that watch over us. Be no shame fall upon us."

The group of knights and squires all erupted into cheers and battle cries as they followed their leader outside and mounted their steeds.

Galzar led the group of eighty-seven thousand Senturians north out of the city and into Krywood. As the army navigated the woods, they saw a few unicorns in the distance just past vacant dens previously belonging to packs of wolves and dubas. A few jackalopes and boars scampered across the ground, weaving in and out of the mare's legs as they trotted by.

277

Rocs and strixes flew overhead, screeching with might.

†

A week after leaving Ringwood, the Senturians had found themselves riding through the chilled region of Frozen Star Keep, where snow still mostly covered the ground and patches of trees.

"No man alive should hath to live in these freezing temperatures," a trembling demon said as he held a torch against his breastplate, trying to stay warm—the embers disintegrating the fur pelt draped over his back and shoulders.

"It's only goin' to get—" The sound of hooves digging into the ground and charging at them silenced Galzar.

A small herd of four pegasi ran from behind the trees to their left and stampeded around the men and their horses. Galzar and his men turned their heads to watch the equines gallop away, disappearing into the white wilderness.

After a loud roar bellowed from just a few strides past their vision, the knights and squires jolted their gaze back in front of them. They sat still and silent, fearing what lurked ahead. After a few moments of nothingness, Galzar motioned for his men to resume their journey.

The flames of the torches raged wildly until they couldn't sustain any longer in the shifting winds and diminished, only leaving a short plume of steam to be carried away by the air. The mares' manes dwindled, leaving just a reddish line traveling down their neck and spine.

"Ser Caski!" Galzar yelled. "Relight their torches!"

The lich tried to obey the command, but only a quick spark of flame left his hands, just to disappear. "They won't relight, Ser! The wind is too strong!"

Galzar's face grew terrified as he turned and glanced at his men, seeing them shaking and quivering in the cold. "I hope ye bundled up tight," he shouted to be heard over the whistling air. He looked over the demons and imps, knowing they wouldn't survive the cold if they didn't get some heat soon. "I fear it's only goin' to get worse! But be perseverant; the warmth of victory is comin'! Be thy gods that guide us! Be thy gods that watch over us! Be no shame fall upon us!"

Decaying State

At the dawn of a new day, the morning sun gleaming through the window of Cornelius's chamber woke him. He rolled over, turning away from the light.

"Trolgar," Cornelius muttered as he pulled the sheets over his eyes. "I would like to break my fast, if you would please."

"As ya bid, m'Lord," one of his guards responded as he left the chamber.

Cornelius tossed the bed sheets to one side and sat up. Bracing himself with his arms on each side—and with his head hung low in front of him—he struggled to rotate his shoulders, feeling the stiffness in his neck and back. He sat quietly, dreading the start of the day. The worries of the impending attack from the Alberians and the frantic state of the townsfolk weighed heavily on his mind.

A few minutes passed, and Trolgar returned with his lord's morning meal on a silver tray. Cornelius took the plate and set it on his bed.

"Would ya like a table, m'Lord?" Trolgar asked as he pointed to a small bedside stand.

Cornelius, sitting in a trance, glanced at his guard. "Yes, please."

Trolgar grabbed the table and placed it in front of Cornelius, then secured the tray on it. Cornelius began to eat. Though his kingdom was falling to ruins and it seemed as if everyone wanted his head on a pike, Cornelius was relieved he could enjoy his delicious meals.

The taste of his creamy, scrambled eggs and lightly cooked bacon warmed his mouth. His biscuits heated to a golden-yellow, placed with peppered gravy in a side bowl.

As he finished his tray of food, a knock came upon the door. Cornelius turned his head toward the doorway. "Morning, Edorin," he greeted his viscount.

"Good morn, my Lord. I am sorry to say, but I bear bad news," the plump elf confessed.

"Of course you do," Cornelius responded, annoyed at the thought of more unsettling news. "Lay it on me."

Edorin surveyed the room, shifting from foot to foot and tugging on his sleeves, stalling for a few seconds as he tried to find the right words.

"What is it, Edorin?" Cornelius demanded.

"Daeavar …" Edorin began, then paused, trying to muster enough courage to finish. "Daeavar was innocent, my Lord."

Cornelius's vision narrowed, and the sound of Edorin's voice distorted. He scanned the room as everything seemed to move in slow motion, and his heart rate increased in his tightening chest. Nauseous, Cornelius grabbed his stomach. With one of his hands still grasping at his belly, Cornelius braced himself on the small table with the other. His breathing became heavy, and his skin turned paler than usual.

Cornelius, in complete fear the murderer still roamed his castle's corridors, spoke. "Are there any other leads?"

"No, my Lord. They examined Lord Brighton's body, and there was no trace of toxins."

Still in shock, Cornelius glanced up. "What are you saying?"

"Our late lord apparently passed from a natural born-illness. That and his age are the suggested cause of his death. He was nine hundred and forty-some-odd years old, after all. But we do still have a group of djinns and liches his body to determine for sure the exact cause."

Cornelius clenched his eyes as he rubbed his forehead. "So, we sentenced an innocent man to death?"

"We sentenced him to the Pit and left his fate to the gods."

"Which was death!" Cornelius snarled as he stood

and paced his chamber. "What will his family think once they find out he was innocent? The news will surely bring more turmoil to the streets outside these walls."

"He may have been innocent for the murder of our late lord, but he was apparently guilty of another crime, my Lord."

"*Guilty?*" Cornelius questioned loudly, growing uneasy with the situation. "All because the gods chose for him to die? The gods don't care if we are innocent or not. We're just puppets for them to toy with. There was no need for that kind of death of an innocent man. The gods even showed that he was innocent, by letting him survive the whole hour. Everyone saw that." Cornelius stopped by his window and glanced at the kingdom. "The gods are cruel. They are like immature children; better yet, they are like cats toying with their prey, causing it to suffer and die slow."

"Forgive me, my Lord, but you should not speak ill of the gods," Edorin said, growing uncomfortable, fearing the gods' retaliation. "We cannot fathom their reasonings for the actions they take."

"We are just pawns in their pathetic game. Look at what they have done to our lands; they've damned this place." Cornelius turned from the window and approached his chamber door. "Let them smite me if they wish. I'm sick of it all. They've punished this innocent man enough. Truthfully, they'd be doing me a favor."

"Maybe you should resign then, my Lord, if it's that

much of a burden on you."

Cornelius, broken and contrite, glanced at Edorin and opened his chamber door. "You may go now, Edorin."

"My Lord, have I—"

"You said what you came to say. Now, it is time for you to leave."

Edorin grew embarrassed and guilty as he nodded in agreement. "As you wish, my Lord."

Edorin exited his lord's chamber. As he left, he passed Duchess Zorie, who urgently needed to talk to their lord.

"Do you bring more bad news?" Cornelius asked annoyed.

Hearing the tone in her lord's voice, Zorie was hesitant to respond. "I do."

Cornelius raised both of his hands and ran his fingers through his golden hair. He rested his palms on his forehead, tense. "What is it this time?"

"Part of the western wall was destroyed overnight," Zorie quietly told him. "It looks as if it were the dragons again."

"Dammit!" Cornelius shouted in frustration. "We need a dome or something, to protect our kingdom."

Zorie's brow furrowed. "A *dome?*"

"Yes, a dome. Like what we have for the Pit," Cornelius clarified. "We need a large, metal cage over this kingdom."

"We don't have enough metal for that. Besides, even if we did, it would take too long to build such a dome.

The dragons could easily jeopardize the construction of it, way before it's complete."

"Well, we need to do something to help protect our kingdom."

"Why don't we get a group of djinns and liches to construct a magical barrier around the kingdom?" Zorie asked.

"We will need a large crew of skilled sorcerers to pull it off, but I suppose that is our only choice right now." Cornelius paused and glanced at his window. "Go gather as many djinns and liches that you can find. Bring them to the throne room this afternoon."

"As you wish." She nodded and exited the room.

Cornelius walked to his bed and sat. His head hung low with despair and depression. He grabbed his glass of juice and took a sip. He twirled the glass in a circular motion, watching the remainder of the liquid slosh. He placed the glass on the table, then glanced at one of his guards.

"Do ya need somethin', m'Lord?"

"Fetch me my daily clothes."

Snow Blows Cold

After waiting for his duchess to return to the castle, Cornelius and Zorie walked to the courtyards and embarked in their royal carriage. They traveled, escorted by another carriage holding four additional guards, through the kingdom streets where many townsfolk were angered and yelling at the carriage as it passed by.

Once the black and white carriage had arrived at the front gate of the barracks, two giant trolls, who drove the cart, opened Cornelius and his duchess's doors. Zorie accepted the assistance as she held the guard's hand and disembarked—unlike Cornelius, who refused any help.

As the eight of them approached the gate, Cornelius turned to his guards. "You all stay with the carriages.

We will be fine on our own."

"But, m'Lord," one of the guards said. "Ya need our protection."

"No. Those dralions need your protection," Cornelius retorted with an assertive tone. "We will be fine without it for now."

"M'Lord, yer people hath grown aggressive. Ya are not safe on yer own—"

"I have Tylon's army inside. If someone wishes to tempt us, we have plenty of protection." Cornelius's anger grew. He had no reason to be enraged, but the stress of being lord was weighing on his mind, causing him to look at every situation with annoyance and hate.

"I understand, m'Lord."

Cornelius and Zorie entered the barracks. Knights sparring with another, running laps around the yard, or doing some other form of workout surrounded them.

As they walked through the barracks' yard, Marquess Tylon greeted them. "Good morning, my Lord. Duchess."

"Morning, Tylon," Zorie replied as she extended her hand for him to kiss.

"What's the news on the Alberians?" Cornelius asked stoically, refusing to make eye contact with anyone, just gazing at the knights train.

"I had a scout go observe them this morning," Tylon said as Cornelius continued to glare at his army. "He affirmed that they haven't changed from their position out in Nuwulf."

Cornelius, with the same cold expression on his face,

turned his gaze toward Tylon. "Why haven't they attacked yet?"

"I don't know, my Lord."

"What could they possibly be waiting on?"

"Again, I don't know."

Cornelius glanced at the men training. "Keep sending scouts out, and inform me if they begin to advance any."

"Will do, my Lord," Tylon responded. "What are we going to do about the kingdom's walls? Another fell during the night."

Zorie cleared her throat, then responded to Tylon's question. "I talked to a group of djinns earlier this morning about conjuring a magical barrier around the kingdom."

"When are they going to have the barrier up?" Tylon asked.

"They, um," Zorie paused as her face grew saddened. "They all laughed. Said that there was no way that they could make one big enough to cover the city."

Tylon's face became tense for a brief moment. "What are we going to do then?"

"We're going to have to start fighting back," Cornelius replied in a flat tone.

"Fight the dragons?" Tylon questioned perplexed. "Are you crazy?"

"We have no other choice," Cornelius said as his cold stare returned to his marquess. "When the dragons approach our kingdom, have your archers let loose their arrows."

"The dragons' scales are too thick; they will just deflect the arrows. There has to be another way to protect ourselves."

"Well, Tylon, whenever you figure out a way, be sure to let me know," Cornelius said in a dry, stern voice. "Until then, you fight them off."

"As you wish, my Lord," Tylon responded as he hung his head, knowing his lord's plan would never work.

"I will check back in with you tomorrow, but I must return to my castle now." Cornelius grabbed Zorie by the wrist and slightly tugged for her to follow him to the carriage.

"You can't possibly believe that fighting the dragons is a good idea, my Lord," Zorie said condescendingly as they traversed the barracks' yard.

Cornelius glared at her with narrowed eyes while remaining silent.

Once they boarded their carriage, Zorie placed her hand on Cornelius's knee and caressed it with her thumb. "My Lord, I know that your role is a tough one—especially since you are so young and inexperienced—but things will get better, I promise."

Cornelius glanced at his duchess. "I don't see how it could ever get better, not for me anyways."

Zorie looked out the carriage window and saw the slushed snow on the ground. She turned toward the young elf. "Being lord is a lot like the snow."

"What do you mean?" Cornelius asked softly, his voice becoming broken as he continued to reflect upon the disastrous state of his land.

Zorie, still rubbing his knee, continued. "When the snow first falls, it's soft and easily molded and manipulated by its surroundings. But over time, it hardens to ice and becomes strong on its own, but it only stays strong for a while before the world around it turns it to slush." Zorie paused and looked at Cornelius's face, his lips slightly trembling.

His icy-blue eyes glazed with the buildup of tears.

"It's so pure and white. So soft and elegant, as if it's heavenly. But it can be easily changed, and its beauty can be quickly taken away."

"What does this have to do with being lord?" Cornelius questioned.

Zorie smiled. "Everyone wants to be lord, because it's so peaceful to look at—all the beauty and fame—but they don't want the responsibilities of being lord. Like the snow, if you are left in it for a period of time, you grow weak and cold, but you will soon become accustomed to the way that it feels. Remember, your mind will break before your body, but as the snow blows cold, it strengthens as it freezes. Thus, so will you as you carry on your reign as lord, but don't allow the world around you to tear you apart and trample over you."

Cornelius remained silent as they continued their travels through the kingdom.

Townsfolk began to crowd the streets, making it impossible for the dralions to walk. The commotion grew loud as they yelled insults at their lord as he passed by, cursing his name. The distempered crowd shoved the carriage, causing it to rock.

An old minotaur, disgruntled about the dragons destroying his business, grabbed the carriage door handle and jerked it open.

Cornelius's guards leaped from the carriages and scurried to protect their lord and duchess. By the time they reached Cornelius's door, the minotaur had drug the lord from the carriage and was commencing to brawl with him.

Cornelius lay on the cold ground—his arms in front of his face, trying to block the punches from the stout minotaur. Two guards grabbed the protester, pulling him off the young elf, while another shoved a blade through the minotaurs husky body.

Cornelius stood and swiped his fingers across his busted lip, looking at his guards and the dead shopkeeper. "What have you done?"

"The harming of the lord is punishable by death, m'Lord," one guard responded.

Cornelius clenched his eyelids shut as he turned from the sight. The violent mob surrounding them had dispersed and returned to their daily work. As the young lord opened his eyes and shambled to the carriage, he caught a glimpse of a cyclops standing in the street throw a large rock. Cornelius watched as the stone passed by his face and impaled Zorie's thigh. Zorie gasped in pain as she grabbed her leg. Cornelius turned toward the cyclops, who was being restrained and cuffed by one of the guards, and ran up to him, delivering a swift punch into his only eye.

The other guards huddled around their lord's body as they secured him into the carriage, then boarded their coaches. By that point, the streets were clear enough for the group to venture through.

†

Later that evening, Cornelius sat at a desk in his cabinet, reading a large leatherback book. As he read the handwritten pages, tears beaded down his pale face. The salty teardrops, one by one, splashed onto the parchment, distorting the ink on the old, yellowed pages.

As Cornelius continued to read, Zorie entered the room. He glanced at her and wiped the moisture from his face. He closed the old book and pushed it to the side of his desk.

"I know that you are under a lot of stress, but I would like to thank you for your actions earlier, though it didn't help with your favorability with the townsfolk."

"I just got caught up in the moment. I know I shouldn't have punched him, but I couldn't control myself. It was all just happening too fast. My guards killed a man for assaulting me but only restrained the one who harmed you. I just couldn't—"

"It's all right," Zorie interrupted as she grinned. "I am thankful that you stood up for me."

"You're welcome." Cornelius looked at the book,

then back at Zorie. "I don't think I can go on with this much longer."

Zorie's smile faded from her freckled face. "What are you saying? You must go on."

"I can't." Cornelius hung his head low and wept. "I can't do it any longer. I'm not cut out to be Lord."

Zorie walked around the desk and placed her hand on Cornelius's back. "It will get better."

"No, it won't." Cornelius glanced over his shoulder and looked into Zorie's dark, forest-green eyes. "The snow is breaking me; can you not see it?"

"My Lord—"

"I've made up my mind. I want to resign."

Zorie removed her hand from his back and walked back around the desk. "Are you sure?"

Cornelius sat there for a brief moment before responding. "Aye. I will meet with the council tomorrow and speak with them about my resignation."

Zorie looked at her distraught lord fleetingly; her eyes filled with sorrow. After watching him for a few moments, she exited the cabinet, sparing him some pride before he broke down in front of her once more.

THE BLACK SHEEP

Cornelius stood in his cabinet with his head pressed against the window that overlooked the kingdom. Tears streamed down his sobbing face as he watched through the foggy glass, his people flocking to the gates of the city, where the knights stopped them. The ever-growing anger led to an outbreak of violence as the townsfolk so strongly wanted to flee the city.

"Look at what I have done to this kingdom," Cornelius said as his duchess entered the room.

"You haven't done anything wrong, my Lord." She tried to comfort him as she approached and placed her hand on his hunched back.

"I've been a horrid lord."

"You have not been a bad ruler. This would've been

the outcome regardless of who was elected."

Cornelius raised his head from the window and turned to face his duchess. "But *I'm* the one they elected to be lord, so all the blame is placed upon me and no one else."

"My Lord—" Zorie began as she wrapped her arms around his thin body.

"They never should've crowned me as lord of this kingdom." He tried to speak through the tears. "I have no awareness of what's going on inside this city."

"You are young, just as I." She tried reasoning with her broken lord as she released his body. "You will learn and grow into a great leader someday, and I will be right beside you. These kinds of things don't just happen overnight."

"It did with Lord Brighton!" he snapped but then returned to his soft toned voice. "He was born ready to be lord, and I ... I can't even stay sane in these trying times."

"I cannot speak on behalf of Lord Brighton's early years, for I was not there, but no one is born to be lord. He had traveled the land and gained vast experience and training from doing so, which molded him to be suited for the throne. But it took time."

"Maybe so, but I am not ready to be lord." Cornelius glanced at his desk where the old leather book sat, then stared out the window. "Being lord isn't something that I can carry on with. Metagore needs a ruler that is able to stand and fight, not an unworthy and disheartened child."

"Nobody said that being lord would be easy."

Cornelius turned to his duchess. "Aye, the snow and ice, but nobody said that I would feel like an outcast in my own kingdom, either." He paused, waiting for a response, but none came. "I must go soon to meet with the viscounts."

"If you must, then go," Zorie responded, saddened by her lord's willingness to give up.

He wrapped his arms around Zorie, squeezing her tight. Then in a tearful voice, he continued. "Thank you for standing beside me these past couple of moons. You've been an incredible duchess. I hope the next lord enjoys your presence as much as I have, but I am not the lord this kingdom needs right now."

Cornelius released his grasp on his duchess. With his head hung low, staring at the floor, he sauntered from his cabinet and through the castle, dragging his feet behind him. Outside the entrance of his home was a carriage waiting to take him to meet with his council in the throne room.

†

In the center of the city, the ten viscounts sat around the throne room's large table, awaiting their lord's arrival.

"I knew we should've never elected a child to wear a man's robe," Barinthus grumbled as he took a sip of his tea.

"He's no child," Mela replied hastily.

"He is too young and inexperienced to be lord over this kingdom."

"Do you think you should have been elected as lord? You are not much older."

"Maybe not, but I've got a better head on top of my shoulders than that boy."

"If we art going to list the next lord whereupon his experience," Efar said, joining the conversation, "then it should be thee. Thou hath served thy time on this council, and now 'tis time for thee to undertake the responsibilities of lord."

"We shall hath a vote like 'tis hast always been done before," the elder lady beside Efar—Coi—proclaimed.

"But we are in a time of war," Kaafel added. "We need someone who has a military background and is experienced with a sword out on the battlefield leading our knights."

The ten viscounts continued to discuss amongst themselves who should be the next lord as the throne room door opened. The room grew silent of chatter as a bronze-skinned lady with fiery-red curls entered the room and approached the stone table.

"Can we be o' help to ya, my Lady?" Efar greeted her.

"What are you all discussing?" Kalama replied with curiosity plastered across her face.

"Lord Cornelius wishes to be renounced as Lord of BrightHelm," Efar informed her as smoke rose from her hair.

Edorin chuckled. "Aye. The poor kid couldn't handle the weight of being lord."

As Kalama's face grew red with anger—the tips of her hair burning with exasperation—Lord Cornelius entered the room, shocked to see the widow back in BrightHelm.

Cornelius managed to summon enough courage to speak. "Lady Kalama, what brings—"

"You wish to *quit*?" Kalama asked irritatingly.

"Aye, my Lady," he responded.

Kalama's ruby eyes grew wide as her hair combusted into a raging blaze. "You pathetic little bastard! You are a disgrace to your title. Lord? Lord of what? Hiding in the walls of your chamber, crying? You should be ashamed of yourself!"

"It's just been so overbearing," Cornelius muttered.

"Do you think my Brighton ever wanted to quit?" She waited a brief second for him to respond, but the moment he opened his mouth, she continued. "No! He led his army into five wars and sat through two rebellions of his own, but he never once uttered the repugnant words: *I quit.*"

The heat of Kalama's flames started to burn Cornelius's pale skin, causing him to take a few steps back. "Your husband was an honorable lord. I … I'll never be as great as he was."

"No, you never will be! You are a disgrace to the throne! Leading this kingdom into war, just to turn around and quit." Kalama paused, trying to control her anger so she wouldn't set the whole room in flames.

"You should be charged with treason and have your head severed off that worthless body of yours or dangled lifelessly for all of the kingdom to see the coward that you are."

"My Lady—"

"Hush! I have wasted enough of my breath speaking to your unworthiness." Kalama turned her stare toward the viscounts. "Now, the reason I have come is to find out when my beloved Brighton's burial will take place."

"Archbishop Bolkan is preparing the service as we speak," Efar told her. "Just a few more weeks, my Lady."

"When?" Kalama asked loudly as tears glazed her eyes. "I want to know the day! It has been over four and a half moons since his passing. A hundred and twenty-eight cold nights I have laid awake, longing for the warmth of my Brighton's touch." Tears poured from her eyes and steamed from her bronze cheeks. "I want you to tell me right now, when can I see my Brighton put to rest?"

Mela stood from her seat on the far side of the table and approached Kalama. "Two more weeks, my Lady."

"Thank you, Mela."

Mela grabbed Kalama's gloved hands and looked into her sorrowed eyes. "I know it must be hard on you. I can only fathom the brokenness that you must be feeling. I, myself, wept every night while our lord laid on his deathbed, just wishing there was something that I could do to make everything right. But our pain will subside, and it will get better, my Lady. That I promise you."

"Thank you, Mela. You have always been such a good friend of mine, and I thank you for that," Kalama responded, still in tears.

"As you have been one of mine," Mela said with a smile. "Now, let's go and discuss how you would like Lord Brighton presented at his burial," she said as she led Kalama from the room.

"Now, Cornelius," Efar began as he turned his attention to the young lord. "Lady Kalama makes a valid statement. Leading us into war then renouncing yerself could very well fall under treason."

"But the war hasn't even begun, nor might it ever will," Cornelius pleaded, trying to look composed in front of the viscounts.

"The hell it hasn't!" Kaafel shouted. "There is an Alberian army knocking at our kingdom's gate."

"No sword has been drawn, nor blood shed," Cornelius replied, trying to defend himself. "The war may be coming, but it has yet to start."

"The decree of war was declared when you, my Lord, declared it in front of the grand dukes and your council after your coronation."

"Words are words, Kaafel, but actions speak far greater than the sounds that come out of a man's mouth."

"Very well," Efar retorted. "As one o' yer councilmen, thou declares that yer action of renouncing is an attack upon this kingdom's well-being. Thus, ya will be held liable of treason and sentenced to the gallows."

Cornelius scanned the room at the other viscounts nodding in agreeance.

"If you all must, then I will stay true until this war passes or my heart ceases to beat. Just know that your hands will be stained with this kingdom's blood and of my own."

"So, ya will retain thy crown o' lordship?" Efar asked.

"For the time being—" Cornelius surveyed the room once more. "Aye, I will remain your lord."

Artus's Ocean

As the sun shimmered over the open waters of the Abyss, Kaprin awoke to the sounds of birds squawking and the waves crashing into the side of his ship. He stood from his hard, lumpy cot and maneuvered to the helm of the ship to meet with Captain Tiberus.

Kaprin approached the djinn and surveyed the vastness of the Abyss.

"How are we comin' along?" Kaprin asked as he glanced at the binnacle and carefully examined the compass.

"We are making good time, my Lord. By my calculations, we should port in Parele in four days."

"'Tis what I wanted to hear. Soon Lord Darius will fall, and may it be by my blade from which he dies."

"I am sure we will prevail, my Lord."

Kaprin patted his captain's back, then headed to the main hull and into the galley. Kaprin fixed himself a plate of food, then joined some of the crew for breakfast.

"Are ye excited? Just under a week 'til we make port," he asked them as he began to eat.

"Aye, m'Lord," one of the warriors responded. "There shall be Senturian blood poured all o'er their black lands."

"There will be blood, 'tis for sure," Kaprin responded as he continued to eat. "But I'm tellin' ya now, I want it to be me who kills Lord Darius. Ya can hurt him, but I want him to fall before me."

"Why dost ya want to be the one who slays him? If he's dead, he's dead. 'Tis that not what we really want?"

"No," Kaprin answered as he glared at the warrior, wondering why he would question his motives. "'Bout five years ago, before Darius became a grand duke, he served in the Taleanic army. At that point, I was already grand duke, with the most beautiful, breathtakin' woman who had ever walked through those swamps by my side—Ky."

"As in, Duchess Ky?" another warrior asked as he had overheard Kaprin's story.

"Aye, but she wasn't the duchess over anythin' at that time."

"Ya and Duchess Ky were a thang?" the warrior asked with a chuckle.

"Aye," Kaprin answered, growing annoyed by the

warrior's disbelief. "Anyhow, after he served as a knight and took the seat of grand duke over Sentries last year, Darius asked Ky to be his duchess. Ky, o' course, said aye. At first, she still came and visited me every few weeks. But 'tis year at the New Life Festival, I noticed some large bruises on her arms." Kaprin's expression slowly grew desolate and bitter. "I brought it to her attention, but she just denied it. Said she had bumped into somethin' that mornin'. But they were in the shape o' fingerprints—Darius's fingerprints. After that, I guess Darius found out, and they left the festival early. I hear that she's locked up in his dungeons now, and he only keeps her for a sex slave."

"I don't recall ever seenin' Ky 'round Medsa'lear b'fore," another warrior interjected.

"O' course ya hadn't," Kaprin responded. "Why would ye've? She was from the northern reaches of Dravendale, 'round the Bonefalls."

An elven warrior approached Kaprin. "M'Lord, the captain wishes to have a word with ya right away."

"O' course."

Kaprin wiped his mouth with a napkin, then returned to the helm.

As he approached Tiberus, Kaprin sarcastically greeted him. "My Captain, could ya not stand me bein' away from yer presence?"

Kaprin's goofy composer drew a slight chuckle from his captain.

"Nay," Tiberus responded as he removed a long, wooden spyglass. Still with a soft laughter in his voice, he continued. "Look out there, about thirty degrees on the port side."

Kaprin took the spyglass from the captain's blue hands. He extended it and placed it against one of his coal-black eyes. In the distance, he saw the silhouette of a landmass protruding from a thick fog.

"'Tis that Sentries?"

"The southernmost tip, my Lord; but aye, that is Sentries."

Kaprin, with a huge smirk on his face, lowered the spyglass. "Four more days, ya said?" He turned and looked at Tiberus. "Get us there in three. I can't wait to shed some Senturian blood."

"As you wish." Tiberus immediately barked commands to the deckhands as Kaprin returned to the hull.

"Three more days, men," Kaprin shouted as he walked past the cabins, banging his webbed hands on the walls and doors.

The warriors in the hull all chatted and shouted battle cries. While everyone was getting jubilant, a sudden crash jolted the ship and everyone staggered and lost their balance.

"What in Artus's ocean was that?" one of the warriors cried out.

Kaprin, who had braced himself in a doorway, stumbled toward the bridge. Once he reached the deck, he ran to the starboard handrail and leaned over. He glanced into the water, looking from the bow to the stern.

"What do you see, my Lord?" Tiberus asked with concern.

"I see nothin'," Kaprin responded as he continued to survey the water for any sign of the cause of the impact.

"A megalodon," one of the warriors shouted as a large group of men climbed to the deck.

"Nay, I don't see any," Kaprin responded.

"Nay. Look o'er there, 'tis a megalodon," the warrior replied with a trembling voice.

"There's another o'er here," a second warrior shouted as he leaned over the portside railing.

As Kaprin rushed to the other side, another crash rattled the ship, knocking everyone off their feet. Kaprin lifted himself and noticed Lucan and many of the warriors on The Mibia frantically panicking as large waves thrashed into the side of their ship.

Kaprin stood there, the deck beneath his webbed feet teetering from side to side as an elven warrior approached him with soaked breeches. "M'Lord, we hath sprung a leak."

Kaprin turned his head toward the elf then over the Abyss, noticing all the gawlers being thrashed by the creatures beneath the waves. His eyes drifted back toward the warrior. "Why are ya not pluggin' the hole?"

"'Tis too big, m'Lord."

"Go find yerself a bigger plug."

"O' course, m'Lord."

Kaprin rushed into the hull. As he passed the cabins, he banged on the walls and doors. "Alright, 'tis time to separate the men from the boys! Get yer weapons ready, and get yer arses suited up! Yer survival lays solely on yer own shoulders. If ya fall into the waters, ya might as well be dead, so watch yerselves!"

After his speech, Kaprin jogged his way to another staircase leading farther down into the ship. As he approached the set of stairs, he stopped and stood traumatized for a brief moment. His mind tried to rationalize their situation as he stared at the water in the keel reaching a fathom deep.

Kaprin turned from the sight and took a step, but another impact knocked him down. Kaprin fell backward and landed in the flooded room. As he stood, he noticed a new leak had sprung from the portside wall.

He quickly returned to the deck, where he noticed the other ships shooting large harpoons into the water in an attempt to kill the giant sea creatures.

Kaprin turned toward his men. "Ready yer cannons! Kill every last one o' them!"

As their lord had commanded, the crew loaded large, wooden bolts into the cannons and fired them into the ocean. Many of the harpoons missed their target, but a few impaled into the giant creatures and caused significant amounts of blood to spill out and mix with the water.

Kaprin quick-stepped to the helm and overlooked his ship. As he analyzed his men and his ship, he noticed something peculiar in his peripheral. He turned and glanced toward one of the other ships. He stood still in horror as he witnessed The Mibia capsizing. The ship's bow stood perpendicular to the water, slowly teetering backward as it fell into the waves.

Another blow caused Kaprin to be shaken from his terrified trance. He glanced at the ship's bow, which had been mostly destroyed.

"M'Lord, we are sinkin'," shouted a member of the crew.

"Keep shootin'! We have no other option," Kaprin responded as he ran into his cabin, his hidden skin completely ashen underneath his blue scales.

He approached the showcase where his sword was on display. He clenched his fist and thrust an elbow into the glass casing. After three blows from his elbow, the glass shattered. Kaprin stood for a brief moment, shaking his arm and rubbing his elbow, which had been cut by the broken glass. After trying to shake off the pain, Kaprin grabbed the sword and ran onto the deck.

"M'Lord, we ain't goin' to make it!" a warrior frantically informed his lord.

"Go! Flee back to Medsa'lear, and tell Alor of the matter. Let her know that none were able to make it to Sentries."

"Aye, as ya bid, m'Lord," the warrior responded as he leaped into the air and morphed into a large bird, beginning his flight to Medsa'lear.

Kaprin gazed at his fleet as his men's dying screams pierced the air as the underwater monsters pulled them under. Kaprin grew numb as sheer terror filled his body.

Kaprin fixed his stare on Lucan and The Mibia as large, scaly arms flung from the water and crashed into the ship's stern. Waves toppled over the ship's starboard side, washing away many of the warriors. Kaprin was heartbroken witnessing such a disaster. His heartbeat grew louder as another large fin raised from the water. Each one had to be at least fifteen strides in length.

"What is that thing?" one of the warriors exclaimed as Kaprin continued to watch in despair.

"A leviathan."

"A what?"

"One o' Artus's servants."

The ship took another hit, and more lumber drifted out to sea.

"M'Lord, we are sinkin' fast, and we are runnin' low on harpoons," another warrior shouted.

Kaprin glanced at his decimated ship. "All hope is lost! Abandon ship!"

"If we abandon ship, m'Lord, we will surely die in these infested waters."

"If we stay, we will die and go down with The Sunete!" Kaprin took one last look at the remainder of his fleet fighting the large monsters. "'Tis yer life and yer decision."

Kaprin turned and dove off the side of the ship, his sword still tight in his grasp. As he plummeted into the water, he began to swim as fast as he could. Every few seconds, he glanced over his shoulder to witness a megalodon swimming after him. He knew looking back would slow him down, but fear and terror took hold of his mind and forced him to check behind him as he dove farther under the waves, hoping to catch a current to propel him from the beast.

At roughly six strides long, Kaprin knew the beast was young, but the megalodon had the advantage as it gained on him. He dove lower into the water and managed to catch a current; elation coursed through his body. As a huge grin blossomed upon his face, the young megalodon caught up to him and grabbed onto his left leg with its great maw. The smile on Kaprin's face turned to pain as he gasped from the agony of the razor-sharp teeth tearing through his lower leg.

Fighting the force of both the current and the beast, Kaprin did the only thing he could think of—stab his sword into one of the megalodon's eye. He pulled the sword from the great shark and prepared to joust it once more when he saw nothing but teeth consuming him and the megalodon.

Sword Play

Darius and Ky stood in a confined, windowless room, barely lit by a few candles. The massive demon examined his many blades resting upon two different wooden sword racks and surveyed his bows set upon another.

"How did the new recruits look this morning?" Ky asked as she moved her fingertips across a steel blade on display.

Darius's eyes sparkled as his gaze followed along the claymore in his right hand and returned the sword to its scabbard. "They looked like children, like scared children wrapped in iron and steel." He fastened the sheath around his waist.

"When do you think they'll be prepared enough to

send into battle?"

Darius grabbed a bow from its rack. "They will never be prepared, not until they go out and experience battle firsthand." He grabbed a quiver full of arrows and draped it and the bow over his shoulder.

He turned to his concerned duchess and placed his hand against her dark cheek as he gazed into her worried, green eyes. "They are grown men, and they will be fighting beside the best knights in the six kingdoms. They will be fine. Okay?"

"Yes, my Lord." Ky nodded as the large hand left her face.

"What's with you always calling me *my Lord?*"

Ky's brow furrowed. "You are the Lord of Sentries."

"Aye, I know this, Ky," Darius grumbled. "But you're not a commoner."

"No, but I do respect your position as lord."

"There is no need for formalities between us," the bulky demon responded as they left his armory. "We are more than just lord and duchess. And if someday you bear my seed, I would rather you not refer to me as Lord. Darius will suffice just fine."

"I understand," Ky said as she placed her hand over her stomach and softly rubbed it, imagining the feeling of carrying a baby in her womb. Ky smiled in the warmth of her imagination. "Oh, speaking of family, your brother has sent another letter."

Darius's eyes grew narrow in anger. "Burn it like the others."

"Do you not wish to see what he has to say?"

"No! He's as good as dead to me."

"But he's your brother," Ky reminded him, though the demon needed no reminders of the past he had shared with his sibling.

"We may have come from the same loins, but that doesn't make us brothers."

"It's been a long time," Ky continued. "It would do you some good to at least see what he has to say."

Darius's fierce face turned toward his duchess. "No, Ky! If you wish to read his dishonorable letters then go right ahead. But by the gods' mercy, you best burn them afterward."

"I have been reading them, my Lord," Ky replied.

"*Darius*," he corrected her as they exited the corridor and entered a courtyard housing a combat practice area with armored-wooden mannequins and archery targets on opposite sides from the other.

"*Whatever*," Ky sassed. "He writes his apologies and wishes to speak with you. I write him back, stating that you do not wish to speak with him, but he keeps pleading that one day you will."

Darius unsheathed his sword and glanced at Ky. "The next time you write to him, tell him to fuck off, or better yet, for him to go get eaten by a death worm or something."

He walked away from her toward one of the mannequins and positioned himself in front of it, spreading his feet apart to keep a better balance with his weapon. He took a step forward with his right foot, bringing his claymore over his head and down against the collar of the dummy, embedding the blade between its pieces of armor. Darius had a look of concentration on his face, blocking all the sounds of the courtyard while he focused on an imaginary battle.

The demon took a breath as he stepped back—his hands on the hilt of his blade, pulling it up and away as he braced his feet again to keep from falling with the weight of his weapon. Though the claymore generally took two hands to fight with, Darius preferred to practice using only one hand as well, in case he became injured in battle. At times he would also practice with a blindfold to learn how to fight with only sound and feel, as war could lead to bouts at any time of the day or night.

Darius held the claymore in his left hand, putting more pressure on his right foot, and swung it in an upward arch from the right, impaling the side of the dummy's head, knocking off its helmet. In one motion, he tossed the blade to his right hand, balancing on his left foot, and swiped the sword down to impale its shoulder. He continued his dance, circling the practice mannequin, switching his weapon from one hand to the other, even using both at times.

Darius spun to the left and flicked out the blade, knocking off the mannequin's breastplate and watching it fly toward a servant walking around the practice yard. Darius chuckled as the young servant yelped in fear when the armor piece nearly collided with him.

"You! Huma! If you're going to come through here while I practice, you might as well make yourself useful.

Put on that breastplate, and pick up a sword. I could use a new opponent, seeing as my mannequin can only do so much."

"Aye, o' course, m'Lord," the boy replied, clumsily putting on the armor before running to the weapons rack. After grabbing an armament, the elf nervously approached his lord, carrying a lightweight metal rod used as a practice sword.

Darius casually circled his servant, raking his blade across the side of the elf's rounded sword, occasionally swinging his sword half speed at his opponent, allowing it to be easily deflected. The two swordsmen continued their movements around the courtyard. With soft clings coming from their weapons, their feet prowled across the ashy ground.

Feeling unthreatened by the elf, Darius quickly glanced at Ky before returning his gaze onto the small figure in front of him. "When I become lord over the six kingdoms, I want all the viscounts removed and killed."

"But you need a council," Ky assured her lord as he swung his blade with more force. "The tasks of upholding the laws would be too much for just you and I."

Darius, holding his sword in his left hand, swung it at the elf's legs. The servant staggered backward as he deflected the mighty swing of Darius's blade. Darius seized the opportunity and stepped forward, ramming his opponent with his shoulder, causing the elf to fall backward from the substantial impact.

Darius stepped over the elf as he walked toward his duchess. "I'll replace them then. I'll replace them with *non*-humas."

"Is it really fair to kill the old viscounts and replace them, just because they are elves?"

Darius glanced at his downed opponent, who had slipped his right arm under the loose breastplate to rub his abdomen as he tried to catch his breath. The demon returned his gaze to the beautiful succubus as he walked backward toward his elven servant.

"It is unfair for them to think they are better than everyone else just because they can live a thousand years—the old selecting the new. Serving their lives to the same shitty order. Growing corrupt in their minds. There has to be a stop to it."

Darius turned after hearing the sound of cloth sliding upon dirt, to see the young elf standing to his feet. He sheathed his claymore and reached behind his back to slip his bow from his black, ashy shoulder. With the silver bow in hand and an arrow in the other, he readied the bolt. The demon concentrated on his target, while his opponent stood stunned and in fear of his life. Within seconds, he released the taut string, and the arrow soared past the pale servant's head, impaling the center of a target at the edge of the courtyard.

The demon's eyes shifted to the elf's wide stare. "Fetch me a glass of mead."

"O' course, m'Lord," the servant hastily replied as he removed his armor.

Darius readied another arrow, then released it at the

target. Slivers of wood separated from the first as it split in two with the arrival of the second bolt.

"That was an excellent shot," Ky congratulated him in a soft voice, still unease with his decision of killing the viscounts.

Darius gave her an uninterested look in response to her comment as he readied a third arrow. Still glaring at his duchess, he raised his bow and released another shot at the target. It took just a split second for the arrow to meet its mark, and a few more for Ky to see the outcome and register the sight of the feathered end of the arrow being the only visible part extruding from the target. The third and final arrow had split the second down the middle, as with the first. It had been released with such high velocity that the bolt impaled the plaque of the wooden target, almost entirely exiting it on the other side.

The demon glanced at the target as his servant returned with his drink. He took the glass and chugged the smooth, dry nectar. After he had swallowed the last drop, he handed the glass to the elf and waved him away.

Darius turned toward his duchess as he wiped his arm across his mouth. "If the viscounts can do that, then they can live."

"My Lord. Duchess," Lucius greeted them as he entered the courtyard. "I have received word that the war may be ending sooner than what some had hoped."

"What do you mean *ending sooner*?"

"I have received word this morning that a small fleet

Learish caravels and gawlers were spotted out in the Abyss, just south of Farshadow—one of the ships being Kaprin's." Lucius removed a scroll and handed it to Darius. "It states that they were seen shooting at the water, but it doesn't say at what exactly. But it does continue on and say that the ships were destroyed at sea."

"They all got destroyed?" Darius asked.

"Aye, my Lord."

Darius smiled. "Artus and the other gods are watching over us, I see."

"It appears that way, my Lord."

✝

The next day, Darius walked to the barracks to meet with his marquess. As he entered the training yard, he saw ten thousand new knights sparring with each other.

Marquess Lucius walked between the sections of recruits, barking commands and trying to prepare the men for war.

"How are the recruits coming along?" Darius asked as he approached the dark demon.

"Their archery skills are insufficient, my Lord, but their physical attributes are compelling."

"Good. We need the strength."

"But I'm not sure if they will hold up in the field."

"Either way, have them suited and ready for departure at the break of dawn."

"They still need a great deal of training before they are battle ready."

Darius scowled. "There is no way to completely get them prepared for battle. I want them sent out tomorrow morning. Do I make myself clear?"

"Aye, my Lord. But what about attire? We don't have near enough chips and pennies to suit them all with armor and weapons."

"Are you saying that Sentries is broke?"

"Aye. Our former treasurer spent all of our purse on whores and expensive wine," Lucius responded as he turned and pointed to a recruit on the far side of the yard, sparring with a mannequin.

"Fucking *huma*," Darius snarled as his nasal cavity flared. "Leave them in their practice attire, and equip them with what we have on hand. If we are short on equipment, send him out bare with a horn of wine."

Off to Valkeri

Alor and Persea sat in the hall of the Learish manor, enjoying each other's company while sipping white wine.

"He said that he could water my fern for me sometime," Persea gossiped about a conversation she had with their lord two weeks prior.

Alor laughed. "Really?"

"Yes. After all of this time, he still surprises me with how blatantly disrespectful and perverted he is toward us women."

"He truly is something. Just too out there, if you know what I mean."

"Trust me. I know *exactly* what you mean."

Alor giggled as she took a sip from her glass. "A few

days before his departure, I was just relaxing and bathing in my tub. The next thing that I knew, he jumped right in with me and wanted me to wash his 'tadpole.'"

The dryad's eyes widened in shock. "So?"

"So, I washed it for him." Alor smirked then paused as Persea spat her drink from the laughter. "And with how big his ego is, I was quite disappointed with how his tadpole was a *tad* pole. Definitely not the Learish death worm that he proclaims to have."

As the two of them continued to talk about their lord they heard a loud screech from outside the manor. Startled by the noise, they turned toward someone opening the hall door. A thin morling entered the room, his feathered face still changing back to its smooth form.

Alor studied the lightly armored morling as he approached them. "Can I assist you with something?"

"Duchess," he greeted her in a pant. "I am Ser Garras. I 'twas with our lord out at sea." He paused for a moment as Alor realized the fear in his eyes and the slight tremble in his stance. "But now ... Now our lord and our armies are dead." The last of his words grew faint as his face tingled with numbness.

Alor's eyes widened as her pulse raced. "Dead?"

"Aye. We were attacked by megalodons, and our ships were destroyed. Lord Kaprin ... Marquess Lucan ... E'erone ... They're all dead," he finished, staring at the floor and shaking his head in disbelief.

Persea turned to her duchess. "This means you are in

charge now."

"Me?" Alor asked as her mind drifted from reality, glancing around the room at the servants passing through. "I don't even know where to begin."

"I know of someone who may be willing to advise you," Persea responded. "She did not favor Lord Kaprin because of how he is—was—but she may be interested in helping you."

Alor perked up as her attention narrowed onto her friend. "Does she know anything about running a kingdom?"

Persea's face drooped. "No."

As disappointment settled onto Alor, she glanced at the warrior. "Ser Garras, go and gather the remaining troops, then prepare yourselves to defend the kingdom."

The two women watched as the thin morling left the hall.

Persea turned toward Alor once more. "She sees things."

"What kind of things?"

Persea glanced at the table, leery her friend wouldn't believe her. "Things that have yet to happen." She paused for a moment, then glanced at Alor, still struck by the confusing concept of someone seeing the future. "Knowledge like that would be a great deal of wealth in these times."

"So, it would. Go ready me a small boat. I need to leave and gather my thoughts on this matter."

"Are you planning on going somewhere?" Persea

asked, shocked by the command given to her.

"I am going home. It will just be for a couple of moons. Rakash will sit in for me in my absence."

"Do you realize you are leaving us in a time of war?"

Alor's gaze sat heavily on her lifelong friend. With a powerful voice—one none had heard from her before—she spoke. "We've lost the majority of our warriors to Artus and the Abyss. We have tens of thousands of men marching to a possible slaughter in Sentries and barely five thousand here. We don't have enough to protect us—to protect *me*, your queen. I'm going to Valkeri to keep myself safe. While I am there, I will ask my father for some of his Valkards to return with me to replenish our military and fleet. But if I stay, I put myself and this kingdom at risk. This is the best option for us; you've got to trust me."

"I do trust you," Persea responded and chuckled. "I definitely trust you more than I did Lord Kaprin. And as you have wished, I will have a small boat ready for you in a few hours."

A faint smile crossed Alor's face. "Thanks, Persea. I will see that you are rewarded for your many services to this kingdom."

As Persea stood and exited the room, Alor approached an ogre who had been keeping guard in the hall.

"Rakash," she addressed him. "I need you to fill in for me in my time of absence."

The huge ogre turned his vision upon the siren. "What dost ya bid me to do whilst ye'r gone?"

"Send off another hunt for the hydra, and keep our kingdom safe. And, if you must, take a knee to any invaders before our military is deplenished."

Rakash's brow furrowed. "Ya bid me to surrender, Duchess?"

"It's Queen now," she corrected. "And if you must, so be it. I'd rather take a knee to another than lose our men to a lost cause."

"As ya bid, my Queen."

Alor stared at the brute. "If anyone comes in search of me, tell them that I've been killed. I will return sometime during the Hiza Moon with a Valkard army sailing at my side. Are we clear?"

A smirk grew upon the ogre's pale-green face. "Aye, my dead Queen."

Alor traveled unaccompanied and riding upon her kelpie to the Seaford docks. The somber siren glanced at the villages around her, fearing they wouldn't be standing when she returned.

Alor glanced at the gawler she would be taking as she took a deep breath and dismounted her mare. She led her kelpie toward Persea waiting at the docks, tears gathering in her eyes as all of her emotions fought to escape.

"Persea," Alor greeted her friend.

"My Queen."

"I pray that you will remain safe while I am away."

"As do I," the dryad responded with a tremble building in her voice. "As do I."

A few tears trickled from Alor's eyes and down her soft cheeks as she tried to force a smile. She wrapped her arms around Persea as they both submitted to their tears. After a few moments of sobbing, they released their grips on each other.

Alor turned from her friend, feeling embarrassed from appearing to be so weak. She slowly trekked toward her rowboat and stepped in. She glanced at Persea as she untied the dock line. After forcing another smile, Alor pushed away from the dock with an oar, then began her journey to her homeland.

Frosted Eyes

A cold, bleak morning greeted the Senturian knights. The air was thick and silent, the wind causing the nightmares to snort whinnies of discomfort. Before the weary soldiers collected their belongings and tended to their empty stomachs, they sorted through their fallen comrades who had succumbed to the bitter coldness of the mountains and alerted their superiors of who had perished during the harsh night.

"Ser Galzar, we need to find some heat or some sort of shelter to recuperate. Our men aren't going to last another day in this cold," Caski informed the elf after being told of another demon succumbing to hypothermia. "If we can locate a cave of sorts, I might be able to heat it."

Galzar analyzed the knights and squires, whose number had been cut by a thousand since leaving Ringwood. His gaze locked onto his squire, Mivros, who sat trembling on his steed, waiting for Nya to have mercy on his soul and take his life.

Galzar sighed. "I've seen nowhere to take up camp. Unfortunately, we must venture on, otherwise more will die in vain."

Galzar's icy-blue eyes continued to scan his army with devastation. Amongst the crowd, he spotted one of his friends, a minotaur, standing beside his fiery horse, packing up his belonging, his muzzled jawline clinched shut. The loss of his squire during the night had broken the minotaur's mental health, but he was conditioned—as well as most of the other knights—to not show much emotion for a lost comrade.

After feeling the burden of the lives lost and the lives still hanging in the balance, Galzar spoke to his men. "I know we have had a few bad nights, but 'tis a new day. We must continue our way through the mountains and hope that we can find a cavern for our night's rest, but for now, we must move on. Keep yer torches close for heat and pray they remain lit for the day." He analyzed the knights and squires one last time, before turning around his mount. "Be thy gods that guide us! Be thy gods that watch over us! Be no shame fall upon us!"

Galzar and his men moved onward, traveling deeper through the snow and slush of Kevward and around the base of Mount Eryn. They were cold and weak. Their spirits were as low as the embers of the flames emitting from their mounts. A squeal broke the forest's dismal silence; the knights glanced at each other as their mounts became frightened.

"Hold yer reigns, men! We don't want to lose any of our mares," Galzar shouted as he drew his bow from his back and readied an arrow.

He tactically led his steed through the trees, toward the sound, and into a clearing ahead of them. As he broke the treeline, he gave a startled gasp and held up his hand, signaling for his men to halt.

Seeing the reason for the squeal silenced any quiet mumbling—the only sounds left were the crunching of bones and the neighs of the frightened mounts. In the middle of the clearing, surrounded by fallen trees and large shards of burning ice protruding from the ground, was the massive form of Tiamus, with a large tirbuck between her two legs—her clawed wings spread around her as she tore a limb from the ram, swallowing it whole.

"By the gods, I thought the Dragon of Eryn was a myth," a squire whispered in awe.

"Steady, men. We do not want to challenge this beast. Let's back up before it spots us and decides that we are its second course," Galzar managed to whisper after finding his voice.

The men in the back muttered as they tried to steady their mounts and have them turn around. One of the nightmares shrieked in fear, rearing back and unsaddling its rider before it galloped away. The noise caused the great dragon's head to whip up and push the half-devoured tirbuck behind her.

She sniffed toward the knights, cocking her smooth, white head, her pupils dilating in her pale-blue irises. She released a rumbling purr, instead of the snarl the men had expected, and stepped toward them, her tail twitching behind her. As she approached, Galzar and his men felt an immense chill surround them, as if her body brought the freezing temperatures with her. Her white oval-shaped head stretched toward Galzar. Placing it near the ground, she sniffed the nightmare's hooves, then traveled toward Galzar's face.

Galzar, struck by fear and amazement at the same time, lowered his bow and arrow and slowly reached out his hand. After a moment of hesitation, he squinted and placed his hand upon her cold snout. The knights around him were as amazed as he was that Tiamus let him touch her.

A smile crossed Galzar's face, until the dragon jerked away, startled by a loud plump. Tiamus swung her head toward the ground where an imp had died from the cold and had fallen from his steed, which scurried away. The dragon's large pale mouth let out a deafening roar—along with a small barrage of tiny pieces of hail—as her legs scattered across the ground, carrying her body backward before she leaped into the air and flew away.

After she took flight, Galzar glanced toward the ground behind him, where his gaze laid sight upon the frosted eyes of Mivros.

329

Slaughtering of Lambs – Daemental
∂e'Ektha

The Alberian warriors, who had set up camp in Nuwulf, were gathered around a giant fire. Ixin had distanced himself from the crowd as he gazed upon the kingdom resting in the distance.

While peering through the spyglass, he heard a loud squawk from above him. He lowered the brass object and glanced at a roc flying across the overcast sky, carrying a scroll in its talons. The lich raised his hand toward the flying creature and projected a large bolt of lightning, striking one of the bird's wings, causing it to plummet to the white powdery ground.

Ixin traversed to where the bird had fallen. As he approached, he tore a strip of fabric from his shirt's hem. Upon reaching the black-feathered creature, he bandaged its wing before retrieving the scroll. He skimmed the letter, then returned to the camp.

"*A roc returned today with word from Lord Azreal. We attack now, and reinforcements will be awaiting us on the far side of the city,*" Ixin informed as he surveyed the hundred and sixty-seven thousand warriors, then shouted their motto as he raised the scroll into the air. "*Until the sun sets in the East, we will defend and serve the West!*"

The warriors all cried out, repeating the motto.

The Alberians began to trek through Nuwulf, anxious about the attack drawing near. As the men navigated the rocky terrain, a few warriors noticed a large feline a few strides away. The creature had a long mane of red and orange fur. Protruding from the middle of the animal's forehead was a single, long, curved horn and from its hind-end were five long tails. The zheng—as they were known to the inhabitants of BrightHelm—just gazed with its golden eyes upon the group as they passed by.

†

Cornelius stood in the center of BrightHelm, staring at the gallows outside his throne room. The thought of giving up still weighed heavily upon him. He could imagine the feel of the rope tightening around his neck as he pictured his young, elven body dangling from one of the nooses. The thought of ordering one of the guards accompanying him to pull the lever played over and over in his mind. It would be a quick death, and perhaps Iden would show him mercy in the afterlife.

His eyes lingered upon the rope's knot, and his mind fell into a deep depression when the sound of snow and ice crunching under giant paws and wooden wheels crept up behind him. A slight snarl from one of the large dralions shook Cornelius from his darkening trance. His sorrowed face turned to witness his royal carriage arriving.

His duchess stepped from the carriage with a sense of urgency across her freckled face. "My Lord, the Alberians are making their way toward the city."

Cornelius's long face returned toward the nooses as his duchess approached him. Her green eyes tried to find her lord's as she wiped a tear from his cheek.

"Tylon is waiting for the orders in your cabinet," she informed him before they both turned and entered the carriage.

†

Several minutes later, Cornelius and Zorie entered his office where his marquess was staring out one of the frosted windows.

"Tylon," Cornelius greeted as he approached his desk.

"My Lord. The Alberians are marching toward us as we speak."

"Zorie has informed me of the matter."

Tylon glanced at his lord. "I have posted all one hundred and seventy thousand of our knights at the western wall. Fifty thousand are on the battlement and the rest just inside the gate, all suited and armed for war."

"Inside the gate?" Cornelius asked with a perplexed look on his pale face. Then with an abrupt voice, he commanded, "Charge and slay every last one of them."

A look of uncertainty crossed over Tylon. "Our archers won't be able to guide their arrows around our men. They will become useless to us."

"We can spare a few lost souls as long as the Alberians don't reach inside our walls."

"But my Lord, I think—"

"Everyone has been wanting me to be more confident with giving orders, so obey them, dammit," the young lord yelled as he knocked off a few loose items that had been placed on his desk.

"I just think that it'd be smarter to wait—"

"It would be smarter if you listened to your lord!"

"Aye," Tylon submissively responded as he glanced out the window before heading toward the room's exit.

"Tylon, wait," Cornelius stopped him. "Do what you think is best for this kingdom and its people."

Tylon stopped at the door and flashed a small smile at his lord. "Beyond the clouds, we shine."

The Helanian knights were in position to defend BrightHelm, awaiting the command to attack the Alberian warriors. The opposition had made steady progress and effortlessly gained ground upon the city walls.

Tylon stepped onto the edge of the battlement as he overlooked the oncoming army. "Archers, take aim!"

The archers, as a single unit around him, docked an arrow, waiting for the call to release them toward the approaching enemy.

The warriors were near the gates before Tylon called for his men to let loose their bolts, hoping the majority of them found their marks. As the arrows rained upon the warriors, a shudder shook the walls surrounding BrightHelm. Tylon's gaze searched for the source of the sound. Seeing nothing, he looked back toward the Alberians as they reached the gates—many had fallen to the onslaught of arrows, but the others were attempting to get through the closed barricades.

A second rumble shook the ground, and a deafening roar split through the sound of raging men. From over the castle flew the massive form of Libras, his great wings carrying him with the clashing sounds of thunder. As one, the knights ducked and covered their ears from the frightening cry.

Libras swooped down, his wings colliding into the smokestacks of buildings as he flew over them. Crimson flames flowed from his mouth, torching buildings and citizens alike. Screams and cries filled the inflamed streets of the kingdom.

The monstrous dragon, whose scales glowed a vivid red from the surrounding flames, landed upon the battlement a few hundred strides from where Tylon and his archers stood guard. Its massive hind feet squished a few of the Helanians. As their God of War and Strength perched itself upon the large wall, giant blocks of stone and rubble fell beneath its weight.

One knight staggered backward in fear of the beast, not paying attention to his footing. After a few quick steps, his waist collided with the stone parapet. Unfortunately, his feet were moving too fast, and by the time he realized he had no farther to go, his feet had already left the structure beneath him as he toppled over the edge and fell to his death.

Another ear-shattering roar pierced the air as Libras waved his head of horns from side to side, causing more men to tumble off the battlement in fear.

From below, Ixin's yellow catlike eyes stared horrified at the massive form of the godlike beast. *"Kik armd,"* he shouted to his men. *"Shul bazh imul wa'taeq!"*

His warriors obeyed his command and retreated from their inevitable death and defeat.

Libras leaped and flew toward the Alberians as they fled helplessly, like a flock of livestock fearing their slaughter. A trail of fire followed behind them as some weren't able to escape, and the blazing flames engulfed them.

Cutting the Head off the Ram – Ideen
Wa'Rayd ush Wa'Ektha

In the afternoon of his one hundred and twelfth day of reign as lord, Cornelius resided in his cabinet along with Tylon and his guards. The young lord stood next to the window and stared at the crumbled wall. His mind—just as broken as his kingdom's borders—ached in sadness and disappointment.

"How are your men holding up?" Cornelius asked brokenly as he turned toward his marquess, slouched in his chair.

"A few less than earlier this week, but their spirits are holding firm."

"Do you think they are capable of protecting us?"

"I do. Even after the events a couple of days ago, we

still match the Alberians man for man, which ours are all far better equipped than they."

While the two elves continued to speak, Zorie entered the room and handed a tattered scroll to Cornelius. "My Lord, your letter has returned back from Ringwood."

Cornelius unrolled the crinkly piece of parchment. His mind filled with horror as his skin became paler than its usual shade of white. His icy eyes glanced from the letter toward Tylon's red eyes. "The Learish are coming."

Tylon straightened his posture. "Spreading our men across the entire southern wall should help protect us from both threats."

"Then go and prepare your men," Cornelius commanded as he motioned for his marquess to leave.

The young lord returned his gaze to the letter. Streaks of blood covered the faded ink of his words—words of hope that had been all for naught. He crumpled the letter into a ball and tossed it into the hearth, watching as the parchment withered to ash amongst the flames.

"The ice is melting," Cornelius began, "and the snow will be gone by morning."

Zorie's brow furrowed. "The snow will be here for at least a few more weeks, my Lord."

"I'm not talking about the slushed powder out on the streets." Cornelius turned his gaze toward his duchess and saw the sorrowed expression upon her face. "The world around us is changing, and as the

Pyqecius Moon grows, a new season is falling over our lands."

"What are you saying?"

"Me—this *Ice Lord* that this kingdom has …" Cornelius's words faded as he glanced at the flames once more. "I can no longer hold strong. I'm melting, and whether it be to water or blood, I'm uncertain. But the snow can't survive."

"But you can, my Lord. I have faith that—"

"No!" Cornelius's attention returned toward Zorie. "War is coming and with it death."

"Then let us pray that it is not our deaths that are coming."

"Some things are inevitable. Save yourself and flee before it's too late."

"I am not abandoning you nor this kingdom."

"Then go and find yourself somewhere safe to hide." Cornelius's focus turned toward his guards. "You all are relieved from your posts. Go help Tylon and his men protect this kingdom."

The guards nodded in agreeance and exited the room while their lord stood staring at the flames.

†

Outside the southwestern wall, Tylon met with his knights. Knowing the Learish were more barbaric and a larger threat than the Alberians, he ordered ninety thousand of his men to head toward the southeastern wall of the kingdom, leaving just over seventy thousand to fight the Alberians.

In Nuwulf, Tylon had seen the Alberians marching along the same slushed path as they had done two days prior. Their strix banners waved in the steady, crisp air.

"Alright, men," Tylon said, pacing behind the rows of knights. "Beyond the clouds, we shine, and beyond these walls, they fall!"

A loud grunt emerged from the knights as they readied themselves in formation. They stood in four long rows. The first two held shields and polearms, while the back two were of archers and bannermen.

As the Alberians advanced closer, Tylon led his men toward them, all four rows marching in unison. The armies drew near to each other, and the knights raised their shields and bows. The Alberians charged at the Helanian knights, yelling and crying out in their native tongue.

When the Alberians were just a few short strides away, Tylon gave his men the order to fire. As he had commanded, the first two rows of knights knelt and covered themselves and their comrades with their shields, while the archers in the back released their arrows.

The two forces collided—harsh clashes from metal and wood echoed through the mountainside. Swords and axes swung through the crowd, denting helmets and dismembering warriors and knights alike.

An Alberian warrior collapsed to his knees while grasping at his chest where a morningstar had punctured his thin armor. Warm red fluids flowed through his fingers as his breaths became harder for him to obtain. The warrior, on his hands and knees, glanced at his adversary as large iron spikes from the morningstar pulverized his face.

A few warriors were able to knock the shields from the Helanians' grasps. The Alberians, in turn, retrieved the protection for themselves and used them as weapons, bunting them against their enemies and stabbing the edges into the open visors of the knights.

The death count rose, and the corpses piled up, causing some of the men to trip over the carcasses—unable to get back onto their feet, they were trampled to death.

Tylon, in the middle of the raging battle, held his glaive in his hands, parrying and slicing any Alberian who came close enough to him. All around him were knights reaching over the heads of other knights just to stab an Alberian with their sword.

As the battle continued, one of the Alberians swung his ax at Tylon, who raised his shield to deflect the blow. Tylon jousted his polearm into the lightly armored elf, then removed it in one swift motion, looking to find his next target.

His red eyes glanced around the battle in front of him when an agonizing pain spread from the back of his neck, down his spine, and around toward his face. He turned to see a blue djinn in golden armor adorned with rubies embedded into the breastplate. The djinn held a falchion sword in each hand. Unable to see the silver hair under his helmet, Tylon was still able to recognize him—Lord Azreal of Talean.

Tylon tried to step toward Azreal but just fell to the bloodstained ground. He lay there wincing in pain as his skin turned darker and began to blister. His red eyes faded as he took his last breath.

Azreal fought through the cluster of warriors and knights, slicing the Helanians with his swords coated with poisonous death worm venom.

Zorie stood in her chamber and stared out the window, witnessing the carnage of the battle drawing closer to the castle's courtyards as she grew worried in the nighttime hours. Amongst the crowd of soldiers, the seventy thousand Helanians fell to the two invading armies, until none remained.

A group of Alberians and Taleanics trooped toward the castle. Zorie grew anxious and scared for her life. As she observed the soldiers nearing the castle entrance, one of them looked toward her, pointed, and notified the others as if he had seen her staring out her window five floors up.

The warriors and Golden Men rushed into the castle as Zorie fled her room. Terror filled her mind as she ran down the passageway toward Cornelius's cabinet. Once she reached the room, she noticed it was vacant, and the flames that had occupied the fireplace had been smothered out. From down the corridor, the sound of the soldiers stampeding toward the room rumbled through the castle. She hid underneath the desk, staying as quiet as her thumping heart and heavy breaths would allow. She listened carefully to the men's footsteps as they passed the room without stopping to investigate any of the chambers. With the sound of the men fading into the distance, Zorie crawled from under the desk and escaped the room.

†

Upon the castle's roof, a group of soldiers approached a young elven figure standing on the edge of the parapet, his blond hair and tunic blowing in the wind.

"Cornelius!" one of the Golden Men shouted. "We hath came, and we hath conquered!"

Cornelius stood with his head hung low. His body shook from weeping and from the disappointment he felt for failing his kingdom.

"If ya bend the knee to Lord Moll'ar, yer life and the lives of yer men will be spared!"

"A bent knee would do nothing to spare my life, only solidify the inevitable," Cornelius said as his voice quavered. "Look at this place. It may be hard to distinguish in the light of the moon, but come morn, you will see the desolation of this city. Winter has proved to be too strong for this kingdom and its Ice Lord."

Cornelius slowly turned his head toward the men, his hair blowing fiercely across his soaked face. He took a deep breath, still shaking from his whimpering. "All I ask is for no more harm or destruction be brought upon this kingdom."

"Bend a knee and all will be permissible to safety."

"May the next lord be not of the cold and ice as I have been, but of fire and passion. All hail Lord Moll'ar," Cornelius said in a brittle tone as he lowered his head and turned.

He took a deep breath, then with a single step, he fell over the parapet. His young body tumbled through the dark sky as it approached the unforgiving ground.

†

From the ground, Azreal watched the young, elven Lord of BrightHelm plummet through the night sky. With a dull thump, Cornelius's body splattered on the stone ground. A small chuckle escaped the djinn before he turned toward a few of his Golden Men.

"BrightHelm is ours!"

Azreal retrieved a small vial from his satchel. He opened the glass container and poured a thick, clear liquid into his gloved hands. After rubbing his hands together, he and some of his Golden Men approached a group of Alberian warriors.

"*Uyi enam du'ya'shuti ghelitha,*" Azreal congratulated them as he placed his hands on two of their necks and gave them a slight rewarding massage. "I am truly honored by all of the hard work you farmlanders showed tonight."

The two Alberians felt a sharp pain in their necks; at first, they dismissed it as stiff muscles getting worked loose, but soon their bodies became numb, and the darkness of the night consumed their sights. Their veins turned black, and their skins boiled with puss, and foam flowed from their mouths.

"Fulken elé rassam su'gleer?" a nearby Alberian asked as he glanced with horror at a smirk on Azreal's face. The warrior removed his sword as his fellow comrades collapsed to the ground. *"Fulken du'uyi du'su'gleer?"*

Azreal, twirling his swords, sliced the surprised and angered Alberians. With each cut from the blades, the poison embedded itself into their foes' skin, decomposing their bodies as it flowed through their bloodstream.

"Alright, men," Azreal said with a devious grin as the nearby Alberians had fallen and the others started to become suspicious. "Let us take what is ours!" He lifted his hand into the air and released a few quick strobes of light.

The Golden Men all knew what the signal meant as they turned on their Alberian brothers in arms. The attack was sudden and caught most of the Alberians off guard. Though many fell at first, they reoriented and began to defend themselves.

"*Kill them all,*" Ixin screamed over the sound of the frenzied fighting. "*Send these traitors straight to their graves!*"

After witnessing some of his warriors fall to Azreal's blades, Ixin concluded they must be poisoned. "*Clothe yeselves with better armor,*" he yelled, hoping it would help defend themselves.

As some men grabbed what armor they could find, others continued to fight against the traitors with the armor they had, as they all hoped to see the unexpected battle through. Though they were initially caught off guard, the Alberians had better numbers and managed to gain the advantage against the traitors they had previously called their allies.

Within the kingdom's ruined walls—close to BrightHelm's throne room—Ixin found himself staring into Azreal's large white eyes. Two warriors—a dryad who still donned his light, leather armor and a satyr who had acquired a breastplate and helmet from a fallen Helanian—accompanied Ixin.

The three warriors surrounded the djinn, ready to fight him to the death.

"*Watch for his swords. A single nick will bring ya to yer knees,*" Ixin snarled, cautiously advancing toward Azreal.

Azreal grinned. "*Do you honestly think your men can defeat me?*"

"*I know we can, traitor,*" Ixin growled as he took slow, small steps toward the blue giant, who stood a leg taller than him.

From the corner of his vision, Azreal saw the dryad

charging him with his weapon drawn. Azreal turned just in time to puncture his chest with one of his swords. The dryad immediately dropped to the ground—sap oozed from his chest, and his bark-like skin turned to ashes as the leaves on his head withered away.

From behind him, the djinn heard both Ixin and the satyr charging closer. He spun around, only to receive a gash in his left arm from one of Ixin's small hatchets, which had been thrown toward him. Azreal screamed, cursing the Alberian lich as he dropped both of his swords and grabbed his wounded arm.

As the two warriors approached the traitor, he struggled to lift his left hand. With his hand finally straight and his palm facing the satyr, Azreal clenched a fist as he twisted his hand toward him. As the djinn made those motions, the dull metal armor on the satyr crushed around his body until the chest underneath gave way, causing blood and fur to explode from under the breastplate.

Ixin, infuriated by the djinn's actions and morals, charged the defenseless being. Unfortunately, as he approached Azreal, a massive minotaur collided into the side of the lich. Ixin's head ricocheted off the stoned street. Standing over him was a Taleanic knight wearing golden armor along with golden, spiked gauntlets on both arms.

The minotaur drew back his fist, ready to impale its spikes into Ixin's thin face when a giant elephant-like creature, known as a baku, stampeded toward the two, impaling one of its tusks through the minotaur's torso.

The baku came to a stop and glanced at Ixin as it morphed into a feminine elf.

"Thanks, Tera." Ixin sighed in relief as he stood to his feet and looked around. *"Where is Lord Azreal?"* he questioned, noticing the djinn's disappearance.

Branded by Battle – Kard biz Dolu

While Ixin walked around the opening where Azreal had previously stood, hoping to see some sign of where the djinn might have fled to, the remaining one hundred and ten thousand Alberians sat around small bonfires in the middle of the streets. They passed around hooked iron rods the chieftains had in their possession for their tribes.

Tera waited and watched as one of the rods circled around the group of warriors until, finally, one of the men presented it to her. She retrieved the rod and a stone and placed the hook into the dancing flames. Her green eyes stared as the metal burned orange, and black flakes appeared around the iron hook. She removed the end of the rod from the fire and smashed the stone onto the hook, causing the slag to break free from the heated iron.

Tera secured the hook around her left wrist. She balled her hand into a fist as the heat neared her arm. The smell of burnt hair and skin filled her nostrils before contact was even made. The pain of her skin searing from the branding iron was more than what she had anticipated. Her eyelids clenched as she removed her wrist, feeling her skin tear away from the metal. Wincing, she bit her quivering lips as she placed the hook on the opposite side of her wrist to complete her voluntary torture.

As she finished and handed the branding iron and the stone to the next warrior, Ixin approached and sat next to her. Her stare shifted from her trembling arm toward a piece of cloth in Ixin's hand.

Ixin scooped some of the remaining snow and rubbed it into the cloth.

"Give me yer wrist."

Tera did as commanded, trying to hold her shaking arm steady.

"How long does the pain stay?" she asked, glancing at Ixin's bandaged bicep.

"The brand will be fully healed in 'bout three weeks, but the initial pain should be gone in a day or two."

Tera continued to grimace as Ixin finished dressing her wrist.

"'Tis not what ya expected, huh? It ne'r is. But ya get used to it. Each time the pain becomes more bearable as the nerves in yer arms are deadened."

"I do not know what I expected having my skin burnt would feel like, but this is far from it."

"Aye, but like I said, the pain will subside in a day or so." Ixin simpered as he observed the only female he had known to be branded by battle. "Ya were right, ya know. I do hold a higher standard of ya now. I know plenty of men who bare the same brands on their faces as I, just because they were scared to be honored with a brand around their wrists, as well as boys who grew old and died as a child because they ne'r took the Walk of Roses. Now, ya can ne'r take the walk, but if they had one for enterin' womanhood, I know ya would be the first to take it."

Tera's eyes glinted behind strands of her black hair, and for a moment, the burning of her wrist fled from her acknowledgment. "That means a lot, Chief."

"Now, do not get all emotional on me, we still have matters to attend to," Ixin stated as he stood. "Give it a couple of hours for everyone to acclimate themselves with their brands, then take fifty thousand of the warriors and return back to Alberon. Tell Lord Moll'ar of Azreal's foul betrayal. I will stay with the remaining men and hold BrightHelm while I continue to search for Azreal."

"You want us to return home just after capturing the city?"

"Aye. Our objective was to take BrightHelm, which we did. I will stay behind with 'bout half our men and hold the city. Ya did far better than what I had expected, and ya deserve to return home to yer ol' lady. Show off yer brand, and let it be known that ya were able to fight alongside the men. And who knows, maybe one day aft' the war, I will come visit and educate all ye northerners on the history of our great land."

Tera's lips curled. "I would enjoy that, and I will be sure to *keep a cot at the ready for your visit."*

A few hours later, as the morning sun began to rise, Tera led her followers out of BrightHelm. They trekked the same path through Nuwulf they had done so the previous day. As they hiked the steep ridges, a loud purr penetrated the winds' howling screams. In the distance, Tera saw a large feline, standing two legs tall, approach them.

With its matted dark brown mane and its bare tail, the dralion waltzed toward the warriors. With each step, its gigantic, hairless paws embedded themselves into the slushed snow. Steam escaped its nostrils with each breath.

Never having seen a dralion before, or even knowing what it was, Tera and the warriors stood frozen. The realization of this possibly being their last seconds to live crossed everyone's mind. The warriors' trembling hands instinctively tightened on their weapons as the massive creature arrived at their position.

The dralion sniffed and smelled a few of the men, examining them and their belongings. After analyzing a dozen warriors, the large feline nuzzled its head against some of the Alberians, staggering them backward with the force of its gentle gesture.

The warriors relaxed and released their grips after realizing the creature was nothing to fear. Many of them ran their hands through the clumps of hair on the dralion's head and back as it continued its way past the group.

After enjoying the peacefulness the giant creature seemed to bring, Tera continued to lead the warriors through the mountains. They approached their previous campsite as the sound of ripping and crunching rung in their ears.

Tera motioned for the group to halt as the noise grew louder. She scanned the surrounding trees as she crept closer toward the sound; her footsteps became heavier as her animal spirit took over.

After advancing a hundred strides ahead of the group, Tera spotted red portions of Libras's dark scales glistening in the array of the rising sun as he devoured chunks of the peryton they had previously dispatched.

Tera, in her baku form, slowly approached the dragon, feasting on the peryton's intestines and organs. Her steps became slow but heavy, shaking the ground as she traversed over it.

The mighty dragon turned his head toward the large creature approaching him. Distributing all his weight onto his front legs, Libras leaned forward, grunting and snarling as the spines traveling down his head and back stood tall. The gaze from his fiery-red eyes targeted the baku as smoke billowed from his snout.

Caught being stuck in-between sheer terror and being protective of the warriors who awaited down the path for her, Tera trumpeted a loud war cry from her short trunk, tempting the mighty god.

He widened his mouth, exposing every tooth that lined the inside, and bellowed a high-pitched cry of his own as a few embers escaped. Tera lowered her head and pointed her tusks toward Libras's thick chest, not completely sure if she'd be strong enough to penetrate his tough scales.

Libras knew what the baku was planning to do as he lowered his own head. A plume of fire collected in his mouth, then released before Tera could try to escape its path.

The fireball hit the ground in front of Tera, causing instant steam as the snow melted upon impact. She scampered backward, trying to keep the heat from burning her face. As the vapors dispersed, Tera saw Libras take flight and vanish into the morning sky.

As she continued to watch Libras's silhouette grow smaller in the orange-colored sky, Tera shifted to her elven form, then returned to the group of warriors.

"We are safe, for now. But we have a long way to go before we are home, and there has been enough red snow painted by our warriors. Do not let your brands be in vain. Keep your eyes open and an ear to the wind."

Torn Banners – Doské Bitham

As the morning light crested over the mountain peaks, Galzar and his men continued north through Nuwulf, the chilled winds still blasting them like needles, as only a handful of demons and imps were left struggling to stay warm.

With the trees dispersed and the number of stone ridges dwindling, their eyes beheld the stone wall that surrounded the city beyond the clouds in the distance, just twenty strides away. Galzar observed the giant wall, noticing a few toppled portions of the structure.

Galzar turned toward his men and had to shout over the howling winds to be heard. "Warmth is just beyond that wall! Hold strong for a few more strides, and we'll all be safe!" He whipped on the reins of his mount as he led the Senturians into the capital.

The knights cautiously trotted through the streets, past frightened citizens as they did their best to avoid the knights. With the blinding light reflecting off the ground and other snow-covered surfaces, Galzar vaguely saw a figure, garnished in some form of armor, moving around in the distance as its hair blew rapidly in the wind. Galzar and Caski dismounted their steeds and crept toward the wandering figure.

The character donned golden armor over its torso and a long maroon skirt dragging across the ground. The figure cautiously surveyed its surroundings before continuing forward a couple more strides, then repeated the nervous act.

Galzar drew an arrow from his quiver and readied his bow. Galzar and Caski advanced toward the unknown being, making sure to stay hidden behind walls and doorways. Once he had determined they were close enough, Galzar pulled his arrow taught, then released it. While in mid-flight, Caski enchanted the arrow as it soared toward its target. The arrow skimmed past the figure, ricocheting off a nearby building.

The figure turned his head toward the two warriors, his eyes glowing bright white. He waved his arm around him as the snow on the ground swept toward the two Senturians, brushing against their faces in an attempt to blind them just enough for him to escape.

Wiping the snow from his eyes, Caski caught a glimpse of the figure running into a nearby home. "There," he shouted as he sprinted after the figure,

Galzar following close behind.

As the two Senturians rushed into the home, an elderly elven man stood frightened near the hearth. Galzar and Caski paid no mind to the homeowner; they just focused on the figure in the golden armor as they chased him through the house.

Coming around a corner of one of the corridors, Galzar spotted the blue-skinned figure darting down the passage. He readied another bolt, and in one steady motion, released it. Once again, Caski cast a spell on it, causing it to glow a dark plum color.

The arrow implanted itself through the red skirt and into the buttocks of the fleeing figure, causing him to stumble to the ground. His face turned toward the Senturians as they approached swiftly.

The knelt figure—which they had come to a realization of being Lord Azreal—reached around and grabbed at the arrow. As he grasped the bolt, it deteriorated into sand; the grains seemed to rapidly fall to the floor but stopped as just a few splinters of the shaft remained protruding from his skin.

Azreal slowly worked the arrow from his flesh. His face grew narrow and his brow furrowed as uncertainty to why all of the arrow hadn't deteriorated from his grasp washed over him.

"What's the matter?" Caski chuckled. "Run out of magic, did ya?"

Azreal scampered farther down the corridor, trying to gain his footing as he went.

Caski extended his arm and swiped down with his

fist clenched shut, ripping a large metal decorative plate from the wall and smashed it into Azreal's staggering body. The djinn collapsed forward onto a small side table, flipping it and spilling its contents into the hallway.

The two Senturians ran to Azreal's sprawled body, blood trickling down the side of his head, just above his right ear. As they clutched his arms, Galzar noticed Azreal's ashen-white hair was covering a large glass vile laying on the floor. He retrieved the vile and examined it thoroughly as he and Caski jerked Azreal to his feet.

The bottom half of the vile had shattered when it had impacted the floor, but the top still remained intact. The label that had once wrapped around the vile hung to the broken piece of glass in Galzar's hand. He tried to read the label, but it was in an unfamiliar language.

Iskah Udet Yehock
Behlúch! Behvlach!
Uchyahgen − Chen toffoch beel. Ahdahytees pug la oazh oneltees
Yaloochyack ood Tets Toph Drumwright
Dames Clechy, Adria, Penora

After glancing at the label, Galzar tore it from the glass and placed it inside his fur cloak before shoving Azreal, escorting him from the building and toward the other knights.

"Ser Darut." Galzar addressed a giant minotaur as he presented them the Taleanic djinn. "Keep siege of Lord

Azreal, and send word to Lord Darius of his capture."

"As ya bid, Ser," Darut responded, taking Azreal and placing him in the cuffs that were bound to his nightmare.

Galzar turned to the rest of his men. "We have their lord, but I am sure the Taleanics are close by, waiting to pounce. BrightHelm has fallen, but the threat to our survival is even more evident now than ever before. So, be thy gods that guide us, and be thy gods that watch over us. For surely, no shame will fall upon us."

The knights and squires roared as they began marching and riding through the city streets but became silent after noticing mangled bodies littering the ground a few blocks ahead of their position. Helanian and Taleanic corpses lay in puddles of red snow, along with a large number of tan-skinned warriors covered in furs and beads.

Caski approached one of the tan carcasses that lay toppled over into his own intestine. With his foot, he rolled the corpse over, revealing the yellow dye smeared across his face.

"Alberians," Caski whispered to himself, then chuckled. "'Tis looks like we're late for the party."

As they ventured through the streets, Galzar spotted the thin stone wall that surrounded the castle.

"Look, BrightHelm rests under the Banner of the Strix." Galzar paused as he glanced around, noticing a few animals down some of the streets, staring at the group of knights. Then with a vibration of panic in his voice, he continued. "Kill everything that moves, civilians and wildlife alike!"

The knights drew their weapons as they advanced toward the castle wall. They filed through the entryway and into the courtyards surrounding the castle. With the entrance of the last Senturian and his steed, a loud blast sounded behind them as the wall above the opening collapsed to the ground.

"There," Caski shouted as he pointed to a decaying lich across the adjacent courtyard, along with a group of sixty thousand warriors spilling out around the castle.

The two armies charged each other—many of the Alberian morlings morphed into their animal spirits and ripped and shredded through the Senturian knights.

Ixin could barely hear the sound of the approaching footsteps over the howling of the wind. He surveyed the courtyards around the castle, spotting a large number of Senturians marching through the gate. He raised both hands and projected a large fireball toward the opening, hoping to cause it to collapse on some of the knights.

After the blast sounded, a Senturian archer informed the others of Ixin's presence.

"*Intruders!*" Ixin shouted as the remaining Alberians quickly joined him in the courtyard.

Ixin led his men into the crowd of Senturians as the air filled with battle cries. Metal clashed with metal, and bodies immediately began to fall, only to be crushed under three hundred thousand stampeding feet.

Men hiding beneath their black armor and swinging flaming weapons surrounded Ixin. Trying to avoid becoming burnt, he brandished his own weapons in an attempt to survive. He hacked away at the knights with his two hatchets, searching for any small opening between their shifting plates as blood splattered his leathery face.

Ixin battled his way farther into the crowd, trudging through flesh and blood as the vomit and feces of his dead allies and foes covered him. As he fought for his survival, Ixin tried to pinpoint the source of the Senturians' fiery weapons.

Upon seeing the Senturian lich igniting the weapons, Ixin's eyes narrowed as he focused on putting a stop to Caski. He blocked and parried swords and maces and reciprocated with a blow of his own axes as his allies fell to the onslaught beside him. The closer he found himself to Caski, however, the thicker the throng of Senturians seemed.

The knights turned their burning blades toward him, forcing Ixin to stop advancing and protect himself. He hissed in pain as a sword cut his arm as he was trying to block a blow aimed for his head. He flipped his hatchets in his hands and swung them at the knight to his right, only to be forced to jump away as an imp swung at his legs with a pair of daggers.

Ixin's jaw clenched with such force that bits of his rotted teeth splintered off. He stomped his foot, sending a shockwave to pulse across the ground, and knocked the knights from him as his skin tightened and strands of hair fell from his head.

The battle waged on, and the Senturians' strength and numbers became too much for the Alberians as their numbers dwindled.

Ixin focused his gaze upon Caski as he slew any Senturian who got in his path until he reached him—the gaze from their slit eyes focused on the other's.

"Kurri uyi daementas!"

As Ixin finished with his words, a sharp pain pierced his torso. His yellow eyes looked down to his abdomen where a long steel blade protruded from under his leather and pelt shirt, dripping blood from the tip.

"'Tis all of 'em," a Senturian knight proclaimed after dislodging his blade from Ixin's back.

After the battle had ended and as the Senturians tended to their wounds, Galzar surveyed the courtyard.

"Go search the castle for any—"

"Ser Galzar!" a troll shouted as he approached. "We found Lord Cornelius's body in a courtyard on the other side o' the castle. 'Tis pretty gruesome to look at, but we found him."

"String him up at the gallows," Caski commanded. "It'll strike fear into the townsfolk."

Galzar glanced at the troll and nodded in agreeance, then faced the rest of the knights. "Tear down them revolting banners! The Burning Tower shall drape these walls!"

As his men dispersed, a large cyclops approached Galzar dragging behind him a young elven lady. "I found the Helanian duchess hidin' in one o' the bedchambers, Ser."

Galzar looked upon the elf's moist green eyes. "Take her back to her chamber and stand guard at the door."

"But Ser," Zorie protested as the cyclops began to drag her away, "my Lord's funeral is in the morn. I wish to attend, if I may."

"Lord Cornelius doesn't deserve a proper funeral; he was a fat-kidneyed huma."

"I am speaking of Lord Brighton's funeral, Ser."

Galzar saw the glossiness of the duchess's eyes build as her body trembled. Sighing, Galzar responded, "Escort her to the funeral and back."

"Thank you, Ser," Zorie said humbly as the cyclops tugged her arm once more and escorted her to the castle.

Galzar watched as the duchess's long brown hair blew wildly in the wind as they went. Lost in a slight daze from the morning's activities, Galzar drifted away in thought as he stood motionless. A loud trumpeting sound echoing through the air, followed by a deeper roar, disrupted his daydreaming. Galzar jolted his head around, surveying the courtyards for the source. At first, he saw nothing, then from beyond the city walls, he saw the vague outline of a massive beast as it flew into the sky.

Galzar rushed up the rampart and glanced into the distance where he saw dark spots in the white snow moving farther away from the capital.

"Caski!" he shouted while keeping his sights on the fleeing warriors. "Ready our men for another advancement. We're going to hunt down the remaining Alberians."

Predators

A week after being deployed toward Talean, a group of thirty-five hundred Senturian recruits convened with Dagrus and his battered-yet-surviving thousand knights in the canyons of Qupar. The recruits were weary and tired from their journey—most of them unconditioned to the long trek they had to make.

As they neared the camp, a squire greeted them. "Yer arrival 'tis a blessin'. Ser Dagrus awaits ye in the war tent to update ye on the battle. Who is yer commander?"

The recruits looked at each other before a troll near the front stepped forward. "My name is Zeke. We were given no commander, just the order to come and assist in the battle."

"Very well. Follow me, Ser Zeke."

"Ser, the men and I are all famished," Zeke confessed before following the squire. "We were barely given enough rations to last us and our mounts the trip here. I apologize for the inconvenience that we may have on yer men."

"No worries. We came across a sickened imugi on our journey to Talean. The flesh had been dried out but is still in good eatin' condition. Ya and yer men will be well fed tonight."

The recruits all murmured in excitement—the thought of enjoying meat after being told they would likely only be able to feast on pieces of bread greatly raised their spirits.

"Thank ya," Zeke said as he began to follow the squire through the canyon.

After arriving at the tent, Zeke entered and found Ser Dagrus sitting behind a table, along with a yellow-skinned djinn. Laid across the table was a large piece of leather cloth with different stones and chips spread on top of it.

"Ser Dagrus, I am Zeke," the troll introduced himself as he removed his helmet—a casque with an extension protecting the nose. "Lord Darius has sent us to aid ya in yer quest to take Talean."

"Good," the hornless demon responded as he moved around a blue chip on the cloth. "We need all the men we can muster up."

Zeke glanced outside the tent at the wounded knights and squires. "It appears that way, Ser."

Dagrus glared at the stones and coins, then turned his vibrant red eyes toward the troll. "Come, look at the war plan I have devised."

Zeke obeyed and made his way around the table and stood beside the seated demon. With all the intention of studying Dagrus's strategy map, Zeke's eyes instead fell upon the large blood-stained bandage wrapped around the demon's right ankle.

Zeke gasped as he stared at the grungy rags. "Yer leg."

Dagrus glanced down at his limb and grumbled. "An arrow sliced it open."

"Why haven't ya returned home? Ya can't fight in this war. Ya can't even walk."

"My men need me here. Many of which are worse off than I, having been cauterized or even amputated. Besides, our lord wouldn't accept anyone back if they had succumbed to defeat," Dagrus stated as his small sunken nostrils flared slightly. "If I can still mount a horse, I can still fight."

Zeke nodded, acknowledging that Lord Darius would make a mockery out of anyone who had returned from a failed quest. He turned his attention from the apparent wound on his new commander toward the group of stones and chips upon the table.

"So, what's the plan, Ser?"

"The last time, they were prepared and waiting for us; this time will be no different," Dagrus mentioned as he pointed at a stack of sun coins on the cloth. "They had fifteen legions of warriors on the ground and a mere third of that upon the battlement. We could outmaneuver them enough to stay out of harm's way, but the battle grew on, and my men grew tired. Then, one by one, our blood was shed."

Dagrus picked up several rubies and shook them in his coal-black hand. "The Taleanics came at us, bargaining for blood. They slaughtered my men like predators, but it won't happen again. We were forced to retreat in hopes of fighting another day—another day that will end in victory. So, this time we are going to only send a few at them, drawing them away from the wall."

He placed a few of the rubies beside the sun coins, then put what remained in a half circle around the two piles. "We will have archers posted up in different spots, surrounding them, to catch them in a crossfire of arrows. This time it'll be their blood that's shed."

✝

Across Metagore, in the plains of Alberon, small farming villages in the region of Redthorn were under attack. The rampaging attackers were not warriors of a foreign land but predators of their own. Typically residing in the region of Kiden Hill, the Kiden lion was one of the most dangerous forms of wildlife the Alberians had to deal with.

The beasts were rampaging through the villages and settlements; they dug up the fields, leaving them riddled with ruts; they clawed at the houses and huts, tearing holes into the walls and knocking down doors; they attacked and pounced upon the herds of cattle, leaving many farmers without.

Terrified villagers grew malicious with the loss of their property. They formed mobs carrying torches and pikes and hoes and shovels and many other kinds of weapon-like tools they had around their homes.

The villagers flocked to the fields, making a useless attempt of attacking the lions. As each probe and blade impaled the felines' thick coats, the lions left the villagers disgruntled as their tools bent and broke and unscathed the lions.

Soon after the villagers had left their demolished homes, they met the same fate as their livestock. The lions tore into their thin flesh and discarded their mangled and bloodied carcasses.

After the beasts had terrorized and killed many inhabitants of a settlement, they fled to the next, just to restart the cycle once more.

†

After being deployed from Sentries with little training, another group of thirty-five hundred recruits rode through the desolate void of Black Rain Forest. The dark landscape and the near silence in the air made the new knights feel eerie. Though they were used to the dull colors and rotted trees, the absence of noise rung loudly in their minds.

A faint chitter echoed around them as a deadened branch cracked overhead, forcing slithers of charcoal and bark to crumble onto their armor. One nervous elf, Briar, looked up to see four pairs of yellow eyes staring down at them—the bright crimson feathers of the strixes contrasted with the gray and black limbs they rested upon. The recruit gasped as he halted and surveyed his surroundings.

Briar's green eyes glanced toward Rosule, a morling wearing peasant clothes, who looked calm as he slowly rode upon one of the few mounts given to the recruits. Briar hurried his pace to near the morling officer, feeling as if he could soak in some of his apparent bravery just by being near him.

"Are ya not scared?" Briar asked, his gaze returning to the red birds.

Rosule was a good head taller than the frightened elf, with brown eyes and long brown hair, which he refused to accidentally damage by wearing the only piece of armor provided to him: a helmet.

Rosule's eyebrows raised in surprise. "What is there to be scared of?"

"The monsters that could be lurkin' 'bout," Briar replied, looking at the ground as the sight of the yellow eyes above them became too much.

"There are no monsters in these woods, just birds and bugs," Rosule said with a chuckle as a long inflamed lizard jolted across the ground. "And salamanders."

"Are ya sure of it?"

369

"Aye, there is nothing to fear here."

"I wish I could have yer courage and bravery."

"I was scared my first time through here—venturing into an uncharted territory for myself. But as my trips stacked up, I realized these woods were barren of any threats. So, I wouldn't call it bravery, just experienced."

"Aye, bravery or not, ya got more courage than I. I would o' ne'r traveled these parts if I weren't forced to."

"Aye, now it's Medsa'lear that I fear."

"Why?" Briar asked as his eyes grew wide. "Wait, 'tis where we are headeth."

"Aye." Rosule's lighthearted tone grew serious and weary. "There is said to be a beast as large as the mighty dragons that hunts in those swamps. It has many heads and eyes so it can track yer every movement. Its venom can burn through trees, and its jowls can bite a man in two."

"Ya can't believe that, can ya?" Briar asked with fear growing in his voice.

"'Tis true," another recruit said. "I've heard the tales o' the many-headed dragon o' the swamps."

Briar looked back at Rosule, fear plastered on his face as he felt his heart pounding rapidly in his chest.

THE MARK

In the early hours of the next morning, before the rising of the sun, the Senturian knights besieged the Kingdom of Talean, advancing in three groups.

Zeke led the recruits toward the kingdom's eastern wall. He glanced to his right, where he saw the torches of the five hundred knights Ser O'Bryon was leading. Looking left, he was unable to see Ser Dagrus and the third group of men waiting for the attack, though he knew they were out there.

Zeke had been informed that he and his men were fodder. Their goal was to draw the Taleanics from the protection of their archers on the battlements. Dagrus and O'Bryon would command their archers to rain their arrows on top of their enemies, risking the lives of their own men just to conquer the kingdom. Zeke supposed it was what they were meant to do, since they were part of the army and their lord had wished to take Talean.

Zeke grew nervous as he sat upon his steed. Being thrown into the face of battle after only a couple of short weeks of preparation and training wasn't the ideal situation. And the feeling of unsettledness by the decision of his commander—and not wanting to be in the middle of a crossfire of arrows by his own men—made him wish he had been born a female. Nonetheless, he knew what would happen to him if he detoured from the discussed plan of attack; he wanted to die honorably and make his family proud of his courage.

Zeke glanced at the recruits behind him. In his best attempt to rally his men, he began, "We are not knights. We are not fighters. Today we shall die, but we shall die honorin' our lord. On 'tis day, we shall put our stamp on history, so that women and children may sing of our songs for years to come. May thy gods guide us, and may they watch over our souls. For on 'tis day, Sentries will prevail with no shame brought upon our names."

He stared at the frightened men who stood behind him. No cheers nor cries came from them, just an unsettling silence. They all knew the battle plan was a suicide mission. Most of them were bakers and ironworkers, even a couple of sales merchants, but none had any experience fighting.

They were not given strong weapons, just old, warped blades that had been laying around the barracks for decades. The armor they were given were extras, intended for archers on the battlement. They did not consist of any metal plates to protect them from deadly blows—merely made of just padded leather with thin cloth sleeves.

Zeke faced the kingdom's wall, where he saw the flames of torches bouncing around on the battlement. He was sure if he could see their lights, they could see his. Nonetheless, he nudged his mount with his heels as he led his men toward the wall with their torches still burning bright.

As they drew closer to the kingdom—just as Dagrus had said—the gates opened, and a flood of ten thousand Golden Men stormed toward them. Arrows from the battlement flew past the foot soldiers and struck the recruits and their mounts; their bodies stumbled as frightened mares tossed off others.

Though the initial attack took just a few moments, Zeke and his remaining men felt as if their death took hours to come upon them. They fought as hard as they could, trying to hold on to the hope of not dying in the onslaught, but their weak blows and inexperience did nothing to alleviate their fears.

Once the Taleanic army engulfed the Senturian recruits, the other two groups of knights approached, and the air filled with the sound of hundreds of whistling metal bolts. In the midst of the storm of arrows, Zeke was pitted against a massive minotaur, who swung his mace toward the troll's head. Zeke parried the strong blow with his sword, but his arms grew weak to the point where he could barely hold up his weapon, but he managed to keep a tight grip and blocked more of the mace's sudden swings until a bolt pierced beneath the minotaur's helmet and into his throat.

The sight of the blood and death shook Zeke as he imagined the bolt could have easily had struck him. He continued to subconsciously swing his blade, only focusing on his own life and the metal bolts hurling through the sky.

As he continued to fight for his survival, his focus trailed toward a fellow recruit lying on the ground with an arrow protruding from his abdomen, pleading for Zeke to euthanize him and put him out of his misery.

While Zeke focused on something other than the battle, a blade ripped through his arm, and blood gushed from the opened wound. With the loss of blood rising, he grew weaker but refused to succumb to the pain and numbness in his limbs. All around him, Zeke saw the large numbers of the Golden Men dwindling down, but at the same time, lay the bodies of his once neighbors and friends.

Zeke continued to fight for his life but quickly felt a series of pinches in his side. His gaze darted down to see three arrows sticking out of him. He removed them from his torso, then turned his attention back to the battle, only to see a mace as it collided into his skull.

Dagrus and O'Bryon viewed their plan as a grand one—sending the recruits as decoys and shooting them and the Golden Men down like jackalopes in a cage. The ambush was quick, and as the last Senturian arrow hit the ground, the recruits and the Golden Men had all fallen.

The two remaining Senturian groups approached the city, picking off the archers placed upon the battlement as they drew near. As they passed through the city gates, a faint sound of a horn blasted, but it was silenced as an arrow impaled the hornblower, his body toppling over the parapet.

The knights stormed through the streets of Talean, slaughtering any civilian they saw outside as they advanced toward Azreal's manor.

O'Bryon led a small group of knights inside while Dagrus and the others remained outside, patrolling the courtyards.

Inside, O'Bryon and his knights split into groups as they scouted the many rooms of the golden palace.

As they explored the manor, O'Bryon and his men discovered an empty bedchamber. The room had a foul, stale smell. In large patches upon the floor, walls, and parts of the ceiling were faint-burgundy and brown stains. Some of the colored spots held deep gash marks embedded in the stone surfaces they covered, as if some great animal had made a kill in the room.

Examining the room, one knight noticed fragments of clay and wood in one corner of the chamber and ran his fingers along one of the gouges. "What could've made this?"

"It could have been a number of things," O'Bryon responded as he glared at the destruction before exiting the room.

As they wandered down one of the corridors, O'Bryon noticed Marquess Solaris. His complexion seemed to be of a heather purple, and he looked unfocused as he moped around, touching random items along the walls as he went. O'Bryon nodded toward two knights and motioned for them to grab the djinn, who made no indication of having noticed the men approaching him. They each grabbed an arm and forced him to turn around as O'Bryon drew a sword and pressed the tip to his throat.

Before he was questioned, Solaris laughed—a crazed and hysterical sound. His once-white eyes were red from irritation.

Much to the Senturians' surprise, Solaris began to ramble. "Kill me if you must, I will die soon anyway. My lord is not here. Duchess Anina is dead, and I will soon join her. So, spare me the wait, and kill me now."

Solaris's legs gave out from under him, his body only staying upright from the knights' grasp on his arms. The Senturians stared at each other, stunned by the djinn's words, before he shrieked, "Do not let me die like she did! Please, just kill me now!"

O'Bryon lowered his sword and motioned for his men to release the djinn.

Solaris raised his collapsed body onto his knees and

hands. His eyes, stinging in his skull, looked at the sword the djinn in front of him was holding, then to his white eyes.

"Kill me!" Solaris screamed, but O'Bryon denied his request and returned his sword to its sheath. "Come on, you piss-stained bastard! Fucking kill me!"

A smirk crossed O'Bryon's face as he knelt. "Who, or what, are you so fearful of?"

Solaris's brow furrowed as he spat onto the yellow djinn's face.

O'Bryon wiped the saliva from around his eyes as he chuckled. "You made a deal with the gods and failed to uphold your end of it. Am I correct?"

Solaris hung his head low, not speaking.

The two knights standing behind him made an *X* in the air with their hands, then in unison, they chanted, *"Remove thy scent, and cleanse thy touch. Protect thee from the debt of the dreshdis. To Nya and Afria, I plea."*

O'Bryon glanced over the crouched djinn and upon the two knights. "What are you doing?"

"Ser, if he is marked by the dreshdis, we risk takin' upon their mark onto our backs," one knight stated with hesitation and fear.

"Dreshdis are monsters, I will give them that, but they hold no stronger power than I with this blade," O'Bryon told his men as he glanced down at Solaris. "I shall spare my blade of your foul blood. After all, you cannot hide from the shadows."

Solaris stayed poised over as O'Bryon and his men left the corridor. As they made their way out, they heard screams and cursing from Solaris, followed by the loud sounds of crashing and banging of Solaris flipping over tables and knocking pictures off the walls.

Once O'Bryon and the other knights had regrouped, he met with Dagrus.

"Lord Azreal is not here, and Duchess Anina is presumed dead," O'Bryon informed. "Marquess Solaris is inside but is marked by the dreshdis. We need to keep him confined within these walls and await Lord Azreal's return."

Flooded Thoughts

Duchess Zorie wept as she watched the denizens of BrightHelm fill the streets and shuffle toward a bank in the region of Galdwulf, passing between the City of BrightHelm and the Abyss Ocean. Her gaze trailed over the large group of mourning residents as the Senturians patrolling the streets heckled them, and she halted as she noticed the banners of a burning tower.

Growing disgusted at the sight of the Senturian banners, Zorie turned from the window. As she traipsed toward the door on the other side of her chamber, she ran her hands down her dress—a unique dress she had made herself just for the occasion—smoothing out the wrinkles. She had used a sleek black material and provided red ribbons for the lace on the back and the red roses embroidered around the cuffs of the sleeves.

Zorie took a deep breath to calm herself before she approached her chamber's door and knocked. A burly Senturian cyclops opened the door and scowled down at her. She detoured her attention to keep the knight from seeing the mournfulness on her face, then raised her gaze after calming herself yet again. "I'm ready to go to my lord's funeral."

The cyclops grunted as he grasped her arm and escorted her down the corridor. Caski had commanded the knights to not speak with the duchess—a prisoner in her own tower, as she was—for her ranking was the only thing protecting her from a cell in the dungeons.

As they continued down the passageway, Zorie gasped as they passed the door to Cornelius's cabinet.

"Ser! Please, I must get something from that room for my Lady Kalama."

The cyclops rolled his eye as he released his grip so the duchess could retrieve whatever it was she felt was needed. Zorie took no time in the room, knowing what she was after and where it was.

Zorie returned with a leather book held tight in her hands as she pressed it against her bosom. The knight scowled at the duchess for grabbing an old book that looked as if it were to fall apart at any second. He shut the door, then nudged her along as he followed behind her through the rest of the castle.

As they exited the castle, Zorie turned her head toward the cyclops. "Will we be taking the carriage?"

she asked, not wanting to walk all the way across the kingdom, but the knight just gave her a slight shove to keep her moving along.

Upon reaching the end of the courtyard, the knight found it within himself to help the duchess over the rubble of the destroyed wall, holding onto her hand as she stepped amongst the stones. Upon traversing the ruins of the castle's wall, Zorie stood frozen in horror.

Down the street, in front of the Kingdom Hall, hung Cornelius's lifeless corpse. His bruised and naked body dangled for all the townsfolk to see. His smoky eyes peered under his open eyelids. His bloodied face caved in—jaw drooped open, exposing the gaps from missing and broken teeth. His neck stretched under the noose, barely holding onto his torso. Deformed limbs slumped from the mangled body.

Still staring at the horrendous sight—with one hand gripped tightly onto the book and the other covering her mouth as she gagged—Zorie felt a nudge on her back from the knight telling her to keep moving. As she began to walk on, her eyes fixated upon the sickening sight of her former lord, unable to look away from the tragedy.

†

Kalama stood trembling in the boudoir of her private estate, just east of the BrightHelm in Nuwulf, and stared at the old, rustic mirror of her vanity. Her bronze figure was dressed in a black satin gown draping to the floor, and long flowing sleeves hid her arms. A silver choker adorned with black diamonds encircled her neck. Her earrings and headdress matched the choker as she placed a sheer black veil over her flaming curls.

Thoughts flooded her mind of all the wondrous memories she'd had with her beloved Brighton. So many centuries they had spent loving and caring for one and another and bearing eleven beautiful children, but as she stared at her reflection, her heart ached in remembrance of her beloved dying in her arms.

Now, after all the cold, lonely nights she had spent laying in bed, the thought of her Brighton being gone was still incomprehensible. Her body became numb as she grew anxious, knowing it would be hard to say goodbye to her Brighton; even with their children there to support her, they could only do so much.

Tears steamed off her cheeks as she remembered their last lovemaking on the morning of the festival. Brighton was not in his younger years, but he was still just as beautiful in her eyes as ever. She knew her beloved would one day grow old and pass from the world, but the knowledge did nothing to lessen the pain she felt knowing she would probably never be reacquainted with her husband. She begged and pleaded to the gods to make her mortal so she could grow old with him, but her wish was never granted.

Kalama took a deep and shuddering breath as she turned from the mirror, wiping the tears from her face. She wanted to look strong in front of her children and for the many people who still looked at her as the Lady of Metagore. She was not the duchess, nor held any authoritative role—just the wife of the late lord—but many still thought of her as their queen and had followed her out of the city when Cornelius had been crowned as the new lord.

Silence filled her chamber as she turned her glossy eyes toward a large window. A shuddering chill traveled through her body as she prepared herself to venture into the dark and cruel kingdom she had grown to love. She sighed as she placed a pair of black satin gloves on her trembling hands. Her children awaited her downstairs, ready to leave for the ceremony.

Kalama exited her chamber and lumbered to the staircase, each step stabbing at her like a shard of glass as she ventured down the staircase of her private mansion Brighton had made for her. One step, then another; with each, the pain grew stronger. Memories of her first pregnancy and how it had pained her to go down the stairs of the castle while carrying twins replayed in her mind. But this time was different—this time Brighton was not here to assist her.

More steps followed along with more memories. One of Brighton chasing Brande, who liked to take off with her father's crown, proclaiming she was the Queen of Metagore. Her auburn curls bounced as Brighton grasped her running body and threw her into the air, catching her as she giggled with joy.

As she approached the bottom of the staircase, her tears had returned and streamed down her face. She gripped onto the silver handrail. Each memory pained her more than the last.

As she reached the ground floor, the most beautiful memory she had of her Brighton replayed through her mind—her and Brighton sharing their first dance as man and wife in the garden behind their old castle.

Kalama collapsed onto the floor as tears gushed from her clenched eyes. "Oh, my Brighton, why did you have to leave me?"

She could not bear it anymore. She wanted her husband back. She wanted to lay by his side at night. She wanted him to watch their children grow old. She wanted her Brighton back.

The pain and sorrow pulsed through her body as her emotions grew rampant, and her skin and gown materialized into raging flames. With all the heartache, she did not care that her engulfing flames were causing destruction to her home. She saw no point to stop her crying. The last time she had seen her husband was the day he had died, cradled in her arms. Now she was going to see him once more—a hundred and forty-three days later—just to see the Abyss carry away his lifeless body.

Rushed footsteps approached her as she kept sobbing. From her glazed eyes, she saw her eldest son, Branton, knelt beside her as he wrapped an arm around her. Kalama buried her face into her son's chest as she tried to calm herself, eventually able to extinguish her flames.

Her heart was shattered, but Kalama did what she

could to stand and compose herself for the sake of her children. She tried to force a smile with her quivering lips as she beheld the sight of her sons and daughters, all except Branton, who was the striking image of his father, for fear of not being able to control her emotions.

"We all miss Father," Branton said in a brittle tone as he gently stroked his mother's back.

"I ... I want him back," Kalama managed to force the words through her sobbing.

"We all do, but we need to be heading off soon. You know how Father was about tardiness."

Kalama nodded as a small laugh managed to escape.

As Kalama gazed upon her children, she noticed her two youngest, Aden and Eira, hiding around the edge of the doorframe. It pained her to see them frightened of their mother's outbursts of despair. She forced another smile as she approached them and placed a hand underneath their chins.

"My darlings, let us be strong for Papa, yes?"

"Yes, Momma," Eira hiccupped as she buried her face into Kalama's bosom.

After a moment of embracing her two youngest, Kalama and her children exited the estate and boarded three carriages.

Senturian knights escorted the carriages through the

streets of BrightHelm, threatening the crowd of people who began to flock to the convoy.

"All praise Lady Kalama!" an elf shouted as he spotted the royal carriages.

Angered by the admiration the citizen showed toward the widow, a Senturian stormed toward him with a dagger in hand. He clenched the back of the elf's neck and thrust the blade into his abdomen.

"If ya art to praise her, then praise her on yer knees," the knight whispered into the elf's ear, then removed his blade.

As the elf collapsed to the ground, the Senturian flung his dagger around at the other townsfolk. "Art there any other humas that wish to meet the same fate?" he grumbled loudly as the denizens retreated into their homes.

A Light in the Waves

Kalama and her family arrived at the Galdwulf coastline, where a small crowd of people had already gathered to witness the ceremony of the Abyss taking away their late lord. The carriage ride to the funeral seemed too short to count. It did not even occur to Kalama that they had entered into the city and passed her once-beautiful castle. It was now a dark and forsaken place, taken charge by the Senturian army. The walls around the castle were crumbling, and innocent blood of those who had opposed the invasion stained the streets.

The pit of her stomach seemed to weigh heavily as she stepped from the carriage. The cliffs around the coastline were thirty legs high and towered over the jagged rocks below them. The banks in Galdwulf had been one of Brighton's favorite places to play hide-and-seek with their children when they were younger.

Kalama felt a jab at her heart as she remembered another memory. She bit her lower lip, trying to subdue the threatening tears she had suppressed during the ride there.

Kalama took a breath and fixed her posture as she approached the crowd, her children following behind. The citizens of BrightHelm still looked upon her with elegance and beauty as she walked broken before them. She tried not to let anyone see the pain she had been suffering.

The crowd, wearing all black and grasping onto small wreaths, heard her steps get closer and heard the crackling of her hair as it sizzled with sparks. Sadness consumed their faces, for they understood what Kalama was going through. She saw some of the villagers Brighton had helped build cottages for outside of BrightHelm to help protect them from the cold. They had never stopped thanking him for his kindness and determination. She also saw some of the rulers from across the Abyss who had been good friends with Brighton throughout the years.

Kalama was brought to tears as each attendee clasped her hands and squeezed them in respect and comfort. She received tight hugs, kisses on the cheeks, and teary smiles as she ventured through the crowd. Her heart burned with love and gratefulness toward the wonderful townsfolk. Her husband had affected so many lives during his reign, in both BrightHelm and the other kingdoms.

As Kalama sauntered to the front of the crowd, a hand gently caught her arm. She turned and came face to face with Duchess Zorie, her eyes rimmed with tears. The two had been good friends even before Zorie had been granted the role of duchess. Kalama had shared many stories and laughs with her, but she never, until then, had shared in sorrow. This day would be their first, and hopefully last, time they would share tears.

Zorie had worn her chocolate hair in a tight coronet adorned with little pinned pearls. Her skin was pale as the snow on the ground, and her freckles seemed to blend in as Kalama studied her face. Zorie's black gown spilled onto the rough terrain like ink flowing from its bottle.

Zorie took a deep breath before speaking, trying to find the right words to say without crying. "My ... Lady Kalama." A shudder came from her voice. "It is so good to see you."

Kalama sniffed back some tears. "Duchess Zorie, it is good to see you too. Thank you for coming to my husband's fu-ner-al." She broke from the word, as it proved too hard to say.

"I am so sorry that you had to go through this loss. Lord Brighton ... he did so much to see everyone happy. Especially to see you happy, my Lady."

Kalama turned away for a moment to gather herself before speaking. "I am sorry for your loss as well. All of us loved him tremendously."

Zorie nodded and squeezed the widow's hand. "I have something for you. I know you had loaned it to Lord Cornelius just before his coronation, but he will no longer be in need of it."

Zorie retrieved a worn leather book from her black coat, sniffling as she brought it out. Kalama knew what it was—one of the many journals Brighton had written in over the course of his life. Kalama clenched her jaw, fighting the horrible sobs that threatened to escape as Zorie handed her the book, the journals being all she had to keep the memories they had shared alive. Kalama embraced Zorie tightly and thanked her for all she had done for her and her family throughout the years.

Kalama's gloved hands shook as she held the old book. She was disheartened to know there would be no more memories written about, but she knew she wanted to spend time with Brighton before the ceremony commenced. It would still be another hour before it would begin, and she wanted to use that time to say her final goodbyes.

Her heartbeat grew stronger as she trudged toward the front of the crowd. Resting in front of everyone lay Brighton's body, glowing with a blue aura. She felt her heart shatter once more as she gazed upon him. He lay on a raft bed beside the gentle waters. Set in the bedding of the raft and surrounding his body were a hundred unlit candles. His aged face still looked beautiful to her as she did not care for the wrinkles under his eyes or the sag of his skin—he would always be young in her eyes.

Brighton wore a white tabard and pants with a golden trim. A pelt of white fur draped over his right shoulder to give him a wealthy stature. His fingers bore the many rings he had worn during his reign. His hair and beard were brushed neatly, and a silver and ivory crown rested on top of his head. His sword was sashed to his hip, displaying the artistic skill and craftsmanship of the obsidian-tipped blade. His appearance was still majestic and powerful as he lay lifeless on the raft bed.

Kalama wanted to stroke his white hair again and braid it into a fine fishtail. She made her way closer to the raft to touch her husband once more. Unfortunately, as she was to touch Brighton's glowing figure, a strong, authoritative hand grabbed her shoulder and jerked her away.

"Ma'am, ya aren't allowed to touch the body," a scratchy voice informed Kalama, her eyes widening in shock as she turned toward the Senturian knight.

"How dare you not let me touch my husband! I am his wife!" she shouted as her hair sparked underneath the veiled headdress.

"I could care less who ya are. My orders are to let no one approach the body," he grumbled as his hand tightened on her shoulder in warning. "That includes ya as well."

Another memory flashed through Kalama's mind of when she and Brighton had first met. They were trapped in a wretched Penéné cell, plotting a way to escape from the labyrinth. They were sore and tired, but they had to stay on their toes, for the guards had only one thing on their minds: to torment and rape them.

Kalama remembered becoming overpowered with rage and how she had latched herself onto one of the guards. Her anger had been so intense that her entire body had engulfed in flames, and the mere touch from her hand had heated a guard's armor to such temperatures that his body burnt and melted inside his steel plating. She had become the monster she never wanted to be, but the only thing on her mind was saving herself and the elf she had just met.

"Ma'am," the raspy voice spoke once more, bringing her back to reality. "Ya must return back to the crowd, or I will have—"

Instinctively, fire radiated from her slender body. The flames startled the knight, and he released his grip. Kalama imagined the guard burning alive under his armor, but she refused to let her emotions get the best of her. She had spent centuries mastering her powers and learning how and when to use them.

"For ya," the guard stammered, "I will allow ya to see the corpse."

Kalama glanced at the other knights approaching her after witnessing the flames, but the first commanded them to stand down.

As the fire around her faded, Kalama glanced at her husband as she sat at his side. Tears swelled once more as she touched Brighton's hand.

Taking a deep breath, she stroked her husband's face. "Hello, my love. I … I have missed you so much. I really did not want to say goodbye to you … Not ever." Her voice broke with the last two words.

She retrieved the journal and rested it in her lap. She was hesitant to open it, afraid she would start falling apart while reading. After a moment of debating, she shook away the thought and opened the book to a random page. In the corner of the page was a small drawing of their wedding day. Kalama looked into the sky, trying to gather all the courage she had to read aloud to her husband.

Before she began, her children gathered around her, tears flowing as they wanted to say their last goodbyes as well. Eira and Aden embraced each other as they looked away. Brighton had loved each of them and taught them many life lessons before he had passed.

Noelle covered her mouth to force away the tears, her hair flaming a little in her sadness. Brande and Titus held each other's hand for comfort as they looked at their father. Branton put his hands on Keegan's shoulders as he cried softly to himself. The children tried hard to control themselves and keep their flames at bay, but it was too hard with their emotions getting the best of them. Branton was the only one who managed to not let his powers control him.

"Now, now children. We are supposed to be proud and thankful for what your father has done for us all. Let us enjoy this time we have together with him one last time before he leaves us," Kalama said through her tears.

"Why is Papa's body blue?" Aden asked as they

settled around his father's body.

Fiammetta wrapped her arm around her younger brother and gave him a quick squeeze. "It's there to preserve his body for the ceremony."

Kalama opened Brighton's journal once more and read the pages aloud. So many adventures and memories flooded back to her as she read each passage. They laughed and cried, sharing in the beautiful moments he had recalled in his writings. He wrote about the wedding and the birth of the twins. He wrote about the times he would gaze at his wife with such adore in his eyes as she would sit in the garden or breastfeed one of the children. Upon each of the pages, he would always mention how beautiful and blessed he was to have Kalama in his life.

The pain that once ached Kalama's heart had all seemed to have disappeared as she read the journal. She was glad Zorie had decided to return the book to her at the funeral and not on some other day. It was just what Kalama needed to make their goodbye a little easier on her and the children.

She finished reading from the journal as the archbishop and two of the viscounts approached the raft bed. The priest looked at Kalama and her family with such sorrow in his yellow catlike eyes, knitting his boned hands together as he bowed humbly to them. He did not tell them to move away, for he knew they would greatly appreciate it if they were allowed to stay beside Brighton until it was time to release him to the Abyss.

The archbishop knelt close to Brighton's body and

chanted something under his breath. The blue glow around the late lord's body vanished as he lay there, looking the same as the day he had passed. The archbishop glanced at Kalama and gave her a reassuring smile, then looked at the mourning crowd.

"Ye art gathered this morn to witness the passing of thy beloved late lord, Lord Brighton," the archbishop addressed the crowd as Kalama and her children rose to their feet.

The widow stood there, tightly grasping onto the journal, tears strolling down from her eyes as the skeletal face of the archbishop glanced at her. "Would ya like to light the first of the candles?"

Kalama responded as she bent over and picked up the candle that rested in the crease of his left shoulder and neck. She cradled the candle in her hand for a moment, then pinched the wick with her fingers as a small flame burned brightly. She closed her eyes and held the candle close to her heart, embracing the warmth of her husband one last time before she returned it to the raft, then kissed Brighton's cold lips.

"I will always love you with all of my heart," Kalama whispered into his ear before standing.

The children each followed her by lighting a single candle and replacing it into the raft.

Once they had concluded lighting their candles, the archbishop waved his left hand over the raft, igniting the wicks of the remaining candles. His yellow eyes scanned the mourning crowd as he spoke. "Unto Iden, we commend the soul of thy majesty, thy late Lord

Brighton, and we commit his glorious body unto Artus's deep waters as Zallah takes thee away. In sure and certain hope that Afria will rest thy fragile minds, for Nya's taken a great soul from thou midst. Libras grant thee thy's strength to carry on with our days upon Trillis's humble earth. May we never forget how humble thy great lord was as Taac guides thou's empty vessel through the crossing to the other side."

The two viscounts standing behind the skeletal lich stepped forward and placed the raft into the water, giving it a slight push as it floated away. Many of the townsfolk placed wreaths into the ocean they had made in remembrance of their late lord and nudged them as they drifted off, following behind their lord's raft.

"Beacon in the darkness," the archbishop said loudly, "light of hope. From the stars we came, to the stars we return. Let thou soul be a light in the waves, and thou's memory a fire unto thy's heart."

The crowd watched as their lord and their wreaths floated into the Abyss and faded away into the horizon as the ceremony, short as it was, had concluded.

The archbishop approached Kalama and her children, giving his condolences before he left. Following behind him was the group of citizens who also wished to say their goodbyes and condolences to the widow and her family.

†

An hour had passed when the last of the attendees had paid their condolences and tried to comfort the family; then alas, only they remained. The children all huddled around their mother as they stared across the empty and still waters. After a moment of gazing at the ocean, Kalama pulled the last memories of her husband from her coat and opened the book once more.

This time, when she opened it, she noticed a page further back, protruding out ever so slightly. She eagerly turned the pages to find a piece of paper placed in-between the sheets. The ink looked fresh and wasn't faded like the other pages. Her brows furrowed as she read the piece of parchment.

Thy darling Kalama,

Please do not be tearful of thy's departure. Thou dost not want to see you cry any more tears than what thou hast already seen. Remember of all the wondrous things we hath experienced together. All of the happiness we hath shared. All of the love we hath shown to each other. Thou art so jubilant to hath been blessed in meeting you in Penora, that forsaken place that it is. Thou had never imagined to hath found a friend and the love of thy life there of all places.

You hath made life such a blessing and a joy. You hath given thee eleven of the most beautiful children to love and cherish. Thou doesn't regret a thing that we hath done together. You hath made thee the happiest and luckiest man in the world.

Thou doesn't want you to remember thy's death in such a horrid way. Thou wants you to remember that even though this is goodbye, thou will always be with you, and thou will always watch over you.

Thy Lady Kalama, oh how thou hast loved you for so many centuries, growing stronger with each passing. You hath been the light of thy's life, the rock that thou sought, the haven that thou needed.

You know thou hates saying goodbye, but Archbishop Bolkan has told thee that there is little hope to surviving 'til the next moon. It breaks thy heart that thou hast to leave you in this world, but know that thou hast loved you unconditionally. There's not been a day that's gone by that thou hasn't thought of how jovial you've made thee.

Kalama, thy love, thou needs you to do me one last favor. Thou needs you to continue to be cheerful and watch over our children as they grow. Thou art blessed to have been called your husband, more so than being given the title of lord.

This is our final goodbye, thy love, but thou will still be with you in your heart and watch over you from the stars. Thou doeth love you, thy darling Kalama. Thou loves you with all of thy heart.

Goodbye from your beloved, Brighton.

As she read the letter, Kalama covered her mouth, trying to keep the sobs from escaping, but she could not stop them. She clutched the letter against her chest as the tears rained down her steaming face.

47

ΠEWS OF FIRE AΠD SAΠD

Ky lay fully exposed next to Darius as he ran his large fingers through her black hair. She trailed her fingers from his broad shoulders, down his chest, and across his chiseled abdomen, examining his collection of scars as she made her way down his body.

"Do you remember how you got all of these?" she asked in a soft and seductive voice.

Darius's large red eyes stared into her's. "I remember a few, but most I have forgotten. The majority of them are from my time as a Golden Man."

Darius glanced to his right thigh and pointed to a circular scar, tracing it with his fingertip. "This one ... This one I received when I was on my first deployment to the Kingdom of Penora. We had taken a small village in Pimi and took up their mounts as our own. We made camp one night, and at one point, I walked behind some of the steeds when one of them got spooked and kicked me in the leg."

Ky's eyes widen as she leaned her head forward. "Were you all right?"

"It nearly broke my leg." Darius turned his attention to a large scar on the side of his abdomen, then to another identical mark running parallel to the first. "These two I got from another trip to Penora. We were in battle on the coast of Tahllua, and one of the Penéné came up behind me and stabbed me in the back. I was moving around, fighting off another Penéné warrior. The blade went all the way through me, but luckily, it missed my insides."

Darius continued to examine his battle wounds, then ran his finger across a scar above his throat. The scar stretched from the bottom of his right jaw, across the top of his Adam's apple, and toward the middle of the left side of his neck.

"This is one of the earlier ones I remember getting. I was young, maybe just a few days after my mother was taken from me. Azreal and I were in one of his father's courtyards, fighting. He pulled a knife on me—it must have been his father's or something. But either way, he stepped toward me and swung his arm out and just barely nicked me with the tip of the blade." Darius chuckled. "That was the closest that he will ever get to killing me. After I had realized that he had sliced my throat, I stomped as hard as I could onto his shin, snapping it in half. He better be glad I didn't kill him right then and there."

"I'm glad that you survived all of your battles," Ky said as she shifted her bare body on top of Darius's, straddling his waist.

A large, warm smile grew upon Ky's thin face as she nibbled her bottom lip. "I felt my stomach move earlier today, and it wasn't in need of food," she informed him as she grabbed his callused hands and placed them on her belly.

Darius's brow furrowed as his eyes widened. He felt unsettling in his stomach as his blood pulsed through his body faster than it had ever done. His dark skin turned a shade lighter from the shock of the news. A smile managed to stretch across his face as he rubbed Ky's stomach with his sweaty palm. Everything in the room turned to a blur—the sounds, the sights, everything. The only thing still in focus was the small bump he softly caressed.

After a moment of being mesmerized by the news, Darius glanced at Ky's face as it glowed with love.

"We're having a baby," she told him as tears of excitement trailed down her tan cheeks.

Darius returned his gaze to where the unborn infant lay resting. "When I become lord over the six kingdoms, I will do away with the election of a new lord for if I perish. I will make it so that he will be my heir by blood and that he will wear the crown and take my spot upon the throne."

Ky rubbed the back of Darius's hands. "But what if

we have a girl?"

"Then she will become the true Queen of Fire."

Ky leaned forward as the two embraced. Darius shifted their bodies so that he was on top as she laid stretched out on the bed. As he began to penetrate her rounding body, a knock came upon the door.

"M'Lord," a feminine voice said from the corridor. "Two scrolls hath arrived for ya today."

"Just a moment," Darius grumbled.

Darius stood from the bed and tossed a sheet over Ky's naked form before grabbing a piece of bedding for himself. After covering his manhood, he shuffled to the door. Opening it, he saw one of his housemaids—a small elf—standing on the other side.

"Let me see them," he stated as he grabbed one of the scrolls and opened it. A smile grew across his face as he skimmed the letter. He dropped the scroll to the floor and grabbed the second.

"What do they say?" Ky asked.

"BrightHelm and Talean have been conquered," he responded with a pep in his voice, then turned to the housemaid. "Send word back to them saying to head west toward Alberon."

"I'm not educated in letterin', m'Lord."

"Then find yourself a scribe to letter it," Darius grumbled in irritation.

"Right away, m'Lord."

The elf started to walk away, but her lord stopped her.

"Huma, when you send word back, tell Ser Darut to

have Azreal brought to me."

"Azreal has been captured?" Ky asked, perplexed how he could have been apprehended, and in BrightHelm of all places.

Darius looked her way, a devious grin anointing his face as a chortle escaped him. "The gods are truly in our favor."

Heed My Warning – Baush Lié Mulstré

As the sun rose, Moll'ar and a large group of Alberian tribe members had begun their seventy-first day of digging the moat.

As the morning grew later, a young, redheaded beauty rode toward the crowd on a kelpie. The young lady had dark green eyes and long copper hair that cascaded to her thighs. Her skin was visible under the few pieces of seaweed wrapping around her boy-like chest, and her short pants appeared to be made from selk hide.

She rode past the crowd and found her lord working.

"*Lord Moll'ar,*" she shouted as she dismounted her kelpie.

Moll'ar turned toward her as she approached him.

"*I am Fiannah. I am from the settlement of Uslana,*" she said with a broken voice as her body trembled.

"*What is the matter?*" Moll'ar asked as he saw the fear in the young lady's eyes and heard the haste in her words.

"*My village. It has been destroyed by the lions. And many others have suffered the same fate, m'Lord.*"

Moll'ar grabbed the young lady by her shoulders, trying to steady her body. "*I was not aware of any villages bordering Kiden Hill.*"

"*There is not, m'Lord. My village is just two leagues upriver from the Fork in Redthorn.*"

Moll'ar released his grip and stood shocked. "*Why were the lions so far from their homeland?*"

"*That is what we were wondering too, m'Lord.*" Fiannah's bottom lip trembled as she wept. "*They came and destroyed our crops and homes. They slaughtered most of our livestock, while the rest were chased away.*" She paused, tears still flowing from her green eyes. "*We now have nothing.*"

Moll'ar turned to the group of workers. "*Pol,*" he shouted, then waved for his duke to join them. He turned back toward the selkie. "*Go with Duke Pol to my manor. You will be safe there.*" He turned to the satyr to confirm he had heard the order.

"*What about my family? They are still out there.*"

Moll'ar looked at her with a reassuring stare. "*I will go gather the rest of the villagers and bring them back safely. Now go and follow Duke Pol.*"

While Pol led Fiannah and her kelpie into the capital, Moll'ar sprinted toward the fields, heading for the closest settlement. As he ran, he transformed into his canine form, knowing he would make faster ground on four legs instead of two. He continued to dash through the rolling hills of the plains. Navigating through Feather's Bow, he visited many settlements, transforming to his elven form to alert any civilian he found to head toward the capital for safety.

All of the settlements he explored seemed unharmed from the attacks—the lions not having migrated westward—but as he ran farther east, moving into Redthorn, the sights drastically changed. Some settlements seemed empty of life; the fallen villagers strolled through the streets, some still gripping pikes and shovels in hand. While other settlements had panicked survivors, struggling to help their wounded family and neighbors.

It was a massacre. The villages were unable to withstand the assault from the bloodthirsty lions. The felines had demolished hut doors. Bloodied gouges adorned the walls and window frames where the lions had attacked the huts to reach the frantic villagers within.

Moll'ar shocked at the desolation, almost forgetting his original mission as he tried helping the survivors before telling them to head toward safety or to wait for the carriages he would send if they couldn't make the journey.

Moll'ar made it to Uslana in Redthorn. Crumbled clay homes and piles of splintered wood riddled the village. Slaughtered bicorn and catoblepones lay amongst the bloodstained fields around the village. As Moll'ar paced into the vandalized village, an elderly couple approached him.

"*Did our daughter, Fiannah, find ya, m'Lord?*" the elderly man asked.

"*Yes,*" Moll'ar responded. "*She is the one who alerted me of the attacks.*"

"*What are ya goin' to do 'bout this?*" an angered troll shouted in disgust as he approached.

Moll'ar turned to the disgruntled villager. "*Go, take shelter in the capital. You will be safe inside the walls. My advisors and I will discuss what future actions will be taken to contain the lion threat.*"

"*Ya want me to leave? What is goin' to be done 'bout m'livestock and crops?*"

"*You would rather protect your livestock than your family?*" Moll'ar asked as the troll's nostrils flared. "*I will compensate each of you for your losses. But I cannot replace your's or your family's lives if you decide to be arrogant and stay here.*"

Moll'ar turned to the few survivors gathered around him. "*Gather all of your belongings! I will send carriages to haul you and your things to the capital. Please, I beg you all to heed my warning. The lions are just the beginnin'. There are more dangerous predators that could come from the mountains and rampage our lands. So, I beg you, please take shelter in the capital.*"

After Moll'ar had talked to the villagers, he returned to his manor, where he convened with his duke.

"*We need all of the kingdom's carriages sent out to all of the villages outside of these walls,*" he urgently told Pol.

"*But, my Lord, we do not have enough catoblepones nor herdbeasts to pull all of the carriages.*"

"*Go to the stables and prepare the kelpie, pegasi, and unicorns. We need those carriages sent out now!*"

"*As you wish, my Lord.*"

As Pol exited the manor, Moll'ar glanced at the selkie from before, who sat on a bench inside the manor's entryway. "*How are you holdin' up?*"

"*Better,*" Fiannah responded, still dejected by the tragedy. "*Did you bring m'parents back?*"

"*No, but I did find them,*" Moll'ar responded as he approached the bench. "*They are packin' what is salvageable, and I am sendin' carriages out to help bring them and their belongings here. They should arrive sometime in the night hours.*"

A great deal of relief fell upon Fiannah as she managed to force a smile. "*Thank you, m'Lord.*"

Moll'ar reached into his pocket and removed a handful of different colored chips. "*Here, take these.*"

"*I cannot accept those from—*"

"*Shh.*" Moll'ar placed a hand over the selkie's lips. "*I do not need these. Take them and buy yourself some food, or a stay at an inn.*"

Fiannah looked at the chips still sitting in Moll'ar's hand, knowing it equated to more than a year's wage for her family. She slowly retrieved the coins. "*Thank you, m'Lord.*"

Moll'ar smiled as he stood and traversed through his manor toward the hall. When he entered the room, his marquess and a warrior greeted him. *"Marquess Terus, what brings you here?"*

"Duke Pol brought it to my attention earlier that there were lion attacks in Redthorn."

"There were probably attacks in Willowgate as well," Moll'ar stated as he approached the dining table and took a seat, Terus and the warrior following behind him. *"I do not know the magnitude of the attacks. But what I did see, it was devastatin'. We have to do something to protect against the lions."*

"If the lions are moving out of Kiden Hill, what is stopping other creatures from doing the same and leaving the mountains?"

"We still have a large number of warriors stationed here, do we not?" Moll'ar asked but didn't wait for an answer. *"Send five thousand men to help with the moat in the morning. The faster we get the moat done, the faster we can protect our tribes."*

"What about the griffins, or the manticores?" Terus asked, concerned for the kingdom. *"Or worse, the dragon?"*

"The only thing we can do is ready our archers and pray to the gods that the dragon of Eryn does not come."

FLASHING FEVER

With the war raging on, Darius revisited the forge deep in the iron veins of Mount Dumas. He was determined to make sure the behemoth-sized weapons were built precisely to his prints. Any obscured changes could be catastrophic and would delay the completion, wasting the workers and Darius's time and money.

"Thou still dost not see the point in havin' these vessels so large," the forgemaster said to his lord. "We will soon have to start movin' the parts to Parele so we can finish with their completions."

Darius glanced over the ironworkers as they banged on the metal, then turned his attention to the cyclops. "It's not your job to grasp the concept of my weapons. It's your job to oversee and make sure they are made to my specifications."

"Thou understands, m'Lord, but—"

"But nothing. And what's this talk about moving the weapons outside the city? I want them created here, close to the kingdom."

"Thou art aware, m'Lord," the forgemaster grumbled as he wiped the sweat from his lone eye's brow. "We would have more room to work across the river where there would be less traffic. Thou hast already secured a piece o' land next to Stone Point—maybe an hour's journey on foot."

Irritated at the potential delay in his plans, Darius accepted that he could do little about the situation. His red eyes squinted in exasperation as he nodded. "Fine, do what you have to. Just know that I'll deduct a gold piece out of everyone's pay for each day that you all are set back."

"I understand, m'Lord."

Darius left the veins and headed toward his manor. While he walked the city's dark, stone streets, his marquess found his way to him.

"My Lord," Lucius greeted. "Three Ajirian ships are pulling into the docks as we speak."

Darius glanced toward the city's eastern wall as a smile grew on his rough face. "So, Princess Abelia has finally arrived."

"Was you expecting her, my Lord?"

"Aye. I sent word to her queen for the need of some resources. Now, we mustn't keep her await."

†

Darius and Lucius traveled to the docks in the eastern part of the city. As they approached, they saw three large ships sitting in port. The hollowed vessels donned a giant sail in the middle, topped with a purple flag featuring an insignia of a golden cross. Shipments of clay jars weighed down two of the ships while the other was the size of the first two combined and commissioned as the royal ship for the Queen of Ajia and her family.

Ten men surrounding a young dryad approached the two demons. The dryad's body looked withered and fragile—not holding any beauty Darius had imagined the Princess of Ajia would have. To each of her four sides stood an incubus, their wings raised to shelter her from the scorching sun, and in their hands, they waved large leaves, trying to keep the princess cool. Walking in front of her, two elves held large urns as they splashed water onto their princess's cracking skin. Four ogres dressed in light armor and carrying large spears led the dryad and her servants.

"Princess Abelia, it is an honor to make your acquaintance," Darius greeted.

"Lord Darius," Abelia said with a sniff of disdain. "We bring a thousand containers of *osami ess* from our queen."

"May we have a look?" Darius asked politely.

Abelia just rolled her eyes and motioned for them to

board the ships.

Lucius followed his lord onto one of the smaller ships, staring strangely at the clay jars. "What's *osami ess*?"

"Translated it means *flashing fever*," Darius answered as he opened a container. He stuck a few fingers inside the jar, feeling the dense, oily liquid. He removed his hand and sniffed the potent odor on his fingertips.

"I'm not familiar with any *flashing fever*."

Darius closed the jar, then glanced at Lucius. "You don't have to be familiar with it. Just know that it will help win this war—and many more to come."

Lucius stared with uncertainty at the jars, then back at his lord as they departed the ship and returned to Princess Abelia.

Growing unpleasant from the heat, Abelia spoke. "Let's talk about payment. My queen has set the price at a yellow chip per barrel of *osami ess*."

Lucius's eyes grew wide from unbelief. "That's ten blood pennies!"

With a slight bow and a subtle tone of voice, Darius responded, "That is fine."

"My Lord," Lucius bluttered as he placed his hand on the large demon's back.

Darius's brow furrowed, and his nasal cavity flared. "That is fine, Lucius." He returned his attention to the feeble princess. "The coins are at my manor for the pay—"

"Then what are we waiting for?" the dryad hissed. "I want to get out of this wretched heat."

†

Once they arrived at the manor, Darius went to gather the coins while Princess Abelia and her servants waited in the hall.

After retrieving the blood pennies, Darius returned to the hall where Ky and Abelia were sitting across the table from each other, both wearing a face of discontent. Darius tried to lighten the mood as he approached. "I see that you have met my duchess."

"I have," Abelia stated viciously. Her eyes narrowed as they focused on Darius's scar-filled body. "She mentioned that you two are going to have an offspring."

"That, we are."

The snobby princess scrunched her nose in disgust as she crossed her arms. "Mutts and bastards are frowned upon in Ajia."

Darius grew tense, trying to keep a professional composure. He glanced quickly at Ky, then back to the dryad. "Good thing this isn't Ajia."

"Maybe for your seed."

Darius stood firm before the princess, his body numbing from the tenseness. Gritting his teeth, he slammed a cloth sack he had brought in with him onto the table. "Here's your queen's pay."

The dryad opened the bag and checked the coins before handing it to one of her guards to carry. "Queen

Aerea will be pleased. We will begin unloading the ships at once." She turned to her servants. "Let's hurry and leave this scorching wasteland before we catch a plague from it."

Abelia's servants accompanied her across the hall to a set of double doors, where two Senturian knights stood guard.

As they exited the room, Darius spoke. "One of your fan serfs needs to make sure to sweep up your withered bark off of my floor on the way out."

Abelia's jaw dropped as her head twisted around toward the demon. "I beg your pardon?"

"This is the Princess of Ajia you are demeaning," one of her guards said, trying to protect the royal family's namesake.

Darius's posture and attitude shifted from professional to sinister. "This is Sentries, and here, I am Lord, and you all are foreigners. I'm just glad that you all don't look like Your Hideousness. Otherwise, I would think that somehow I got lost in Black Rain Forest with all of those rotted trees."

"And yet, you chose to remain in this desolate hellhole with your pregnant wench," Abelia responded, still in shock by the outburst from the filthy being in front of her.

"Honestly," Ky chimed in, unable to sit quietly any longer, "I'm glad that my mutt of a bastard child will be becometh and won't bring shame and ill fortune to us, unlike you for your incestual parents."

"The nerve you have—" one of the princess's guards

began, but Darius interrupted him.

"Guards! Remove these disrespectful afterlings from my kingdom."

The two guards closed the doors to the hall, and, accompanied by four more guards, escorted the Ajirians to their ships.

Seven Faces of Darkness

After two weeks of traveling through Ringwood's thick forests, the Senturian recruits entered the murky swamplands of Medsa'lear, where they trudged through the muddy grounds for four days. While the woods of Ringwood seemed to be full of life, the swamplands appeared to be as dead as Black Rain Forest regarding sound. Where they should have heard the fauna of the swamps, all they heard was the squelching of their boots and the hooves of their mounts in the puddles and mud. The farther into the swamps they traveled, the quieter everything seemed to get, as if the air around them stopped making a sound; Medsa'lear itself appeared to be holding its breath.

A low rumble shook the ground, followed by the

snapping of a large tree branch as it fell. Looking to where the limb had fallen, the knights beheld a massive serpentine head seeming to appear from the darkness. Its forked tongue flicked to smell their presence, and its golden eyes honed in on their movements as they slowed their stride.

The Senturian knights stopped in their tracks, mesmerized and fearful of the massive creature. Six other heads emerged from behind the collection of trees—some much shorter than the first, others a bit longer.

Briar's eyes widened within his steel helmet as he nervously turned toward Rosule, hoping to be reassured by his bravery but to no prevail. Rosule sat slouched forward upon his mount. His hands gripped tight onto the reins. His parted jaw quivered in fear.

"'Tis that the—" Briar whispered, then grew quiet as the seven pairs of eyes stared at the group, seeming to target him.

"'Tis the dragon o' the swamps," another stated in awe of the beast.

The hydra lunged forward, snapping limbs as it passed the nearby trees. Its seven heads swayed in random directions as its large body stomped through the muddy grounds.

"Attack!" Rosule commanded, trying to overcome his body's numbness and his pounding heart as adrenaline rushed through his veins.

The thirty-five hundred Senturians drew their rusted weapons and charged the oncoming creature. The giant beast plowed over some of the mares, trampling them under its massive feet. Its serpentine heads snatched a few knights from their mounts and crushed their armored bodies in its jowls.

One of the four smaller heads darted forward; its fangs dripped with steaming venom, melting armor from the recruits unlucky enough to be in its path. Its scales seemed brighter than the three longer heads and lacked the scars and burns the larger ones bared.

It snatched a knight from the ground, just to drop him in an attempt to bite another of its smaller heads when it tried to take the same soldier from it. The knight, dead from the initial bite, dissolved as the potent venom melted through to his skin and bones—his muscles and blood boiled from the toxins.

The large beast had spooked the few mounts they had been allowed to bring, fleeing into the swamps to never be seen again. The remaining knights continued to fight for their lives. Some of them noticed scarring on the hydra's flank and teamed together to stab and hack at the weak scales, bringing sharp and pained shrieks from the beast. The archers stayed their grounds toward the back of the group, shooting arrow after arrow toward the serpent's many eyes. One metal bolt slammed into a pasty-brown eye, causing the massive head to jerk and bite in the direction the arrow came from.

Cries from both the Senturians and the beast filled the air. Bloodied bodies decaying with venom and other debris from the fight littered the ground as both sides fought to survive.

Launching from far in the distance, flaming arrows rained on the hydra. Warriors dressed in leather armor rushed toward the recruits and helped to bring down the great beast once and for all. A large ogre wearing a maroon leather breastplate, with a light-blue serpent head painted on the left side approached one of the struggling heads. The flames of the arrows glinted off the scales surrounding them. The Learish ogre drew back his warhammer and slammed it upon the hydra's burning head. Near instantaneously, the massive creature collapsed into the mud, its hide burning as it lay dying before the two armies.

"Kill them!" Rosule shouted, pointing his spear toward the Learish army.

Much to the Senturians' surprise, the Learish warriors immediately knelt to the ground, their heads hanging low in humbleness. Rosule surveyed the kneeling warriors, then glanced at his men, then back at the Learish.

Rosule cautiously approached a warrior and lifted the Learish's head with the tip of his spear. "Who are you? And why do you kneel before us?"

"I am Ser Garras of Medsa'lear," the warrior responded as he motioned to the blue serpent head painted on his chest. "And we surrender unto you."

Rosule kept his spear pressed against Garras's neck as he examined the warrior. "Why do you surrender like a yellowbelly? Be it not better for you to fight?"

Garras felt the tip of the spear slowly puncturing his

throat as he tried not to swallow. "We're just doing as we were commanded."

Rosule's sweat glistening brow furrowed. "By who?"

"Rakash," he intoned.

Rosule tilted Garras's head a little farther. "Who's Rakash?"

Straining his neck and trying not to move, Garras responded, "Rakash is a royal guard at Lord Kaprin's manor."

Puzzled by the response, Rosule stayed persistent with his questioning. "Why did he give you the command to surrender?"

"That is something you would have to ask him yourself. I can take you to him if you wish."

"Take us," Rosule commanded as he nudged Garras to his feet.

All the Learish stood and began marching toward the city, the Senturians following close behind. As they walked, Rosule kept his spear pressed to the back of Garras's neck, in case the journey turned into an ambush.

Later that evening, the two armies arrived at the manor, where Garras took Rosule and twenty other Senturian knights inside to meet with Rakash—the remainder of the troops waited outside in the estate's courtyards.

"Rakash," Garras greeted the large ogre as they

entered the great hall. "The Senturians would like to have a word with you."

The plump giant stood and waved for them to approach. "Whom am I having the honor of speaking with?" he asked the morling in front of the group who still had his spear pressed to the back of Garras's neck.

"I am Ser Rosule, former Treasurer of Sentries."

The ogre placed his fist over his heart and introduced himself. "I am Rakash, Royal Guard of the Learish realm. You wish to have a word with me?"

"Did you give the command to your warriors to surrender?"

Rakash sat down at the table and responded, "Indeed I did."

Rosule's brow furrowed. "Why did your lord not give the command?"

The ogre's yellow eyes peered at the table, and his broad snout scrunched tight. "Lord Kaprin died at sea, sailing toward your homeland."

Rosule studied the ogre, feeling as if he was putting on a show to trick him into letting down his guard. "And how do you know of his death?"

The gaze from the ogre's large eyes fell upon the knight. "Ser Garras here had returned to us a few weeks back with the news of being the only survivor of the voyage."

"What about your duchess?" Rosule questioned. "Why did she not give the command?"

The ogre's pale-green head drooped, and his voice cracked. "Duchess Alor, along with Marquess Lucan, were both on the ships with our lord."

Rosule's tan face grew tense and distrusting. "Why would they all leave their kingdom behind to fight in a war of knights?"

"I don't know." Rakash's eyes focused on the Senturian again. "Lord Kaprin was always one to demand the most unwise of things of his servants."

"So, you're in charge now?"

"No, by no means. I would just rather see this kingdom stay standing than to lose it without a chance of survival."

The gaze from Rosule's brown eyes narrowed in on Rakash's. He slowly pulled his spear from Garras's neck, then jousted it back into it, piercing all the way through. He yanked his weapon from the dead warrior.

"Throw Rakash and all of the Learish army into their cells," Rosule commanded. "If there's no room for them all, slaughter the remaining men. Then go and burn down their villages."

"But we surrendered unto you," Rakash pleaded.

A smirk grew upon the Senturian's face. "That was very polite of you, but this is *war*, not peace. Next time, pick who you are willing to surrender to. Besides, surrendering holds no value in war, now does it?"

51

Sɪᴢᴢʟᴇ ɪᴨ ᴛʜᴇ Pᴀᴨ

In the dungeons of Sentries, two elven prisoners hung from the ceiling by shackles around their wrists. Their bodies dangled exposed over a cauldron of boiling water still sitting over a burning fire. They had acquired an assortment of cuts and scars and bruises over their emaciated bodies during their imprisonment. The blemishes ranged in colors from blues and blacks to pale greens and yellows and covered most of the prisoners' bodies. Where there wasn't a bruise, cuts and gashes lay, some showing visible signs of infection and bearing larvae eating the infected flesh. One of the elves' joints were swollen, as if they had been dislocated and repositioned multiple times, while the other's legs hung crooked with a broken bone protruding from his still-bleeding leg. Thin metal bands with four tiny hooks attached to the bottom donned each of the elves' heads. The hooks punctured the prisoners' eyelids, forcing them to keep their eyes open or risk ripping holes into them.

A few strides away lay another prisoner—a djinn—bearing old and new burns from head to toe. His skin was disfigured, and it was impossible to tell what color he had been from the blackened flesh and discolored scars that marred his body. He lay stretched out on a table, the shackles around his wrists were attached to a chain wrapped around a gear at one end of the table and his legs attached to another on the far end.

The djinn breathed heavily as tears leaked from his closed eyes; he clenched his jaw to try and keep the sounds of agony he wished to make from escaping. His freshly flayed leg burned as the humid air came into contact with the skinless patch on his thigh.

Darius circled the table, wiping his hands and knife on a grimy rag as he spoke to the djinn. "Is today the day that I kill you? No, but I promise that day is drawing near." He smirked at his prisoner and tossed the rag on the table beside him before he grabbed the lever attached to the gears and cranked it, slowly stretching the djinn's body.

Parts of the still-healing flesh on the injured figure broke open, leaking fresh blood and causing him to hiss and cry in pain as the blood touched the flayed leg.

"You cry worse than a wench giving birth."

Darius walked across the room and examined a rack

on the wall equipped with various rods and straps and spiked chains. His fingers trailed over a whip with nine heads embedded with hundreds of sharpened pieces of stone and metal. As he scanned the torture rack, his eyes lit up when they came to an iron rod bearing a rounded, hollow bulb on one end. The bulb had five small holes clustered together on half of it.

Darius removed the torture device and returned to the djinn. "What bone shall I break today? Oh, I know …" Darius's gaze trailed across the naked form in front of him. "Your favorite one." He smirked as he slammed the iron bulb into the djinn's genitals.

The prisoner's head lifted from the table, and his swollen eyes clenched shut as he gasped in agony, feeling a sharp pain course through his body—every muscle, regardless of how bruised or damaged, tensed as his groin throbbed in excruciating pain. After a moment of not being able to move or breathe, the djinn opened his eyes. His head turned toward the demon, who was dunking the bulb on the rod into the boiling water.

Darius returned to the djinn, holding the bulb over his waist. He dripped the boiling water onto the djinn's scarred abdomen. The prisoner twisted and turned, trying to keep from being burned, but there was no way to escape the torture.

"I can only imagine the pain you are going through," Darius said with a flatness in his voice as he stared at the djinn's bubbling skin. "But, then again, I don't want to know, and I really don't care."

Darius continued to insult the djinn as his duchess entered the dungeons, and he greeted her.

"My Lord," Ky responded as a shudder of horror and disgust crossed her body. "Ser Darut has returned and is waiting for you in the great hall."

"Aye, good."

Darius lay the iron rod on the table, the bulb resting against the djinn's ribcage just below the armpit. As the djinn cried out, Darius picked up the bloodied rag and shoved it into the prisoner's mouth. "I would have thought after thirty-four years, you would have manned up, but I guess there's only one man in the family."

Darius stood straight and approached his duchess.

"Are you going to leave them out of their cells?" Ky asked.

Darius's large fiery eyes glanced at the two elves draped from the stone ceiling, then at the long djinn stretched across the torture rack. "I don't think they're going anywhere anytime soon."

†

Above Darius's keeps, Ser Darut stood tall and firm. One hand held a chain attached to a metal collar around Azreal's neck; in the other, he held a leather bag with the two swords the djinn had with him in BrightHelm.

Before him stood Lord Azreal. His pinched face was swollen around the right eye, and his temple was a dark purple from a bruise. He had been stripped of his armor, left to wear just his breeches and a cotton shirt. A collar with small spikes on the inside that pricked his throat each time Darut tugged the chain hung around his neck. A solid cuff that molded itself together once it had became latched clamped his wrists.

Darius entered the hall as a smirk grew on his face. He lay his stare upon his new prisoner and slowly approached him. "It's funny how all of this worked out in my favor. You wrote to me wishing to make an alliance between Sentries and Talean, willing to give me all the resources my men and I would need. I declined your offer, sent my men to Talean, and had them take all of your resources anyways. Now you stand before me, my new prisoner of war. Why don't you make this easier on all of us and bend a knee to your new lord?"

Azreal clenched his jaw and narrowed his eyes at Darius, refusing to speak.

"I said, bend a knee, peasant," Darius growled.

Azreal straightened his back and raised his chin in defiance, still ignoring Darius's command. Darut stomped in Azreal's left knee, causing him to collapse to the ground with a grunt.

"Now, that wasn't so hard. Surely you can see the power I have over you?"

"You have no power over me," Azreal snarled, his lip upturning in anger.

"Oh, but I do. I now control five of the six kingdoms, including Talean, thanks to your generous marquess. But don't worry, my men kept him alive and free. They say he has gone mad, ranting and raving

428

about monsters in the shadows. I guess he couldn't handle dealing with the gods."

Azreal's eyes widened, and his mouth dropped open. He shook his head and began to speak before Darius cut him off.

"What? Did you think I wouldn't find out about your planned assassination of our sister? I've made bargains with the gods before, I know how they work—what to do and what not to do. They each require a payment. And if Solaris is anything like you, he won't last the moon."

Darius retrieved the chain from Darut. "Thank you for your services, Ser Darut. Take those blades to my cabinet; I will examine them later."

"Aye, my Lord," the minotaur responded. "There is one more thing I think you should see." Darut retrieved the label from the broken vial. "We believe it to be in Pauchyano or Penishi."

Darius studied the label and determined it was indeed Pauchyano. He studied the script, translating it in his mind.

Age After Beauty
Poison! Caution!
Antidote − *No known cure. Effects last thirty-six hours*
Property of Tets Toph Drumwright
Dames Point, Adria, Penora

"Where did you find this?"
"It was found with Lord Azreal."

"How did you come to possess such a poison?" Darius questioned. "Was the act of pairing the eastern lands against each other no longer fun for you?"

Azreal gathered a mouthful of saliva and spat it at Darius's feet.

Darius glanced at the floor before him, then back at his prisoner. "I guess meddling in the affairs of the Penéné people wasn't enough anymore, so you had to follow in your father's footsteps and create a divide in the six kingdoms."

"That is not my vial," Azreal lashed out as he approached the demon, but Darut kicked the back of Azreal's knee once more, causing him to collapse back to the ground.

"So, you want me to believe that some huma from beyond the clouds has access to vials only available to the Tets of Penora?"

"I tell you, it is not mine," Azreal stated through clenched teeth.

"So be it," Darius stated as he yanked Azreal's chain, causing him to fall to the ground from his kneeled position, the spikes probing into the back of the djinn's neck, drawing blood. "Come, there is someone I would like for you to meet."

He dragged Azreal through the manor grounds and down to the dungeons. Every so often, Darius pulled harder on the chain to make Azreal lose his balance and fall again, drawing more blood from around his neck. They reached the stairway leading to the dungeons, and Darius shoved Azreal forward, causing him to stumble down the stairs, smacking his head on the hard steps and wall, the collar ripping at his throat as blood streamed down his chest.

Darius led his new prisoner through the passageway and noticed a large cyclops returning the elven prisoners to their stone cells. He was closing the steel door and getting ready to lock it as Darius came upon him.

"Kitroz, you could have left them out. They weren't hurting anyone but themselves where they were."

"Apologies, m'Lord. I can return 'em back to where they were if ya bid so?"

"No need, they are already down and in their rooms. Besides, their cells won't occupy themselves."

"As ya bid."

Darius walked farther down the passageway and came to an empty cell. He unlocked Azreal's collar and shoved him into his new room. He laughed at the sound the djinn made when he collided with the stone wall before he slammed the door shut and locked it.

He walked to the cell across from Azreal's and banged his fist on it. "I brought you some company. Let's just call it a reunion." Darius gave a sinister laugh and navigated out of the dungeons.

Across from Azreal's cell, the other djinn prisoner struggled as he spoke in a raspy voice. "What did you do to become Lord Darius's prisoner?"

Azreal approached the door and peered through the window. The old voice seemed vaguely familiar, but he couldn't distinguish whose it was. "I am a prisoner of war."

The djinn in the opposite cell gasped as he recognized the voice. His eyes glazed over as he thought of Azreal being held captive in the keeps. "I did not think Darius took prisoners of war. He usually just has them slain in battle."

A snicker escaped from Azreal as he glanced down the passage toward the wall of torture devices. "I would much rather have that been the case. So, what is your name?" he asked, still trying to match the voice to a face.

The mysterious prisoner, who had been laying on the floor of his cell with cuffs around his wrists and ankles, clenched his jaw as he scooted toward the door. After a brief struggle to stand up, the gaze from his white eyes met Azreal's. "Valek, of Talean."

Azreal studied the burn scars and boils on Valek's swollen face. Scars on each side of his mouth stretched across his cheeks, caused by a device used to spread apart his mouth, resulting in tears and a shattered jaw. "Father? I thought you were dead."

"Oh, how I wish I was," Valek stated as he lowered his head, his mangled raven hair draping over his face.

"You have been gone for decades."

Valek's legs grew weak, and he was forced to sit. "All of which I have been in your brother's company."

"Why have you not escaped?"

"Of course, at first, I tried. But with no magic and being in bondage for all of eternity, I was unable to succeed." Valek paused to wince, still in pain from his previous torture. "Now, Darius tortures me daily, usually twice a day. I do not have the strength to do anything anymore. All I want is to die, but he will not grant me that freedom."

Azreal glanced at the shackles around his wrists. "I have never seen a cuff of this making before. It molded itself into a single piece."

"There are only a hundred cuffs like these made, and Darius owns all one hundred."

"How did he come upon them?"

"He went to Afria, seeking her help with my capture."

Azreal raised his head and looked out the window once more. "What was her price for such cuffs?"

"The death of a Taleanic ruler within the first five years of holding the title. One ruler for each cuff, hence the Curse of a Hundred Rulers."

"What?" Azreal shouted in disgust. "Darius is the cause of the curse placed on our land?"

"He is," Valek responded, hanging his head low. "I heard that you became a grand duke four years ago."

"I did."

Valek leaned his head back, resting it against the metal door. "Darius drug me from the far reaches of the Qupar canyons, where he had me stowed away in a shack, to this forsaken city when you took upon the title. That is until last year when he became grand duke over Sentries and moved me into these dungeons."

"I had no knowledge of it. If I had known you were alive and were a captive of his, I would have freed you years ago."

"It is all right, son."

"No, it is not," Azreal shouted as he banged his fists against the door. "Darius has to pay!"

"There is no hope of us seeking vengeance now."

"There has to be something we can do," Azreal stated as he sat down.

Valek's eyes grew wide as he remembered something he had heard. "You picked your sister … Um … What name did her mother give her? Anina? Aye. You picked Anina as your duchess, right? He will listen to her. We need to get word to her somehow to plea for our release."

Upon hearing the statement, Azreal's face became despaired.

The Gods' Betrayal – Wa'Shulvelki Barlie

After a vigorous journey through BrightHelm's rough terrain, Tera led the Alberian warriors along the banks of Lake Sound where the snow had all melted. The rhythmic sounds of the waves crashing into the rocky shores seemed to relax the tired warriors. In the distance, a morgawr swam in the lake, occasionally diving to catch a fish, then resurfacing.

Tera admired the beautiful scenery as they continued their march. With the betrayal of Lord Azreal and the Taleanic army weighing heavily on her mind, she tried to distract herself with the views of the mountains and the new forms of wildlife she had never seen before.

Her attention turned toward a soft

nickering—almost like chiming bells—where she saw an equine covered in thick scales and patches of fur around the face. The creature was larger than any equine she had ever seen, and it bore two horns upon its head, so she knew it couldn't be a kelpie, but her mind wasn't able to comprehend what she was looking at.

"*Kirins are gorgeous animals, aye?*" a voice said beside her.

Tera turned her head toward the warrior. "*Kirins? Is that what they are called?*"

"*Aye. They are excellent game as well, but they are intelligent creatures and are hard to hunt down. Some say they can camouflage themselves and walk on clouds, though I do believe those to be old hunter tales to impress the youngins.*"

"*That may be so, but I will have to try it sometime,*" Tera responded as the group continued around the lake.

As the days passed, the warriors returned to the plains of Alberon, entering into the region of Willowgate. The fifty thousand Alberians were relieved to be just a few days from home.

Jolly from their long travels, the warriors sang ditties in anticipation of seeing their family and friends once more. One of the songs began with just one warrior singing a few lines, then another would add to the song, and before they knew it, the song spread across the majority of the warriors, lasting an hour.

"Off to our homes we go
Where the fields are green
And the weather not cold
Off to our homes we go

We slayed a beast, the biggest there was
And made a fire, we eat it on up
Its fat kept us warm, more than making love
Now off to our homes we go

We climbed above the clouds and conquered a kingdom
We fight for our lord, and we fight for our freedom
Raise our banners to the sky, so that all may see them
And when I get home, a drink I need them
Off to our homes we go ..."

The warriors' cheering and rejoicing halted abruptly as their gaze beheld the destruction of the villages. Homes and markets were in ruin. Herdbeasts and catoblepones alike lay slaughtered in their fields and pastures. Bloodied limbs and intestines strolled amongst the carnage filled the air with the stench of decaying flesh and rotting corpses. Peppered amongst the destruction were strixes as they scavenged on the carcasses polluting the lands.

Tera approached one of the herdbeasts, shooing the strixes feeding upon its wounds with her club. She knelt beside it and ran her fingers across the gashes on its neck, feeling the deepness of the tears. *"The cuts are embedded deep, and the body's cold and mucusy. It's been dead for several days, and whatever killed it had to have been very powerful."* Tera grew intrigued as she examined the creature, checking its face, legs, and stomach. *"There is no indication it was fed upon before the strixes arrived."*

"What does that mean?" a warrior standing behind her asked.

"It means that it was killed for sport, not food."

"It could have been the nundus or the lions."

"Kiden lions?" she questioned while staring at the carcass. *"Why would they be in Willowgate?"*

"What else could it have been?"

While the warriors stood among the collection of strolled bodies, staring in horror and disgust, a rumble shook the ground. The group turned and stared in disbelief at what they saw. Stampeding upon black-as-coal mares, twenty thousand Senturian knights and squires, led by Ser Galzar, charged with their lances and other polearms pointed at the Alberians.

The warriors readied themselves, drawing their weapons and bracing for the collision of the approaching Senturians. With the larger army, the Alberians still feared for the worse. The majority of their armor was merely thick leather, while the higher-ranked warriors were blessed with thin plates of metal covering their chests and backs. On the other hand, the Senturians were dressed in full metal suits, including helms and visors, with the exceptions of the archers, who were dressed in thick leather armor and breastplates constructed of metal and pieces of testudine shells.

Tera clenched her jaw tight, preparing herself to morph into her animal spirit, when a roar, louder than the rumbling war cry of the stampeding army, came from the sky above them. She glanced to see the large dragonic body of Libras swoop down and land in the field.

The dragon spooked Galzar and his men's mounts, and they reared back and turned away. The Senturians tried with all their might to calm and steady their mares, but many bucked off their riders and cantered toward the mountains.

Libras scanned his blood-thirsty gaze over the two armies as he released another screeching roar. The Alberians stood frozen, too terrified to move a muscle, hoping their god would leave them alone and return to its godly duties. The Senturians, however, were thankful for the arrival of the god that had granted them his blessing four moons prior.

Galzar continued to lead his men closer toward the warriors who couldn't pull their gaze from the massive god. The great dragon turned his horned head toward the Senturian army—his snout wrinkled as he snarled loudly and spat a burst of flame at the armored knights. Their mounts whimpered in fear, throwing their riders from their backs as the knights retreated, enraged that their god would forsake them.

Libras turned his long head toward the Alberian warriors, still amidst the scattered carcasses of the villagers and animals. He gave a mighty roar, then pounced upon the warriors—his tail crashed and flung some of them through the air while his body crushed many others. The Alberians scattered as they all tried to avoid the fangs and flame of the great beast.

As he swiped at the Alberians, Libras noticed some Senturians still nearby, and his eyes flashed crimson as he heaved more flames toward the knights, who fled farther from their god.

The minor distraction gave the surviving Alberian army a chance to flee from the enraged god, fearful for their lives and for the injured comrades unable to escape the wrath of Libras.

With both armies abandoning the area, Libras turned his head toward the carcasses upon the ground and feasted upon the death and destruction around him.

A Dish Best Served Boiling

Three weeks after receiving Azreal as his new prisoner, Darius stood on his balcony as Meek lay across his shoulder. The gaze from his red eyes scanned the stone city he had sworn to protect for the past four years, then he looked into the sky.

Darkness engulfed Sentries as night fell over the land; the clouds of smoke coming from Mount Dumas blocked the stars and the Oticius Moon. The air was crisper than usual, brought on by a storm brewing over the ever-moving waters of the Abyss. Though the smoke clouds were thick, from a distance, purple streaks of light flashed across the dark skies.

The night progressed and Darius, smiling, remained studying the city as the wind carried the sounds of faint rumbles through the air. The townsfolk were returning to their homes, settling in for the night. A few guards patrolled the streets, their steel armor glinting in the arrays from torches hung on the side of buildings.

Darius glanced back into his chamber as a noise came from within the room. His gaze fell upon his duchess, who stood bare. Her petite figure was starting to round—a small bump showing the life growing inside her, now noticeable. In her hands, she held a scroll tied with a simple piece of twine.

"You're still up?" he asked as Ky approached. "You need your rest."

"As do you, my Lord."

"Aye, I do," he responded, his smile never leaving his face. "How are you and Cháy doing?"

"We are doing well," Ky responded as she subconsciously rubbed her bump. "I felt her kick earlier in the day."

Darius glanced back over his kingdom, propping himself against the railing. Ky stood next to him, wrapping one of her wings around his tall figure.

Ky trailed a finger across a newly formed stretch mark. "Do you know of any apothecaries that could help with my growing belly?"

"No, I don't. Just ask around. I'm sure one of the humas or house servants couldn't keep their legs shut and has spawned a new peasant lately."

"I have, but none have reproduced."

"Go to the brothels," Darius grumbled, his voice becoming irate. "Ask any of the wenches there; they are always spawning little pests."

Ky's body shifted, and her expression changed slightly. "Why must you be so negative and belittle others?"

"They are a waste of space. They do nothing to help this kingdom thrive, aside from making one weak at their knees for a few chips, which in turn makes more wastes of space. I can do that off this balcony for free if I so desired, without bringing more useless cretins to this land."

"But your prisoners. Why do you have to torture them so?"

"They have wronged me and this kingdom. They get what they justly deserve."

"Do you think that your tortures are justifiable?"

"When they steal, I remove their fingers so they will never steal again. If they continue, then I remove their hands. When they speak blasphemously about their lord, I remove their tongue so that they will never be capable of cursing anyone else for as long as they may live."

"What about your prisoners that you torture daily? What had they done?"

"You know of the actions Valek did to my mother."

"Those elves though ... their eyes. You've had them for as long as I have known you, yet you have never mentioned what they did. What deeds must have been done for them to be punished so?"

"When I was younger, Valek would invade my home, bringing them with him. They would restrain me and force me to watch as Valek assaulted my mother. I would try to look away, but those animals would hold my head and pry open my eyes. I had to watch as he beat and raped my mother, week after week." Darius closed his eyes as he clenched his fist, trying to suppress the grieving anger within.

"I … I never knew …" Ky whispered as the wind ruffled her ink-colored feathers.

"Now, I force them to suffer and watch as I torture Valek," Darius snarled as he forcefully grasped the stone rail in front of him.

After a moment of uncomfortable silence, Ky held out the scroll. "This missive came for you today."

Darius reviewed the letter, his eyes hardening as he read each line. "Return to your chamber at once and rest," he stated, turning from her as he strode inside, where he placed Meek on the floor.

"Where are you going?"

"To the dungeons."

"My Lord! Why—"

"Do not follow me!" Darius roared and turned to face her. "Go to your chambers and remain there for the night. I will see you come morn. And for fuck's sake, Ky, call me *Darius*!"

"But, what do you plan—"

"I said go to your chambers at once!" The demon spun around—his nasal cavity flared with intensity—and stormed away, heading toward the stairwell and cursing the gods as he went.

Darius stalked to the dungeons, his prisoner guard,

Kitroz, following behind him. Once they reached the keeps, they approached the torture rack on the wall, and each retrieved two spiked collars; from there, the duo made their way to the cells. Kitroz grabbed the two elves, while Darius retrieved the two djinns.

Darius unlocked Azreal's cell first and entered with a collar in his hand. Azreal, sitting upon a thick plate of metal intended as a bed, glanced with narrowed eyes at the demon.

"What do you want?"

"You're coming with me."

Azreal turned his head from Darius, then in a defiant tone stated, "I am not going anywhere."

Darius grasped Azreal's arm with his free hand.

The djinn turned toward him and shoved the large demon backward, pushing him with his legs.

As Darius staggered, Azreal stood to his feet and slammed his closed fists and cuff into the side of Darius's large head, just below the horns. Darius's eyes burned fiercely as he looked at the djinn, feeling the throbbing of his temple. He tightly clenched his fist as he reared back, then swung with all of his might at Azreal, colliding into his pinched face.

The djinn's body spun from the impact as he fell backward onto the metal platform. Azreal's eyes rolled to the back of his skull, and his jaw sagged from the force of the blow.

Darius stepped forward and placed the collar around Azreal's neck as the djinn's head wobbled, stunned and in a daze.

"Stand," Darius barked, but Azreal's white eyes just glanced at him, then looked away, still refusing to submit to the demon. "Fine, if you don't wish to stand, then fall at my feet, and kiss my boot." Darius grabbed the chain with both hands and jerked the djinn off the bed and onto the floor and drug him from his cell, the spikes on the collar piercing Azreal's throat and releasing small trickles of blood.

Darius began to unlock Valek's cell when he noticed Azreal starting to push himself up. Darius swiftly kicked Azreal's mouth, causing him to collapse onto the dungeon's dingy floor.

He squatted beside the djinn, who had lifted himself onto his hands and knees once more before spitting out a glob of blood.

"I told you: here, I have power over you."

Darius stood as he stared at his prisoner's face, blood streaming from the djinn's lips. His right eye was nearly swollen shut in the middle of a dark purple patch of bruised skin.

"That's right," Darius began in a commanding tone. "Stay on your knees where you belong, you fucking disgrace." Darius turned toward Valek's cell door and opened it. "To your feet," he ordered as he approached the djinn with blackened, burn scars all over his once green body.

Valek unsteadily rose to his feet—his legs shook in pain and weakness—as Darius placed the collar around his neck. As Darius began to exit the cell, Valek's feeble body collapsed to the ground.

"Stand! You know the drill!"

"He cannot stand," Azreal stated as he stood. "He is too weak, and you can clearly see that."

"If he can't stand, then I will have to drag him."

Darius wrapped the chain attached to Valek's collar tightly around his hand as he began to drag the prisoner's mangled and scarred body across the stone floor.

"Stop," Azreal pleaded. "May I carry our father? He cannot walk properly."

Darius's brow furrowed and his gaze narrowed onto Azreal's. "No!" he blurted as he yanked on both chains. "Stay on your feet, or I will drag you up the stairs as well." He paused as he looked over at Valek's gruesome figure. "We will be riding horseback soon enough. If you fall off your horse, I will have Kitroz trample you with his."

An hour later, the six of them, riding upon four mares, had reached a break in Mount Dumas's crater where it met a river of lava flowing down the side of the great volcano. The storm over the Abyss had gotten closer to land, and the wind had picked up. Next to the edge of the pool of molten flames rested two piles of stone rubble, where the offering had taken place over four moons prior.

They all dismounted from the mares, and the

prisoners were ushered toward the crater as Darius retrieved a sword from a sheath strapped to the saddlebag of his steed. As they walked, Valek stumbled onto the soggy ground—embers of flames danced into the smoky air as his body impacted the ashy terrain. Kitroz lifted the djinn by his arm and carried him the rest of the way.

Lightning continued to flash across the cloudy night sky as the winds howled through the air. Rain had begun to fall, and the night seemed darker than usual. The billowing shapes of the large storm clouds swirled in the sky. The air felt heavy, and the massive storm falling upon Sentries seemed to intensify the volcano's sulfuric smell.

While Kitroz held the chains of all four of the prisoners, Darius approached the edge of the lava-filled crater.

"What kind of god are you?" Darius yelled with his arms stretched out to both sides. "You accept our offering for the bloodlust of battle, but then you betrayed us! What god does that? No, you are no god of mine. I will never bend a knee or take up a sword in your name again." As he finished the sentence, he lifted his sword. "Unto the Six I may bid, but to you, I never will. I don't need a mindless beast charading around as a god to win wars for me."

Darius lowered his sword, still staring across the pool of fire—flashes of light from the storm around him lit across his face.

"Libras!" he shouted at the top of his lungs; his voice

echoed off the mountain until a loud clash of thunder drowned out his words. Darius paced along the ridge of the crater. "Come out and face me!"

When no answer came from the dragonic god, Darius's face darkened in anger. "Are you too scared and weak to face a mortal? Or is your fist-sized brain too small to know when you've been ousted?"

After a brief moment of nothing happening, Darius stomped toward the prisoners. Thunder boomed, shaking the volcano with its force as the sky illuminated with streaks of electricity.

"Maybe Iden will appreciate my offerings!" Darius roared, thrusting his sword through the back of Valek's neck as he sat hunched forward on the ground.

Seeing the life being stolen from his father, Azreal screamed and charged Darius. The gaze from the demon's red eyes locked onto Azreal's approaching figure. He pulled the sword from the djinn and swung it at Azreal, slicing his face from side to side. Azreal lifted his hands over his new gash, wincing in pain. Nothing could be heard over the gale of wind and the crash of thunder over Sentries. The cavern walls in Mount Dumas lit up brighter with each flash of lightning, and the air seemed to thicken.

Darius dropped his sword as he pounced onto Azreal, toppling him onto the ground. With his callused hands clinched, the demon pounded his fists into Azreal's bloodied face. One after another, they pulverized into the djinn's skull—blood oozed from the fresh cuts. Azreal's cheekbones cracked from the force.

Darius saw the consciousness leaving his prisoner, but he was lost to the bloodlust of torture and revenge to care enough to stop.

"Don't ya think 'tis enough, m'Lord?" Kitroz spoke in a booming voice, barely overheard from the raging tempest.

Darius, breathing heavily and still heated with anger, glanced over at his guard, then back to Azreal's disfigured face. After a final punch, he stood and trooped to Valek's crumpled body. Pulling the corpse by its collar's chain, Darius drug his body into the burning lava. He stepped onto the molten rock; his feet slowly sank as if it were thick mud. The magma's intense heat ignited Valek's body, causing his skin to boil and char as the scent of burning flesh mixed with the rich sulfuric odor of the mountain. He watched with a smirk as the burning corpse disintegrated into ash before him.

Darius stepped out of the crater—unphased by the heat of the lava—and returned to Azreal, still lying on the ground unconscious. He grabbed the chain to his collar and began to drag him closer to the lava, the spikes ripping at Azreal's torn flesh. Darius leaned forward and grasped him by the throat and lifted him into the air, blood streaming down his hand.

"Go join your father in the ever-burning flames of Sentries," Darius stated in a normal voice—seeming as if he was finally at peace with the djinns—as he tossed the body into the flaming pit of Mount Dumas.

After a few moments of staring at Azreal's blue flesh burning as it lay upon the boiling lava, Darius turned to

Kitroz and the two elven prisoners. "I guess I'll leave you two here as food. I'm sure Libras is too stupid to go hunt for his own."

"But he's not here," one of the elves said.

Darius glanced behind him at the cave across the crater, then back at the prisoners. "Other creatures roam these parts; maybe they will find you just as appetizing."

Darius retrieved his sword from the ground and approached the prisoners. He grabbed one of them as he stood behind him, and with a quick slice, he slit the elf's throat, then did the same to the other, leaving them to gurgle in their blood as they died.

ΠEAR AΠδ AFAR – Ε88iϯ ΟΠδ ZHUΠ8

After hearing about the lion attacks that occurred six weeks prior, Lord Moll'ar decided to take advantage of the influx of wildlife fleeing south and visited the fields to enjoy one of his many passions: hunting.

That afternoon, after returning to his manor, Moll'ar went to the larder to skin an achlis he had killed as it hung from a hook in the ceiling. As he peeled the skin from the neck, his lovely wife waltzed into the cool underground room.

"*I see you made a kill,*" Laurelin spoke as she analyzed the achlis.

"*Aye, I also managed to kill a jackalope for Onnan,*" Moll'ar stated as he pointed his knife toward a stone table where he had laid a small hare. "*He loves collectin' their feet.*"

She smiled. "*That he does. 'Tis makes him feel like some o' the elders who keep trophies o' their kills.*"

Moll'ar chuckled as he worked on removing the hide from the achlis. "*He wants to grow up too fast.*"

Laurelin leaned against one of the stone walls and smiled. "*Marquess Terus came by while you were out. He said they finished the moat last night. They just need the barriers to be removed so the water can flow through.*"

"*I shall do that first thing in the mornin',*" he said as he finished removing the achlis's hide. "*And, all the while, here is some hide for you to start tannin'.*"

Laurelin's hazel eyes narrowed as her nose scrunched. "*You better clean the fur before you bring it to me.*"

"*Aye, I will,*" Moll'ar stated as a satyr entered the chilled room.

"*My Lord. My Lady. Our warriors have returned from BrightHelm.*"

Moll'ar lay the hide onto the stone table beside the jackalope. "*Where are they gathered?*"

"*The casemate, my Lord.*"

†

Moll'ar had made his way to a large room with a vaulted ceiling built into the wall around the capital—the casemate. As he entered the room, he realized just an eighth of his warriors had returned from their journey. He grieved the loss of close friends.

453

"*I can see that the battle was a tough one,*" he said, scanning the group to see who all had been lost to the battle.

"*Lord Azreal is a traitor!*" a large group of the warriors retorted.

"*A traitor? What happened in the North?*"

"*We attacked BrightHelm from the West, while Lord Azreal led an attack from the East,*" Tera replied. "*After we had taken the capital, the Taleanics turned and started to kill our men. After we had gained knowledge of their betrayal, we stood our ground and defended ourselves and sieged control over the city ourselves. Lord Azreal, though, fled while his men were being butchered.*"

"*So, we have BrightHelm?*" Moll'ar questioned.

"*Aye, my Lord. Chief Ixin stayed behind with sixty thousand of our people to keep control of the city.*"

"*Good. I have yet received word on the state of the other kingdoms. But if we hold BrightHelm, then we hold the crown.*"

The group of warriors cheered. "*Until the sun sets in the East, we will defend and serve the West!*"

†

As the light of a new day crept through the window, Moll'ar lay awake to the sounds of his wife's soft breaths. He looked at her, studying her every curve and dimple—the way the sun glinted in her hair and the rise and fall of her chest as she took another breath. He eased out of bed, careful to not disturb her as he began to dress himself. He left his manor and traveled toward the edge of the capital, on the border of Feather's Bow and the Abyss Ocean.

When Moll'ar rode up to the edge of the moat, he saw a large crowd of serfs and warriors, waiting for their lord to raise the barriers.

One serf approached Moll'ar and greeted his arrival. *"M'Lord, 'tis hast been an honor to do our kingdom such a favor."*

"It warms me deeply that you were able to help with this project," Moll'ar responded.

"I took the liberty o' checkin' and double checkin' the trenches, and as far as I art aware, m'Lord, there is nobody inside the moat."

"I appreciate your services for our kingdom," Moll'ar stated as he reached into his pocket and retrieved a sun coin and handed it to the serf.

Moll'ar climbed the barrier in front of the crowd—to one side of him stood Marquess Terus, on the other Duke Pol. He glanced at Terus. *"Raise the gate."*

As commanded, the giant minotaur cranked a lever that lifted the gate, allowing the force of the Abyss to gush into the wide trench around the capital.

Moll'ar scanned the crowd. *"You all have done such great work. This moat will ensure that no army will breach our kingdom's walls, that I can assure you. For your pay, as promised, meet with Duke Pol later today at the manor; there will be a sun coin for each of you there."*

The denizens all cheered and applauded their lord for the gratitude he bestowed upon them.

"I would give out the coins myself," Moll'ar continued, *"but there is a war out beyond these fields, and I cannot just stand by in*

my safe haven while my tribes are gettin' slaughtered and betrayed by other realms." He paused for a brief moment, then continued in bursts of shouts. *"Lord Darius's knights are sweeping across Metagore, seizing what they will! I have to put a stop to his run! Or Metagore will burn by his hands, and our people will fall beneath his feet! But mark my words as true: by my blade, his reign will end!"*

The crowd shouted and cheered, showing as much enthusiasm as their lord.

Moll'ar, louder than before, concluded, *"Until the sun sets in the East, we will defend and serve the West!"*

†

After filling the moat with water, Moll'ar returned to his manor, where Laurelin was outside removing the achlis hide from the drying rack. He entered their house and headed to their bedchamber. As he entered the room, his eyes focused on a large wooden cabinet that sat across from his bed.

Moll'ar opened the cabinet doors and retrieved his various weapons. He grabbed two hunting knives and placed them in their sheaths, then attached them around his shins. He removed a hatchet and placed it in a sling around his waist, then a small sword with two white crystals embedded into the handle and strapped its holder onto his belt. Lastly, he retrieved a spear with red feathers tied just behind the head of the polearm from the cabinet.

The Alberian Lord made his way back outside to where Laurelin was sitting in a wooden chair, shaving the coarse hair from the dried hide with a rounded steel blade.

"*Are you going on another hunt, Husband?*" she asked peculiarly as she noticed the many weapons Moll'ar had retrieved.

"*No, I am preparin' for the war.*"

"*The war?*" Laurelin asked as she set down the blade and hide and stood. "*You cannot be serious.*"

"*But I am.*" Moll'ar approached his wife as her eyes analyzed his body in disbelief. "*I said if the war ever came to Alberon, I would pick up my blade and I would fight.*"

Tears seeped from her hazel eyes. "*What am I supposed to do while you are gone? I cannot raise two children on my own.*"

Moll'ar grasped his wife in his arms as she lay her head against his chest. "*The serfs and housemaids will be able to help you. Besides, I will not be gone for too long.*"

Laurelin sobbed softly into the divot of her husband's chest. "*How long do you think the war will last?*"

"*I do not know how long. But I promise you, I will return home every moon for a few days.*"

"*I wish you would not go,*" Laurelin pleaded as she pulled away from her husband's warm embrace, her cheeks still moist from the sobs. "*Can Marquess Terus not take your spot out on the field?*"

"*Terus's duty is to protect our capital from invading armies. It is my duty to protect all of the tribes of Alberon, near and afar. Which is why I must be the one to fight the great fight.*"

As the two of them stood there, their young,

shaggy-haired son approached them, dragging a twig behind him. Onnan saw the sadness and worry on his parents' faces. *"What is wrong? Is everything okay?"*

Moll'ar turned toward the boy and knelt before him. *"I am goin' away for a short period of time, and I need you to watch after your mother for me while I am away and help with your sister."*

Onnan's green eyes studied his father's expression, then trailed down toward his weapons. *"Are you going to fight the bad people, Pappi?"*

Moll'ar nodded in response, trying to not upset or worry Onnan.

A smile grew across Onnan's face. *"Can I come? I have been practicing my spear throwing."* Onnan turned and hurled his twig through the air, then turned back to his father. *"See, I am getting better."*

Moll'ar chuckled. *"Maybe when you are older and have taken the Walk of Roses, you can fight by my side, but for now, I need you to be the lord of the house."* He smiled as he ran his fingers through his son's black and red hair. *"And who knows, when I return, maybe you will have found your animal spirit and can show me your transformation."*

Onnan's rounded face scowled at his father. *"Okay …"*

Moll'ar stood to his feet. *"Now, go run off and play."*

As his son went into the house, he turned back toward Laurelin, who had sat down and started removing more hair from the hide. *"I am goin' to go get suited for armor. Please try to stay strong for the children."*

Laurelin remained silent as she stroked the curved

blade across the hide, never looking up as her husband walked away.

THREE-TIPPED DAGGER

Six weeks after conquering Talean, the Senturians were still enjoying their spoils of war, taking what they could from the frightened citizens and shopkeepers. From food to wine and from women to blood pennies, the knights took pleasure from everything Talean had to offer. The beautiful landscape and marvelous buildings were the perfect descriptions of paradise for the nine hundred Senturians.

While most of the knights were gallivanting in the brothels and gambling houses, Dagrus and O'Bryon convened in one of the manor's cabinets they had commandeered from Solaris. The two Senturians sat at a desk across from each other and began to plan their next course of action.

"We need to make our way to BrightHelm," Dagrus mentioned as he looked at the map sprawled in front of him. "Once we take the high city, Lord Darius will hold the crown."

"Aye," O'Bryon acknowledged. "Do you wish to stay here with a handful of men and hold control over the city while I lead the rest beyond the clouds?"

"Nay," Dagrus grumbled, then glanced at his right leg. "This splint won't keep me immobile."

"I am aware of this, Ser. I meant nothing by it," the djinn humbly stated. "But who will keep the Taleanics loyal in our absence? You cannot trust they won't start an uprising against Lord Darius's name."

"Nay. With Talean only being led by some ogre that Solaris appointed, the kingdom will fall on its own without any guidance."

"If you believe it is true, then it is so."

"Aye, it is," Dagrus stated as he rolled up the map. "Go round up the rest of the knights and have them meet me in the garden around back."

"As you have commanded, Ser."

"I hope they are sobered up, because today we ride for BrightHelm."

†

Twelve days after being betrayed by their god, the eighteen thousand Senturians on the northern edge of Willowgate in Alberon maneuvered south once more.

Only left with two hundred steeds, they traversed the fields, leaving their mares to carry all their gear.

As they marched, they found settlements desolated and in ruins. Homes had been torn to shreds, and the fields were riddled with ruts. Carcasses of residents and cattle littered the ground—their bodies picked clean of any flesh from the local scavengers. Bent and broken tools and weapons were strolled amongst the corpses of the tribes who had tried to defend themselves from the attacks.

"Do ya think Libras did 'tis?" one knight asked as the group passed through the village.

"Surely, it 'twas him helpin' us with the war," another knight said. "What else could it hath been?"

"Are we still in the gods' favor?" the first knight questioned. "Libras did turn on us."

"Aye, the Gods of the Eight Divides gave us their blessin's. They wouldn't not keep their word."

Caski, who had overheard part of the conversation, spoke up. "Maybe they gave us their favor to weaken us."

"What? Why would they do that?" another knight asked.

Caski looked across the destroyed village with his yellow catlike eyes. "Maybe the Gods of the Eight want us to fail."

"That would be cruel o' them."

"Are we any better?" Galzar asked, hearing his men speculating the betrayal of their god.

"Are they even gods?" Caski asked in a hysterical

voice. "Maybe we just worship the idea of something greater than us, when the truth is: Libras is just a dragon that we fear and feed for when we feel we need something to rest our guilt upon after slaying the innocent. As if that would release us from any punishment that would be justly given for our heinous crimes."

One of the knights' brows raised underneath his steel helmet. "If 'tis true, then we are responsible for our own actions, and we deserve to die for the villages that we've burnt."

Galzar gazed around him, fearing the mighty dragon could return at any moment. "Quiet with your dishonoring of the gods. If Lord Darius heard word of your distrust, he would have your head on a pike—or worse, lock you in his dungeons and torture you for all of eternity."

"One could only survive so long in those dungeons," another knight said. "Our suffering would all come to a quick end."

"Aye," Caski reentered the conversation, "but Lord Darius has prisoners that he's tortured for thirty-four years. He will find a way to keep you alive well enough to be tortured."

As the Senturian recruits trudged through the swamps of Medsa'lear, they heard a faint hiss over the sound of crackling from the burning village they had left in Vaseere. The sound echoed around them, gradually getting louder before it faded into silence and then started back up moments later.

Briar—nervous and in fear of his life—looked around and noticed a few shadows moving in the deeper parts of the water. The shadows seemed to circle around as bubbles floated to the surface of the murky water. Every so often, he saw what looked like a vine whip out of the water and splash back in.

"Bunyips, nasty little beasts," a demon remarked.

"Pardon?" Briar asked, glancing at the knight.

"Those creatures ye'r watchin', they're bunyips. Ya don't see 'em very often outside of Medsa'lear; they flourish here."

"What are they?"

"They are 'bout as long as that salamander of Lord Darius's and as big as a droyaid—fast too. Ya don't want 'em to catch ya off guard, or they'll devour ya in a heartbeat."

Just as the demon finished talking, one of the shadows detached from the rest and slithered to the bank of the pond. The bunyip climbed out of the water and raised its head, looking toward the group of knights. The creature hissed loudly and raised its frill around its neck, making it look twice as large.

"See the tail? See how it splits in two? Means it's a male; females just have the one. And they have a bunch of eyes too, so they can watch ya better."

"How do you know so much about them?"

"Traveled 'round in m'days, studied the beasts m'self. Just watch yerself 'round 'em. If ya get too close to their nests, they'll swarm ya. They ain't fearful of nothin' but that damn hydra we killed."

The bunyip flicked his tail and eased back into the water after realizing the troops were not heading toward him—his shadow returned to the others.

After passing the hive of bunyips, the recruits arrived at a dry patch of land. As they continued through Vaseere, one recruit yelled, bringing the other men to a halt. Exclamations traveled through the knights as they gathered to see what had caused the commotion. With a gasp, they came upon a dead Learish death worm. Its light-brown skin was now a dull gray. Its long slimy body had visible signs other animals had feasted off it.

"I thought I'd never see one of those in my lifetime. Thanks to the gods its dead, otherwise we'd be goners for sure!" Briar exclaimed.

"Don't be ridiculous. They don't eat meat, just the dirt that it digs," one recruit replied.

"Look at those teeth! You can't tell me it doesn't kill, with teeth like that."

"I'm telling ya, they don't eat meat. My uncle told me stories about them."

"And my brother told me a story about a man who was swallowed alive by one of those beasts!" Briar responded as he stepped away from the worm, trying to avoid contact with its skin. "And the venom in its teeth is potent enough to dry a man's body of all blood and leave him in ashes."

"Both of you knock it off. Damn worms haven't been seen in decades, and this one obviously didn't eat whatever killed it. Let's just move on," Rosule snarled as he continued the trek; the rest of the knights followed behind him.

While walking down the path, the group heard the roaring of the Diamond River. The river was massive—eighty chains in width—and it stretched from Lake Sound in the mountains of BrightHelm all the way to the Abyss Ocean, dividing the plains of Alberon from the swamplands of Medsa'lear.

As they approached a large wooden bridge, Rosule turned to his men and pointed across the clear waters of the river. "There it is. Alberon, the land of the strix. Our destination is upon us. For in just a few short nights, we will arrive at Lord Moll'ar's doorsteps, and he will bend a knee in Lord Darius's name."

The recruits shouted in excitement. "Be thy gods that guide us. Be thy gods that watch over us. Be no shame fall upon us!"

56

An Icy Blaze – Ya'Yajirae Fið'ka

Galzar continued to lead his remaining group of knights and squires through the hills of Willowgate. Their minds were weary and lacked hope of lasting through another major battle, but the Senturians knew returning home would mean certain death under Lord Darius's rule. They marched in two columns of eighteen rows—five hundred men in each row—with two hundred and fifty squires lined up in the center of the columns, holding high banners of a burning tower. Less than half of the men had maintained possession of their shield during their long journey, leaving the first nine rows to be comprised with the knights who had their shields. The next six rows featured archers, while the last three were mostly injured knights and unarmed squires.

The day was silent; the only sounds they heard were their marching feet and labored breaths. As they continued and traversed a massive hill, they saw a large mass of Alberians spread out ahead of them.

Galzar halted his men. "We have the favor of the gods! They may have weakened us, but by the Eight Divides, the gods will see our victory true!" His blue eyes analyzed his troops, studying their slouched posture and the doubt they wore on their faces. "We are the best knights in all of the six kingdoms! And if the gods see to it that we must die today, then we shall all die heroes!"

He saw the morale of his men rise as they all shouted and clashed their weapons against their steel armor. "Be thy gods that guide us. Be thy gods that watch over us. Be no shame fall upon us!"

Galzar turned to face the opposing army as they grew closer. He saw the silhouettes of morlings in their animal form standing behind the group of tribal warriors. The Alberians halted as a pair of dire wolves, a nundu, and a duba emerged from the pack. His men heard faint shouts in Oacari—as well as the howls and roars from the morlings—over the vast distance between the two forces.

Galzar studied the Alberians' formation and the landscape surrounding them as a soft whistling sound rang through the air, signaling an arrow puncturing one of their banners.

"Shields ready!" he barked as bolts began to rain

upon them, a few impaling the bannermen.

The first row of Senturians knelt behind their shields; the next eight rows, placed theirs above the first, making a barrier between them and the onslaught of arrows.

Once the sound of arrows ricocheting off the metal shields had ended, the rumble of shouts from the stampeding army emerged from the silence. The Senturians broke formation and readied their weapons. The archers pulled their arrows taught, then released them into the air, while the few liches enchanted them with fire, electricity, and poisons, causing a handful of the massive Alberian army to fall from their impact.

"Charge!" Galzar shouted as he readied an arrow of his own, but a high-pitched shriek, followed by the flapping of wings, drowned out his voice.

A second screech penetrated the air, and in moments, the pale body of Tiamus landed behind the Senturians, her tail lashing out behind her in agitation. Her arrival caused the Alberian warriors to stop their charge as they all stared in awe and fear of the massive dragon.

Tiamus extended her long neck, leaning over the Senturians as she began to nudge them with her cold snout, taking in and remembering their scent. The gaze from her icy blue eyes found Galzar in the center of the clustered knights as she tilted her head and released a rumbling purr. The pale dragon unfurled her great wings, encircling the Senturian army.

"*Dolu!*" an Alberian minotaur shouted as he lifted a

giant ax.

Tiamus raised her body and released a third roar, her anger bringing a sudden drop in temperature as ice formed around her feet. She pounced over the Senturians, landing in front of the Alberians. Sharp ice particles flew from her mouth as she roared, impacting against the warriors.

The tribal warriors snapped from their stupor as they attacked the new threat—many of them falling to her icy breath and sharp claws. As Tiamus spat plumes of burning ice, freezing more warriors, a bellow broke through the commotion, followed by a crash, as the dark form of Libras collided into Tiamus, crushing many of the Alberians in the process.

Both dragons tumbled across the fields as Tiamus fought to free herself from Libras's firm grasp. She kicked and clawed at his face, sinking her nails in-between his scales, prying them from his flesh, until he released her to attend to his new wounds. Tiamus lept into the air and fled from the battle; Libras chased after her, breathing flames in her wake. As the two dragons moved farther away from the armies, one lone Senturian chose to shoot an enchanted arrow toward the Alberians, resuming their battle.

Tiamus, being smaller than Libras, was agiler in the air, but the god was quicker and caught up to her within moments. He grabbed onto her back, his hind legs digging into her rump and ripping off pale blue and white scales while releasing a stream of blood from her flank. Tiamus screeched and turned her head toward

Libras, biting his neck to force him to release her.

Libras flew higher into the air, shaking his head and scratching at his neck—the puncture wounds on him freezing from Tiamus's icy saliva. At his retreat, Tiamus darted after him, but his spiked tail collided into her head, forcing her to plummet to the fields.

As she fell, Tiamus tried to straighten her body to better land on her legs, but the force of his blow and the speed of her plummet made the task difficult. The crackling rush of Libras's fire chased after her body. Libras swooped down on top of her, nipping at her shoulders and ripping long gashes into her back. Tiamus turned her body as much as she could and exhaled an icy burst of air, forming ice particles on Libras's scales and causing him to roar as the inflicted wounds began to bleed.

Libras reared back, scratching his wounds and trying to remove the ice, as Tiamus limped in retreat. She took a staggering run, crushing Alberians in her path, before she leaped into the air. Her wings forced a few of the nearby warriors to fall, and others dropped their weapons as the air around them seemed to freeze. She shrieked and flew high into the sky, trying to flee her large opponent.

†

Galzar stood amongst the chaos of the two battling armies, watching the dragons fight in the sky—Libras and Tiamus breathing their flames and ice. His men were burning alive all around him, succumbing to their deaths; unknown to him, only a few hundred Senturians remained on their wobbling legs.

As Galzar stood in horror, a small knife pierced his left bicep, then pulled out. His attention turned to a satyr grabbing hold of his elven body, and soon, his attacker swung him off his feet and onto the ground.

Galzar glanced at the warrior, hearing him shout to the others, "*Dakamd uyi ek'uyi killi, bie kik uli yaemeem su'wa'bryadae dragon omd razh occalé shulveki!*"

Galzar clinched his eyes shut, bracing for his impending fate, only to open his eyes moments later to see the satyr a few strides away, charging with the other Alberians toward the two dragons wrestling in the fields.

While he lay amongst the trampled weeds, Galzar's blue eyes scanned the carnage of the engagement. The thirty thousand native warriors all advanced north, following the fleeing dragons, while the few remaining knights and squires burned around him.

Galzar, lost in thought, tried to figure out what they could have done to anger the gods. With each passing day, Galzar's faith in the Eight dwindled as he was persuaded by overhearing his fellow comrades diminish their gods, calling them vicious monsters. He was uncertain if he believed the gods were just dominant creatures they feared and revered for no purpose, but he had come to the assumption that the gods—especially Libras—had no adoration for their subjects.

Amongst the destruction the armies and the dragons brought, Galzar spotted a thin figure staggering through the smoke and flames. As the silhouette became more apparent, he recognized it to be Caski, peeling the burning gambeson from his body. The lich's bare torso was now scattered with fresh burns—some of the flesh on his right side had burned off completely, leaving part of his rib cage exposed to the elements.

"We've gotta go if we wish to live," Caski stated as he extended an arm as he approached. As he reached the downed elf, he grasped his hand and pulled him to his feet.

Galzar stared at the chaos in a daze as Caski tugged on his arm, trying to get him to flee.

"Did you hear me? We've gotta go!"

"But the others," Galzar stated in exasperation as he tried to pull away. "There might be others out there."

"They're all dead!"

"You don't know that," Galzar grumbled as he freed himself and sprinted toward the heaps of carcasses.

Caski raised both hands, causing a fire to engulf the mounds of fallen bodies. With the use of his magic, the lich's body undertook the strain of his powers. His skin drew tighter as the magical decay ate some of his flesh, exposing more of the skeleton underneath.

Caught off guard by the sudden burst of flames, Galzar jolted his head toward Caski. As the lich lowered his hands, the skin on his right forearm sagged exponentially, drooping over his bony hand.

Caski's gaze shifted toward the shaken elf. "Magic

doesn't work on the living. They're dead."

The young archer stood in horror as he gazed upon the arm of the lich; the skin ripped and tore as it slowly slid down. Caski glanced at his arm, apathetic to the sleeve of flesh peeling from his body. Without a second thought, he reached up with his other hand and grasped the loose flesh, pulling it from the bone as if it was an old bandage covering a wound.

Caski glanced back toward Galzar, who was staring in shock at the flesh still in the hands of his fellow knight. "That's just a downfall of being birthed a lich instead of a djinn."

Galzar's gaze trailed up the lich's emaciated body, seeing the insouciant look upon Caski's face as a clash of shrieks and roars broke his attention, causing him to turn toward the dragons and the Alberians.

"They're all monsters," he stated, his speech crackling with uncertainty.

"War makes everyone into monsters."

"Not them," Galzar responded with a numbness in his voice. "The gods."

"Gods or monsters, whatever their title, we need to go," Caski rebutted as he placed a hand on Galzar's shoulder.

The elf nodded in agreeance as they both fled eastward.

†

As the final two Senturians fled, the roars of the massive beasts echoed across the plains. The remaining Alberian warriors marched toward the fight; the archers readied their arrows as they came upon the dragons.

Libras had wrapped his front legs around Tiamus's body, bringing them both to the ground. He grabbed at one of her wings with his front claws and ripped into it, biting holes into the thin membrane as she shrieked and tried to fight back.

Tiamus frantically shook her hindquarters, freeing her backside of Libras. She leaped into the air with hopes of flying away, only to drop back to the ground—the holes in her wing rendered itself useless to her. She tried to crawl away as arrows fell upon them. She lifted her tattered wing, trying to shield her body from the onslaught.

Libras jumped into the sky, circling her as he flew, and released a bellow of flames. He dashed toward his adversary, grabbing her lithe body with his four legs and lifted her off the ground. Tiamus raised her head toward him and released a gust of ice at his face, only to have her neck trapped in his jaws as he thrashed her from side to side. Tiamus roared, trying to fight off the god, only to shriek as he released her body.

A few unlucky archers on the ground shouted in fear just before being pinned under the weight of Tiamus's wyvern-like figure—many froze from her very proximity as shards of ice danced through the air from the impact. She lifted her head—weak from Libras's assault—and growled at the men around her before the massive red dragon mounted onto her limp body. Libras released a plume of fire, her opal scales searing from the intense heat of his attack. He snapped at her neck once more, sinking his sharp fangs into her throat, and ripped away a large chunk of flesh as her body became lifeless in his grasp.

The Alberians soon realized their god's foe had been conquered. Their cheers and shouts of victory rang through the air, alerting their presence to the massive dragon.

Libras's head swung toward the vast army as he bellowed a deafening roar, followed by a projection of flames sweeping onto the crowd of warriors.

This is Our Land – Arya elé Occalé Stavek

A week had passed since Moll'ar had left his family and home behind to join the war. He had plans to return to them after a full turning of the moon, but even the few days he had been gone had been hard enough on him. As he rode through Feather's Bow, passing by deserted villages, Moll'ar thought of his family, wondering if Onnan had come any closer to becoming one with his animal spirit and if Athana had begun to crawl yet.

He feared for his life, knowing he could die in any of the battles awaiting them. He heard the marching of twenty-five thousand warriors as they stomped through the plains lands, nearing the Uniun River. The grunts of the catoblepones and herdbeasts mixed with his men's heavy breathing and loud footfalls, but Moll'ar's mind was leagues away. He didn't notice the still smoldering huts from the lion attacks, nor the smells of the decaying corpses around them. He fell in a trance as he tried imagining what his wife was doing and how she was handling the possibility of being a widow soon, but his thoughts were jolted to the present when he heard a feminine voice come from beside him.

"My Lord, are you all right?" Tera asked.

"Aye, my mind is just far from me right now."

"I can tell. You are starting to lag behind the rest of the troops," she said and smiled as she glanced at his feathered war bonnet.

Moll'ar's crown featured the red feathers from strixes. Against the headband, green and red beads decorated the black down feathers of rocs. Stitched onto the leather band was the Oacari phrase: *Gravoul de'wa'Lléish (Warrior of the Strix)*. Upon his face, he wore the city of Alberon's warpaint—black across his green eyes and a line from his lips down his chin.

"Aye, but I will be fine," Moll'ar stated as he guided his mount closer to the other warriors, noticing a halt in their march.

From down the dirt road, a centaur galloped toward him, slowing as he approached.

"M'Lord," the centaur greeted.

"Ser Clythis, why have my people stopped?"

"A small platoon of Senturian knights have been spotted just o'er the hill."

Moll'ar healed his mount's sides as he and Clythis

galloped past the long line of warriors and maneuvered to the top of the hill before them.

Moll'ar halted his steed as he stared upon the Senturian army posed in the valley. In the center of the crevice stood merely three thousand Senturian knights—the majority on foot, with only twenty on horseback. In front of the Senturians, Moll'ar saw an elven knight sitting upon a kelpie with indigo-colored scales, marsh weeds for a mane and a maroon cloth draped across its back so the knight wouldn't get glued to its sticky coat of scales.

The knight held a short spear in one hand and a rounded shield with spiked rivets around the boss in the other. The shield was wooden and painted red with a blue serpent head striking at its foe. Moll'ar recognized that the equipment had once belonged to the Learish as he studied the remainder of the knights, many of whom had also acquired weapons and armor from the Learish they had conquered.

Moll'ar turned to his men, the feathers on his headdress blew fiercely in the warm summer air. *"There marches our adversaries. We outnumber them, but they see us comin' as we see them. The Senturians in the midst of battle are as strong as ten men, so never underestimate them by the count of their heads or you will lose yours."* Moll'ar studied his warriors' determined faces. *"But we have somethin' that they do not—heart! They lust for the warmth of victory, but we lust after the safety of our tribes! Now let us fight and show Lord Darius and his heartless knights that this is our land! The land of our fathers and of our fathers' fathers! The land that we live and survive by!*

The land that we will grow old and die upon, or die protectin' what is ours! Until the sun sets in the East, we will defend and serve the West!"

Upon seeing the Alberian tribes stampeding down the hillside, the outnumbered Senturians turned and began to flee.

"Stop them!" Moll'ar shouted as his warriors charged passed him. *"Do not let a man escape, nor a bird fly, for they will surely return with reinforcements! Take them, and let them know that this is our land!"*

The Alberian army quickly caught up with the fleeing Senturians. Adrenaline coursed through the veins of knights and warriors alike. The Alberians overtook the Senturian recruits as the vast number of stampeding warriors overwhelmed them. Their pointed ears—tucked behind wool and steel—rung with the intensity of each strike and parry. All of their training to become part of the most celebrated knighthood of the six kingdoms fled their minds as the only thing they could focus on was trying to make it out alive.

As the Alberians flooded the recruited knights, drowning them under their charging feet, Moll'ar examined his men from afar. Two highly decorated chieftains had stayed back to protect their lord. Moll'ar led his mount in a trot down the dirt path; the warm air brushed against his tan skin as his face showed only determination. He did not care that his warriors were defeating the strongest knights in all of Metagore, though the victory tasted bittersweet. He had grown hardened with the numerous lives of his people being lost to a war he had been against—a war he only allowed himself to be drug into in the event of a possible attack by the invaders they were slaughtering.

"*Look there,*" one of Moll'ar's guards said as he pointed toward another hilltop. "*It appears like reinforcements are a-comin'.*"

Moll'ar's gaze tethered to his left. Upon the hill, north of the battle, two silhouettes stood against the darkening sky. The two knights stopped on top of the hill's crest, looking upon the battle. One knight was clothed in armor from head to toe, while the other was nothing more than a skeleton of bones, holding up a metal cross gripped onto a small portion of a shredded banner—no sigil noticeable, just the blackened gray fabric remained.

"*Reinforcements, aye?*" the other guard questioned with a laugh. "*Appears to be two more ironclads that are ready to die today.*"

Flashes of light flickered amongst the clouds, followed by a clash of thunder rumbling over the ground. The wind howled as Moll'ar reached for the spear draped across his back. He gripped its wooden shaft tight in his fist as he stared at the two silhouettes standing still upon the hill.

"*Do not underestimate what a Senturian has under his iron sleeves,*" Moll'ar informed the two warriors.

"*What?*" one of the warriors asked and chuckled. "*That one does not even have sleeves; just mere flesh and bones, he is.*"

As the wind halted and another streak of lightning

illuminated the sky, a single arrow pierced the chest of
the naive warrior, causing the three mounts to buck off
their riders. Moll'ar quickly stood and unstrapped the
wooden shield latched to the back of his belt and
protected his body with it. With the fall of the first
warrior by his side came another bolt, but the second
missed its mark, impaling the soggy ground. Moll'ar
peered around his shield, trying to make out the source
of the arrows, only to see the sky raining metal bolts
onto his current position.

With no other option, Moll'ar sprinted down the hill
toward the brewing battle. As he ran, his war bonnet
ruffled through the air as he glanced at the two lone
knights standing upon the summit, but as his gaze
found them, they were no longer alone. A hoard of
knights mounted upon fiery steeds crested over the hill.
They guided their mares around the battle, enclosing
the Alberians and the recruits into a confined circle.

Moll'ar found himself amongst his warriors,
stabbing and deflecting the knights' jabs. Fear from the
intensity of battle entered Moll'ar's mind. He still had
the numbers, but deep down, he was well aware there
was little hope for him to emerge as the victor.

Sweat dripped from his soaked hair and into his eyes.
His body and tanned clothing became stained with
blood and gore sprayed out from the fallen. Nothing
but a storm of disorder and violence surrounded
him—a chaotic blur of colors. He heard a cohesion of
chants and screams of injured men and beasts alike over
the thunderous sounds of stone striking steel.

What was left of the Alberian warriors—after the continuous onslaught of arrows bombarding them—managed to surround their lord, trying to protect him from the tips of their enemies' blades.

Moll'ar nervously followed the mounted knights, circling them with his gaze. Studying their speed and position, Moll'ar maneuvered his way from the crowded warriors and took aim with his spear. As he noticed the archers ready their arrows, he propelled his weapon through the air, until it impaled itself into the front shoulder of one of the nightmares, causing it to topple over and sending its demon rider hurling into the fields.

Soon after, Moll'ar knelt behind his shield as it absorbed a few of the metal bolts. While he was kneeling, a fellow Alberian fell beside him—his face so crushed and deformed, Moll'ar could not decipher who it had been.

Startled by the reveal of the dead warrior, Moll'ar's focus shifted as he stood, only to witness a massive war hammer swinging toward him. He immediately lifted his shield and lunged backward as the hammer struck the wooden plate of protection, shattering half of it into splinters. Moll'ar staggered from the great blow but managed to obtain his balance as he drew his sword and hatchet.

The Senturian approached Moll'ar once more, swinging his hammer with as much force as before. Moll'ar ducked and glided his torso under the large blunt weapon and sliced the Senturian's leg just above the kneecap—one of the few places a plate of metal didn't cover his body. The knight collapsed, holding his leg in agony as the Alberian lord stood straight and delivered a mighty swing of his hatchet into the knight's neck.

Moll'ar's feat of killing the Senturian didn't last long as a large troll rammed into him, knocking him onto his back. Moll'ar retrieved one of his hunting knives as he raised himself up, but the troll thrust his knee into his face, Moll'ar's head ricocheting off the metal greave and onto the muddy ground. Upon the impact, the troll stomped Moll'ar's hand gripping the knife, crushing his fingers and hand under his heavy weight.

Moll'ar gasped in pain as he lifted his torso off the ground, blood streaming from his nose and mouth. Before he could become upright, the troll pinned his neck to the ground with a trident he had obtained from the Learish—one of the prongs grazed the side of Moll'ar's neck as it passed by. By that point, the pain from the fresh gash didn't even register in his mind. The heightened throbbing of his crushed hand still restrained under the troll's massive boot distracted the pain from the nicks and cuts.

Even in all the pain, Moll'ar grabbed the trident and fought to remove it from around his throat, but the weight of the troll leaning upon it proved too much. Moll'ar's dark-tinted face grew to a faint shade of purple underneath the caked-on dirt and blood.

As Moll'ar still squirmed on the ground—beginning to gag and gasp for air—a hornless demon with a slight limp approached him. The demon knelt beside him and inhaled deeply through his nostril cavity. "Do ya smell that? The scent of sweat and shit from afterlings and humas that don't know their place in society. That smells like victory." He spoke with a sense of mockery in his voice. "Yer tongue can taste the metallic of the bloodshed in these fields, of the liquids drained by yer men, fighting to serve ya as their lord. I guess 'tis a blessing they won't see their land taken from them. So, why don't ya just go ahead and bend the knee and end all of this?"

"I will never bend the knee to Lord Darius," Moll'ar managed to say. "You will have to kill me first."

"Alberon will be Lord Darius's whether ya bend the knee or not," the demon knight told him as he rose to his feet and surveyed Moll'ar's body. "Look around ya. Ya don't have enough men to keep yer kingdom safe."

"Smite me if you must," Moll'ar grumbled as he scanned the field to see his men with fewer numbers than the Senturians. "But I will not just give over my land."

"Yer land?" the demon bellowed in a laugh. "Maybe I wasn't clear. I am Ser Dagrus, and 'tis is *our* land now! If I want these fields torched, then they shall, and Alberon will be known as the Sentries of the West."

"If you burn our fields, then there will be no food for either of our kingdoms."

"Food? We survive off of meat, not roots in the ground." The demon knight turned his attention to the troll standing over Moll'ar. "Let him stand."

The troll yanked the trident from the ground and

removed his foot.

Moll'ar stood, panting, as he held his shattered hand close to his waist while he rubbed his throat with the other.

"Now," Dagrus began to speak once more, "have yer men drop their weapons, and there will be no more blood shed here today."

THE RED CROWN

Inside his manor, Darius bathed his duchess in her chamber. Ky sat on one of the steps that descended into the stone tub built into a third of her room's floor. The water's depth would have reached the top of Ky's breasts if she had chosen to stand, but with the swelling of her ankles, she had wished to rest on one of the steps instead.

Darius filled a large drinking horn with the warm liquid from the tub and poured it over Ky's beaded black hair. The water cascaded over her face as she leaned forward, and her wings stretched above the water, looking fluffier than usual as they had gained a darker silk since she had become pregnant. The water continued down her body, streaming over her growing belly and around her protruding navel.

Darius filled the horn once more, then poured its content over Ky's back as he rubbed a sponge across her hazelnut skin. As he bathed her, she moaned in pain as she leaned forward and farther away from his hand.

"Was I scrubbing too hard?" he asked caringly.

"No," she responded as she straightened back up, grabbing at her hip. "Cháy was stretching and pinched a nerve, but I am fine now."

"Are you sure? Can I get you anything?"

"I am fine," she assured him as he began to bathe her once more.

Darius continued to wash the mother of his future child when a voice came from the passageway outside her door. "Lord Darius, may I have a moment with you?"

The demon turned toward the door but saw no one standing in-between its frames. He placed the horn on the stone floor and walked into the corridor. Awaiting him—knelt down on one knee—was his marquess with his head bowed before his lord.

"What are you doing?" Darius questioned the elder demon.

"I'm kneeling before my lord," Lucius responded as he remained knelt.

"Stand. You look foolish. Why have you come for a moment with me this early in the morning?"

Lucius stood and handed a scroll he had been holding to Darius. "We have taken siege of all the kingdoms, my Lord."

As Darius read the letter, Ky exited her room wrapped in a towel—her arms cradled her growing stomach as if she was holding the baby within. "You mean—"

"The war is over," Lucius answered. "Ten days have passed since Alberon's fall. It was the last of the kingdoms to be taken by our knights."

Darius handed the letter to Ky so she may read the words for herself.

"Send rocs to the five capitals," Darius commanded Lucius. "I want to know how many men I have in each of the realms and how wounded they are."

"Right away, my Lord," the elder demon replied as he turned to attend to his new assignment.

"And Lucius," Darius said, stopping him. "When you finish, go to the smithy and demand a crown to be made for your lord. I will not wear a circlet that a huma has soiled with their wretched locks."

"Will do, my Lord."

As Lucius made his way down the passageway, Ky looked toward Darius's radiating face. "You did well, my Lord."

Darius's large red eyes sparkled as they focused on Ky. "Thank you. Now, go clothe yourself and gather the servants around the manor. Have them prepare a small banquet for tonight in honor of our victory."

"As you wish," Ky stated before re-entering her room.

Darius walked down the corridor to his chamber. He entered his room and headed toward the balcony. He surveyed the stone city before him. The knowledge of triumph grew warm within his body as the morning sun burned brightly over the kingdom.

After some time of standing on the balcony and embracing the joy of being the new lord over the six kingdoms, shrieks from the sky disrupted Darius's rejoicing. As the demon looked toward the heavens, he saw the dark scales of Libras, glowing red in the sunlight as his former god passed over the kingdom.

Darius's brow furrowed, and every pleasant thought that had once occupied his mind fled. "You should have never returned," he grumbled, then stormed into his chamber.

Later that evening at the banquet, Darius sat at a table elevated higher than the others by a stone step, his lovely duchess and his trusted marquess accompanying him. Darius stood from his chair as he scanned the audience in attendance—mostly servants and guards, with a few knights who had been kept behind to protect the city from invaders.

Darius raised his chalice of mead in a toast. "We have conquered the six kingdoms and have won all of the spoils of war!" He lowered his glass and took a sip from it before placing it on the table. "All the bellies and blood pennies in the bank of Talean is ours. It will soon be time for us to rebuild the six kingdoms, but first, I will pay any family who has had a loved one die serving to protect us in this war four sun coins. Then after, I will rebuild Metagore to be the perfect kingdom that our founders once had hoped it would be." He raised his goblet once more as he concluded with their motto. "Be thy gods that guide us. Be thy gods that watch over us. Be no shame fall upon us."

The large demon took a swig of his mead, then sat beside his duchess as she stood. "I think I am going to go turn in for the night," she informed him before kissing him on the forehead and exiting the hall.

A few moments after Ky's departure, Darius downed his mead and finished the steak he had been eating. He rose from his seat and quickly surveyed the room of servants and guards. Though he'd had a status of power and leadership over them for the past eleven moons, he was now bestowed with greater power than before, and it brought warmth to his chest.

He turned and departed the hall, nodding to the guards stationed at the entrance as he passed by. Once he was out of sight from the lesser beings in attendance, a smile grew across his face as he felt more confident in himself. He knew he would be a far better lord than that huma child and knew his rule would lead the kingdoms to great prosperity.

Darius's grin grew wider when his presence granted a bow from the guard patrolling the corridor of his bedchamber. "Rise, Ser Keir."

As he had commanded, the guard straightened his stance.

"I trust Ky has already made her way to bed?"

"Aye, m'Lord. She passed me by not too long ago."

"Good. You are granted leave from your post. Go enjoy the festivities in the banquet hall."

Surprised by the unexpected reward, the guard thanked his lord before bowing once more, then made his way to the feast.

Darius approached his chamber as a new smile spread across his face. He pushed open the door and looked to the bed—expecting to see Ky laying upon it—only to straighten in surprise when he found it empty. With furrowed brows, he skimmed the room devoid of any inhabitants but himself. As the demon entered the chamber, his pleasure and excitement of being the new lord faded.

On his balcony, the ethereal purple figure of Afria waited patiently for his arrival to the chamber.

"Where's Ky?" Darius asked in haste as he approached the goddess.

Afria's eyes narrowed in confusion. "I do believe she is asleep in her bed, but I may be mistaken."

"What are you doing here?"

"You seem quite tense for a man who has just conquered all of Metagore," Afria retorted as she turned to look at the city before them.

"Aye, I am," Darius responded as he stood beside the wisp, looking over Sentries. "For your presence is never in good standing."

"What?" Afria scoffed as she turned toward Darius, baffled by the statement. "Are you not pleased to see me? I just came to congratulate you on your victory."

"I am grateful to the gods that I have been blessed with being the victor, but your presence isn't welcomed here."

Afria floated into Darius's chamber. "Ahh, yes, the gods and our favors that we just bestow onto any who is willing to just ask of it," she said while making gestures with her hands and arms. "To the Eight you pray—"

"To the *Six*," Darius corrected her.

The wisp grew still as her brow sat low. "Six, is it?"

"Aye," Darius confirmed. "I only pray to the Six now."

"Well, I do hope I am one of the six."

"You are not," Darius stated, hesitant by the context of Afria's statement. "I thought you knew all things."

"I tend to not listen to the silent words that your mind speaks, for I wish to not know of such foul and private things. But I do know all the things that have happened and that will come to pass. Such as Libras's two perceived betrayals of your men in Willowgate, or the fact that you will conquer a god before you are to die." Afria paused as she noticed that her last statement sparked an interest in Darius's mind.

"I will conquer a god? Which god? Tell me! You must know!"

Afria approached the large demon. "I did not think you prayed to me anymore, for I have not heard your words in my ears for many moons now."

"You have wronged my family, and I know what you are capable of," Darius said hastily. "Now, which god will I conquer?"

"Have you not wronged your own family as well? As for the god, I will leave that for you to decide."

"What?" The demon's deep voice echoed through the room. "You must tell me. I am the lord now!"

"My apologies, *Lord* Darius. I was unaware of the fact that the title of Lord—one in which you took from another—had power over the title of Goddess, that you have bestowed upon me," Afria mocked. "And I do hope no one prays to me for your death, as they did Duchess Anina's. She was a kind and gentle spirit, didn't you think?"

Darius's eyes widened as their red shade seemed to dance like raging flames. "It will take more than your walking shadows to kill me."

A broad smile grew across Afria's translucent face. "Enjoy your rule over *Talean* and the other kingdoms," she said and chuckled as she vanished.

Darius stood infuriated as terror slowly invaded his thoughts. As he reflected on the wisp's last statement, he realized a fact that had completely slipped his mind until that moment: becoming lord over all six kingdoms included him as a ruler over Talean and made him susceptible to the Curse of a Hundred Rulers.

In fear, Darius rushed out of his room and down the passageway leading to Ky's chamber. Once he reached the entrance, he barged in, flinging open the door.

The loud commotion startled Ky awake, and she rolled over in bed to face Darius. "Are you all right, my Lord?" she asked in her drowsy state.

Relieved she was alive and unharmed, Darius inhaled a few deep breaths as his adrenaline dissipated. "I thought you would have slept in my chamber."

"I chose to sleep in my own bed tonight," Ky responded as she struggled to sit up. "I know I take up a lot of room, and it must be uncomfortable for you."

Darius approached the bed and sat beside her. He wrapped an arm around her body and gently pulled her close. "You are what comforts me."

A smile spread across Ky's dark face as she leaned against Darius's chest. "So, why did you barge in here?"

"Afria just visited me in my chambers."

Ky pulled her head from Darius's body as she looked at his dark face. "What did she want?"

Darius released his grasp of his duchess and stood to his feet. "She came to mock my lordship and to bring certainty of my sister's death. Honestly, I was fearful that she might have gotten to you as well."

"I'm okay," Ky replied softly as she took Darius's callused hands. "And I'm sorry. I know you and Anina used to be real close."

"Aye. We hadn't spoken in a few years, but she was my sister and someone whom I wanted to call family nonetheless. But Solaris and Azreal prayed for the gods to take her life."

"I still can't believe the gods would actually follow through with the execution of such—"

"These are the same gods who cursed Talean," his crackling voice interrupted her. "They will do whatever is asked of them, just so they can remain in the high, utmost power. But one day soon, I will become a god above all others, and I will see to it that they bend to my will and not to the wills of others."

"But, my Lord, one cannot just become a god."

"But I will become a god; I am certain of this." Darius raised Ky to her feet as he looked into her green eyes. "And I will make you my goddess, and we will rule over all the lands of the Abyss."

"How are you sure of such a thing?"

"Afria has told me so, and she knows all things that are going to happen. She is a goddess, after all."

Ky's gaze shifted about, unbelieving what her ears were hearing. Her stomach grew tighter than what it already was, and questions flooded her mind. How could an ordinary mortal become one of the gods? And why would Afria willingly tell such a drastic future event to anyone?

†

Three weeks later, Darius knelt on the elevated stage in the great hall of his manor; an archbishop—an aged djinn with skin the color of the sun's kiss—stood before him. A black robe held to his waist by a scarlet ribbon covered his pale-red flesh, and the garment's ruffles draped to the floor. Ky and Lucius stood behind them.

Ky wore a black elegant dress with sleeves of lace-embroidered nets and a black satin band crossed above her protruding belly that forced up her enlarged breasts, making them appear rounder than what they were. She stood with her hands held behind her back as she subconsciously stroked her fingers through the feathers on her wings. She was anxious for what was to come of Darius being the lord over the six kingdoms and was even more concerned about how the other lands would react to his victory.

The archbishop finished the ceremony by holding up a metal circlet with large peaks placed around the top. The crown glowed a vibrant red as an illusion of flames danced across its surface—enchanted to appear on fire but produced no heat so it could be endowed to Darius's heiress in the future without any harm coming to her.

"We crown thee with a crown of passion and fire. The crown of thy new lord, pressed in the bowels of Mount Dumas," the djinn proclaimed as he placed the crest onto Darius's flowing hair. "We place thee upon thy head, to restore thy kingdom to a state of high power. Now, rise to thy feet and go forth and rule thy lands with a sharp mind."

Darius stood as he turned to look at the crowd as they cheered loudly for their newly crowned lord.

"'Tis my honor and duty to present to ye, Lord Darius—the lord of fire and ruler of the six kingdoms," the archbishop announced, then stepped off stage to allow his new lord enjoyment of the spotlight.

"It has been exactly one year to this day since the six kingdoms have had a *real* lord," Darius announced to the crowd. "And as the new lord, I will unify the kingdom's six armies. I will do away with the viscounts and hold them liable of treason for starting the war amongst the realms. I may even throw them in that pit they are so fond of." Darius's voice grew louder as he continued his speech. "There will never be a corrupt election ever again, for from this day forward, the crown will be passed down to the holder's heir, and the heir's heir as follows. There will be no more tributes to the gods for their favor in war, for they have betrayed us and spat upon our offerings. Finally, I am doing away with all the statues and monuments obtaining to Libras and Afria within this city's walls, for they are no gods to me. If you must pray and worship in their names, then so be it, but I will not see them praised in the temples of my city." Darius paused as he scanned the crowd for a moment before concluding with their motto, but this time it slightly varied from what it had once been. "Be thy Six that guide us. Be thy Six that watch over us. Be no shame fall upon us."

—TO BE CONTINUED—

EPILOGUE:

Waves crashed upon Aikia's sandy beaches, bringing with it a mass of water quickly forming into a humanoid figure, materializing into skin and cloth—an ellestrian.

As the ellestrian ambled along the coast, she approached a blue-scaled figure sprawled out in the sand, who appeared to have been amputated beneath his left knee.

As the ellestrian approached the cryter crawling across the wet sand, she knelt beside him and looked into his black eyes.

"I heard you were dead."

The cryter smiled. "I heard ya were a great oracle who sees everything."

"I only see what is asked to be seen."

"What if I asked to see what wonders lay under yer clothes?"

The ellestrian scoffed as she stood. "The Abyss was too kind to you."

"Aye, but she cares for me; much like I predict that ya will care for me."

"I can't escape you, can I?"

"'Tis fate, I reckon."

The ellestrian shook her head as she reached to lift the cryter onto his only leg.

ACKNOWLEDGEMENTS

I have to start by thanking my wonderful and supportive wife, Amber. From helping flesh out some of the details, to reading and critiquing early drafts and helping write parts where I struggled to get the right words down on the page, and allowing me some quiet time away from the kids so I could work on this book, she is just as much to thank for the completion of this book as I am. Thank you so much, babe.

Thanks to Mary Lee and Fay, as well as everyone else from Writers Ink of Northeast Arkansas, for sharing all your journeys and wisdom with me. I have learned so much from you all over the course of time I've been a part of this amazing group of writers.

Special thanks to Brian, my ever-patient editor, who is, I'm sure, very pleased this book wasn't 400,000 words long—but it might have been better with a steam-powered train ... or a taco or two.

Thanks to Claire Marie and Chris Lucas for the amazing cover and interior formatting. I couldn't have asked for anything better than what you both provided me with.

There are many others who helped bring this book to life. I would like to thank the Booksie community for your overwhelming support of this book. The AuthorTube community for all of your wonderful videos of inspiration and advice that helped guide me through the struggles of writing my first novel.

Thanks to my awesome beta readers for pointing out weak points in my manuscript and for providing input on how to strengthen the story arc and character development.

Lastly, I would like to thank all my coworkers and close friends for listening to me ramble on and on about this book over the past three years. I know at times you probably got annoyed being around me, but your continued support and interest in the story are what really motivated me to finish and publish it for all to see.

Again, to everyone named and not: THANK YOU!

www.ingramcontent.com/pod-product-compliance
Lightning Source LLC
Chambersburg PA
CBHW070926100726
47908CB00001B/119